1972

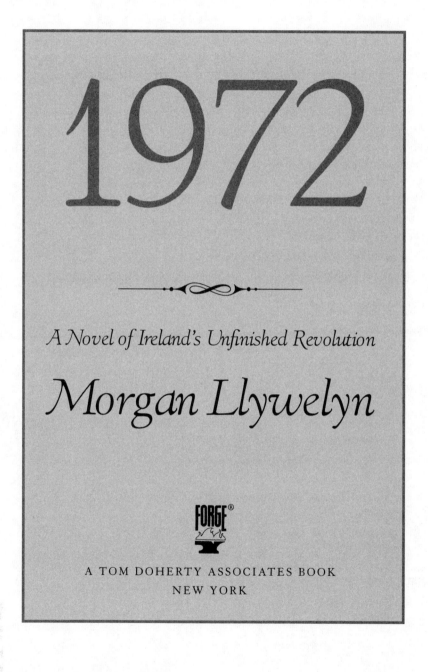

1972

A Novel of Ireland's Unfinished Revolution

Morgan Llywelyn

FORGE®

A TOM DOHERTY ASSOCIATES BOOK
NEW YORK

1972: A NOVEL OF IRELAND'S UNFINISHED REVOLUTION

Copyright © 2005 by Morgan Llywelyn

Edited by David G. Hartwell

Map by Mark Stein Studios

A Forge Book
Published by Tom Doherty Associates, LLC
175 Fifth Avenue
New York, NY 10010

www.tor.com

Forge® is a registered trademark of Tom Doherty Associates, LLC.

Library of Congress Cataloging-in-Publication Data

Llywelyn, Morgan.
    1972 : a novel of Ireland's unfinished revolution / Morgan Llywelyn.—1st ed.
        p.   cm.
    "A Tom Doherty Associates book."
    ISBN 0-312-87857-5 (acid-free paper)
    EAN 978-0312-87857-3
        1. Photographers—Fiction.   2. Demonstrations—Fiction.   3. Political violence—Fiction.
    4. Derry (Northern Ireland)—Fiction.   5. Ireland—Fiction.   I. Title: Nineteen seventy-two.
    II. Title.

    PS3562.L94A65   2005
    813'.54—dc22

                                                                        2004051246

First Edition: February 2005

Printed in the United States of America

0 9 8 7 6 5 4 3 2 1

In Memory of Marcella Curran
and Éamonn MacThomáis
God bless

Acknowledgements

The author gratefully acknowledges the immense contribution made to this book by a number of men and women who took part in the events depicted. Their generosity in sharing their memories with me is deeply appreciated. Every effort has been made to present the truth as they saw it. In many instances I have not given the names of real people, either at their own request or for the sake of their families.

My heartfelt appreciation goes to Rosaleen MacThomáis, who unselfishly gave me the handwritten, unpublished memoirs of her late husband, Éamonn MacThomáis.

Special thanks are due to the historians and academics from both sides of the political divide who took time to read various portions of the work in progress and correct any factual errors. Those errors which may remain are totally my own.

Last but not least, I owe a huge debt to the real "Séamus McCoy." You know who you are. This book could not have been written without you.

Dramatis Personae—1972

Fictional Characters (in order of mention):

Finbar Lewis Halloran, "Barry": Born in Switzerland on April 6, 1939.

Séamus McCoy: Born 1918 in West Belfast; IRA training officer during the Border Campaign of 1956–57.

Edward Joseph Halloran, "Ned": Born in Clare in 1897; joined the Irish Volunteers in 1913; fought in the Easter Rising; married Síle Duffy; fought in the War of Independence, the Irish Civil War, and the Spanish Civil War; died in Clare in 1948.

Ursula Jervis Halloran: Born approximately 1910 in Dublin; foster child of Ned and Síle Halloran, who called her "Precious."

Eileen Halloran Mulvaney: Ned Halloran's youngest sister.

Henry Price Mooney: Born in Clare in 1883; journalist; married Ella Mansell Rutledge, who was born in Dublin in 1890; emigrated to America after the Irish Civil War.

Gerry and George Ryan: Brothers who work on Ursula's farm.

"Mickey": IRA explosives expert.

Isabella Mooney Kavanagh: Henry Mooney's older daughter, born in Dublin in 1923; widow of Michael Kavanagh.

Pearl and Opal: Employees in the Mooney household.

Henrietta "Hank" Mooney Rice: Henry Mooney's younger daughter, born in America in 1926; married to John Rice.

Barbara Kavanagh: Daughter of Michael and Isabella Mooney Kavanagh, born in America in 1947.

Claire MacNamara: A very pretty girl from Cork.

Miriam Fogarty: Claire's widowed aunt.

Gilbert Fitzmaurice: Barry's roommate at Trinity.

Father Aloysius: A priest in Derry.

Terence Roche: A doctor in Derry.

May Coogan: Father Aloysius's housekeeper.

Margaret "Peg" Reddan: Woman living in Killaloe.

Dennis Cassidy: Journalism student at Trinity.

Alice Green: Another journalism student; marries Dennis Cassidy.

Mr. Philpott: Owner of a boardinghouse in Harold's Cross.

Jeremy Seyboldt: Music promoter.

Paudie Coates: Automobile mechanic.

Historical Characters

Adams, Gerry (senior) (d. 2003): A lifelong republican; he and his wife Annie had thirteen children; three boys died at birth, but they succeeded in raising five daughters and five sons, one of whom, also named Gerry Adams, became president of Sinn Féin.

Aiken, Frank (1898–1983): Born in County Armagh; joined the Irish Volunteers in 1914; commandant of 4th Northern Division of the IRA in 1921;

when the Civil War broke out in June 1922 he tried to bring about reconciliation and kept his own division neutral as long as he could; was appointed chief of staff of the IRA following the death of Liam Lynch; subsequently served as minister for defence in the Fianna Fáil government, then as minister for finance, minister for external affairs, and finally as tánaiste.

Austin, Campbell: Owner of department store in Derry.

Bates, Dawson: Minister for home affairs in the Stormont government in 1934.

Behan, Brendan (1923–64): Dublin-born writer who left school at fourteen to become a house painter; joined the IRA; arrested in Liverpool in 1939 for possessing explosives and sentenced to three years Borstal detention; arrested in Dublin in 1942 for shooting at a policeman; learned Irish in Mountjoy Jail; eventually began making his living as a writer. His autobiographical novel *Borstal Boy* was an international best-seller.

Belloc, Hilaire (1870–1953): English Catholic historian.

Berry, Charles Edward "Chuck" (b. 1926): American rock and roll singer who shot to the top of the charts in 1955 with a song called "Maybellene."

Blaney, Neil T. (1922–95): Born in Donegal; his father was a prisoner of the British, under sentence of death, during the War of Independence. Blaney was TD for North-East Donegal and minister for agriculture in the Lynch cabinet.

Brookeborough, Lord (Alan Francis Brooke) (1883–1963): Chief of the British Imperial General Staff during World War Two; titled Baron Alanbrooke of Brookeborough in 1945; created a viscount in 1946; prime minister of Northern Ireland during the border campaign of 1956–57.

Cahill, Joe (1920–2004): Belfast-born member of the IRA; O/C of the Provisionals' Belfast Brigade in 1971.

Casement, Sir Roger David (1864–1916): Born in Dublin; in 1892 joined British Colonial Service in Africa, where he exposed the inhumane treatment of African workers in the Belgian Congo; promoted to consul general at Rio de Janeiro; knighted in 1911 for distinguished public service. His published reports on the cruelties practiced by white traders on the native population caused an international sensation in 1912; retired from the colonial service that same year;

joined Sinn Féin; joined the Irish National Volunteers in 1913; tried to obtain German help and arms for the 1916 Rising; hanged as a traitor by the British.

Churchill, Winston Leonard Spencer (1874–1965): British politician, author, and statesman; prime minister 1940–45, and 1951–55.

Clutterbuck, Sir Alexander: British ambassador to Ireland in 1956.

Collins, Michael (1890–1922): Born in County Cork; member and later president of the Irish Republican Brotherhood; aide-de-camp to Joseph Plunkett during the 1916 Rising; minister for home affairs, 1918; minister for finance, 1919–22; organiser of the Irish intelligence system; member of the Treaty delegation; chairman of the Provisional Government of the Irish Free State, 1922; commander in chief of Free State forces, 1922; shot dead in County Cork, 1922.

Conlon, Vincent: IRA Volunteer.

Connolly, James (1870–1916): Born in Edinburgh, Scotland; socialist, labor leader, and journalist; founder of the Citizen Army; commandant general of Dublin Forces during the 1916 Rising; executed by the British.

Cooper, Ivan: Northern Ireland Protestant.

Costello, John Aloysius (1891–1976): Dublin-born lawyer; Free State attorney general 1926–32; joined Fine Gael in 1933; represented the government at the League of Nations; became taoiseach in 1948; declared the Irish state a republic during a press conference in Canada that same year; served again as taoiseach 1954–57.

Craig, William: Minister for home affairs in the Stormont government under Terence O'Neill.

Currie, Austin (b. 1939): Born County Tyrone; Nationalist MP (Stormont) for East Tyrone 1964–72; founder-member of the SDLP in 1970.

Daly, Seán: IRA commandant.

Dealey, Ted: Publisher of *The Dallas Morning News*, 1950–60.

de Gaulle, Charles Andre Marie Joseph (1890–1970): French soldier, writer, and statesman; trained at the Military Academy of St. Cyr; brigadier general in World War Two; architect of France's Fifth Republic; president of France 1958–69.

de Valera, Eamon (1882–1975): Born in New York City, raised in County Limerick; joined the Irish National Volunteers in 1913; commanded the Third Battalion of the Dublin Brigade during the 1916 Rising; elected Sinn Féin TD for Clare; president of the first Dáil 1919–21; president of the second Dáil 1922; rejected the Anglo-Irish Treaty; president of the Executive Council of the Irish Free State 1932–37; spearheaded the Constitution of 1937; taoiseach 1937–48, 1951–54, 1957–59; president of the Republic of Ireland 1959–73.

Devlin, Josephine Bernadette (b. 1947): Tyrone-born civil rights activist; youngest woman ever elected to Westminster (1969–74); seriously injured in a loyalist gun attack in 1981.

Doherty, Patrick "Paddy Bogside" (b. 1926): Born in the Bogside; a builder by profession; a leading member of the Derry Citizens' Defence Association.

Dorati, Anton (1906–88): Hungarian-born orchestra conductor who made his American debut in 1937 with the National Symphony of Washington, D.C.

Eden, Robert Anthony (1897–1977): British prime minister 1955–57; resigned over the Suez Canal crisis; was created earl of Avon in 1961.

Eisenhower, Dwight David (1890–1969): Born in Denison, Texas; graduate of West Point Military Academy; appointed supreme commander of the Allied Expeditionary Forces in World War Two; elected thirty-fourth president of the United States in 1953.

Elizabeth II (b. 1926): Queen of the United Kingdom of Great Britain and Northern Ireland from 1952.

Emmet, Robert (1778–1803): Dublin-born Protestant; educated at Trinity College, Dublin; a member of the College Historical Society until he was expelled for radicalism in 1798; discussed plans for liberating Ireland with Napoleon and Talleyrand; at the age of twenty-five, he became involved in the conspiracy for a new Irish rebellion; his attempt to seize Dublin failed and he was arrested by the British. His speech from the dock guaranteed him immortality as one of Ireland's most romantic heroes. Condemned to a public hanging, Emmet slowly strangled to death, after which his body was beheaded.

Faubus, Orval: Governor of the state of Arkansas in the 1950s.

Faulkner, Brian (1921–77): Born in County Down; Unionist member of British parliament; became prime minister of Northern Ireland in 1971.

Ferrier, Kathleen (1912–53): English contralto; one of the most beloved singers of her time.

Fitt, Gerry: Labour MP for West Belfast.

Fitzgerald, Ella (1918–96): American jazz singer who became internationally famous for the wide range and sweetness of her voice.

Gageby, Douglas (b. 1918): Dublin-born journalist; son-in-law of Seán Lester; editor-in-chief of the Irish News Agency; editor of the *Evening Press*; joint managing director and then editor of *The Irish Times*.

Gandhi, Mohandas K. (1869–1948): Known as "Mahatma," which means Great-Souled, Gandhi was the leader of the Indian nationalist movement to put an end to British rule, and is considered the father of modern India.

Garland, Seán: Commandant of the Lynch column during the border campaign of 1956.

George V (1865–1936): Born George Frederick Ernest Albert Saxe-Coburg-Gotha. Crowned king of the United Kingdom of Great Britain and Ireland in 1910; in 1917 the king renounced his German name and titles for himself and his progeny, and the family name was changed to Windsor, after Windsor Castle.

Gilchrist, Sir Andrew: British ambassador to Ireland in 1969.

Goulding, Cathal: Joined the republican movement in 1927; imprisoned and also interned for IRA membership; elected chief of staff of the IRA in 1962; after the split in 1969 became chief of staff of the "Official" IRA.

Haughey, Charles J. (b. 1925): Born in County Mayo (both parents were involved in the War of Independence); joined Fianna Fáil; married Maureen Lemass, daughter of Seán Lemass; elected to the Dáil in 1957; became minister for justice in 1961; minister for agriculture 1964–66; minister for finance 1966–70; dismissed from cabinet in 1970, arrested and charged with conspiring to import arms into Northern Ireland, acquitted of all charges; elected taoiseach in 1979 and again in 1982 and 1987.

Heath, Edward Richard George (b. 1916): Born in Kent, England; educated at Oxford; elected to the British parliament as a Conservative in 1950; prime minister of Great Britain from 1970 to 1974.

Hitler, Adolf (1889–1945): Born in Austria; leader of the National Socialist Party (Nazi), 1920–21; dictator of Germany from 1933; assumed the twin titles of chancellor and führer in 1934; died by his own hand as Allied forces entered Berlin in 1945.

Hume, John (b. 1937): Born in Derry; taught French at St. Columb's School; active in the credit union movement, the Derry Housing Association, and the Northern Ireland Civil Rights Association; elected vice chairman of Derry Citizens' Action Committee in 1968; elected to Stormont in 1969; in 1970 cofounded the Social Democratic and Labour Party (SDLP); elected to Northern Ireland Assembly, 1973–74; the NI Convention, 1976–77; the new Assembly, 1982–86; minister for commerce, 1974; elected to European parliament in 1979; elected to UK parliament in 1983; in 1988 entered into dialogue with Gerry Adams, which led to IRA ceasefire in 1994. Awarded the Nobel Peace Prize in December 1998.

Johnson, Lyndon Baines (1908–73): Born in Texas; congressman, senator, then vice president; became thirty-sixth president of the United States following the assassination of John Kennedy.

Johnston, Dr. Roy: Marxist socialist in Britain; Trinity College lecturer.

Kavanagh, Noel: IRA commandant.

Kelly, Captain James (d. 2002): An intelligence officer in the Irish army; arrested for gunrunning in 1970, he spent the rest of his life working to prove he had been under government orders.

Kelly, John: A leader of the Belfast Citizens' Defence Committee and one of those arrested for gunrunning in 1970.

Kelly, Mick: IRA Volunteer.

Kennedy, John Fitzgerald (1917–63): Born in Massachusetts; World War Two war hero; author of *Profiles in Courage*; congressman, senator, then thirty-fifth president of the United States.

King, Martin Luther, Jr. (1929–68): American civil rights leader; assassinated in 1968.

Ledwidge, Francis (1887–1917): Poet born in County Meath; his lament for Thomas MacDonagh is one of his best-known works; killed in World War One.

Lemass, Seán Francis (1899–1971): Born in County Dublin; joined the Irish Volunteers at fifteen; fought in the GPO in 1916; subsequently became an officer; took the republican side after the Treaty; fought in the Civil War; founder-member of Fianna Fáil; elected TD for Dublin in 1925; minister for industry and commerce in de Valera's first government, a post he held until his election as taoiseach in 1959; a specialist in economics, Lemass promoted the turf industry (Bord na Mona), the national airline (Aer Lingus) and was instrumental in developing Irish shipping; in 1965 he reestablished free trade with England.

Lester, John Ernest "Seán" (1888–1959): Born in County Antrim; member of the Gaelic League and the Irish National Volunteers; news editor on the *Freeman's Journal*; publicist for the Irish Free State; appointed Irish representative to the League of Nations, Lester was the last secretary-general of the League.

London, Julie: American entertainer and jazz singer.

Luykx, Albert: Belgian-born businessman arrested in 1970 for gunrunning.

Lynch, John Mary "Jack" (1917–99): Born in Cork; one of the county's most outstanding athletes, winning one All-Ireland Gaelic football championship and five All-Ireland hurling championships; qualified as a barrister while working in Dublin as a civil servant; elected to the Dáil in 1948; parliamentary secretary, 1951–54; minister for education, 1957–59; minister for industry and commerce, 1959–65; minister for finance, 1965–66; elected leader of Fianna Fáil and taoiseach in 1966; re-elected in 1969.

McCluskey, Con, and his wife, Patricia: Founders of the Campaign for Social Justice in Northern Ireland.

McGirl, John Joe (1921–88): Born in Leitrim; member of the IRA Army Council during the border campaign; Sinn Féin TD for South Leitrim, 1957–61; central figure in the Provisional IRA after the split; vice president of Sinn Féin at the time of his death.

McGuinness, Martin (b. 1950): Born in Derry; joined the Official IRA in 1970 but was with them for only a few weeks before joining the Provisionals instead; second in command in Derry on Bloody Sunday.

McKee, Billy: Born in Belfast; joined the IRA; Belfast O/C in the early 1960s; Belfast commander of the Provisional IRA in 1970.

McQuaid, John Charles (1895–1973): Born in County Cavan; ordained in 1924; president of Blackrock College; a close friend of Eamon de Valera; had a strong hand in framing the 1937 Constitution; appointed archbishop of Dublin by Pope Pius XII in 1940.

MacBride, Seán (1904–88): Born in Paris, son of John MacBride and Maud Gonne MacBride, two of the foremost figures in the Irish revolution; joined the Irish Volunteers and fought in the War of Independence; opposed the Treaty; worked as a journalist in Paris and London; returned to Dublin and became chief of staff of the IRA in 1936; called to the bar in 1937; resigned from the IRA upon enactment of the new Constitution; founded Clan na Poblachta in 1946; in 1948 became minister for external affairs; in 1949 founded the Irish News Agency; increasingly vocal as a defender of human rights and campaigner for peace; founder-member of Amnesty International; served as UN Commissioner for Namibia, 1973–76; recipient in 1974 of the Nobel Prize for Peace; was awarded the Lenin Peace Prize in 1977 and the American Medal for Justice in 1978.

MacGiolla, Tomás (Thomas Gill): Member of the IRA; president of Sinn Féin in 1966.

MacStiofáin, Seán (John Stephenson): London-born and half English; joined the IRA; became chief of staff of the Provisional IRA after the split.

MacSwiney, Terence (1879–1920): Lord mayor of Cork, commander of the Cork No. 1 Brigade of the IRA. Arrested by the British in 1920; died on hunger strike in Brixton Prison.

MacThomáis, Éamonn (Éamonn Patrick Thomas) (1927–2002): Patriot, historian, writer, Dubliner. Joined both Sinn Féin and the IRA in the fifties; became treasurer of Sinn Féin; manager and contributor to the *United Irishman*; Dublin O/C at the start of the border campaign; arrested in 1957 and interned in Curragh Camp; released in 1959; became editor of *An Phoblacht* in 1972; arrested again in 1973; upon release was again editor of *An Phoblacht*; rearrested within two months and sentenced to fifteen months in prison for allegedly possessing an IRA press bulletin; author of numerous books about Dublin; creator and presenter of RTE series during the seventies on the history of Dublin; conducted numerous walking tours of Dublin; lecturer and Keeper of the House of Lords Chamber in the Bank of Ireland on College Green, Dublin, 1988–2002.

Markievicz, Constance (1868–1927): Daughter of Sir Henry Gore-Booth, wife of Count Casimir Markievicz; cofounder of na Fianna Éireann; member of Cumann na mBan and the Citizen Army; second in command to Michael Mallin in Saint Stephen's Green during the 1916 Rising; first woman to win election to the British Parliament although she never took her seat; subsequently served as the world's first female minister of labour in the Irish parliament.

Murphy, Charlie: Member of IRA general headquarters staff.

Ní Ghráda, Mairead: Irish language playwright; member of staff of the first Dáil; the first female announcer on radio.

Nixon, Richard Milhous (1913–94): Thirty-seventh president of the United States.

Ó Brádaigh, Ruairí (Rory Brady) (b. 1932): Sinn Féin TD for Longford-Westmeath, 1975; IRA chief of staff, 1958–59 and 1961–62, when the republican movement split in 1970 became the first president of Provisional Sinn Féin; lost leadership to Gerry Adams in 1983; became leader of faction which left Sinn Féin to form Republican Sinn Féin.

O'Brien, Dr. Conor Cruise (b. 1917): Dublin-born politician, diplomat, and writer; active in the anti-partition campaign in the forties; seconded to the United Nations during the Congo crisis; after a long period out of Ireland he returned to win a seat for Labour in 1969; minister for posts and telegraphs, 1973–77, during which time he developed an abiding hatred for Irish republicanism; in 1966 joined the U.K. Unionist Party.

O'Brien, Mick: IRA Volunteer.

Ó Ceallaigh, Seán T. (Seán T. O'Kelly) (1882–1966): Born in Dublin; joined the Gaelic League in 1898; subsequently joined and recruited for the IRB; founder-member of Sinn Féin in 1905; elected to Dublin city council; staff captain to Pearse in 1916; elected in 1918 as Sinn Féin MP; envoy to the Peace Conference in Paris; opposed the Treaty; served as minister for local government and public health; minister for finance; elected as second president of Ireland in 1945.

Ó Conaill, Dáithí (David O'Connell) (1938–91): Schoolteacher from Cork; joined Sinn Féin in 1955; subsequently joined the IRA; second in command to Seán Garland in the 1956 border campaign; lost a lung to a bullet wound.

O'Donnell, Mary: Noted Irish fashion designer born in County Donegal; trained with Mainbocher and with Sybil Connolly before going into business for herself in 1963.

O'Donoghue, Phillip: IRA Volunteer.

O'Hanlon, Feargal (d. 1957): IRA Volunteer killed during the Brookeborough raid.

O'Malley, Ernie (1898–1957): Born in County Mayo; fought in the 1916 Rising; commanded 2nd southern division of the IRA during the War of Independence; took the anti-Treaty side in the Civil War; arrested after the siege of the Four Courts, he later escaped; became IRA director of organisation; travelled widely as a writer and broadcaster; published to critical acclaim *On Another Man's Wound,* his account of the War of Independence, and *The Singing Flame,* about the Civil War.

O'Neill, Terence (1914–90): Born in County Antrim; captain in the Irish Guards, serving in the British Army during World War Two; leader of Unionist Party and prime minister of Northern Ireland 1963–69.

O'Regan, Paddy: IRA Volunteer.

O Riada, Seán (1931–71): Cork-born composer; joined the staff of Radio Éireann as assistant director of music; studied music in Paris and Italy; in 1953 became music director of the Abbey Theatre; composed the musical score for the film documentary *Mise Éire.*

O Súilleabháin, Muiris (Maurice O'Sullivan) (1904–50): Born on Great Blasket Island off the coast of Kerry; went to Dublin in 1927 to join the civic guard; his biography, written in Irish, *Fiche Blian ag Fás,* was published in English as *Twenty Years A Growing* and translated in many languages.

Paisley, Ian Richard Kyle (b. 1926): Born in Armagh, Northern Ireland, the son of a former Baptist minister. Paisley studied at the Reformed Presbyterian Theological Hall in Belfast; was ordained at the Ravenhill Evangelical Mission Church in 1946; cofounded his own new sect, the Free Presbyterian Church of Ulster, in 1951; from 1960 became the voice of extreme Protestant opinion; elected to the parliament of Northern Ireland; elected to the British House of Commons; cofounded the Democratic Unionist Party (DUP); elected to the European parliament.

Pearse, Senator Margaret Mary (1878–1968): Sister of Pádraic and Willie Pearse; helped in the establishment and maintenance of St. Enda's; was one of those who kept the school open for seventeen years after the execution of her brothers; TD for County Dublin 1933–37; in 1938 elected to Seanad Éireann; in 1967 she bequeathed St. Enda's to the nation.

Pearse, Pádraic (Patrick Henry Pearse) (1879–1916): Born in Dublin. Patriot, educationlist, writer, republican; founder of Saint Enda's College; member of the military council of the IRB; founding member of the Irish National Volunteers; signatory of the Proclamation of the Irish Republic; president of the Irish Republic and commander in chief of republican forces during the 1916 Rising; executed by the British in 1916.

Pope John XXIII (Angelo Giuseppi Roncalli) (1881–1963): Leader of the attempt to modernise the Roman Catholic Church.

Rooney, Patrick: Nine-year-old Catholic boy killed by the B-Specials.

Scott, Michael (1905–89): Born in Drogheda; architect of the Irish pavilion of the New York World's Fair in 1939; leading figure in the introduction of modern architecture to Ireland.

Shackleton, Sir Ernest Henry (1874–1922): Born in County Kildare; member of Scott's Antarctic expedition 1901–04; led his own Antarctic expedition in 1907–09; was knighted upon returning to England; led his second expedition to the Antarctic in 1914 aboard the ship *Endurance,* which was caught and crushed in the ice; in an act of an almost superhuman heroism Shackleton managed to keep all his men alive and bring them to safety.

Sheen, Archbishop Fulton J. (d. 1981): American cleric considered to be one of the most influential Catholics in America in the twentieth century, Sheen popularised radio and television ministries. Millions regularly tuned in to his programme, *The Catholic Hour.*

Solomons, Estella (1882–1968): Dublin-born painter of Jewish extraction; educated in a finishing school in Germany; joined Cumann na mBan; active behind the scenes during the 1916 Rising; her home became a safe house for republicans on the run.

South, Seán (d. 1957): Born in Limerick; joined the IRA; killed during the Brookeborough raid.

Thatcher, Margaret Hilda (b. 1925): British politician and member of the Conservative Party; prime minister 1979–90, the first female prime minister in European history.

Truman, Harry S. (1884–1972): Thirty-third president of the United States.

Yeats, William Butler (1865–1939): Dublin-born poet and dramatist; awarded the Nobel Prize for literature in 1923.

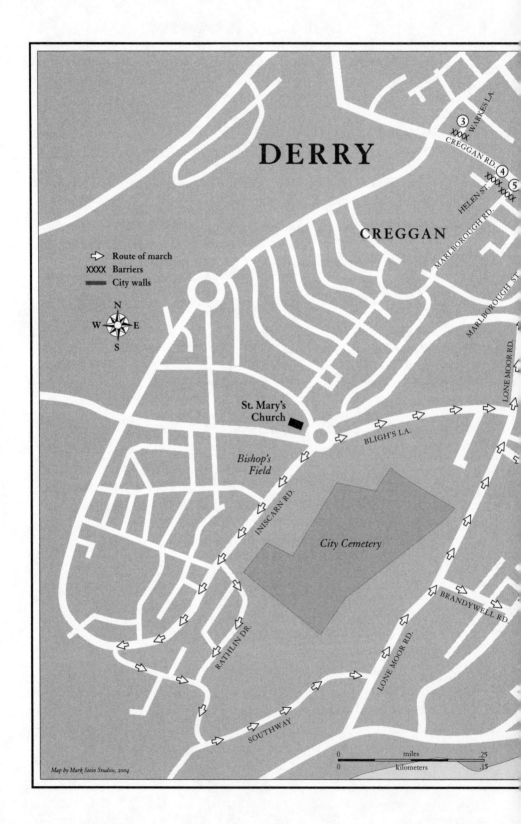

Map by Mark Stein Studios, 2004

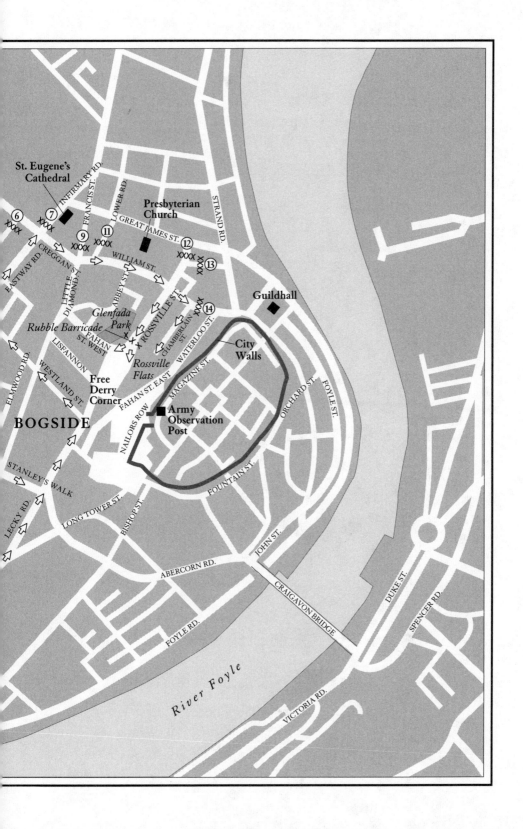

Bipartisan Declaration

———•·•❦•·•———

Unanimously adopted on the proposition of the Taoiseach, John A. Costello, and the Leader of the Opposition, Eamon de Valera, on 10 May, 1949

Dáil Éireann, SOLEMNLY RE-ASSERTING the indefeasible right of the Irish nation to the unity and integrity of the national territory,

REAFFIRMING the sovereign right of the people of Ireland to choose its own form of Government and, through its democratic institutions, to decide all questions of national policy, free from outside interference,

REPUDIATING the claim of the British Parliament to enact legislation affecting Ireland's territorial integrity in violation of those rights, and

PLEDGING the determination of the Irish people to continue to struggle against the unjust and unnatural partition of our country until it is brought to a successful conclusion;

PLACES ON RECORD its indignant protest against the introduction in the British Parliament of legislation purporting to endorse and continue the existing Partition of Ireland, and

CALLS ON the British Government and people to end the present occupation of our Six North-Eastern Counties, and thereby enable the unity of Ireland to be restored and the age-long differences between the two nations brought to an end.

Chapter One

THE crack of rifle fire splintered the frosty morning.

Barry gave a violent start. *Where the hell did that come from?*

He was in an overgrown hazel thicket near the top of a steep hill. In ages past, the many-stemmed little trees had been rigorously pruned by men from the village at the foot of the hill. The coppiced hazel provided a bountiful supply of flexible rods which the villagers wove into baskets and cradles and seats for stools, sheep pens and turf creels and nest boxes for hens.

Then the Great Famine stalked across Ireland.

A century later all that remained of the village were tumbled stones and a bit of gable wall. The neglected coppice was dying.

Peering out between brittle stems, Barry saw that the only footprints on the frost-rimed slope were his own. In the ruins of the village below, three crows perched on the broken wall. There was no other sign of life.

The hairs prickled on the back of his neck.

WHEN his company broke camp at dawn Barry had been sent ahead to reconnoitre. Séamus McCoy's orders were, "Use your compass to take a line due north. Mark your trail the way I taught you. After an hour take up a position on high ground—someplace where you'd be hidden from a casual observer—and watch for us. Don't move a muscle until we come up to you."

"Are we expecting trouble?" Barry asked eagerly.

McCoy laughed. "Sorry, lad, this is just an exercise. There'll be no fighting 'til we cross the border."

After an hour's brisk walk, Barry had chosen this site as his lookout because of the abandoned village. Throughout his life there had been certain places which spoke to him in a way he could not explain.

The echoes of the gunshot died away among the hills. *It might be someone out hunting,* Barry told himself. But he knew better. He knew his arrival had been observed by the enemy.

Easing his finger into the trigger guard of his rifle, he waited.

B ARRY Halloran had grown up leaning against the wind the way men do in the west of Ireland. He had been a chubby, cheerful toddler. Then a little boy who ran everywhere he went—and was usually up to mischief.

On the brink of manhood, Barry was tall and rangy and restless, a lightly freckled lad with red-gold hair and dark grey eyes. "Hair like summer, eyes like winter," his grandfather had once said of him. Like many Irishmen, the late Ned Halloran had possessed a poetic turn of phrase.

When great winter storms came roaring out of the Atlantic, Barry hitched a ride to Lahinch to watch the ocean attack the west coast of Ireland. The drama of nature enthralled him. In the crests of the mammoth breakers he glimpsed the white-maned horses of the sea god, Manannán mac Lir. Indomitable and mythic and splendid.

On summer nights Barry liked to lie embedded in clover and gaze at the moon. He returned from the fields with his clothes drenched in dew. His great-aunt Eileen invariably warned, "You'll catch your death for sure." But what did that matter compared to seeing a goddess? Beautiful and remote, indifferent to man, pulling the tides of the earth this way and that. A step beyond earth and halfway to heaven.

Barry's full name was Finbar Lewis Halloran. Eight Irish saints had been called Finbar, but the Church disapproved of Barry's surname because it had come to him from his unmarried mother.

Barry's mother disapproved of the way the Church held Ireland in a domineering fist and called it beneficence. Roman Catholicism no longer had any influence over Ursula Halloran.

When the second shot rang out Barry assured himself, *I'm not afraid, I'm Ned Halloran's grandson.* He did not really expect anything awful to happen to him. It never had in all of his seventeen years.

Besides, he thought, *the column must be near enough by now to hear the gunfire. They'll realise some feckin' Prod's trying to kill me and come at the run.*

If his mother heard him say feckin' she would tear strips off him. Ursula strictly forbade him to use bad language—though she uttered the occasional profanity herself.

None of the rules applied to Ursula Halloran.

She owned a dairy farm in County Clare with a profitable sideline in horse breeding. Although she employed hired men, she boasted that she could do anything they did except for shearing sheep, which required more sheer physical strength than she possessed. But Ursula milked cows, mended fences, trained the young horses, and kept the farm accounts, yet still found time to be active in *Banracht na Tuaithe.**

Barry regarded his mother with awe.

During the Irish Civil War, Ursula Halloran—known to her family as "Precious"—had been a courier for the republicans. A fifteen-year-old girl on a grey horse, galloping across Clare with messages for the IRA tucked inside her knickers.

After the Civil War, Ursula had gone to school in Switzerland. Two years in a finishing school were a gift from her father's best friend, Henry Mooney, and his wife, Ella. The time spent in Europe would forever set Ursula apart from most Irish women of her era. When she returned to Ireland she went to work for Radio Éireann in Dublin and took an active part in the first days of Irish radio. She remained a devotee of the wireless, arranging her farm work around news broadcasts and programmes of classical music.

The wireless—which the rest of the world knew as the radio—had been part of Barry's life for as long as he could remember. Some of his earliest memories were of listening to Radio Luxembourg when his mother was not around. They played foreign music from exotic places like France and Germany and America.

Listening to music, a boy could close his eyes and escape into his imagination.

AT the outbreak of World War Two, Ursula had been employed in the secretariat of the League of Nations in Geneva. Occasionally she told her son something of those nerve-racking months when the fate of the world hung in the balance. He was fascinated by her stories but resented their brevity. "You always leave out the best parts," he accused his mother.

"You don't need to know everything," she retorted.

Ursula retained a number of friendships from those days and was still interested in international politics. National politics infuriated her. The Civil War had left Ursula with a permanent loathing for the government established in its aftermath. She never had a kind word to say about "the Free Staters" as she called them. Barry enjoyed her rants; he deliberately introduced topics into the conversation which he knew would set her off. A casual mention of the Emergency might elicit, "During World War Two the Free State government didn't have the industrial resources to make gas masks. They couldn't provide for

*The Irish Countrywomen's Association.

their own citizens! Finally they had to bring the masks in from Britain as they bring everything in from Britain. They're West Brits to a man, every one of the Free Staters."

To call someone a West Brit was the ultimate insult.

As soon as Barry was old enough to ride a bicycle he was sent to the news-agency in the nearby village of Clarecastle every morning to collect the newspapers. Ursula bought all the major Irish papers and those from Northern Ireland as well.

Her conversation frequently involved events across the border. "There was another arson attack in Belfast yesterday. The police looked the other way, of course. Catholics in the north can't get jobs, so they're forced to live in slums that aren't fit for human habitation. Then they're burned out of them by Protestant mobs. Those are our people up there, and they're being treated worse than dogs in the country that once was theirs. Where are The Boys when we need them?"

The question was rhetorical. Ursula knew full well what had happened to The Boys—otherwise known as the Volunteers. The soldiers of the Irish Republican Army.

Following the Irish Civil War in 1922, supporters of the Anglo-Irish Treaty had tried to eliminate every trace of physical-force republicanism. Throughout the twenties and thirties the government of the Irish Free State had conducted a relentless campaign against the IRA. When he became *taoiseach*,* Eamon de Valera, a former Volunteer himself and the last surviving commandant of the Easter Rising in 1916, had not hesitated to send former comrades to the firing squad. Some saw this as the ultimate act of betrayal. But as peace replaced decades of turmoil, public support for militant republicanism had faded.

By the early 1940s the IRA was—almost—moribund. Its leaders were either dead or in prison. While detectives searched for him in Dublin with an arrest order, the last free member of the headquarters staff was playing banjo with a dance band in Derry.[1] Little remained of the IRA but a mixture of romantic myth and rusting weapons hidden in ditches and outhouses. Independence for twenty-six of Ireland's thirty-two counties had long since been won . . .

By the now outlawed Irish Republican Army.

Six counties designated as Northern Ireland remained part of the United Kingdom. Northern Ireland had its own parliament at Stormont, which had been opened with great fanfare by King George and Queen Mary in 1921. Stormont claimed to represent all the people, yet in actuality it was a Protestant parliament for Protestants. Catholics constituted a sizable minority of the population but they had almost no voice. The Unionist Party, which was exclu-

*Irish prime minister.

sively Protestant and dedicated to keeping Northern Ireland in the United Kingdom at all costs, controlled Stormont. The tiny Nationalist Party, which was mainly Catholic and supported the dream of an independent Ireland, had minimal representation.

Periodically Ireland's conscience was tormented by her amputated limb. Outbreaks of sectarian violence in the north caused waves of grief and guilt in the south.

The little boy who was Barry Halloran was aware that his mother was troubled from time to time. But he was busy with his own small adventures and soon forgot.

IN 1947 Irish Americans sent a petition signed by two hundred thousand people to President Truman, asking him to use his efforts to bring an end to Ireland's quarter century of partition.[2] Stating emphatically that it did not meddle in the affairs of other countries, the U.S. government declined.

ON Easter Monday, 1949, the Irish Free State—otherwise known as Éire— was officially declared to be the Republic of Ireland and was so recognised by the United Kingdom.

Other countries were redefining themselves that year. When China became Red China, the Soviet Union triumphantly predicted a coming world revolution that would see communism cover the globe.

By September the Russians had the atomic bomb.

THE newly named Republic of Ireland was poor but peaceful. There was only one recorded murder in 1949. The police were armed with batons and the goodwill of the people. Across the border in Northern Ireland there were plenty of legally held guns, though none was allowed to Catholics.

Many believed that the partition of the island could be ended by political negotiation. But, although they engaged in anti-partition rhetoric at election time, politicians in the Republic showed no real inclination to confront Britain on the issue.

"We won our independence in the same way America did," Ursula Halloran said angrily, "yet we're still tiptoeing around Britain! When are we going to stop being afraid of the old enemy?"

A united Ireland became a dream denied, receding into the past with all the other might-have-beens of Irish history.

.   .   .

JOHN Charles McQuaid, the authoritarian archbishop of Dublin and close friend of Eamon de Valera, was a dominant figure in Irish life. His influence was felt everywhere in the Republic. Among the crusades Archbishop Mc-Quaid undertook was a relentless battle to stamp out the mortal sin of sexuality among the Irish.

Under his rule the clergy also frowned on all secular forms of art. The theatre was considered an occasion of sin, and strict censorship laws enforced by the State ensured that all but the most inoffensive books were denied to the public. An average of 840 books a year were condemned as dangerous.

Through contacts abroad, Ursula Halloran acquired books that no one else read. Her ever-expanding library overflowed the bookshelves of the farmhouse and was stacked in tottering piles on the floor. Ursula and her father, Ned Halloran, had always encouraged Barry to read anything he wanted. By the time he was ten he was beginning to leaf through Shakespeare. At first the language was almost unintelligible to him, but when he discovered the sword fights he was hooked.

He organised the boys from neighbouring farms into Montagues and Capulets and staged ferocious battles, in which his side—though he was sometimes a Capulet and sometimes a Montague—always won. He could not bear to lose, and would simply try harder than anyone else.

In his blood, in his bones, was memory. Like music played beyond audible range. Yet when the light fell a certain way or he caught a whiff of some hauntingly familiar smell, Barry was struck dumb by its power.

The overlapping of his grandfather's life with his own, and his boyhood on what remained essentially a nineteenth-century farm in spite of its twentieth-century improvements, gave him a sense of connection with the past. On more than one occasion he had wandered down some lonely boreen until there was neither house nor barn in sight, then stopped and stood quietly, waiting. Obeying an instinct. Reaching out with something beyond flesh. Touching a past so distant that telephone poles and automobiles were unimaginable, and houses were made of wattle and daub. Circular walls, conical thatched roofs, pens of woven hurdles to keep the livestock safe from raiders. The smell of venison roasting on a spit flooded his mouth with saliva. He knew with certainty that the fire was being fed with the bounteous timber of ancient Ireland, which the *sasanach** had long since destroyed.

Against his hip he felt weight of the sword. *Fight back! You were born to . . .*

The fragile moment burst like a bubble and was gone.

·   ·   ·

*English.

IN August of 1950 Winston Churchill proposed to the Council of Europe at Strasbourg the creation of a European army. The Irish voted against the plan on the grounds that Britain maintained an occupying army in the north of Ireland.

IN the early 1950s Sinn Féin,* the political party of Irish republicans, began holding summer schools in Dublin. The subjects offered were as diverse as ancient Irish history and modern agricultural techniques. Party headquarters was on the top floor of 3 Lower Abbey Street—accommodations shared with the Legion of Mary. When the president of Sinn Féin addressed a meeting, the statue of the Virgin was standing right behind him. Her serene face looming over his shoulder lent an ironically symbolic weight to his words.

NINETEEN fifty-four was designated as the Marian Year. Throughout the Republic of Ireland special events were held in honour of the Virgin Mary. Thousands of children bedecked her altars with thousands of flowers and sang hymns in praise of Christ's gentle mother. Barry took part with skinned knees plainly visible below his short trousers, and afterwards he eagerly returned to playing soldiers with his friends.

He was always the general.

When he pointed his finger at someone and went "Bang," they obediently fell on the ground and rolled around moaning and groaning. In the end everyone walked away.

IN March, Ursula was furious to read in the papers that Northern Ireland Catholics on their way south to take part in the Marian celebrations had been savagely assaulted by sectarian thugs in a village called Portadown.

*Ourselves Alone.

Chapter Two

ON the sixth day of April, 1954, Ursula Halloran had carried a long, bulky parcel into the kitchen and set it on the table. Her fifteen-year-old son, Barry, wearing long trousers by now, had watched in fascination as she unwrapped layers of oiled cloth.

His mother took a long look at his plump cheeks and rounded chin, as if it was the last time she would see her son as a child. Then she unfolded the final layer of fabric.

Barry caught his breath.

The rifle was old but not neglected; the stock was still polished, the barrel still gleamed. Ursula lifted the weapon and cradled it against her body for a moment, then handed it to Barry.

The thrilling war stories the late Ned Halloran used to tell came flooding back to the boy. "Is this the rifle Granda carried in the IRA? The one he called his Fenian gun?"

Ursula nodded. "It's a short magazine Lee-Enfield .303 made during the First World War. Papa wanted me to give it to you on your fifteenth birthday, because that's when boys in ancient Ireland took up arms."

Barry examined the rifle with fascination. "Winchester Repeating Arms Co., New Haven, Connecticut," he read aloud from a small brass plate. "This was manufactured in America! How did Granda get it?"

"One wouldn't know." Ursula's lips tightened over her teeth. Barry recognised her expression; it meant she knew but would not tell.

"Is there any ammunition to go with it?"

She retrieved a cartridge box from among the wrappings. "So much time has passed, these may not be any good. Leave them in the box."

Barry sighted along the barrel and swung it slowly around the kitchen. "Granda's rifle, and now you're mine," he murmured to the stock pressed against his cheek. "All mine. What shall we do together?"

The answer sprang to Ursula's lips—fight for a united Ireland—but she choked the words back. The trumpets still sounded in her blood, but she was not prepared to give Barry to the cause. Not yet, when he was so young. Not yet, when he was her only child. She caught hold of the rifle barrel and pushed it toward the floor. "You're not going to do anything with this rifle, young man! That's history you hold in your hands. Pack it away and take good care of it so you can pass it on to your own children someday."

Barry was always obedient—to the degree that suited him. He took very good care of the rifle. He, who usually was as quick and impatient as any other boy his age, painstakingly disassembled the weapon, thoroughly cleaned and oiled every part, and then taught himself to put it back together again. But he did not pack the Lee-Enfield away.

A few weeks later one of the hired men discovered him in the farthest corner of the farthest pasture, shooting pebbles off the top of a field wall.

Gerry Ryan ambled over to watch.

A short, thickset man in his sixties, Ryan had a huge nose that sprawled at random across his face. He and his brother, George, had worked on the Halloran farm for many years; Barry had grown up under their avuncular gaze. "You make those pebbles dance for sure," Ryan commented. "First time I took you bird huntin' with my old shotgun I knew you had a keen eye. What else you plannin' to shoot with that rifle?"

"Vermin," Barry said without taking his eye off the target.

Ryan raised an elbow and gave his armpit a satisfying scratch. "That's Ned Halloran's old rifle, I'd know it anywhere. He carried it in the war against the Tans,* and then against the Free Staters.† Could tell some stories itself, that gun could."

"You won't say anything to Ursula about my firing it, will you? She told me not to."

Gerry Ryan looked offended. "I know how to hold my whist. Always have done. Never told all I knew about your granda, neither."

"Did you know a lot?"

"Happen I did. I saw things, heard things. Nothing he told me outright, mind. He always played his cards close to his vest."

"Exactly what do you know about him and those days?" Barry asked eagerly.

---

*The so-called Black and Tans, Bristish irregulars notorious for their brutality.

†Government forces during the Irish Civil War.

"Why you askin'?"

"I'm curious about, well, about what makes people the way they are. People like my mother, and Aunt Eileen, and you, and . . ."

"Get your nose broke," Ryan said curtly, "shoving it into other people's business."

IN 1955, twelve thousand members of the anti-Catholic Orange Order staged a triumphalist march through a solidly Catholic area in south County Down. Jeering at terrified residents, beating a relentless tattoo on massive Lambeg drums. The march was led by Brian Faulkner, a member of British Parliament, and protected by three hundred armed policemen of the Royal Ulster Constabulary. Better known as the RUC, that organisation saw itself as both a police constabulary and a paramilitary force answerable to the unionist majority.

The following day The Boys went looking for their rusted guns.

MEANWHILE the Republic of Ireland was being admitted to the United Nations. The Irish delegation avoided any mention of the rampant sectarianism in Northern Ireland. The government, now led by Taoiseach John A. Costello, was making a concerted effort to attract American tourists and did not want to call attention to violence anywhere on the island. The image being sold was one of thatched cottages, leprechauns, and forty shades of green.

BARRY Halloran, who did not live in a thatched cottage and knew better than to believe in leprechauns, was aware of at least forty shades of green. Maybe more. He loved the land unthinkingly. The shape of the hills, the weight of the wind, were dear to him. He never said anything so fanciful to his friends, though; boys did not talk like that.

STUDENTS in Hungary initiated an uprising in 1956, rebelling against the oppressive Soviet regime that had occupied their country since the end of World War Two. Lacking sophisticated weaponry, the would-be revolutionaries hurled invective, paving stones, and Molotov cocktails. The Hungarians called them freedom fighters. The Soviet Union called them terrorists.

That year Irish audiences were flocking to see a documentary titled *Mise Éire*.* The film was made up of newsreel footage from the 1916 Rising and the

---

*"I Am Ireland," from the poem by Patrick Pears.

subsequent War of Independence. No leprechauns here, only stark reality in monochrome. Legendary men and women straight from the history books came alive again on the screen, ready to sacrifice their lives for their country's freedom.

With the film's transcendent musical score, composer Seán O Riada redefined Irish music. His majestic, luminous vision of Ireland made people fall in love with their own country.

Ursula took Barry to see *Mise Éire* at the cinema in Ennis. "That's where Papa fought in 1916," she whispered when the General Post Office appeared on the screen. "Mama was with him. It was the adventure of a lifetime."

Spellbound, Barry watched as the GPO collapsed in flames and the centre of Dublin was demolished by British artillery.

These horrific scenes were followed by grainy images of the Irish rebels being marched to jail at gunpoint, grimy and smoke stained and staggering with weariness. Ursula clutched Barry's arm. "There's your grandfather! The thin lad in shirtsleeves."

As if he could hear her across the years, a young man with a bloody bandage wrapped around his forehead turned and gazed straight at the camera. A shiver ran up Barry's spine. *He's looking at me!*

When Barry Halloran stepped from the darkness of the theatre into a blaze of afternoon sunshine, he felt the entire weight of republican tradition like a hand on the small of his back, propelling him forward.

THE big radio in its highly varnished case glowed and crackled in the parlour. Many people kept their wireless machines in the kitchen, the heart of the Irish house, but Ursula would not allow domestic noises to drown out news broadcasts. The news was sacrosanct.

Besides, the kitchen was Great-aunt Eileen's territory. Therefore Ursula claimed the parlour.

When it was announced that Irish representatives had, for the first time, taken seats in the General Assembly of the United Nations, Ursula gave a cry that was heard throughout the house.

"Robert Emmet!" she cried gleefully.

Barry came running into the room. "What's wrong?"

"Emmet's famous speech in the dock! Surely Papa taught it to you. Before the British hanged Robert Emmet he said, 'When my country takes her place amongst the nations of the earth, then, and not 'til then, let my epitaph be written.'[1] Now's the time, Barry; now someone can write Emmet's epitaph."

Her eyes were shining. Her enthusiasm was contagious.

·   ·   ·

ON the fifth of November, 1956, Soviet tanks were rumbling through the streets of Budapest. Ursula and Barry listened together to the final desperate transmission from Radio Budapest.

"Help Hungary . . . Help . . . Help . . . Help . . ."[2]

Then silence.

Mother and son looked at each other. "That's the story of Ireland," Ursula remarked. "Since the sixteenth century every desperate attempt to regain our freedom was crushed. Until—"

"Until 1916 inspired the War of Independence in 1921," Barry interrupted. "And now we're free."

"Almost free," his mother replied. "There's still a way to go."

That evening Barry went upstairs and took Ned's rifle from under his bed. Breathlessly balanced between boy and man, he sat looking at the weapon as a cold blue twilight filled the room.

IN the halcyon years of Irish nationalism, the patriotism and fervour of the people had been a model for the rest of the world.[3] The policies of early nationalist governments, however, had not lived up to the dream of an egalitarian republic. Economic and social disaster resulted.

The 1950s were grim years in the Republic, blighted by chronic unemployment and endemic tuberculosis. America's post-war technological boom had not reached Ireland. Over one hundred thousand homes had telephones by 1953, but vacuum cleaners were unknown. A motorised farm vehicle was an object of envy. On countless small farms hay and grain were still being harvested with a scythe as they had been since the Bronze Age.

A married woman was expected to devote all her energies to home and family. She could not buy property or open an account in the local market without her husband's signature. If her husband failed to support her economically— even if he abused her physically—there was little she could do about it under the law. This attitude toward women was not unique to Ireland. In 1954, Commander Hatherill of Scotland Yard remarked, when assessing the annual crime figures in London, "There are only about twenty murders a year in London and not all are serious—some are just husbands killing their wives."

In Ireland a labourer was lucky to earn five pounds a month. Eamon de Valera, the dominant Irish political figure in the first half of the twentieth century, had envisioned a Celtic utopia, but young people found his frugal pastoralism stifling. Lack of employment and social stagnation drove them to seek their futures elsewhere. Emigration soared as more than twenty-five thousand a year left the country for America, for Australia, for England. For jobs. Neither the government nor the Church made any effort to stop them. The Republic of Ireland was hemorrhaging the generation that should have been its future.

A common sight was a single *garda** cycling along an otherwise empty road where nothing ever happened. In the garda station his sergeant would be doing what shop owners and cottage owners were doing in every town: standing in the doorway gazing idly out on streets where nothing ever happened.

This was the Ireland young Barry Halloran knew, and it was not good enough; not good enough by half.

THE day after the Hungarian revolution was crushed beneath the treads of Red Army tanks, Barry slipped out of the house before dawn. His mother was still asleep when he tiptoed past her door, carrying his boots in his hand. *I'm not a child anymore so I don't have to ask her permission. She'd approve anyway, no one's a more ardent republican than Ursula.*

As he strapped the rifle to his bicycle only the last stars were watching. *Are you up there too, Granda? Can you see me?*

In addition to his grandfather's rifle, Barry carried something else of Ned Halloran's. Ned had rarely been found without a book of poetry in his pocket, a habit he had inherited from his own father. As Barry set out on his new adventure, a copy of the poems of Francis Ledwidge was in his back pocket.

He cycled to a farmstead east of Ennis that rumour identified as a secret IRA camp. No sentry was on duty. Barry searched several outbuildings before the sound of snoring led him to a dilapidated cowshed. From the doorway he made out several dim shapes lying on the ground, wrapped in blankets. Abruptly one of them sat up. "Who the hell are you?" he demanded as he reached for his pistol.

"I'm Barry Halloran and IwannabeaVolunteer!" Barry's words tumbled over one another in his haste to get them out.

Séamus McCoy glowered at him. McCoy was short in stature but stronger than he looked. A little weary, a little worn; a hard man with some of the hard edges rubbed off. "I'm the officer in charge," he told Barry, "and you nearly got yourself killed walking in here like that. We don't like surprises and we don't welcome uninvited callers."

"I'm not a stranger, I'm Ned Halloran's grandson. I've even brought his rifle with me. It's out of ammunition but I thought you'd be able to . . ."

"Stand over there," McCoy snapped, "and keep your gob shut. I won't talk Army business 'til I have my boots on."

Barry self-consciously shifted his weight from one foot to the other while McCoy and the three men with him dressed. Because they slept in their clothes, dressing consisted of putting on footgear and coats. One man then went outside

---

*Member of the Garda Siochana, the "guardians of the peace" or civic guards.

to build a fire and make tea. Another opened a canvas backpack and took out some bread and hard cheese. "Give the lad a wee bit too," McCoy said. "He must be hungry."

Barry observed that the man's accent, with its flattened vowels and rising inflection, was not local. *Northern Ireland?* "Thank you, sir. I didn't have any breakfast before I came away."

One of the other men sniggered. Barry heard him whisper derisively, "Sir!"

McCoy said, "You'd best eat hearty before you go."

"Go?" Barry's heart sank. "But in Ennis I heard you were looking for recruits."

"Aye, you heard right. GHQ sent me down here to find a couple of good Clare men. Men, mind you, not lads with fuzz on their faces."

"But I'm eighteen."

McCoy looked sceptical. "And I'm the pope's daughter. When's your eighteenth birthday? The truth, now."

"Ah . . . next April."

"Think seventeen's old enough to be a soldier, do you?"

Barry felt his ears redden. "In ancient Ireland boys were warriors at fifteen."

"I wouldn't know, I wasn't there myself." McCoy busied himself with lighting a cigarette while he covertly assessed the potential recruit. Although the newcomer had a boy's unfinished face, he was well over six feet tall. Broad shoulders, big feet; he's probably still growing, McCoy concluded. Might make a hell of a soldier. Scare 'em to death with his size anyway.

A tin cup brimming with black tea was thrust at the officer, interrupting his ruminations. He scowled down at the brew. "No milk, Martin?"

"No cow."

"But this is a farm, damn it."

"No sugar, either," Martin said. "War's hell, ain't it?"

Between puffs on his cigarette and swallows of scalding tea, McCoy told Barry, "We're opening a new campaign in the north, mostly along the border. It'll be called Operation Harvest. You know what flying columns are, Seventeen?"

Barry's knowledge of Irish history had been acquired at Ned Halloran's knee. He could hardly wait to show how much he knew. "They're mobile attack units consisting of two dozen men. The original flying column was developed by an American-born Fenian, Captain Mackey, who used it against the British in Cork in the last century.[4] Michael Collins took up the idea and ran rings around the British in the War of Independence."

When McCoy smiled, the baring of teeth in his unshaven face gave him the expression of a jovial wolf. "Fair play to you, lad; that's one less lesson the Army'll have to teach you. We want our people to know Irish history. It explains why we're fighting and what we're fighting for. We'll be at war against Britain until they finish giving our country back.

"But for your information, Collins wasn't the only one responsible for forcing them to the truce table in 1921. He operated mainly in Dublin. The lads down the country ran their own war and a good fist they made of it.

"As for the future, initially this new campaign will employ four flying columns: Pearse, Clarke, Teeling, and Lynch. We plan to develop more later. The overall size of a column's been reduced to fifteen or so, but those fifteen have to be choice. We're waiting for units from Cork and Limerick to join us to make up the Lynch column."

"Named for Liam Lynch?"

McCoy squinted at Barry through a veil of cigarette smoke. "Aye. Commander of republican forces during the Civil War. Well, tomorrow I'll be taking the Lynch column north for a period of training. Then I'll turn them over to their permanent O/C for active service.

"This is an army, Seventeen, with a definite chain of command. We're fighting a war and no mistake, you have to understand that from the beginning. The Army Convention meets every four years, or when the need arises, and is our supreme policy-making authority. It's very democratic. Senior officers serve as voting delegates representing their men. They elect an executive body composed of veterans, and the committee appoints the Army Council. The council in turn appoints both the chief-of-staff and the headquarters staff. In the field the IRA is organised into brigades, each with its own staff, and a brigade may be divided into battalions. You got all that?"

"I do, sir."

"Unh-hunh," said McCoy, sounding unconvinced. "Be warned: This new campaign's not going to be a stroll in the sunshine. There's a lot of hard and dangerous work to be done. I'm talking about kill or be killed, Seventeen. Think you're able for it?"

"Indeed I am!"

THAT same afternoon Barry took the oath of the Irish Republican Army. Reverently holding a folded Irish tricolour in his hands, he recited, "I do solemnly swear that to the best of my knowledge and ability I will support and defend the Irish Republic against all enemies, foreign and domestic, and that I will bear true faith and allegiance to the same. I further swear that I do not and shall not yield a voluntary support to any pretended government, authority, or power within Ireland hostile or inimical to that Republic."

McCoy shook his hand with grave formality. "Congratulations, Volunteer Halloran. You're a member of *Oglaigh na h-Éireann*."*

Barry had felt ten feet tall that day. Entering the company of giants.

---

*The Irish Republican Army.

·   ·   ·

A week later found him on a lonely hillside in County Leitrim, listening to the echoes of the second rifle shot dying away. Then it was quiet. Too quiet. Warily, Barry edged out of the hazel thicket.

The rifle barked again. This time he felt the wind of the bullet's passage.

Someone *was* trying to kill him! This was for real!

He flung himself facedown on the ground. As he pitched forward he accidentally dropped his weapon.

Over the pounding of his heart he heard the thud of running boots. Coming closer.

Barry grabbed for his rifle. His fingertips just brushed the stock, but it was enough to send it sliding away from him down the icy slope.

For the first time in his life he knew what fear was. Fear squeezed the breath out of your lungs. Fear locked your muscles and left you helpless.

Barry struggled to remember the words of the Act of Contrition, but all he could think was, *God. Oh God*.

Then someone was standing over him. Helplessly, he waited for the bullet in the back of the head. Time telescoped into one heartbeat, his last on earth. And then another.

And another.

No great adventure for me after all. Suddenly he was angry. *Go ahead and shoot, damn you! Don't drag this out any longer!*

"Seventeen!" bellowed a familiar voice. "What the hell do you think you're doing?"

Rolling onto his back, Barry stared up at Séamus McCoy. The scale of Barry's relief told him how frightened he had been. *Cowering on the ground like a baby*. Disgust scalded him.

"When you've been ordered to stay still, stay still," the officer grated. "Don't move, don't even blink. D'ye understand?"

"I thought the unionists were trying to kill me."

The officer briefly glanced heavenwards. "Come down off the Cross and put me up there, I'm crucified by stupidity!" He lowered his eyes to the young man on the ground. "We're still miles from the border, Halloran. It was me shooting to give you the experience of being under fire. If I'd meant to kill you you'd be dead by now.

"You broke every rule there is, d'ye know that? You disregarded orders, you stepped into the line of fire, and you threw your weapon away." He looked pointedly at Barry's crotch. "I'm surprised you didn't piss your pants for good measure."

Barry heard a loud guffaw. The rest of the column was coming over the crest of the hill. He realised they had been there for quite some time, just out of sight. Laughing at him.

At that moment Barry made a vow to himself: *I'll never let anyone see me afraid again. I'd rather die first.*

Something shifted in his eyes; long-lidded grey eyes from which the youth suddenly vanished. Someone older, sterner, savage, glared up at McCoy. "Is this how you train recruits? By shooting at them?" Even Barry's voice had changed. It was a low growl, curiously unnerving.

McCoy squared his shoulders in a conscious effort to reassert his authority. "Unh ... better me than the enemy, Halloran. A soldier's no use 'til he's been shot at a time or two. Then we know what he's made of." He reached a hand down to Barry and was relieved when the boy accepted it. "On your feet now, *avic.** We have a way to go before nightfall."

Still laughing, the other Volunteers gathered around Barry. Feargal O'Han-lon gave him a ferocious punch on the shoulder. "Ye've been baptised good and proper now, Seventeen."

Barry tossed his hair out of his eyes. With a reckless, devil-may-care grin, he returned the blow in full measure. His fist was hard and his arm was strong and the blood was singing in his veins.

He felt all alive under his skin.

*My son.

Chapter Three

WHEN Ursula realised that her son was missing she went looking for Ned's rifle. It was missing too.

"I'm sorry I ever gave that gun to Barry," Ursula told Eileen. "Now he's run off to join the IRA."

The two women were in the kitchen, the one place where their separate worlds overlapped. The farm was Ursula's dominion. Eileen, the youngest of Ned Halloran's sisters, kept house.

Ursula Halloran was thin. A small woman with greying hair cut like a boy's and an abundance of nervous energy. The angular planes of her face were ageless. Ursula wore that face like a shield with the real woman hidden behind it. Only in rare unguarded moments did her eyes reveal banked fires.

Eileen Halloran Mulvaney was fat. In her youth Eileen had been pretty, but she had married a drunkard and borne eight children in quick succession. One had died in infancy and two more succumbed to tuberculosis before her husband beat her into a final miscarriage and deserted her. Since then she and her family had been dependent on Ursula's charity.

The surviving children, who should have been a consolation in Eileen's old age, had left home as soon they could. The boys had emigrated; Ursula paid their fares. The girls had married as soon as they were old enough; Ursula paid for their weddings.

Eileen sought solace in her faith and comfort in her food. She ate too fast to taste her meals. The important thing was swallowing, cramming material into an emptiness that could never be filled.

As she spooned thick cream onto a scone slathered with butter, she reminded Ursula, "You had to give Ned's rifle to the boy, he made you promise to. But why do think he's gone to the IRA?"

"Barry's been impulsive ever since he could walk. Half the time we never knew where he was. Do you recall the day—he wasn't more than six years old—when he strolled all the way to Ennis without saying a word to anybody?"

Eileen chuckled. "When you finally found him he was exhausted, but indignant that you'd come after him. He claimed he just wanted to know where the road went."

"He's taken some other road now, I'm afraid," said Ursula, "and God knows where it will lead him. He's disappeared along with the rifle and the compass Henry Mooney sent him for Christmas. What do you think?"

Eileen swallowed and reached for another scone. "I think you're proud of Barry. There's nothing would please you more than having a son in the IRA."

"I am proud of him," Ursula conceded. "More proud than I've ever been of anything in my life. But if he gets himself killed I'll never forgive him."

Two days later she found Barry's bicycle leaning against the side of the barn, returned anonymously in the night.

IN the years leading up to Operation Harvest, the IRA—or the Army, as it called itself, ignoring the fact that the Republic had a national army under government control—had been acquiring new ordnance. Daring arms raids were staged on military installations in both England and Northern Ireland. Sympathisers abroad were purchasing arms and arranging to have them smuggled into Ireland. In smoky Irish pubs in New York and Boston and Manchester the children and grandchildren of immigrants sang songs about Ireland's tragic history, then passed the hat to buy guns for The Boys.

In the Republic of Ireland, members of the IRA were arrested on a sporadic basis by a government which did not know what else to do with them.

ON the day that Barry was sworn into the Volunteers, men from Cork and Limerick began arriving at McCoy's encampment. By nightfall there were a full dozen of them. A few were new recruits but most were veterans. They came from varied backgrounds. Students, farm labourers, a schoolteacher, a shop assistant, a bank clerk.

Barry had fancifully imagined the IRA as a uniformed army marching in formation like the British or American troops in the newsreels. However, the reconstructed IRA was a guerrilla force. The officer in command was called the O/C rather than the C/O because, as McCoy said scathingly, "C/O is the British term."

They would be a column in name only. No uniforms, no marching in formation. "You'll wear your own clothes," McCoy informed the new recruits. "GHQ's provided us with light arms, a few rifles and pistols and some ammunition. Not enough, but some. Any of you know how to shoot?" He did not wait for an answer. "Once we're across the border we'll have target practice. As for transport, you're going to walk. I want every one of you as fit as a butcher's dog by the time we reach the border. There'll be no hitching rides."

Walking was still the most common form of travel in rural Ireland. Men thought nothing of driving cattle on foot for twelve miles to market, then returning home by the same method.

"You'll carry everything you need on your backs," McCoy said. "You may not know how to put together a comfortable pack now, but I guarantee you will by the time we get there. Walk in groups of two or three, no more than four at the most. You'll be less conspicuous that way. Remember to keep an eye out for the *gardai*. If a garda stops you for any reason, you don't know the names of the lads walking with you, understand? They're just some men you met on the road. You know nothing about them. If you're questioned be polite, but give no details.

"Which brings up an important point. As a Volunteer the first lesson you must learn is: Whatever you say, say nothing. Even to your families. That's safest for everyone.

"We'll spend the night in safe houses when we can, but we're just as likely to be billeted in hedgerows. The important thing is to keep out of sight. We have plenty of friends on this side of the border who'll see that you don't go hungry, but in the Six Counties it'll be a different story."

At dawn the next morning the column set out for the north. The pistols were concealed beneath their clothing. McCoy stowed the rifles and ammunition, together with a shotgun belonging to a Volunteer from Cork, in a large handcart. He covered them with a tarpaulin and piled turnips on top. "If anyone asks, you're taking these to market. If we're discovered, try to get the weapons safely away. If for some reason you can't, disable them."

Pairs of men took turns pushing the cart.

McCoy chose a route that followed farm roads for the most part, avoiding towns and large villages. At unexpected moments he would order the men to run. Sometimes he did this when they were cutting across open fields, which was hard on the men pushing the cart. More than once they had to stop and go back for their turnips.

During that first day the veterans regaled the recruits with their Army experiences. Their exploits reminded Barry of games he had played as a small boy. Cowboys and Red Indians. *This is fun!*

Hard on the heels of that thought came another: *But if no one enjoyed soldiering, how could we have wars?*

The makeup of the small groups changed frequently. Some moved forward, others fell back. When it was Barry's turn to help push the cart he was teamed with a Limerick man called Seán South. South, who was twenty-seven, came from the republican stronghold of Garryowen. He was a member of the Irish-speaking branch of the Legion of Mary and preferred to speak that language.

Barry took the opportunity to practice his own language skills. "How are you employed when you are not with the Army?" he asked in careful Irish.

"I am a social worker in Limerick. I paint, and play the violin. And go to Mass every day of course."

Before Barry could frame a response South continued, "I also publish an Irish language magazine, *An Gath*. We address such topics as the decline of the Irish language, the problems of western Ireland, and the future of the nation. In the last issue I wrote, 'There is an end to foolishness; the time for talk has ended!'[1] So here I am in the Army. The true Irish Republican Army, the only one dedicated to this island as a whole."

Confronted by a man who was living his life so fully, Barry fell back on his one asset. "Perhaps you have heard of my grandfather, Ned Halloran? He was in the GPO in 1916 with Pádraic Pearse, and during the War of Independence he fought the Tans in Limerick."

"You're leaving out the most important part of the story," South replied. "Without Ned Halloran the IRA might not have survived. In the late thirties and forties we were holding on by our toenails. It was your grandfather, working in secret, who kept the scattered fragments of the Army in contact with one another."

The cart slewed to a halt as Barry stopped in his tracks. "My granda did that?" he said in English. "He never mentioned . . . How'd he do it?"

"Halloran knew just about everyone in the Volunteers and where they were at any given time. He even had connections in America, or so I've heard. Perhaps he held all the information in his head, but more likely he kept written records. That would have been desperately dangerous, of course. But if what they say about him is true, he paid danger no mind."

"Did you ever meet him?"

Seán South replied, "I never had the privilege; Ned Halloran was before my time. I envy you, being his grandson."

At twilight they made camp in a secluded strip of woodland. McCoy collected the weapons and stashed them away under the tarp and a pile of brush, keeping out his own pistol in case of emergency. Barry was reluctant to surrender his precious rifle. McCoy said brusquely, "This is Oglaigh na h-Éireann. Discipline is all-important. You respect the rank, not the individual, and if your commandant says do something you do it. Accept the rules or go home, Seventeen."

Barry handed over the rifle.

"Another thing," said McCoy. "In 1954, Standing Order Number Eight was incorporated into the IRA's General Army Orders, and I want every one of you to memorise it. 'Volunteers are strictly forbidden to take any military action against the twenty-six county forces in any circumstances whatsoever.' "[2]

"Does that mean if the Free State Army shoots at us we can't shoot back?" someone asked.

"Indeed it does. And if the gardai arrest you, go quietly. We have no quarrel with them, no matter what they think about us. Our enemy is the army of occupation in the Six Counties. Which brings up another point. Our enemy is *not* the Protestants. This isn't about religion, not with us. Religious wars have caused too damned much trouble as it is. The Protestant civilians across the border are Irish just the same as we are, and don't you forget it."

There were other rules to learn. McCoy drilled them into his men from the beginning. Piety, courtesy to women, and sobriety while on active duty were imperative. "The Brits accuse the Irish of being ignorant, drunken louts," McCoy said, "so the Volunteers have to prove them wrong. Anyone who lets the Army down is gone."

Once the day's activities were over, rank was set aside. The evening was devoted to conversation. Topics ranged from discovering familial connections to swapping amusing anecdotes to "country matters"—the euphemism for sex.

When Barry asked about his accent, Séamus McCoy said, "I was reared in West Belfast, but now I have a wee bolthole in a village in Tipperary. Place called Ballina."

"What brought you down here?"

"To be closer to the heart of the campaign. These days the Belfast IRA consists of little more than one man with a rifle—and that an old Martini Henry. There's the Felons' Club, of course, but . . ."

"What's that?"

McCoy smiled. "The Irish Republican Felons' Association, comprised of what you might call retired Volunteers. They have a clubhouse on the Falls Road. A friend of mine, Gerry Adams, Senior—he has a young son by the same name—was one of the founders. He was shot and wounded by the RUC in forty-two. When the last major release of republican prisoners took place in the north, Gerry and some others decided to organise a place where they could meet and socialise. Talk about old times, tell each other war stories. To thumb their noses at the Brits they named it the Felons' Association, turning an insult into something to be proud of."

Barry grinned. *I'm part of this!* he silently congratulated himself. *This spirit. These men.*

Conversation circled and spiralled while McCoy smoked cigarette after cigarette, listening to his little group talk about old times, tell each other war stories. Watching his charges coalesce into the band of brothers they must become.

Occasionally he threw in a few words of encouragement. "We're going to have the Irish Republic yet, lads, don't ever doubt it."

"I thought we'd been a republic since 1949," one of the recruits said.

McCoy gave a snort. "Don't you believe it. The Twenty-Six Counties are just the Free State under another name, they don't begin to measure up to the republican ideal. The government down here's still run along British lines, aping the British Parliament, with British-style bureaucrats determined to preserve the status quo."

"That's what my mother says," Barry whispered to the man sitting next to him.

McCoy cleared his throat. "How much do any of you actually know about republicanism?"

The men glanced self-consciously at one another. The moment lengthened, became uncomfortable. At last Barry spoke up. "My grandfather went to Saint Enda's College and studied with Pádraic Pearse, so he knew all about Irish republicanism. He told me it began way back in—"

"Don't be making a show of yourself, Halloran," one of the veterans interrupted.

Barry was forcibly reminded of one of Ned Halloran's favourite sayings: "A man never learns anything with his mouth open."

He said nothing else that evening. But he listened—avidly. One of the older veterans made a comment he committed to memory: "Wars are like women. They're all the same yet every one's different."

When I know enough women I'll test that theory, Barry promised himself.

A few days later he overheard McCoy remark, "That Seventeen's a deep one. Doesn't talk much, but you can tell he's thinking underneath." Although it was flattering, the comment made Barry vaguely uncomfortable. It placed him under an obligation to be more serious than he felt.

Because the Army *was* fun.

The Boys often sang to pass the time. While they were trudging across a ploughed field in County Roscommon, painfully negotiating the cart over the broken earth, a tenor from Cork led a rendition of "Four Green Fields" that brought a lump to Barry's throat. *My fourth green field will bloom once again, said she.*

Séamus McCoy broke the mood by demanding, "Don't you lads know anything livelier?"

With a receding hairline and permanently bloodshot eyes, McCoy seemed old to Barry. He was all of thirty-eight. But a common saying was, "It's the old dog for the hard road." The campaign in the north promised to be a hard road indeed. Séamus McCoy was determined to have his men well prepared before handing them over; prepared spiritually as well as physically.

He insisted they attend Mass. "Slip quietly into church and stand at the back.

Attract no attention and leave before anyone else does, lads. As for confession . . . best not. For the sake of your fellow Volunteers say nothing to outsiders."

URSULA Halloran was a rebel. From time to time she tried to shock Eileen Mulvaney out of her unquestioning Catholicism. "Institutionalised religion is a poor substitute for spirituality, Eileen. People should listen to the spirit within themselves, that's the voice of God. It doesn't come from some male spinster in a long dress."

"Och now, that's not fair." The older woman knew she could not debate Ned's educated daughter. Her defensive technique was to let her lips quiver and her eyes fill with tears.

"I blame Eamon de Valera," Ursula countered, warming to the topic. "He fought to free Ireland from England in 1916, only to hand the country over to the Church as soon as he got into power."

"Sure we've always belonged to the Church," Eileen said.

"That's what's wrong. The Church is supposed to belong to its *people*. But for centuries the English forced the Irish to be deferential until it became part of our nature. Now that quality has delivered us to McQuaid's theological terrorism." Ursula liked that phrase. She said it again, savouring the words: "Theological terrorism. McQuaid's policies are designed to protect the institution, not to enhance the life of the spirit. Anyone who doesn't agree with them is publicly condemned from the altar.

"Fear and abnegation, that's what the Church in this country demands of us. It's not like that in other countries. I've been to Europe, I've seen with my own eyes what Catholicism is like in places like Italy and Switzerland. It's joyous! Not here, though. In Ireland people are not only frightened of the clergy, they're even afraid of their own bodies. And who taught us to be that way? The priests!

"Do you think it's natural for men to sit on one side in the church and their wives on the other, as if they didn't sleep in the same bed at night? Or for boys and girls to have to enter the school by different doors? Is it an act of Christian charity when the priest reads out in public how much each family gave to the collection, shaming those who could not afford to give enough—in his opinion? The Church does everything it can to keep us terrified."

Ursula had proved that she was not afraid. She had borne a son out of wedlock and raised him in defiance of both the Church and social convention. When she met a priest in town she held her head up proudly and looked him right in the eyes.

Usually it was the priest who looked away first.

Yet Ursula had insisted that Barry have a Catholic upbringing. At first the Church was glad to have him, seeing him as a sort of token penitence on the part of his mother. He had even spent a year as an altar boy in surplice and soutane—until dismissed by the parish priest. "Your nephew has too much energy to serve on the altar," the priest told Eileen. "It's like trying to contain a whirlwind in a bottle."

"Don't think this means you can get out of Mass and midweek Benediction," Ursula had warned Barry. "We live in a Catholic country. Whatever about me, I don't want you to grow up feeling like an outsider."

Yet Barry, fatherless in a patriarchal country, an only child in a land of large families, a dreamer given to wandering off by himself, did feel like an outsider. Until the moment when he stood on a frozen hillside in County Leitrim and Feargal O'Hanlon punched his shoulder.

WHEN the column moved off from the deserted village, Feargal and Barry walked together. Feargal, two years older than Barry, was a merry young man with a lopsided smile. His unfailing good nature had already made him popular with the rest of the column.

As the pair strode along he asked, "D'ye play much football, Seventeen?"

"Some. You?"

"Senior for Monaghan," O'Hanlon said proudly. "We were almost unbeatable last year."

"Good on you. Actually I'm more of a hurling man myself."

Feargal glanced sideways at his companion. "You have that look about you. Clever and quick for such a tall fellow. But . . ."

"But what?"

"To tell the truth, you have the oddest ears I ever saw."

Barry took no offence. "Inherited 'em from my father. His ears came to a peak at the top too, or so I'm told."

"Is he dead then?"

"He is dead."

"I'm sorry," Feargal murmured. He said no more on the subject. A person never pried into another's grief.

AS a small boy Barry had simply accepted that his father was dead, in the way young children accept everything adults tell them. When he grew old enough to ask questions Ursula's replies were unsatisfying. "What was my father like?" elicited only, "He was a good man."

That was not enough of a description. "Do you have a picture of him?"

"I do not."

"Well, do I look like him?"

"A little."

"How?"

"You have his ears."

"What else?" Barry persisted. "What about his hair?"

"Redder than yours, with less gold in it."

"Was his name Halloran too?"

The flesh around Ursula's eyes tightened. "His name was Cassidy. Finbar Cassidy."

"So you're Mrs. Cassidy?"

"I was never Mrs. Cassidy."

"Why not?"

"I did not choose to marry." She clamped her mouth shut. There was to be no further discussion.

Barry questioned both Ned and Eileen but could not reconstruct his father from their memories. Neither had ever met Finbar Cassidy. "Leave it be," Ned had advised. "Your mother will tell you what she wants you to know."

"She doesn't want to talk about him."

"Then you must respect her wishes. Perhaps someday she'll change her mind."

BRILLIANT in black and white plumage, a magpie alit on the path of the two Volunteers and strutted along ahead of them, puffed with its own importance. "Hello, Mr. Magpie!" Barry called. A lone magpie was said to bring bad luck unless spoken to respectfully.

Feargal snorted. "That's just an old *piseog*.* You'd best fly away," he warned the bird, "or you'll be the one with the bad luck. I'll pluck your feathers for my girl's hat."

"Your girl?"

"A little sweetheart back in Monaghan who I see at the dances sometimes. You know how it is, Halloran. One of the show bands comes 'round and we all go to the parish hall. Fellows on one side, girls on the other. Lads talking to lads, girls giggling and pretending not to look at us. Us pretending not to look at them. Someday I'll ask her for a dance, though."

TREAT all women like you would the Virgin Mary," the priests said. But they didn't say how that applied to the thoughts that came to a boy at night in his bed; the thoughts that burned and thrilled . . . and shamed.

So far Barry's only experience of the opposite sex had been with a shopkeep-

---

*Superstition.

er's daughter in Ennis, who stood with her back against the wall in a narrow laneway off Parnell Street. Afterwards Barry had wondered, *Is that all?* Weeks of covert glances and sweating every time he saw her had resulted in a brief explosion that left his knees trembling, then faded before he could savour it.

The girl had darted anxious glances left and right while she pulled up her knickers. "Do ye love me, Barry? Say you love me so."

What has this to do with love? At that moment Barry had wanted only to be somewhere, anywhere, else.

As he strode along beside Feargal O'Hanlon, Barry was in high spirits. Childhood playfellows were behind him, as were the days of Montague and Capulet. His companions were real soldiers now. Bending, he seized a stick from the ground and used it to slash the dead meadow grasses. "Here's a sword for our enemies!" He laughed aloud.

"Up the IRA!" cried Feargal.

The column continued northward in no particular order. All that was required was that they keep going until they reached their destination. A few more miles would take them to the border. Beyond the border lay Northern Ireland. The fourth green field of Erin; in strangers' hands, as the song said.

"Why'd you join the Army, Feargal?"

"It was that or get a job, and work for Catholic boys in Monaghan is thin on the ground."

"I mean why did you really join?"

Feargal hesitated for a moment. "To finish what they started," he said soberly.

Barry did not need to ask who "they" were. Their bodies lay in quicklime in Arbour Hill cemetery but their names were engraved on Irish hearts. *Pearse, Plunkett, MacDonagh, MacDermott, Connolly, Clarke, Ceannt.*

The signatories of the 1916 Proclamation had been inspired by the Gaelic Revival and fired with the romantic nationalism that swept the world at the dawn of the twentieth century. Like most Irishmen of their generation, they were avid readers. Several were poets of considerable merit. Intelligent and idealistic, they had dreamed of a nonsectarian Irish Republic where all children were cherished and all citizens equal.

Ned Halloran had insisted that Barry memorise the entire Proclamation.

The men with Barry and Feargal came of a different generation from that of Ned Halloran. The Great War had put paid to romantic nationalism. The Irish Civil War had changed Ireland's image of herself, fragmenting her politically. The Second World War with its concentration camps and atomic bombs had provided a foretaste of hell. People were more cynical now and far less sentimental.

Yet in spite of all this, Ireland's unfinished revolution went on.

• • •

WHEN the column came to the border there was no sign to indicate that they were entering a foreign country. Fifteen men snaked along the southern bank of a stream until they came to a wooden footbridge closed off by two strands of rusty wire. Lifting the top strand, McCoy said, "Duck under, lads. Anyone entering the Six Counties from the Republic is required to have a passport, or at least a document signed by the authorities, but we have our own ways of getting in. And out."

Almost at once Barry could see a difference. The unkempt countryside in the Republic was a patchwork of irregularly shaped fields bounded by tangled hedgerows teeming with wildlife. Fields in Northern Ireland were neat, geometrically precise, and divided by well-maintained walls and fences. Yet the air was the same on both sides of the border. The earth was the same too, even if the enemy insisted it was part of Britain.

The Enemy. Barry knew who they were. Everything was simple, black and white. Like the magpie.

The column trudged along a country road. From a farmhouse chimney came a whiff of burning turf. The haunting fragrance reminded Barry of home. And Mam.

He called her Mam only in his thoughts. Aloud she was always Ursula, a preference she had expressed long ago.

A mile farther on brought them to a meadow in the lap of sheltering hills. "We'll camp here for the night," McCoy said. "There's a farm up the road that belongs to some of our crowd, so we'll ask them for spades and a pickaxe. It's time you had practice making dugouts for yourselves."

At first building dugouts was fun. The men made jokes as they worked. Later Barry thought he was too excited to sleep, but between one thought and the next the world slipped away and he knew nothing until he awoke cold and stiff in the pre-dawn dark. McCoy was prodding the sole of his foot with a rifle. "Crawl out from under that blanket, Seventeen. Things are about to get serious."

Barry leapt to his feet while his mind was still cobwebbed with sleep. From that day on he made sure to be the first one up. Eyes open, brain alert, ready to learn.

It was easy to tell the difference between Catholic and Protestant areas. In Protestant areas the houses were better, the roads were better, the schools were better. There were other, more subtle differences as well, such as the fact that northern Catholics said they went to chapel rather than church because *church* was the Protestant term.

During the next two weeks the column was constantly on the move, roving the Six Counties and learning their way around while simultaneously practicing guerrilla tactics and avoiding the police. At night they gathered around tiny campfires and talked. Talked politics and war.

McCoy explained that the IRA had a long-standing tradition of political abstention. "Politics is a waste of time. Britain became an empire through force of arms, and that's all the British respect. There's no way for Ireland to end the injustice of partition except through the armed struggle."

A recruit chimed in, "That means the IRA, since the current government are too cowardly to fight for the country that was taken away from them."

"Right you are," said one of the veterans. "Furthermore, we're fighting a monster with two heads. One is the government at Stormont, and the other's the government at Westminster that props it up. That's why the Army needs to carry the war to England."

Stories were told, in voices hushed with admiration, of brave men who crossed the Irish Sea to attack the enemy on their own home soil. Planting bombs in Britain was a tactic that dated from the preceding century. There was rarely any real damage due to incompetence on the part of the bombers, but it served to keep the British public aware of "the Irish problem."

Chapter Four

———•·❧·•———

OUTSIDE Derry City the Volunteers came upon a ramshackle community known as Tin Town. Rusting Nissan huts that had been used during World War Two for housing troops in transit to Europe were filled to overflowing with impoverished Catholic families. The place was a sea of mud, stinking of cesspools and running with rats. Amidst scenes of appalling squalor, parents struggled to raise their children as best they could.

"If you ever wonder what this war's really about, here's your answer," McCoy told his men.

Two-thirds of the north's population were staunchly unionist in their views. Learning how to make contact with nationalists who wanted to see their fractured country reunited was an essential part of a Volunteer's training. "You'll be relying on the locals for intelligence and supplies," McCoy said. "Some of the most dedicated republicans are in the north; it's their home ground they're fighting for. Be careful, though. The Brits have paid informers everywhere, often the person you'd least expect. The wrong word in the wrong ear and you could wake up in one of Her Majesty's holiday hotels." The wolfish smile flickered.

"Were you ever arrested yourself?" a recruit wanted to know.

"I've been lifted once or twice. Can't say I'd recommend royal hospitality. Being kept in a darkened cell for weeks on end plays hell with your eyesight."

Suddenly Barry understood McCoy's constant squinting.

In spite of his damaged vision, McCoy usually saw the bright side. He often said, "Don't worry, lads, everything will come right in the end." And made them believe it.

Such optimism was essential. The winter of 1956 was cold. Rain fell almost every day, turning overnight to frozen mud. Physical discomfort was a constant and hunger was never far away.

Training sessions did not include weapons practice because the sound of gunfire could draw the RUC,* but McCoy directed mock attacks and ambushes, advances and retreats. The men memorised maps and practiced infiltrating areas under cover of darkness. During the day they hid out in dugouts in the woods.

Barry and Feargal usually shared a dugout. Sitting side by side in a damp, dark hole that smelled of earth, they used conversation to ease the tedium. They told each other silly things and serious things, laughed at jokes that had meaning only for themselves, and exchanged dreams and hopes and fears they would admit to no one else.

They enjoyed comparing their childhood foibles. "I would do just about anything for the pure divvil of it," Barry admitted without shame. "And I was a fearful dreamer. I spent more time gazing out the window than I ever did learning my lessons."

Feargal said, "I was sports mad. Mitched school every chance I got to play ball. Used to steal a few coppers from the old man's pocket to buy bits and pieces of equipment. He never even noticed."

Barry began to boast, "My mother never knew what I . . ." then stopped in mid-sentence as a more mature realisation dawned on him. "I thought my mother never knew what I was up to," he amended. "But looking back now, I believe she did."

EVERY move the Volunteers made carried an awareness of imminent danger. "Even the dogs in the street are watching you," McCoy stressed. "Up here the IRA's the enemy."

At a rural crossroads in County Tyrone, McCoy raised his hand to signal a halt. "At ease, lads. We'll be waiting here for Commandant Garland, if the bloody RUC haven't picked him up. He'll be your permanent O/C."

McCoy sat down by a signpost that gave directions in English only, and in imperial miles rather than the longer Irish mile. Grunting with pleasure, McCoy scratched his back against the signpost while his men lounged along the verge at the side of the road. The recruits began removing their shoes to examine their feet for blisters.

Barry was unlacing his boots when Seán South put out a staying hand. "I wouldn't," he advised. "Wait until we camp for the night. If you take them off

*Royal Ulster Constabulary, the police force of Northern Ireland.

now your feet will be too swollen to put them back on." Barry tried to pass the warning on to Feargal but the young man from Monaghan was too involved in a discussion about the fine points of Gaelic football to hear him.

Barry took out the slim volume of Ledwidge's poetry and began to read. By now he knew all the poems by heart, but revisiting them was like talking with old friends.

McCoy smoked a cigarette until it burned down to his fingers, then got to his feet and brushed off his pants. "Listen up, lads." Barry put his book back in his pocket. "Seán Garland's a good skin," McCoy went on. "He has an orderly mind and a good eye for the lay of the land. A few years ago GHQ decided to send a member of the Dublin brigade up to Armagh to enlist in the British Army, and they chose Garland. He made a very convincing recruit, and the Brits accepted him into the Royal Irish Fusiliers without question. Almost at once he began passing valuable information to GHQ. Documents, maps, even photographs taken with a mini-camera.

"The intelligence Garland provided was responsible for one of the most successful arms raids we ever had. Our lads lifted two hundred and fifty new rifles, thirty-seven Stens, nine Brens, and a bunch of training rifles from the Armagh barracks and got them safely back across the border. The British Army was left with egg on its face."

Several Volunteers sniggered. "I wish I'd been there to throw the eggs," Barry whispered to Seán South, who nodded agreement.

McCoy continued, "Eventually the IRA withdrew Garland from the British Army before they could sniff him out. Now he's going to be in charge of you lot, and I expect you to make me proud of you.

"Your second in command will be David O'Connell. Dave's only nineteen but don't let that fool you. He joined Sinn Féin in 1955 and then the Volunteers. He was appointed over Vincent Conlon, the former quartermaster general of the IRA, so that tells you how highly he's regarded at headquarters."

The Volunteers waited with heightened anticipation. For a long time nothing happened. At last a redheaded man on a motorbike appeared around the bend in the road. A second man was riding pillion with his knees drawn up to keep his feet from dragging the ground.

Séamus McCoy gave a relieved shout: "Hullo, you two! I was beginning to think you'd got lost."

The bike growled to a halt. The pillion passenger unfolded himself and nimbly stepped aside so the driver could dismount.

The redhead strode up to McCoy. "Shay, you old rogue," he said in a hard Dublin accent. "What d'ye have for me?"

"You're looking at them, Seán. This unlikely lot sprawled all over the road."

Seán Garland gestured toward his former passenger. "This is—"

"Dáithí Ó Conaill, in the Irish," the man interrupted, stepping forward. "My friends call me Dave."

O'Connell had a domed forehead and receding hairline that gave him the appearance of a much older man. But this was not the reason the Volunteers were staring at him.

Dave O'Connell was six and a half feet tall.

"They must feed 'em good where he comes from," Feargal murmured in awe.

SEÁN Garland took over the column with smooth professionalism. "We're getting you out of sight as soon as possible," he told the men. "I don't want to lose you to the RUC before I've had time to learn your names. Down the road now, and on the double."

Barry cast a pitying glance at Feargal, who winced as he crammed his swollen feet back into his shoes.

Within an hour the Volunteers were snugly billeted in a barn belonging to a republican family. "From now on you'll take your orders from me or Dave," Garland told them, "and no one else. Each column is relatively autonomous. The Army wants to keep them as separate as possible because the less one group knows about another, the less chance there is of an informer giving out valuable information."

The mention of informers gave Barry a jolt. His vision of the Irish Republican Army was pure and noble. Ned Halloran had never said anything about informers within.

"Our primary mission," Garland continued, "is to disable and demoralise the enemy. That will involve cutting their communications, obstructing roads and railways, and putting their facilities out of commission. In short, making matters as difficult as possible for the occupying forces. We'll use explosives to gain entry to their military installations and . . ."

"And blow open the odd prison door?" McCoy suggested.

Garland gave him a wintry smile. "The only explosives we have right now are gelignite and paxo. Paxo's made from potassium chloride and paraffin wax and it's pretty volatile stuff. Of course we can always make Molotov cocktails with glass bottles and petrol," *like the freedom fighters in Hungary,* thought Barry, "but they're almost as dangerous to the man who throws them as they are to his target.

"Our friends across the pond are buying American war surplus for us—anyone with dollars can buy American war surplus—but we don't have any mortars. Other weapons are coming on stream, though. We'll take whatever we can get. So let's have a look at your ordnance."

Frowning, Garland had examined the column's small stock of rifles and pistols. "Is this all you brought, Shay?"

"It's everything GHQ sent us, plus one old rifle and a sawn-off shotgun that two of the lads brought with them."

"What, no pitchforks?"

"Not unless we steal some from this barn."

Garland chuckled. "We won't need to, thank God. Every attack group's being supplied with machine guns. We've two Thompson submachine guns and a Bren tucked away a few miles from here."

"What's a Bren?" asked one of the recruits.

"An infantry weapon really, and more reliable than the Thompson. Thompsons have a tendency to pull to the left unless you know how to allow for it. You fire a Thompson standing up and spray the bullets around, but the Bren's mounted on a bipod and you lie on your belly to shoot. It's much steadier, and can take the same ammunition as the Lee-Enfield .303."

"I have a Lee-Enfield .303!" Barry cried. "I could handle a Bren."

Garland slanted a look in his direction. "Keen as mustard, are you? Ever used any class of machine gun?"

"Not yet, but I can . . ."

"Halloran's quite a marksman with his own rifle," McCoy commented. "He could be a sniper."

Sniper. Me! I told Gerry Ryan I was going to shoot vermin. That's what the enemy does to our crowd, kills them like vermin. It's only fair they get back what they give.

Sniper. Barry liked the sound of the word. Adventurous and heroic.

Seán Garland was saying, "In the finish-up, we can't hope to defeat the enemy through conventional warfare. Britain will always be able to supply more men and more weapons. But we can do what Michael Collins did: we can break down the machinery of administration until the British are unable to govern. Then they'll have to withdraw from Northern Ireland."

"However long it takes, we'll get our country back," Séamus McCoy added. His voice rang with conviction.

This is for real. Sitting on a barrel in a barn. Legs aching. Stomach rumbling. Adrenaline prickling beneath the skin. *However long it takes, we'll get our country back.*

The barn smelled of hay and chickens.

"One more thing," said Garland. "Up here labels are a matter of life and death. Keep that in mind. You have Catholics and nationalists and republicans; Protestants and unionists and loyalists. Those are, broadly speaking, the two sides, with the government soundly on the latter. Within those two divisions there's a lot of crossover. All Catholics aren't nationalists; many are just people who want to work and bring up their families in safety. Nationalists may or may not be practicing Catholics, but they want to see this island reunited."

"A nation once again!" whooped one of the recruits.

Garland suppressed a smile. "Exactly. I don't have to explain who the republicans are: that's us. We want the Irish Republic we fought for in 1916 and again in 1921, not some diluted version like the Free State.

"Now about the unionists: Only a small percentage are members of the Ulster Unionist Party, but the vast majority of northern Protestants would describe themselves as 'unionist' because they want to remain within the United Kingdom. 'Loyalist' refers to an extremely sectarian group that's developed in the Protestant working class. You could call them supremacists, like the Ku Klux Klan in America. Loyalists bash and bludgeon Catholics and claim they're doing it to protect their Protestant heritage. Many loyalists belong to the Orange Order, one of the most virulent anti-Catholic organisations in the world. They consider themselves above the law with some justification, since the RUC lets them get away with murder. Sometimes literally. A lot of RUC men belong to the Orange Order too, you see."

O'Connell spoke up. "I think it's important to make a point here. The real divide in Northern Ireland is more economic than religious. One reason unionists are adamant about remaining part of the United Kingdom is because their financial well-being depends on it. When the British controlled this entire island they located all the heavy industry in the northeastern corner of the country to benefit the Protestant majority there. The rest of Ireland, 'Catholic Ireland,' was left with a largely rural and impoverished economy.

"After World War Two a lot of formerly profitable industries in the north began to have to tighten their belts as well. But Britain is subsidising the Six Counties, so the unionists still have jobs. They don't want to find themselves thrust into a united Ireland because the south has nothing comparable to offer them."

"Even if it did," said Séamus McCoy, "it wouldn't make any difference. As far as the unionists are concerned the Republic is a foreign country like darkest Africa. Some of the younger ones are unaware that this island was partitioned less than forty years ago. They assume there's always been a Northern Ireland, a place where the best land and the best jobs are theirs practically by divine right."

A man sitting near Barry muttered, "Damn the Prods."

Dave O'Connell silenced him with a frown. "In fairness," O'Connell said, "the vast majority of Protestants are decent people who have no desire to persecute anyone. The problem is with the sectarian bigots like the Orange Order. Unfortunately, they control just about everything in the Six Counties, including the parliament at Stormont."

Before Barry fell asleep that night he thought about what he had heard.

The face of the enemy was becoming more specific.

In the morning the column lined up to bid farewell to Séamus McCoy. McCoy and the other training officers were being recalled to Dublin to brief

GHQ. A Morris Minor driven by a middle-aged woman who looked like a schoolteacher was waiting to take him across the border. McCoy tossed his pack inside the car, returned the salute of the column, and settled himself in the passenger seat. The door slammed with the sound of finality.

"There goes a good man," said Feargal O'Hanlon. "We're going to miss him."

As the car began to pull away Barry shouted, "*Slán leat,** Séamus!"

McCoy thrust his arm out the window and waved his hand. "*Slán,*" he called. But he never looked back.

Half an hour later a creamery wagon drove up. While O'Connell and the driver were tying the motorbike to the bumper, the other Volunteers clambered onto the flat-bed wagon and tried to find space for themselves among the metal milk cans. A jolting ride along rural byways terminated at an abandoned flour mill. The old red brick walls were slimy with moss; the wooden millwheel was gently rotting.

Standing outside the mill were two men in shabby overcoats. Garland introduced one as Charlie Murphy, a member of headquarters staff with extensive experience in the north. Murphy, a short man with blunt features and no interest in small talk, brought further instructions from Dublin. He stared off into space while Garland read them. The other man went into the mill and brought out a cardboard box filled with sandwiches.

Garland looked up. "Get that food inside you in a hurry, men. We're pulling out soon."

"Where are we going, sir?"

"To set up a base camp for the first phase of the campaign. It's better if you don't know exactly where until we get there. That way if you're lifted, you can't tell them anything."

I wouldn't tell them anything anyway, thought Barry. *Not even if they tortured me like they did Kevin Barry in 1920!*

*Good-bye.

Chapter Five

◦═◦∞◦═◦

December 10, 1956

HUNGARY PUT UNDER SOVIET MARTIAL LAW

Soviet Army once again threatens to turn its guns on the people.

T HE second week of December found Seán Garland and his men encamped in a secluded valley just south of the Armagh border. The area was strongly republican. Instead of dugouts the column had the use of an old barn, and the village at the head of the valley kept them supplied with food and cigarettes. The men took turns cooking meals with the ingredients provided. When Barry solicited comments on his contribution, Paddy O'Regan said, "It's marginally better than being poked in the eye with a sharp stick."

"I inherited my cooking skills from my mother."

"God have mercy on your family, then," O'Regan replied in sepulchral tones.

The village women thought having the IRA camped nearby was incredibly romantic. "We could stroll over there and give the girls a thrill," Feargal suggested to Barry. "What d'ye say?"

"Sounds good to me. Do you have a comb? I've lost mine someplace."

Seán Garland overheard the exchange. "You two Romeos leave the local girls alone. We're here to be a plague to the British, not to decent Irish women."

Target practice was held in an empty field amidst winter-grey stubble. The Bren was assigned to Seán South while the officers kept the Thompsons for themselves. "I don't mind about the Bren," Barry lied to Feargal. "My chance will come."

It will, I know it will. It must.

Waiting for the call to action was the hardest part. Being Irish, they filled the time with talk. Still, and always, talk of politics. The addition of Garland and O'Connell added depth to the conversation.

"England's been our enemy from the beginning, taking the best we had and leaving the dregs for us. The English never paid a blind bit of mind to how we felt."

"You can't blame the ordinary punter in the streets for that. It's their bloody government that's responsible."

"I've often wondered how a people as essentially decent as the English can tolerate a succession of governments which habitually practice deceit in domestic policy and use genocide as a tool of foreign policy."

"That's pretty harsh."

"You think so? Ask the Boers in South Africa. For that matter, ask the Irish. Doesn't Britain realise those sins might come home to roost someday?"

"Ah, you forget—every government has a finite life and acts in its own self-interest. Which isn't necessarily the national self-interest."

"Please God the sins of the Free State government will come home to roost someday too, and we'll have a true republic on this island."

"Up the Republic!"

"Can anyone spare a pair of dry socks?"

On the afternoon of the tenth, Seán Garland announced, "There's a major attack scheduled for tomorrow night. The flying columns will hit enemy installations all across the north. Seán Daly's men are going to join us in an attack on Gough Barracks. The Royal Irish is my old regiment, so I know the place."

The next morning Garland and O'Connell went to the nearby village and returned laden with bulky parcels wrapped in butcher's paper. They were unwrapped to reveal a number of military uniforms. Barry recognised both British and American, but there were also a couple stolen from the Irish Army.

The Free State Army, Barry mentally corrected.

"We're going to wear these as disguises," Garland said. "They won't fool anyone for long, but they may add to the confusion and that's what we need."

Dave O'Connell and Barry Halloran were the tallest men in the column; only the American uniforms would fit them. Everyone shied away from the British outfits until Barry picked up one of the jackets. "I dare you to wear this," he said, tossing the garment to Feargal. "Surely to God a bold lad like you isn't afraid of a bit of cloth."

The British uniforms were quickly claimed.

Seán Garland passed out black berets for the Volunteers to wear. He explained, "It's Army policy to conform with the Geneva Convention, which demands active-service headgear to make combatants identifiable.[1] As members of an organised army fighting a legitimate war to regain stolen territory we must obey international law. Even if the other side doesn't," he added sourly.

"We commence operations at Gough Barracks sharply at midnight. The time's been coordinated with the other columns because GHQ wants simultaneous attacks on British Army installations and the RUC. If this thing runs like clockwork we'll knock 'em off their pins.

"Two covered lorries will be here to collect us by ten tonight. Bring your packs with you, you never know where we may finish up. We'll rendezvous with Daly and his men at the barracks. Some of the locals will meet us with a mine so we can blow open the front gate. Once we're inside, break down the doors, rip out the electrical wiring, destroy the telephones, set fire to files and mattresses—in short, do everything you can to make the damned place unusable. Then seize all the weapons you can carry and get out."

"The soldiers aren't going to stand idly by while we destroy their barracks," Paddy O'Regan said.

"Threaten and intimidate 'em all you like," Garland retorted. "But don't shoot anyone unless you have to."

Feargal whispered to Barry, "The O/C just doesn't want to kill any of his old pals."

Seán Garland glared in his direction. "I heard that, O'Hanlon. I never *want* to kill anyone, and neither should you. Disable and demoralise, remember?"

THE day was heavily overcast. As the light died a bitter wind blew in from the Irish Sea. In the barn where they waited the temperature dropped steadily, forcing them to put their coats over the borrowed uniforms. By eight o'clock they were blowing on their hands and stamping their feet.

Barry, who thought smoking made him look more mature, lit a cigarette as much for the warmth as the comfort, and puffed ostentatiously to conceal his excitement. *Now it begins. Now it really begins!*

Ten o'clock came and passed. The men grew restless. Several went outside to urinate. The Limerick contingent broke out a pack of cards and enjoyed a furious argument over which game to play.

Dragging its feet, another hour crept by.

Garland was consulting his watch every ten minutes.

"Where d'you think our transport is, Seventeen?" Feargal wondered.

"How should I know? If it doesn't come I suppose we can always walk."

Feargal took him seriously. "Anything's better than waiting."

"My granda said a lot of being in the Army was just waiting."

Seán Garland's temper neared the boiling point. "Isn't this bloody typical!" he snarled to his second in command. "Another Army cock-up." He glanced toward the waiting men to be sure they did not overhear him. "Dave, run to the village and scare up some sort of transportation for us. We're going to be late as it is."

O'Connell looked dubious. "The locals may feel they've done enough by getting those uniforms. They were certainly taking a ri—"

"Nobody's done enough until the war's won!" Garland exploded.

O'Connell hastily left the shed.

Garland's watch ticked on.

After another half hour a dilapidated cattle truck appeared, lurching along uncertainly, backfiring and belching fumes. The exhaust pipe was only an ancient memory. Dave O'Connell leaned out the window. "Borrowed this from a farmyard," he called to Seán Garland.

"Did you have the farmer's permission?"

"Not exactly." O'Connell climbed gingerly from the cab, then turned and glared at the rusty springs protruding from the dung-smeared seat. "I'm not familiar with this class of vehicle, Seán. You'd best ask someone else to do the driving."

Vince Conlon was duly appointed as driver. The other Volunteers scrambled into the back of the lorry. The stench was appalling. "Pigs was in here last," a farm boy commented. "We'll smell just like 'em before we get out of here." The floor was slippery with pig manure. The Volunteers kept their packs on their backs rather than set them down.

With an appalling screech of metal Conlon engaged the gears and they were off. "Should the engine sound like it's full of gravel?" Feargal asked Barry.

"I don't think so. My mam won't let me touch her Ford, but I've tinkered with it a bit when she's not around, so I know a thing or two. An engine should purr, not cough."

"Will this one get us there anyway, d'ye think?"

"I'm sure," replied Barry. Who was not at all sure. But he did not really care. The here and now was wonderful. A huge adventure!

As the lorry clattered across the border into Armagh, sleet spattered against the windscreen with a sound like shotgun pellets. The bald tyres skidded on the icy road. The Volunteers clutched at anything they could hold on to.

"Faster," Garland urged. "Faster!"

When they were within a mile of Gough Barracks the truck's misaligned headlamps picked out two figures in overcoats standing by the side of the road. One of them waved twice, briskly, then once more.

Garland ordered Conlon to stop. He slammed on the brakes and the lorry slewed sideways on ice.

"Fuckin' Jaysus!" someone gasped.

The men on the roadside were carrying a mine wrapped in a flowered quilt. Garland spoke with them from the back of the lorry. "Haven't seen the other crowd at all," one man said in response to his query about Daly. "They're prob-

ably waiting for you up ahead somewhere. Here, would you take this? We have
to make a move, we've been here too long already."

Garland reached down and lifted the mine into the truck. The other Volunteers quickly edged away from him.

A hundred yards farther on, Garland directed Conlon to a dirt track that
branched off from the main road. "This will take us to a hill behind the barracks. There's no guard post there. We can park without being seen, then sneak
around on foot and blow the gate. If Daly's anywhere in the area he'll hear the
explosion and come at the double."

As they started up the hill, Conlon throttled down to the lowest gear.

The headlamps promptly failed.

In the darkness they did not realise they were parking below a watchtower
that had been erected since Garland's days at the barracks. The sentry in the
tower peeped over the edge. After one glimpse of the invaders, he fired his rifle
into the air and ducked back down out of sight.

A Klaxon blared. Lights shone from every window. Officers could be heard
shouting orders and a five-man patrol came running along the wall, weapons at
the ready.

Seán Garland tossed the mine out the back of the lorry. "Let's get the hell out
of here!"

His men sprayed the barracks wall with bullets as the truck lurched away.
When it built up enough speed the headlamps came on again.

Seán Garland was cursing under his breath. "They're too well prepared,
damn them. Didn't used to be that way."

Halfway to the main road they met another truck coming toward them.
The access road was too narrow to allow the two vehicles to pass each other.
Brakes squealed.

The driver of the second lorry stuck his head out the window and called,
"Garland, is that you?"

WE didn't even get out of the lorry," Feargal complained.

"Don't worry," Barry consoled his friend. "I'm sure we'll see plenty of action
soon."

Privately his disappointment was intense. The high excitement of anticipation, the sudden burst of adrenaline when things began to happen, the racing
blood, the pounding heart, and then . . . and then nothing.

Damn, damn, damn it!

THE attack on Gough Barracks had to be abandoned, but at midnight ten
other targets, in a ring from Antrim to Derry, were hit. In spite of a substan-

tial network of paid informers, the RUC did not have adequate warning. Operation Harvest began with the chatter of machine guns and the roar of explosives.

A raiding party destroyed a BBC transmitting station. After moving the caretaker and his family to safety outside, another group set fire to a courthouse full of government documents. A post used by B-Specials was burned to the ground. Originally recruited under orders from Winston Churchill, the B-Specials were a fanatically pro-British militia with a taste for violence. Although they were called "police reservists," this was only a flag of convenience. In reality the B-Specials dispensed punishment as they saw fit and had a well-earned reputation for savagery to Catholics.

Not all IRA operations that night went smoothly. A plan to blow up bridges in County Fermanagh went awry because the mines used were not powerful enough to destroy the concrete pillars. An attack on the RAF radar installation at Torr Head was intercepted at the last moment; gunshots were exchanged and three Volunteers were arrested.

But the opening salvo of the campaign could be considered a qualified success.

The combined Garland-Daly column fell back to South Armagh to await new orders. Irritable and frustrated, the men put together a makeshift camp and tried to get some sleep. The only dry place was inside the lorries.

In the morning Phil O'Donoghue went to the nearest village for milk for their tea, and a newspaper. He returned in a state of elation. "This made the early edition!" he said, waving the paper.

The men crowded around him. Barry read over Feargal's shoulder.

December 12, 1956

IRA ISSUES CAMPAIGN PROCLAMATION

Spearheaded by Ireland's freedom fighters, our people in the Six Counties have carried the fight to the enemy. We seek an independent, united, democratic Irish Republic. For this we shall fight until the invader is driven from our soil and victory is ours.[2]

The words swelled in Barry's soul like a balloon going up.

That afternoon new orders arrived. "We'll be moving out again," Garland told them. "We're going to attack Lisnaskea Barracks in County Fermanagh tomorrow night."

For once the promised transport—three small trucks and a bakery van—arrived on time. The men piled inside. Their route led through Monaghan, where IRA field headquarters had been set up, to Fermanagh. Along the way Dave O'Connell "liberated" fifty pounds of gelignite from a small-town armoury and Charlie Murphy used the explosive to construct a large mine.

. . .

AT Lisnaskea the members of the Royal Ulster Constabulary were billeted together with a squad of B-Specials. The Lisnaskea Barracks was a three-storey building in the main street of the town, with civilian houses on either side. Across the road from the barracks was a house occupied by the parish priest. On this evening the bitter cold and sleet were keeping everyone indoors.

At dusk a couple of Volunteers knocked at the priest's door. "We're here to free occupied Ireland, Father. Would you kindly remove yourself for a little while to avoid accidental injury?"[3]

"If the time of my death has come," the old man replied, "I'll meet it here in my own house, thank you."

The rest of the group parked behind an outhouse not far from the barracks. As soon as darkness fell, the attack party advanced on their target while the drivers waited with their vehicles, ready to make a getaway. As Charlie Murphy was lifting the mine from the back of a lorry the driver's foot slipped off the brake and hit the accelerator. The truck lurched forward. The mine fell at Murphy's feet. Mercifully, it failed to explode—the detonator was not yet attached.

Breathing hard, Murphy completed the arming of his device. Barry Halloran and Seán South carried it to the entrance porch of the barracks, then ran back to crouch behind the lorries while Charlie Murphy triggered the detonator.

Fifty pounds of gelignite blasted open the barracks door. The porch collapsed into the street in a cloud of dust and splinters. The brick walls of the building remained standing, however, protecting the RUC as they opened fire through the windows.

The Volunteers shot back as best they could. Unfortunately the Garland and Daly contingents had not yet drilled together and kept getting in each other's way. To make matters worse, when Seán South tried to fire the Bren, the usually reliable weapon failed to operate.

"We can't move closer without getting right in their line of fire," Seán Garland said in frustration. Murphy suggested they pull out and O'Connell agreed. "The chief constable's probably on the radio right now, calling for reinforcements."

The Volunteers climbed back into the trucks and roared away.

"All that effort and we only destroyed a porch. A porch!" Barry lamented.

It was Feargal's turn to console him. "At least we fired at the enemy this time, that's something."

THEY arrived at field headquarters in Monaghan shortly after daylight, eager to hear how other operations were doing. "Kavanagh's column hit the Derrylin Barracks last night," they were told, "and walked straight into an RUC ambush. Kavanagh himself was shot, but when they arrived here a little while ago we found the bullet had only destroyed his belt buckle and left a mighty bruise on his belly."

Field headquarters had a radio, so, after some food and a brief rest, Garland and his men crowded around to listen. It became obvious that the coordinated attacks of the twelfth and thirteenth had caught everyone off guard. Northern Ireland was in turmoil.

The RUC was mobilising on an emergency basis. The B-Specials, however, were having difficulties. Some of the militia were eager to fight but a significant number wanted to go home. They might enjoy battering individual Catholics in their homes and shops, but they did not relish confronting an organised army.

After dark, country roads were abandoned to the IRA. Businesses closed early. Tens of thousands of legally held guns belonging to northern Protestants—Catholics were not allowed to have guns—were loaded in the name of self-defence. More than one nervous householder shot his dog or his own foot by mistake.

The prime minister of Northern Ireland left for London to confer urgently with Anthony Eden and the British government. The British ambassador to the Republic, Sir Alexander Clutterbuck, gave the Irish minister for external affairs a stiff note expressing Her Majesty's displeasure.

John A. Costello disapproved of the IRA's actions, but refused to order wholesale arrests of republicans just to satisfy the British. The taoiseach knew that such an action might cause a major public outcry. Following the IRA announcement of intent, the Irish people were experiencing a resurgence of patriotism.

BY the fifteenth of December, Operation Harvest had moved out of field headquarters and dispersed throughout the region.

Chapter Six

IN Rostrevor, County Down, Barry Halloran stood in the doorway of a small hardware store and gazed out at the empty street. Nearby Carlingford Lough, where a flotilla of fishing boats rode at anchor, was leaden beneath a leaden sky.

"Drismal," Barry commented.

Feargal was sitting on a high stool behind the counter, mending a pair of socks. "Drismal?"

"A word my mam concocted. Drizzly and dismal."

"Better than the snow we had yesterday."

"I'd rather have the snow, it makes everything a fairyland."

Feargal clucked his tongue. "A hopeless romantic, you. I'm more the practical type meself. How are your socks?"

"Full of holes."

"Hand 'em over, then. It'll pass the time."

"I thought you offered to mind the store while the owner visits his wife in hospital."

"I am minding it, there just aren't any customers. Catholic area, Catholic pockets. Empty."

Barry perched on the end of the counter while he took off his boots. "These fit fine when I left home, but they're getting tight now," he complained. He peeled off his socks and tossed them to his friend.

"Whew!" Feargal wrinkled his nose. "D'ye ever wash these at all?"

"They're every bit as clean as yours."

"That's not saying much."

Dave O'Connell strode purposefully up the street and into the store. "New orders just arrived. We're being pulled out of the north for the Christmas. That means you can go home for a few days, lads."

Feargal winked at Barry. "God works in mysterious ways. Now your mammy can wash your socks for you."

WHILE she waited for the spuds to boil, Eileen Mulvaney fanned her face with her apron. Even in December a morning's baking made the kitchen uncomfortably hot for a fat woman.

The newspapers that came down from Dublin carried adverts for "gleaming white fridges with plastic trays for ice cubes." Ice in cubes. The image was deliciously cooling. What a triumph it would be to announce the acquisition of a modern refrigerator to her friends over cups of tea! An event for serving caraway seed cake and looking smug.

The most common method of keeping food cool, in both town and country, was the meat safe: a raised wooden box outside the back door for storing milk and meat. None of the neighbouring farms had electric refrigerators. Few even had telephones. If someone needed to make a call he went to the kiosk at the post office. The telephone had to be cranked with a heavy black handle like the handle of a skillet, and as the caller shouted down the line, the operator unashamedly listened in to the conversation.

Ursula had installed a telephone for the sake of business. The Halloran farmhouse had an indoor toilet as well, the ultimate mark of rural sophistication. But Eileen knew that Ursula would never consent to buying a gleaming white fridge. The only creatures she provided with luxuries were her horses.

Eileen sighed. Heaving her bulk off the chair, she went to the dresser to get the bowl of freshly laid eggs. She smeared her palms with butter, then rolled the eggs between them until the shells were thoroughly coated. Thus sealed, they would last for weeks. A box of buttered eggs packed in straw would fetch a premium price at the market.

The horses and cattle were Ursula's enterprise, but the butter-and-egg money was Eileen's.

She was tucking the last greasy egg into its straw nest when Ursula entered the kitchen. She was still wearing her riding boots. Eileen began to scold her for tracking mud on the flagstone floor. Then she saw Ursula's face. "What's wrong?" she asked in alarm.

"There's a telegram. I met the boy in the lane."

Eileen put her hand to her heart. "Mother of God." No one ever received telegrams unless there was dreadful news. "Who is it?" she whispered. "Has something happened to Barry?"

Wordlessly, Ursula extended her hand.

Eileen took the crumpled yellow paper from her and read, "Captain dead.

Cancer. Funeral yesterday. My life is over. Henry." She looked up. "What captain? What can this mean?"

"It's Ella Mooney. Henry always called his wife Cap'n, but I suppose the telegrapher couldn't use a contraction."

"Oh, Ursula, I am sorry! I know you were fond of both of them."

"Henry was Papa's best friend. And mine. When I was a child he called me Little Business, did you know that? And it was Ella's money that sent me to school in Europe and opened the world to me. Now . . ."

"Now you can't even go to the funeral."

Ursula clenched her thumbs in her fists, an old habit when under stress. "I could have taken an aeroplane if only I'd known in time."

"You mean *fly* to America?" Eileen was astonished. Flying was as exotic as an electric refrigerator.

Without pausing to take off her boots, Ursula went upstairs to her room and began composing a letter.

My dearest Henry,

Words are no good at a time like this, yet they are all I have to offer. My heart aches for you. From having been Ella's bridesmaid, I know that October marked your thirty-fourth wedding anniversary. I hope you celebrated, Henry. I pray that wretched disease allowed you some final, happy time together.

Please do not say your life is over. You may feel like that now, but remember how much Papa accomplished after Síle died. Remember also how much you are loved by

Your devoted
Little Business

Ursula put down her pen and turned toward the window. With unseeing eyes she gazed across a succession of paddocks. When the broodmares were turned out with their foals in the spring the paddocks would fill with new life. But she was thinking about death. Henry was seventy-three. Realistically, how long could he be expected to survive the woman he had adored? His feelings ran very deep. When Ned lay dying, Henry had made the long journey from America to be with him and put an end to their ancient quarrel.

Ned. How surprising that a man like Ned Halloran had died peacefully in his bed! Ursula, who knew his soul, had wished a warrior's death for him.

Barry.

She did not want a warrior's death for Barry. The only child she would ever have. Had the republican movement asked for her last drop of blood she would have given it without hesitation, but she did not want them to take so much as a hair from Barry's head. She knew she was being hypocritical—Ursula never lied to herself—but she yearned to have her son home this very minute, safe beneath her roof.

When he came striding down the lane the next morning it was as if the power of her thoughts had summoned him.

"I've come home for a new book of poetry," he jauntily announced. "My copy of Ledwidge has gone to pieces."

Ursula longed to hug him. Instead she cried, "How dare you give me such a fright! You put the heart crossways in me, going off without a word. I didn't know where you were, or how you were, or if you were lying dead in a ditch someplace. I should take a horsewhip to you!"

Barry waited until the tirade ended, then observed mildly, "A simple *Dia dhuit** would have been enough."

THE prodigal was welcomed home with a prodigious meal. The big table in the kitchen groaned beneath roast chicken and ham, brown bread and soda bread and fruit scones, roasted potatoes and mashed potatoes, runner beans, carrots with parsnips, bowls of crisp breadcrumb stuffing, a jug of glossy brown gravy. When Barry protested he could eat no more, Eileen produced an apple tart hot from the oven and smothered it with thick yellow cream.

At last Barry pushed his chair back with a satisfied sigh. "I haven't eaten like that since I joined the Army."

"I should think not," his mother said with asperity. "You've just devoured the ingredients for our Christmas dinner."

Eileen said, "Och, don't begrudge it to him. It does my heart good to have a man's appetite at table again."

"He's not a man, he's a boy."

"I'm a man, Ursula," Barry contradicted. He pitched his voice as low as he could and was pleased with the way it resonated in his chest.

"A man wouldn't sneak out of here in the dead of night without telling anyone. That was a boy's prank."

"If I told you I was going to join the Army, would you have let me go?"

"Of course not. You're too young."

"There's younger than me in the IRA. Lads of only fourteen fought in the Rising."

"That's different," said Ursula.

"How is it different? You and I listened to the radio while boys of fifteen and sixteen fought the Red Army in the streets of Budapest. You thought they were heroic, you said so."

Eileen's eyes twinkled. "He has you there, Ursula."

*Hello; good day.

· · ·

AN anomaly amongst the women of her era, when Ursula became pregnant with Barry she had defied priest-ridden, patriarchal Ireland to keep her child. Other women gave up their babies at birth, or even committed secret, desperate infanticides to keep from being disowned by their families, but Ursula Halloran had raised her son with her head held high. For years he was all she had.

With the passage of time, however, the relationship between mother and son had changed. Since inheriting the old Halloran farm Ursula had ruled it well and wisely; ruled the farm and everyone on it. But now Barry had escaped her benevolent dictatorship without her knowledge and she was upset.

Yet she loved him more than ever.

Centuries of harsh colonial rule that denigrated everything Irish had stripped the people of self-esteem. Ursula Halloran had rebelled against this tendency from earliest childhood, breaking the shackles that limited so many others. Perhaps this was what had given her the strength to keep Barry.

Throughout her son's childhood she had told him that he was intelligent and worthwhile. She had praised his achievements and encouraged him to be his own man.

Now he was. And more than that: He had embraced the republicanism that was her heart and soul.

THE morning after Barry's return he went on a tour of the farm. Familiar buildings, familiar fields; tangible reality that made his recent experiences seem a dream. *Did it really happen? Was I shooting at the RUC from behind a lorry? Were they shooting at me?*

Back in his room, he sniffed the muzzle of his rifle and caught the faint, lingering smell of gunpowder.

THAT night at table he remarked, "Did you know there's a donkey in the upper pasture? A little piebald jack. I thought that field was set aside for next season's yearlings."

"Donkeys have a right to eat too," said Eileen. "Have another roast potato."

"But where did he come from?"

"I met a tinker family in the road a few weeks ago," Ursula told him. "Their horse had died and all they had left was a donkey. He was too small to pull a caravan but it didn't matter because their caravan was rotten clear through and falling apart. The family was living in appalling conditions even for tinkers. The adults were wretched enough, but the children were practically starving.

"I collected our old pots and pans for the tinker to mend and I offered to buy the donkey from him. I gave him more money than the creature was worth, it was almost as starved as the rest of them. But at least they will be able to eat for a while. And besides, Christmas is coming."

Barry said, "I didn't know you had such a soft heart."

"There's a lot about me you don't know."

This, Barry mentally agreed, was true. Sometimes he thought his mother was like an onion. If you peeled away one layer there was another one underneath. On the farm she habitually dressed in shabby clothing and wore an old pair of men's trousers belted around her narrow waist. She walked with a long, unladylike stride. With her cropped hair and boyish figure she could have been mistaken for a farm labourer.

Yet she insisted on elegant table manners. By the time he was four the rules had been deeply ingrained in Barry. If soup or a bit of fish was served before the meat, it was called the first course and not "starters." The knife must not be held like a writing pen. Elbows were not allowed on the table. One did not speak with food in one's mouth. When one finished eating, the cutlery must be arranged on the plate at "half past six," to indicate that the plate could be carried away. A small portion of food must be left on the plate, however, to show that one was not greedy.

Born into an Ireland where memories of the Famine were still vivid, Eileen disapproved of the latter precept. Wasting food was a mortal sin. Before she washed the dishes she surreptitiously ate everything Ursula and Barry had left on their plates.

TWO days after Christmas found Barry on his way back to the north. His mother had said, "Leave Papa's rifle behind this time, the Army will give you another rifle. And please, take care of yourself."

"Oh, I intend to," Barry had assured her.

But the rifle was already disassembled and stowed in his pack.

He did not know that she was watching from an upstairs window as he went whistling away down the lane. Whistling "The Old Fenian Gun."

WHEN Barry rejoined the column in Tyrone, Feargal gave him the now-familiar punch on the shoulder. Phil O'Donoghue offered a drink of Christmas brandy brought from home. The Volunteers melded together as smoothly as if they had never been apart. They no longer called themselves the Lynch column. They were Seán Garland's men.

.   .   .

DURING Christmas there had been little peace in the north. Attacks on Catholics continued through the holy season. Instead of making any effort to prevent them, the RUC banned the Sinn Féin political party and raided their headquarters in Belfast. The office soon was quietly reopened, however.

Sinn Féin offices in the north tended to be located in dark, unfrequented laneways or over derelict shops where they attracted no attention. But northern Catholics always knew how to find them. Sinn Féin was all they had in times of need—when there was no work, no food for the children, no shelter for the family.

If a man's life was threatened, Sinn Féin knew how to get in touch with the IRA.

ALERTED by the start of the border campaign, unionists were beefing up their forces. The RUC now numbered three thousand men and was actively re-cruiting. The B-Specials claimed a thousand men full-time and more than ten thousand part-time. They were eager and untrained. When an excited B-Special patrol fired in error on an RUC jeep, which it somehow mistook for "the enemy," a constable was seriously wounded.

In late December, Noel Kavanagh decided on a second raid of the Derrylin Barracks to make up for the failure of the first. This time the raid came as a complete surprise, catching the RUC unprepared. In the bloody attack that fol-lowed, several men died. The barracks was reduced to a smoking ruin. The column made a desperate getaway through a snowstorm, but Kavanagh him-self was captured. There were claims that he was being tortured.

Garland's column was in South Fermanagh, laying one ambush after an-other for RUC patrols that never showed up. The rumours of Kavanagh's tor-ture upset Seán Garland. "We're freezing our arses off with nothing to show for it," he told his second in command. "The nearest RUC barracks is at Brookeborough. Let's strike a blow for Noel!"

Dave O'Connell urged caution. "The town's solidly Orange, Seán. I have a planner's map of Brookeborough but we don't have anyone in place to provide us with reliable intelligence. We'd be going in blind."

"We'll rely on the element of surprise," Garland told him. "Until now the IRA's been attacking late at night. We'll attack at dusk, at tea time on New Year's Day, when they're inside having their meal. I only want sixteen on the assault team. There won't be many men in the barracks anyway because of the holiday, and we can't afford another mob scene with Volunteers falling over each other and wasting ammunition.

"When we reach the town we'll drop off a couple of lookouts at the top of the main street. The barracks will be somewhere on that street; the constables like to be in the heart of town. We'll park well beyond the building, run back and set a mine against the door. Have Murphy make two; we can keep the second one in reserve.

"And incidentally, this time we won't wear those military uniforms. They've brought us nothing but bad luck. We'll wear our own clothes."

Amongst the men Garland selected for the raid were Halloran and O'Hanlon. "We're back in the war!" Feargal enthused. "I've been bored to bits, how about you?"

"Bored to bits," Barry agreed.

Chapter Seven

THE big red lorry drove slowly along the main street of Brookeborough. The roads were icy again and it was past seven by the time they arrived. Darkness had long since fallen, but powerful streetlamps cast wide pools of light on the pavement.

"We're not what ye'd call sneaking in," Vince Conlon commented. He wiped the inside of the fogged-up windscreen with his forearm. "Where's the damned barracks?"

"I think that's it," said Garland beside him, pointing. "See that low two-storey house?"

"There's a whole row of them. Which one?"

"Right th—"

Conlon slammed on the brakes, halting the lorry at a forty-five-degree angle to the barracks and much closer than Garland wanted. They were no more than forty feet away. The Volunteers shrugged off their packs to be ready for action. Dragging the wire that led back to the detonator, two men ran to place a mine against the front door of the barracks. As soon as they were in the clear Murphy hit the plunger.

Nothing happened.

"Damn wire must be kinked," Murphy said with disgust. "Or the battery's dead. Give me a minute and I'll—"

The door opened and an RUC sergeant stepped out for a breath of air after his meal. The startled Volunteers greeted him with a hail of bullets. Shouting a warning, he leapt back inside and slammed the door.

"The second mine, hurry!" cried Garland. "Put it against the wall!"

From the back of the truck Seán South provided covering fire with the Bren. Paddy O'Regan knelt beside him, feeding the gun ammunition. The first burst from the Bren shattered windows across the front of the barracks. Within seconds the constables inside were shooting back.

WHEN they reached Brookeborough, Garland had surveyed the layout of the town from the top of the main street, then decided that three lookouts would be necessary. To Barry's disappointment, he was assigned to keep watch with Mick O'Brien and Mick Kelly. "Deploy in a wide arc at the upper end of town," Garland ordered them, "and stay in shouting distance of one another. If you see any more RUC men headed toward the barracks, or anything else that might interfere with our plan, give the loudest whistle you can."

Barry had fully intended to obey orders. But when he heard the voice of the Bren he found himself running toward the action.

"Where are you going?" shouted Mick Kelly. Mick O'Brien added, "We're supposed to stay here," but they both began to follow Barry.

"*You* stay here!" Barry cried in a commanding voice that stopped the other two in their tracks.

He ran on alone. *I'll never let anyone see me afraid again.*

THE second mine also failed to detonate. In desperation Dave O'Connell began shooting it with his Thompson. The others crowded around Garland, straining to hear his orders. "O'Hanlon, you have the Molotov cocktails. Lob some through the—"

From an upstairs window an RUC machine gun opened fire. Garland pivoted and looked up. He and O'Connell returned fire simultaneously.

The Volunteers had been told to make every bullet count, but, feverish with pent-up tension, they shot wildly. Bullets ricocheted off the cast-iron casements of the windows. While the raiders were clearly visible in the light of the streetlamps, the constables inside the barracks were no more than shadowy figures behind broken glass panes. Theirs was the superior strategic position. They took time, took aim, and placed their shots well.

The gunfire rose to a crescendo. Seán South tried to take out the RUC machine gun but could not get enough elevation with the Bren.

Garland heard one of his men scream.

He made a split-second decision. "Back to the lorry, now!" As he herded them toward cover, the machine gunner in the upstairs window squeezed off a long burst of fire. A full twenty-five rounds were pumped into the assault team.

AS Barry pelted down the main street of Brookeborough the sound of gunfire dwindled away. Stopped.

The world stopped.

Streetlamps bathed the scene with overlapping pools of light, creating a series of vignettes. Alarmed townspeople peering out of windows. A terrier sitting on the kerb with its head cocked, one ear up, one ear down. An overturned ash can spilling refuse onto the footpath like a mouth vomiting filth.

Frozen in time. *Like the horses in the snapshots Ursula sends to prospective buyers.*

A hundred yards away was the red lorry with the back wide open. Grouped around it was a motionless tableau, halted in the act of lifting a man into the truck. Then Barry realised they were moving. Scrambling into the lorry in the same way he was running: in a nightmarish slow motion.

Conlon revved the engine for a getaway.

An eternity passed before Barry reached the lorry. He vaulted over the tailboard just as the truck lurched forward. Conlon was trying to turn and go back the way they had come.

Light streaming from the barracks cruelly illuminated the interior. A final snapshot burned into Barry's brain, a scene from a slaughterhouse.

Inside the bullet-riddled lorry, blood was splashed as high as a man's head. Seán South sprawled motionless across the Bren. Beside him lay Paddy O'Regan, gasping with pain. Phillip O'Donoghue sat cross-legged with his face bathed in blood. Seán Garland's trousers were soaked with it, but he was still standing.

Barry slipped in a puddle of blood and almost fell over Feargal O'Hanlon. The young footballer from Monaghan was lying on his back. A bullet had smashed his femur. Blood fountained in spurts from a severed artery.

"Feargal?" Barry dropped to his knees. "Feargal! Can you hear me?"

Feargal's eyes opened. "You missed it again, Seventeen," he said in a whisper.

Vince Conlon cursed through gritted teeth as he struggled with the gears. The lorry was all but unmanageable. Two tyres had been burst by gunfire and the undercarriage was damaged. When the vehicle started forward, the rear end tipped up violently, throwing men about. Seán Garland sat down hard beside Phil O'Donoghue.

A lone constable ran after the lorry, shouting, "Come back, you fuckin' Fenians!"

KNEELING beside his friend, Barry saw Feargal's eyes go blank.

IT was no longer about making the British give back the Six Counties. Or protecting northern Catholics or getting even for eight hundred years of oppression. Everything dwindled down to Feargal O'Hanlon's face with the light going out of it. Barry gave a terrible cry and leapt to his feet. Somehow he had the rifle in his hands. Just beyond the tailboard was a figure in an RUC uniform.

Do it do it do it do it do it!

He pulled the trigger he shot the bolt he pulled the trigger he pulled the trigger he pulled the trigger and the thunder of the rifle rang through his living bones.

come morning they'll be looking for us with helicopters. Halloran, you still have that compass?"

"I do."

"Hand it here and we'll take a bearing."

The officers consulted Barry's compass by the light of the electric torch. After a few calculations O'Connell said, "Even going at a snail's pace for the sake of the wounded, we should reach the border in four hours."

"You will, I won't," Garland told him. "I can't go any farther whether you carry me or not. This time it's an order: Leave me here. The bastards won't find me, I'll go to ground like a badger."

As the Volunteers were dragging themselves to their feet flares began exploding in the night sky.

O'Connell had underestimated the time it would take to reach the border. Almost five hours passed before they were certain they were in Monaghan. They collapsed again and lay unmoving while the dawn slowly broke around them.

True to Garland's prediction, two British Army helicopters took to the air as soon as there was enough light. Four hundred members of the RUC, together with B-Specials and British Army units, joined in the ground search.[1]

THE priest who administered the last rites to Seán South and Feargal O'Hanlon had gone straight from the farm shed to the nearest telephone. Within a matter of hours the bodies had been collected and their families notified.

Washed and dressed in fresh clothing, the corpses were wrapped in blankets and inconspicuously returned to the Republic in the back of a small delivery van.

Two hearses were waiting at the border with members of the IRA, accompanied by Seán South's brother. He was openly hostile to the Volunteers, whom he blamed for misleading and destroying an exceptional man.

The Volunteers tenderly placed the blanket-wrapped bodies in coffins, then covered them with the Irish tricolour. The sombre procession set out. Soon clusters of people began to appear along the roadside. Men uncovered their heads as the hearses passed. Women wept.

South's brother observed the tribute with amazement.

At midnight on the fourth of January, the lord mayor of Limerick and twenty thousand mourners came out to meet the hearse bearing the man from Garryowen. The next day an estimated fifty thousand followed the casket to Mount Saint Laurence Cemetery, where a Celtic Cross was to be erected over Seán South's grave.

Within days his brother joined the republican movement.[2]

Feargal O'Hanlon also was given a huge funeral and a graveside eulogy befitting a martyred hero. The Monaghan lad had been extremely popular; his many friends crowded the cemetery. Anonymous amidst the ruddy footballers was a tall young man wearing a woollen cap pulled over his bright hair. There were tears in his eyes, but no one paid any attention. Many were weeping that day.

IN spite of the nationwide outpouring of emotion, Operation Harvest brought an end to any support by the Irish government for the anti-partition campaign. Speaking in the Dáil on January 6, Eamon de Valera said, "To allow any military body not subject to Dáil Éireann to be enrolled, organised and equipped is to pave the way to anarchy and ruin."[3]

Many Irish people agreed with him. "At best," one veteran of 1916 told another in the Bleeding Horse Pub in Dublin's Camden Street, "the border campaign was an exercise in bravado. At worst it was damned irresponsible."

The taoiseach, John Costello, spoke with great sadness on Radio Éireann about the lives that had been lost at Brookeborough. Ireland could have but one government and one army, he stressed, adding that the police had been instructed to round up all known republican activists under the Offences Against the State Act.

URSULA Halloran was a light sleeper. She claimed to keep one ear open so she could hear her animals. Swollen like ripe fruit, broodmares and dairy cows were dreaming milky dreams and awaiting the miracle of birth.

On the night of January seventh Ursula retired earlier than usual, worn out with tension. All week the broadcasters had kept up a steady drip-feed of items about the Brookeborough raid. Ursula did not need anyone to tell her that Barry was involved. She simply knew.

Sometime after midnight she heard a startled whinny in the broodmare barn nearest the house. She rolled off the bed in one smooth motion, flung her coat over her nightgown, put her pistol in the pocket, and ran barefoot down the stairs. When she switched on the electric light bulb in the barn the mares blinked in their loose boxes. Only one did not stretch her neck over the half door in greeting. The big bay mare stayed at the back of her stall, apparently watching something out of sight below the door.

"Who's there?" Ursula called. "I warn you, I have a gun."

"So do I," said a voice.

Barry stood up with the rifle in his hands.

Ursula gave a sharp intake of breath. "Home safe, thank God," she murmured.

A faint smile flickered across Barry's face. His mother's hands were shaking. To steady them she unlatched the door and swung it open. "Come out here and let's have a look at you."

When the tall young man stepped from the stall she reached out to hug him, then hesitated. His face had changed more than she would have thought possible in so short a time. The boyish softness had melted away, revealing an aquiline nose, jutting cheekbones, and a strong chin. Wind and weather had scoured his freckles. His eyes were set deep in their sockets.

In the shadowy barn Barry looked dangerous.

Ursula drew an unsteady breath. "What are you doing out here in the middle of the night?"

"I thought the house might be watched."

"It isn't."

"How can you tell?"

"I just know."

Barry nodded. Within the family Ursula was famous for "knowing."

She gingerly took him by the arm—half expecting him to pull away from her—and drew him into the cobbled yard. "You can see for yourself, there's no one here but us. Why, you're shivering! You're as cold as well water. Come into the house and I'll light a fire in your room. Quietly now, we don't want to wake Eileen. You know how nosy she is."

In his bedroom Barry leaned the rifle against the wall and sat down heavily on the bed, watching while his mother lit a fire in the grate. When the blaze took hold she asked Barry, "What are those stains on your coat?"

"Just stains."

"They look like . . . they are, they're blood. You tried to wash them off, didn't you? Then smeared them with dirt?"

He made no effort to deny it.

"Take off your coat and we'll have Eileen give it a proper cleaning." Barry removed the coat. Ursula's eyes widened. "No wonder you're cold! What's become of your shirt?"

"You don't want to know."

After Barry was in bed with quilts piled over him and a hot water bottle at his feet, his mother lingered in the doorway. "You were at Brookeborough, were you not?"

"I'd rather not talk about it."

"There's been hardly anything else on the wireless. They said an RUC man was killed, and the northern authorities insisted the raiders be arrested if they tried to enter the Republic. The taoiseach gave in—I don't know what pressures were brought against him—and the gardai, the Army, and Special Branch were all alerted. Then we heard that some wounded fugitives were captured in a house just this side of the border."

Barry wriggled his toes against the hot water bottle but could not feel its heat. He knew she would never give up unless he said something. "We left those men there while we went for medical help," he told her. "Instead we ran into an Army patrol. My pals surrendered quietly, as we'd been taught. But I still had Granda's rifle and I wasn't about to give it up, so I scarpered."

"A good thing too!" said Ursula. "The wounded were taken to hospital but the rest are being held in the Bridewell Garda Station in Dublin. Twelve of them altogether, awaiting trial. God knows what they'll do to them."

Twelve. That must mean they haven't found Seán Garland yet.

Barry faked a huge yawn to encourage his mother to leave. She stayed where she was. He rolled over so his back was to her and pulled the covers over his head. At last, and reluctantly, she turned out the light and left the room.

He burrowed deeper under the covers. He longed for sleep but it eluded him. Whenever he closed his eyes it was not Feargal's dying face he saw. Like a strip of film projected on the inside of his eyelids, he was forced to watch, over and over again, as the RUC man threw up both arms and pitched backwards onto the road.

BARRY might be unwilling to talk about Brookeborough, but Ursula was not naïve enough to believe that her son could escape the consequences of whatever had happened there. Sooner or later someone would come looking for him.

The next morning she tucked her pistol into the waistband of her trousers before leaving the house. From that day on she carried it everywhere.

Like Ned's Lee-Enfield, Ursula's Mauser had a history of its own.*

WHEN Barry looked at his grandfather's rifle he saw, superimposed over the weapon, the RUC man running toward him. Heard the crack of the rifle. Watched a human face explode into red mush.

He shoved the Lee-Enfield out of sight under his mattress.

Formerly he had equated violence with action, the magnetic pole to which boys were drawn. At Brookeborough he had learned the true nature of violence. The passion of patriotism had exploded in a shower of blood. Barry had taken life and seen life taken, and none of it was the way he had imagined when he was a small boy playing soldiers.

Yet underneath everything the passion was still there. Or rather, the need for the passion was still there. Without an intense, thrilling focus such as the Army, what was the point of existence?

I killed a man who wanted to live as much as Feargal. Yet that man or someone like him killed Feargal.

I killed a man. And for one brief moment . . . Barry forced himself to be hon-

*See *1921* and *1949* by this author.

est . . . *the sense of power was tremendous. Like nothing I ever experienced before. Then he was just a heap of clothes lying in the road.*

The same as Feargal lying in the lorry.

Bit by bit, in fractured thoughts and tormented dreams, the pain began to work its way to the surface. When his mother chided him for ignoring something she said, he replied, "Sorry, I wasn't listening."

"Am I boring you?"

"It isn't that. It's just . . . Feargal's dying the way he did and . . . and everything . . . it's pulled me up by the roots."

"Feargal O'Hanlon?"

"He was my friend. And the first person I ever saw die." Barry's voice faded away; returned: "I wanted to fight for a united Ireland. I just never thought it would become so . . . personal."

"Sooner or later," Ursula said sadly, "all wars become personal."

BY government order, known or suspected republicans throughout the country were being arrested. On the thirteenth of January several prominent members of the IRA were seized during a raid on Charlie Murphy's house in Dublin. By the end of January the staff of GHQ and most of the Army Council were in the Bridewell, from which they soon were transferred to Mountjoy Prison.

No one came for Barry Halloran. He did not want to go to prison yet resented being excluded from the band of brothers. He tensed when a car turned into the laneway and looked around for the nearest escape route, but at the same time he wanted to stand in the middle of the road and shout, "I was at Brookeborough too!"

The more Barry thought about Brookeborough the more he reproached himself. He had dreamed of being a hero like Ned Halloran, yet he had disobeyed orders—again—and compounded his crime by deserting his post. To make matters worse, he had run away while his comrades were being taken prisoner.

We were supposed to disable and demoralise the enemy. We're the ones who ended up disabled and demoralised. How could such good intentions have such a bad outcome?

He ached to talk about the contradictory feelings roiling through him. But how could anyone understand who had not been there? Feargal would understand, but he was dead. Seán Garland would understand, but to go looking for him would subject them both to almost certain capture. Barry thought of speaking to his parish priest until he recalled the words of Séamus McCoy: *You never know who might be an informer.*

Chapter Nine

FOR the first time in Barry's memory the door to the bedroom that had been Ned Halloran's was ajar. Ursula kept it closed out of deference to her father, and it was firmly understood that no one aside from herself and Eileen was allowed inside. During his lifetime Ned had discouraged visitors, particularly noisy and nosy children. His room was a private sanctuary where he sorted amongst his memories and grappled with whatever demons still haunted him.

Barry clearly recalled the only time he had been inside. *The day Granda died. Mam brought me up here to kiss him good-bye.*

It had not been an occasion for exploring the room.

Barry stood listening to the sounds of the house; faraway kitchen sounds. Ursula was outside with her horses. No one would know if he entered the room, yet it took a surprising amount of courage.

Once he was inside he quickly closed the door.

The bedroom was Spartan in its simplicity. On the wall instead of the usual portraits of the pope and Mr. de Valera was a framed sepia photograph of a young couple. Because he had seen *Mise Éire,* Barry recognised his grandfather in the lanky man with a tousle of black curls tumbling onto his forehead. There was strength in the gaunt face. *And courage. The camera captured his courage perfectly.*

Barry had never seen a picture of the grandmother who had been killed by the Black and Tans before he was born. Ursula had once explained, "My mother wasn't the sort of woman who liked having her photograph taken." Now Barry identified Síle Halloran by the wifely deference in her posture as she leaned against Ned. But there was nothing submissive in her face. Slanting eyes like a cat's eyes, and a wide, sensuous mouth. *She doesn't look like anyone's grandmother. The camera must have captured her soul.*

The only other ornament on the wall was a copy of the Proclamation of the Irish Republic. One corner of the document was torn. The paper was yellowed with age and seamed where it had been folded small enough to fit in a man's notebook. Barry caught his breath. *This must be one of the copies they put up all over Dublin during Easter Week, 1916!* With reverent fingers he removed the frame from the hook and turned it over. Written on the brown paper backing was, "Ned, this rightly belongs with you and not me. Henry."

Ned's personal belongings were still in the room, not because Ursula kept the place as a shrine, but because she never threw anything away. They were few enough. A bone-handled pocket knife, a shaving mug and straight razor, a pair of military brushes with a few grey hairs still tangled in the bristles. A tweed cap with a sweat-stained label that read MORGAN'S, 19 DUKE STREET, DUBLIN—BEST IN 1768, BETTER IN 1928. A scuffed leather wallet that contained a few old banknotes and a Dublin pawn ticket, but no identification of any kind.

I wonder what he pawned. And why he never reclaimed it.

Barry's curiosity was growing.

Hanging from pegs in the wardrobe were the clothes Ned had worn in his latter years, and a uniform of much earlier vintage: a single-breasted tunic with brass buttons embossed with a harp, and matching trousers cut like riding breeches. Pinned to the tunic was a bronze Volunteer's badge.

Time had faded the grey-green serge to the colour of moss in winter. When Barry pressed the fabric to his nose it smelled of the little bag of camphor someone had placed in a pocket to prevent moths. *Eileen probably. Mam's not that domestic.*

In the bottom of the wardrobe were Wellington boots and two pairs of leather shoes grown stiff with age. Shoved in behind them was a canvas back-pack. Barry swung the pack onto the bed and sat down beside it. The buckles were rusted and difficult to open. Underneath several woollen jumpers was a large metal box. Try as he might, he could not force the lock. A diligent search uncovered the key in the drawer of the bedside locker, attached to a thin leather cord that Ned used to wear around his neck.

Barry unlocked the box with mounting excitement and flung back the lid. The first thing he saw was a folded square of paper with "Síle" written on it. When he unfolded the paper a curl of russet-coloured hair tumbled out. Barry bent to pick it up; the curl twined around his fingers like a living thing. Feeling as if he had committed sacrilege, he returned the little memento to its wrapping. The other contents of the box were the marriage certificate of Edward Joseph Halloran and Síle Duffy and two thick bundles of school copybooks tightly bound together with twine.

Before he left the room Barry took a last long look at the photograph of Ned and Síle. Dead for years, as the world reckoned dead, yet still vibrantly alive in the picture.

In the privacy of his own room Barry examined the copybooks at length. Ned had used them as his personal notebooks, and they contained a mixture of diary entries, political commentary, and philosophical musings. Plus a number of pages that appeared to be written in code. The earliest book—recognisable as such because it was worn and faded with age—comprised the opening chapters of a novel. The handwriting was clear and forceful, a young man's handwriting.

Turning back to the first page, Barry began to read. He had not gone far before he encountered his grandmother, she of the cat's eyes and sensuous mouth. Ned had called her "Sinéad" in his novel, but made no other attempt at disguise. Ned Halloran's passion for her fairly leapt off the page. Barry closed the book in embarrassment. It was like feeling her hair curl around his finger again.

When he heard Eileen's cracked voice calling him down to the table he thrust the notebooks into a drawer, knowing he would come back to them later. Come back again and again, reading a bit at a time, like having conversations with his grandfather. If he could not be with his comrades, at least he could be, in some sense, with a man who understood.

During dinner Barry felt his mother's eyes on him. "Are you ill? You've hardly touched your food."

"I'm all right." He took a roast potato he did not want and forced himself to eat it.

"You're worrying about going back," she speculated.

He felt her silently pulling at him, seeking information. "I'm not worried about going back."

"But . . . ?"

"But nothing. I told you, I'm not worried." Barry helped himself to another potato. *Whatever you say, say nothing.*

"The government's determined to destroy the IRA once and for all. It might be best if you kept out of sight for a while."

"Umm." As long as Barry kept his mouth full she would not expect him to speak. *The Garland column's broken up, I'll have to find another company.* But even as he considered the possibility his thoughts went skittering off in another direction.

Until the afternoon he spent amongst his grandfather's memories, Barry, like most youngsters, had given little thought to the personal lives of the adults he knew. But the belongings Ned Halloran had treasured touched him deeply. He found himself thinking about them at the oddest moments. A photograph. A curl of living hair. Someone else's reality, as valid as his own.

Ursula had seen her son lose himself in daydreams before. She set her teacup in its saucer with a commanding clatter. "A third-level education is a fine thing," she said in a voice that commanded attention.

Barry looked up. His mother never made idle remarks.

"You could go to university, you know," Ursula went on. "Trinity College would be perfect. There was a time when a Catholic had to get special permission to attend Trinity because the Church considered it dangerous to faith and morals.[1] I don't know if the ecclesiastical ban is still in effect, but if it is, I'm sure we can find a way around it."

Eileen had put down her knife and fork and was staring fixedly at Ursula.

"I'm not interested anyway," Barry said. He had been a man amongst men; he was not willing to be demoted to the rank of student. "And even if I were willing to go to a college it wouldn't be that one. Granda told me Trinity flew the Union Jack during the Rising in 1916."

"All the more reason to enrol you there; you'll be a secret viper in their bosoms," Ursula said with a laugh. "Seriously, though—you'll receive an excellent education and be out of harm's way for a while."

"I'm not supposed to be out of harm's way, Ursula. I'm a soldier."

"I'm not suggesting you give up the Army, just take sensible precautions in the current situation. The gardai probably have your name by now, but they'd never think to look for you at Trinity. It's still a symbol of the Protestant ruling class. We'll enrol you as an undergraduate and . . ."

Barry pushed back his chair and stood up. "No, Ursula," he said. For the first time in his life. He shot his mother a look which she would think of, forever after, as Barry's dangerous look. Then he left the room.

When he had gone Eileen caught Ursula by the elbow. "You never told me there was that sort of money," the older woman hissed.

"What sort of money?"

"Enough to send the lad to university."

"The farm's not doing too badly, and I'm careful."

"This farm's the most productive for miles around and you're not careful, you're mean!" Eileen burst out. "Philomena Pinchpenny, you."

"How can you say that? Do you not have plenty of food and clothes and a roof over your head, all provided by me?"

Eileen thrust out her lower lip in the pout that was the sole remnant of her girlish charm. "And never a shilling in my pocket."

"What about your butter-and-egg money?"

"That goes to the Church, as you very well know. The Mass offerings and the Poor Box."

"Well, if you need something else you have only to ask."

"There's need and there's want, Ursula. I don't *need* anything, but there's things I want."

"We both remember a time when merely being able to provide for one's needs was a triumph," Ursula reminded the other woman. "Since I took over this place in 1940 I've worked night and day to build security for all of us. I've denied myself a lot of things I wanted, books and smart clothes and travel."

"You travel up to Dublin," Eileen reminded her. Few of their neighbours in

Clare had ever been to Dublin, yet Ursula took the train across the island to the capital twice a year. Gerry Ryan maintained that the trips were strictly farm business but local conjecture was rife as to what that might include. "Ned Halloran used to do a lot of business in Dublin," men reminded one another in the pubs of Ennis. "IRA business." Knowing winks.

Women were not as quick to ascribe a political motive to Ursula's actions. "The bishop says Dublin is a bog of temptation," they whispered to one another in the corner shop in Clarecastle. "You know what her past must have been." "Any woman who goes off to Europe and comes back with a baby . . ." Fingers tapping sides of noses.

"Why don't you ever take me to Dublin with you?" Eileen asked resentfully. "The only time I've been there was when we buried my brother."

Two graves side by side in the republican plot in Glasnevin Cemetery. Ned and Síle Halloran. Ursula always went to the cemetery first, straight from the train.

"Is that what you want, Eileen? To visit Papa's grave?" Ursula sounded exasperated. "We've been all through that before. I'd take you to Dublin but you'd be bored to tears. I go to meet potential buyers at the spring horse sales and the big horse show in the autumn. You're not interested in horses, so what would you do with yourself all day?"

Eileen pleated her apron between fingers knotted by arthritis. She had never stood up to Ursula before; few people did. But Barry's rebellion had inspired her. "Perhaps I'd get a nice cup of tea and find someone to chat with in the hotel lobby."

"I stay in a poky little commercial hotel whose guests are usually out during the day. Salesmen, most of them, working on commission; hardly the sort to enjoy a leisurely chat with an old woman."

Eileen bristled. "I thought you stopped at the Shelbourne."

"I don't know where you got that idea. I never stop at the Shelbourne."

Eileen was not the most sensitive of women, but something in Ursula's voice warned her off. "Well, you needn't worry," she said. "I'm not asking you to take me to Dublin. All I want is a fridge."

Ursula's mouth dropped open. "A what?"

"A fridge. Re-frig-er-ator. With plastic ice trays."

As they were scrubbing the milk cans in the dairy Ursula told Gerry Ryan, "I'll never understand people. Animals make sense but humans don't. Take Barry. He's intelligent enough to have a career in any profession he likes, but he refuses to go to university. Then there's Eileen, who has more now than she's ever had in her life but thinks I'm mean because I won't buy an electric refrigerator."

Ryan cocked an eye in her direction. "You're not exactly *flaithiúlach,** missus, but I wouldn't call you mean. You plan to get one of those contraptions for her?"

"I certainly am not, there's no need. Eileen wouldn't use it anyway. That woman's as set in her ways as an old hen; she's still suspicious of the electric light. Barry's a different class of animal altogether. The future belongs to him and I want to see that he has one."

BARRY spent a restless night. His thoughts ran in circles, exhausting him. He got up next morning more tired than when he went to bed, keenly aware that he was in danger of being pressured into the life his mother planned for him.

He was certain of only one thing: whatever he did with his life, it must be his own choice.

THE spatter of gravel against a windowpane brought Séamus McCoy instantly awake. He reached under his pillow for his pistol. Flattening against the wall, he crept toward the window and peered down at an angle. The grey light of early morning revealed a man standing in the road below with a bicycle.

McCoy lowered the pistol and opened the window.

"Seventeen? Is that you down there?"

"I need to talk with you, sir."

"Forget the 'sir,' I'm Séamus. You're not in my command anymore. How'd you find me?"

"You once mentioned having a bolthole in Ballina, so I came looking for you. When I saw the strategic location of this place I was sure . . ."

"Jesus God. Stay there and I'll come down."

McCoy's hideaway was a brick-fronted pub on the road that ran through the centre of the village. On the other side of the road was the bridge spanning the Shannon between Ballina in County Tipperary and Killaloe in County Clare. The pub's upstairs windows thus commanded a view of the main street of Ballina in both directions and the full length of the bridge, as well as the village on the opposite bank.

In one of those windows was a faded notice proclaiming FURNISHED ROOMS TO LET.

McCoy emerged from a side door. "Whew! The wind off the river this morning would strip the feathers off a goose. Why aren't you in a warm bed, Seventeen? For that matter, why aren't I in a warm bed? What's this all about, anyway?"

*Lavish; extravagant.

Barry hunched his shoulders against the cold. The cold inside, not outside. "Brookeborough."

"So you were there. I wondered, but there was no Halloran named amongst the prisoners taken."

"Because I wasn't caught. I ran away to save my rifle." Barry spat out the words with surprising vehemence.

McCoy took him by the arm. "Don't tell the world and his wife, lad. Come inside where we can talk. It's safe; a friend of mine owns this place."

The room above the pub was larger than Barry had expected. A cast-iron fireplace, its black mantelpiece piled with books, stood opposite the door. Stools that looked suspiciously like bar stools were placed on either side of the hearth. Between two windows was a table holding a teapot, an empty milk jug, a bowl of sugar, and several cups. The surface of the table was marred with overlapping rings where tea and milk had been spilled. On the wall above the bedstead were yellowed newspaper photographs of James Connolly and Countess Markievicz, and a framed print of Estella Solomons's brooding portrait of Frank Aiken, former IRA chief-of-staff.

McCoy lifted more books—topped, Barry noticed, by a dog-eared copy of *On Another Man's Wound,* Ernie O'Malley's classic memoir of the Irish War of Independence—off a chair by the table. He beckoned to Barry to sit down while he coaxed a fire from the coals banked in the grate. When McCoy produced a pack of cigarettes Barry took two, one to smoke now and one tucked behind his ear for later. McCoy lit a cigarette for himself and perched one buttock on a stool. "All right, Seventeen. Tell me about it."

He listened without comment until Barry stopped talking and sat staring at the floor. The older man flipped the stub of his cigarette into the fireplace. "Even if I can't condone it, I can understand why you abandoned your post. You were desperate to be part of the action. I might have done the same thing at your age. But why come to me now?"

"I need advice, and you're the only officer I know who isn't in jail or on the run."

"You want to leave the Army, is that it? Did Brookeborough put the frighteners on you?"

Barry lifted his head. His eyes were clear and calm. "I wasn't afraid then and I'm not afraid now." *Except of myself and what I've discovered about me.* "I love being part of the Army. But I shot a man and saw him die right in front of me, and I won't do that again."

McCoy gave a snort. "And here's me thinking you were such a clever fellow. I even told GHQ you had the makings of officer material. Maybe I was wrong. This is war. If you didn't regret having to kill a man I wouldn't want to know you, but if you want to be part of the Army you'll learn to live with it."

"Last night on my way here . . ."

"You cycled all the way from Clarecastle in the dark? Trying to avoid the gardai?"

"Not at all, I don't even think they're looking for me. And I didn't set out in the dark, it was late afternoon when I left the farm." He had waited until Ursula was preoccupied with her horses. The broodmares would be foaling soon.

"By the time I reached Lough Derg the night was drawing in. I don't have a light on my bicycle, so I camped a couple of miles north of Killaloe. I found the perfect campsite, Séamus. There's a little promontory overlooking the Shannon with a deep hollow like a bowl in the centre and oak and beech trees growing all around the rim. The trees form a huge dome I could see from the Scariff road even at dusk."

"According to the locals," said McCoy, "that's the remains of an ancient Irish ring fort. What you call the rim is an earth embankment now, but under the mud and ivy are the stones of a wall built over a thousand years ago."

"Last night . . ." Barry began again, then stopped himself. Some experiences were too amorphous to articulate. But he would remember. He would remember always.

Sitting on a fallen tree at the bottom of the hollow. Too troubled to sleep. Alone while the night closed around him. Burying his face in his hands and trying to drive the memories of Brookeborough from his mind.

I killed a man and I hated it.

But . . . for just one moment it felt wonderful.

Killing the enemy is what heroes are supposed to do.

But . . . I was raised to obey the Ten Commandments.

Thou shalt not kill.

But . . . what about Feargal and Seán South, and all the other Irish men and women the British have killed over the years? Don't they have a right to be avenged?

Vengeance is mine, sayeth the Lord.

But . . . who better to dispense the Lord's vengeance than the creatures he made in his image? If God didn't want me to kill that man, why'd he make me so I'd enjoy it?

Barry beat his knuckles against his skull in an effort to silence the voices inside, but they went on praising and condemning, denying and justifying.

Then, slowly, a sort of music eased into his overheated brain. It overrode his tortured thoughts with an arpeggio of branches played by the wind. A largo of river flowing to the ocean.

His tense muscles began to relax.

The earthwork bank encircled him with protective arms. His nostrils were filled with the clean fragrance of damp soil and the pungency of rotting wood. All around him were the rustlings of nocturnal life, the hunters and the hunted acting out the roles decreed for them since the dawn of time.

The site possessed an almost palpable atmosphere. Layered, complex. There was a degree of peace in this place, but not tranquillity. In addition to life and death on an elemental level, a haunting echo of emotion persisted. Barry strove to identify it. Intense excitement; yes. Joy amounting to exultation. There was also a residue of terrible grief. And futility; the flat, unpleasant, familiar taste of futility.

As the hours passed, Barry no longer felt alone. He was in the company of silent multitudes. There was neither past nor future, only now, an eternal Now in which he and the place and all it contained existed in and through one another. Perhaps he dreamed. Perhaps not. It seemed possible, even desirable, to remain where he was forever. To be one with the earth and the river.

Shortly before dawn, clear, unimpeded thought came like a gift.

MCCOY'S voice brought him back to the present. "What were you saying about last night?"

"I did some serious thinking and I realised something I hadn't realised before. Listen here to me, Séamus. We want to unite Ireland in order to make life better for everybody on this island, right?"

McCoy nodded.

"And the purpose of a gun is to destroy life, right?"

McCoy nodded again.

"Logic tells me it's futile to use one to achieve the other. Therefore, the gun is the problem."

Chapter Ten

MᴄCOY threw back his head and laughed. "You're as daft as a brush, Seventeen! The gun's not the problem, the British are. As long as they control even a fraction of Ireland they can pretend they're still the almighty Empire. They've proved time and again that they don't respect anything but force or the threat of force. Without guns we haven't a hope of getting them to give back the north."

"That well may be," said Barry, "but what I'm saying is, I personally don't want to use a gun anymore. A man doesn't have to be a gunman to be a hero. In 1916, with the British doing their level best to kill him, Pádraic Pearse didn't fire his Browning once. Tom Clarke was carrying an old revolver that might have killed him if he tried to use it,[1] but he never did either."

McCoy rolled his eyes heavenward in a now-familiar gesture. "You're a terrible trial to me, lad. A terrible trial." Barry's gaze was so intense that McCoy could feel it burning into his face. "Let me get this straight. You don't want to carry firearms, is that right?"

"It is right."

"But you're still a republican?"

"I am. And I want to stay in the Army."

"Jaysus." McCoy lit a fresh cigarette and took a thoughtful drag. "Well. There is an alternative, but it's bloody dangerous."

"I don't mind. I'll do anything except shoot another human being."

"I'll hold you to that," said McCoy.

UʀSULA intercepted her son as he wheeled the bicycle into the yard. "Where have you been this time?"

"Army business."

"I thought we decided you were going to college."

"You decided, Ursula, I didn't. School's out of the question for now because I have a new assignment starting tomorrow. Granda always said we couldn't have won the War of Independence without the republican women, so I expect you to support me in this."

Ursula realised she was outmanoeuvred.

Her son had not been strictly honest about having an assignment, however. That would come later, McCoy promised, after he completed his training.

McCoy had given Barry a name and an address on the outskirts of Limerick. "Mickey's probably the best explosives engineer the Army ever had. He and his wife are keeping an IRA call house now—a safe house—I'll give you the password. Mickey can teach you everything you need to know. If you dance him around he'll take against you, so be straight with him from the beginning."

Barry set out early the following morning. As he sped south on his bicycle he was aware of the countryside flashing past. In the hedgerows tiny birds were gathering strength for their spring courtship. The fields on either side of the road lay open and empty, anticipating the plough. Ireland was a land waiting to be reborn.

When the conquerors finally give up and go home.

THE middle-aged woman who came to the door was decidedly suspicious until Barry gave the password. Standing aside, she beckoned him into a narrow front hall. "Someone for Mick," she called to the interior of the house.

A door opened and a man peered out. "Who's looking for him?"

"I am," said Barry. "Séamus McCoy sent me."

The man was sixtyish and paunchy, with a tuft of colourless hair like a clump of withered grass atop his otherwise bald head. "Come on through," he said, indicating the small parlour behind him.

Over the fireplace someone had hung an old hammer as if it were a sword.

Barry glanced curiously at the hammer but made no comment. The other man saw the glance. Keeping both hands in his pockets, he looked Barry up and down. "How do you know Séamus McCoy?"

"He swore me into the Army and was my first training officer."

"And you would be . . . ?"

"Halloran. Barry."

"McCoy give you any message for this Mickey fellow?"

"He said to tell him there are a hundred potholes in the Falls Road."

"Nothing changes, then. Nothing ever bloody changes. Sit down over there, Halloran. I'm Mickey. What can I do for you?"

"Teach me what I need to know. Séamus says you're the best engineer in the country."

"Was," Mickey corrected. "Was the best. I'm retired now."

"How'd you learn your trade?"

"You don't care about all that."

"But I do," Barry assured him. "I've always been curious about other people's lives."

Mickey slouched against the doorjamb with his hands still in his pockets. He did not often talk about himself, but Barry's obvious interest was irresistible. "I was born and reared in Larne, in County Antrim—you know Antrim?— when this whole island was still part of the United Kingdom. Larne was mostly Protestant in those days. Still is, of course. Because we were Catholic my father couldn't get work, so like a lot of others he took the boat to England and hired on with a construction crew building roads for the government.

"He came home once a year, for Christmas. My mother always cried. That's how I remember Christmas: my mother crying and my father turning out his pockets on the table and telling her everything would be all right. 'Just keep your faith, Peggy,' he'd say. 'Just keep your faith.'

"When I was fourteen I went back with him to work on the road crew. There were seven children still at home and my mother needed the money. As soon as I realised that the men who handled the explosives made the most money, I apprenticed myself to one of them. I was smart and I grew up fast.

"After a couple of years my father was beat to death by some thugs in an alley. The police didn't want to know. To them, the killing of an immigrant Paddy was no more than the killing of a dog." Mickey's level, unemotional voice concealed a lifetime of rage.

"I came back to Ireland after that. But I couldn't stomach life in the north anymore, so I made my way south and joined the Irish Volunteers. When I wasn't much older than you are now I was blowing up train tracks to keep the Black and Tans from getting supplies. During the Civil War, I took the republican side and kept on fighting. I really was the best with explosives in those days. If I wanted, I could blow the chin whiskers off a man and not singe his eyebrows.

"When Frank Aiken gave the order to dump arms, I thought I'd put all that behind me. I married the missus and settled down. Then things started up again a few years ago, so I went back on active service. Unfortunately my reflexes weren't as sharp as they used to be. One day my age caught up with me."

Mickey took his right hand from his pocket and held it out for Barry to see. The hand shook uncontrollably. The thumb and first two fingers were missing and the remainder was cobwebbed with angry red scars. "I don't work with explosives anymore. No prizes for guessing why."

Barry tore his gaze away from the mutilated hand. "You can still teach me," he said.

MICKEY led the way to a woodshed behind the house. He propped a log against the door to prevent its being opened from the outside, then switched on the single light bulb hanging from the ceiling. Shelves lining one wall were crammed with empty tins, jam pots, glass bottles, and stacks of old newspapers.

"Hold out your hands," Mickey ordered. He carefully examined Barry's palms and fingertips. "Those long fingers could be an advantage if they're flexible."

"They are."

"For your sake I hope you're right. D'you smoke?"

"I do."

"I wouldn't," Mickey retorted. "These aren't toys you'll be playing with. Now help me shift this woodpile."

With Barry doing most of the lifting, they moved a stack of timber from one side of the shed to the other, uncovering a trapdoor in the floor. "Lie down on your belly," Mickey instructed, "and feel around in the crawl space down there until you find two big boxes. Bring them up."

Barry watched curiously while Mickey took an odd assortment of items from the first box. Wooden clothes pegs, nails, corks, a roll of corrugated wrapping paper, kitchen matches, a narrow plastic tube with holes drilled in it, a mousetrap, some strips of solder, and a roll of blue-grey cord. At the bottom of the box were several battered alarm clocks.

"This," said Mickey, "is a bomb-making kit."

"You're not serious."

"Oh, but I am. Deadly serious. The British government gives the RUC and the B-Specials all the weapons they want, and thousands of them are passed on to loyalist gangs. To counter that we've had to become resourceful in the true meaning of the word. A resourceful man can construct a bomb with little more than an old alarm clock, a clothes peg, and two drawing pins. Of course one other ingredient is necessary." He opened the second box, revealing sticks of a substance wrapped in cellophane.

"Gelignite," Mickey said. "It comes either like this or in a sort of sausage. Either way, it'll blow. If you know what you're doing."

He took a small tin from the shelf and removed the lid. "If you pack this full of gelignite you can make a handy little throwing bomb by poking a hole in it and inserting a length of commercial fuse—that's this over here." He indicated the roll of cord. "There's a core of black powder inside a waterproof casing. Don't let it kink, whatever you do, and be sure to cut the fuse at an angle to expose the core."

By way of demonstration Mickey deftly put together five more dummy bombs of various sizes, with a running commentary on each. "This one may look simple, but you'd want to mind what you're doing. More than one bomb's failed to explode because somebody forgot to wind the clock."

As he worked, the man issued almost as many warnings as instructions. "You'd want to be careful about static electricity. A wool jumper, a cheap nylon shirt—dangerous as hell. I knew a lad who combed his hair too close to an explosive device and set it off."

"What happened?"

"He lost the hair. And the head it grew on."

Barry swallowed hard.

One tiny device made from the workings of a writing pen, was, Mickey claimed, sufficient to blow open an old-fashioned door lock when inserted in place of a skeleton key. "You tailor your explosives to the situation. Some blow upward, some blow out, some'll even blow under if you place 'em right. A tiny charge can open a safe as slick as surgery. A large mine can take the front off a building, but if you're using a battery-operated detonator things can always go pear-shaped."

"I know," Barry said ruefully. "I've seen it happen."

"Unfortunately I can't give you any real practice. Since I blew my hand off, the authorities think I'm harmless, but one explosion in my back garden and there'd be swarms of gardai around here. I'd be in prison before I could bless myself left-handed. So just listen and learn, Halloran. Listen and learn."

During the next few hours Barry asked so many questions that Mickey finally said, "You don't have to make such a meal of this, Halloran."

"Did you not claim you could blow the chin whiskers off a man without singeing his eyebrows?"

Mickey dug in one ear with the little finger of his ruined hand. "Did I?"

"You did. And I want you to make me as good as you were. Don't hold anything back."

He was rewarded with a terse nod of approval.

Barry stayed for a week, absorbing all Mickey could teach him. The man was a consummate craftsman. He spent a whole day on timing. "All fuses aren't alike, Barry. A roll of commercial fuse will have slight chemical differences from every other roll. The weather can affect it, too. In a damp climate like ours, fuse that's out in the open can absorb a surprising amount of moisture from the air. That will affect how fast it burns. Cut off an exact twelve inches, then burn it and measure the time it takes with a good watch. Actually you should burn three pieces to be sure."

Barry slept on a battered couch in an otherwise unfurnished back room. He took his meals with Mickey in the kitchen while the woman stood by the hob, watching them. She rarely spoke and never called Mickey by name, but she always served him first. Once or twice her hand lingered on his.

She touched the mutilated hand as lovingly as she touched the other.

Along with his expertise Mickey shared a number of anecdotes. "Three or four of us were creeping up on an RUC station, planning to lob a bomb through the window. Just as I was about to throw the thing, I stumbled. It rolled away down the street with the fuse burning and a little mongrel came racing out of nowhere to chase it. He caught it at the worst possible moment. I like dogs; I didn't know whether to laugh or cry."

At the end of three days Mickey admitted, "You're all right, Halloran. Most men haven't the temperament to work with explosives. It's fiddly work at the best of times, but never forget: good workmanship is essential to success."

What Mickey called fiddly, Barry called precise. The painstaking detail appealed to a certain orderly quality he was discovering in his own nature: the counterbalance to the wild and reckless side.

HE returned to the farm eager to utilise his new skills. "When Mickey's finished with you," McCoy had said, "get word to me. Then wait for your assignment."

When Barry telephoned the pub in Ballina he was told, "Never heard of anyone called McCoy."

Damned Army secrecy. "I have a message for him anyway. Tell him Seventeen rang and he's ready."

"If your man turns up, we'll tell him." Click.

Days passed, became a week, became a fortnight.

FORCED by events and public opinion, Costello called for an election. The Sinn Féin party received an impressive 65,640 votes. But spearheaded by de Valera, a man even more implacably opposed to the IRA than Costello had been, Fianna Fáil won seventy-eight seats in the Dáil and swept back into power.

On the twentieth of March, Eamon de Valera began his third term as taoiseach of Ireland.

IN one of Ned's notebooks Barry read, "I believe I know what turned de Valera against his former comrades in the IRA. It was not simply political expediency. Dev blamed inadequate planning by the Irish Republican Brotherhood for the failure of the Easter Rising. Pádraic Pearse was large-spirited enough to accept the responsibility himself, gallantly exonerating his fellow republicans, but that was not in de Valera's nature. Since he could not punish the

IRB directly he took out his spite on the Irish Republican Army because it had been the tool of the Brotherhood."

WHILE he waited to hear from McCoy, Barry threw himself into farm work. He liked animals and had been riding horses for as long as he could remember, since the first time Ursula sat him on a broad, warm back and closed his chubby fist around a clump of mane. But Barry's thoughts kept running back to his former comrades. He felt as if the greater part of himself was still with the column.

In the evenings Barry went to his room, closed the door, and sat down with his grandfather's notebooks. He did not return to Ned's unfinished novel but skipped around in the other books, reading whatever caught his eye. He was intrigued by Ned Halloran's evolution from passionate warrior to thoughtful observer.

Toward the end of the Spanish Civil War, while he was fighting with the International Brigades against Franco's fascists, Ned had written, "There is a terrible irony here. In Ireland the republicans fought against the official government and lost. In Spain the republicans are fighting on behalf of the official government and are losing. Why are we so addicted to lost causes?"

I'm not, thought Barry defiantly. *I intend to be on the winning side.*

He began stocking a remote outbuilding with empty containers he took from the kitchen when no one was looking.

Shortly before America entered the Second World War, Ned had stated emphatically, "The Easter Rising was not only a military revolution, but also the physical manifestation of a yearning on the part of the Irish to be *themselves,* to create a society where the native Irish imagination and potential would be unfettered!"

An entry dated 1943: "If we had been given Home Rule there would have been no Rising, but in the long run that would have been a tragedy for Ireland. Home Rule would have replaced the tyrannical Act of Union with an only slightly more palatable version of colonialism, giving us the delusion of self-government while keeping our resources firmly within the British realm. Victorian values and culture would have been the only models allowed us. The colonial class system would have kept the native Irish on the lowest rung of the ladder."

A few months later Ned had written, "Republicanism rejects the obsession with class. The republican philosophy threatened both the northern Protestants and the southern Ascendancy, who, under British rule, were enjoying economic and social privilege they did not want to lose. Quite understandably, they resented the Rising and hated its leaders."

An entry in 1945 pointed out, "After independence the southern Protestants became an important part of this state. They made and continue to make valuable contributions in the professions, in business, and in politics. Their religious beliefs are never questioned or challenged. I do not know the religious affiliations of many of my acquaintances. Here, it is not important.

"Tragically, in Northern Ireland the division between Protestant and Catholic has become a chasm. For their own purposes northern politicians cynically encourage hatred and mistrust between the two. If the ordinary people of England knew what was being done in their names on this island, they would be appalled. But they will never learn the truth. Their government will see to it."

A solitary paragraph on a single page, dated August 1946: "World War Two is over. But how much hatred is being stored up for the next time? This war was a direct result of the First World War, which left such deep resentments. The longer one hates the deeper it goes. Hatred is passed on to the children and the children's children until it becomes a religion in itself."

Chapter Eleven

March 25, 1957

EUROPEAN COMMON MARKET CREATED BY
TREATY OF ROME

URSULA was sitting on the farmyard gate—which she cryptically referred to as "the blesséd gate"—watching Barry approach from the fields. Her face was expressionless but the set of her shoulders warned him.

I'm in trouble.

As he came up to the gate she said, "I went into that shed on the far side of the orchard today. I was looking for a pruning saw George misplaced."

"And was it there?" Barry asked politely. He waited for her to step down from the gate so he could swing it open and enter the farmyard. She did not move.

Deep trouble.

"I found some other things instead. Rather odd things, actually. Did you put them there, Barry?"

He offered his jauntiest grin. "You know me, I'm like a magpie, I collect bits and bobs that appeal to me."

The grin failed to melt her. "To what purpose? Don't lie to me, young man, I didn't just come down in a shower of roses."

"It's Army business."

"If it's on my farm it's my business. Exactly what are you using that shed for?"

Might as well bite the bullet. Except there's no bullet. "I'm practising. Constructing a few simple explosive devices out of things we have lying around the place. It's safe, I know what I'm doing."

"That's your new assignment? Making bombs for the IRA?"

He nodded.

Her features seemed to collapse in on themselves, as if the strong bones underneath were crumbling. "Do you have any idea what a bomb can do? Your own father . . ."

He seized on the word. "My father? What about him? Was he in the IRA?"

"Hardly; he was the least militant of men. If he knew what you're planning . . ."

"I'm not planning to kill anybody. My job will be to help break down the machinery of administration," Barry explained, quoting Seán Garland. "I'll blow up roads and bridges and telephone lines. And if there's any danger of people getting hurt, I'm going to give warnings first."

Although she was not yet fifty, Ursula stepped down from the gate like an old woman afraid for her brittle bones. "You're going to give warnings first," she repeated.

"I am."

"That's your idea of how to conduct a war?"

"It's how I'm going to conduct this one."

Ursula studied his face with narrowed eyes. *Is she seeing my father in me?* Barry wondered.

Then she turned away.

THAT night Barry trawled through Ned Halloran's notebooks seeking some mention of his father. The name Finbar Cassidy never appeared. Stranger still, after 1926 the only entry concerning Ursula was a newspaper clipping that listed her amongst the Irish working in Geneva for the League of Nations. There was no reference to her pregnancy or Barry's birth in 1939.

Mystified, Barry kept searching until he came to an entry dated 15 June, 1941: "Precious and I are fully reconciled at last. She has forgiven me."

She forgave him? What the hell for?

After that Ursula and Barry made frequent appearances in Ned's writings. But nothing explained the silent years.

BARRY was keenly aware of time passing. *I was stupid, saying what I did about guns. Séamus must have passed it on to General Headquarters and they've decided I don't belong in the Army. But I do.*

Eileen complained that he was neglecting his food. "Perhaps the milk's gone off," she suggested during dinner one Sunday.

"No refrigerator," Ursula said without looking up from her plate.

In early April, Barry at last received a letter postmarked Ballina. He eagerly tore the envelope open. A single sheet of paper bore two words: "Saturday morning."

Now it begins, Barry told himself. But there was not the heart-pounding excitement of the past, nor the sense of high adventure. Not even the purity of intent. This was a compromise and he knew it. He envied the men of 1916 for whom everything had been simple.

In Ballina, Séamus McCoy greeted him with, "Mickey tells us you're ready to do the business, is that right?"

"It is. When do I begin?"

"Not so fast, Seventeen. Here, have a fag."

"I don't smoke anymore."

"Wish I didn't," McCoy said wryly. "Cigarettes use up money better spent on whiskey. But back to business. The Army Council's called a temporary halt to attacks. Reluctantly, I must say. John Joe's particularly upset about it, but . . ."

"John Joe?"

"John Joe McGirl. He's been very committed to the border campaign, he was even chief-of-staff for a wee while. But things are too hot for us right now, too many of our lads are in prison. We need to spend a few months regrouping. When the nights begin to be longer, we'll send fresh active-service units across the border."

"Including me?"

"Aye, but you won't be assigned to one particular group. We're short on explosives engineers so you'll be a floater, sent wherever requested."

The disappointment Barry felt told him how much he had been looking forward to the camaraderie, the sense of cohesion, that came with being part of a unit. Instead he was being cut loose. *An outsider again.*

He let none of this show in his face. "How do I get my orders?"

"My friend Éamonn Thomas wears a lot of republican hats. In addition to being the Dublin O/C, he's the treasurer of Sinn Féin and the manager of the party newspaper, the *United Irishman,* for which he also writes historical articles. Since you're interested in history Éamonn suggests you buy a subscription."

Barry laughed. "For once I'm ahead of you, Séamus. My mother already has a subscription. She takes every republican periodical in the country."

"Then make sure you get to that copy of the *Irishman* before anyone else does. There'll be notes in code for you tucked between the pages."

"Thank Éamonn Thomas for me, will you?"

"Thank him yourself if you ever come up to Dublin," McCoy said, "though I think you'll soon be too busy."

As Barry was about to leave the room above the pub McCoy stopped him. "One more thing, Seventeen. It's a stroke of luck that your name doesn't seem to be on any arrest list. Mind you keep it that way. *I ngan fhios don dlí is fearr bheith ann.*"

"It's better to exist unknown to the law," Barry translated. "I didn't know you had any Irish, Séamus."

"Even an old dog can learn. It's my language too."

In response to the lessening of IRA activity, the Irish government began to release republican prisoners. Eamon de Valera, however, remained personally determined to stamp out the organisation. At his order the old prison camp on the Curragh in Kildare was reopened and made ready.

In the north the loyalists, convinced that the IRA was a spent force, renewed their attacks on Catholic families. People were beaten and houses burned with such regularity that the incidents were rarely even reported in the newspapers anymore.

In May a large republican rally was held in Dublin. Ex-prisoners assured a cheering crowd that the war was far from over; Ireland would be reunited yet. The government was alarmed by the size of the crowd and dispatched the Special Branch to take down names, though no arrests followed. "The government hopes," stated a radio announcer, "that the declining number of incidents in the north signals an end to republican violence." He made no mention of ongoing loyalist violence.

Throughout June, Barry waited, spending his ferocious energy on farm work during the day, then joining his contemporaries for a round of socialising in Ennis until late at night. He drank more than most and talked less. The life of the local young people seemed far removed from his own. Their conversation was about sports—which he once had followed avidly—and the latest popular music on the wireless and the newest motion picture from America. Barry soon drifted away to spend his evenings reading Ned's notebooks. He lived a rich fantasy life as the young Ned Halloran, doing valiant deeds.

To his disappointment, the next small, blurred issue of the *United Irishman* arrived with no message inside for him. But a few days later a large box of what appeared to be stable supplies—curiously addressed to Barry Halloran rather than Ursula Halloran—was delivered to the farm. When Barry opened the box, he found, beneath two horse blankets that were neither clean nor new, a roll of commercial fuse and some detonators.

On the fourth of July an RUC patrol unexpectedly encountered a fully armed IRA unit in County Armagh. In an exchange of fire, the Volunteers killed one constable and severely wounded another. The next day the newspapers were filled with condemnation of "the Forkhill Ambush."

The match was put to the tinderbox. Without hesitation, de Valera issued an order for internment. The gardai and the Special Branch fanned out across

Dublin. At Sinn Féin headquarters in Wicklow Street they arrested twelve men, then went on to clean out the offices of the *United Irishman* in Gardiner Row. Éamonn Thomas temporarily eluded them and went on the run, but was soon captured.

The sweep continued throughout the week. Most of the Sinn Féin executive committee, the Army Council, and the staff of GHQ were sent to the Bridewell to await transfer to Curragh Camp. Only a few highly ranked republicans escaped, fleeing to a hideaway in the hills of Limerick.

Ordinary men and women were shocked by the number of arrests. The Bishop of Clonfert commented, "Our version of history has tended to make us think of freedom as an end in itself and of independent government—like marriage in a fairy story—as the solution of all ills."[1]

AN outraged Ursula Halloran cried, "How dare they imprison people without any charge, just on suspicion of what they *might* do! Do we have a government or a dictatorship?"

In Curragh Camp the internees soon were following a well-established republican tradition, one that dated back to the days of Michael Collins: using their time to study the Irish language and the arts of subversion.

THAT summer Bill Haley and his Comets brought rock-and-roll to Dublin. They performed to packed audiences in the Theatre Royal. The music was condemned as "anarchic" by the Church and hailed as "revolutionary" by the young people, who loved it. Their idea of revolution was different from that of their grandfathers. To boys and girls growing up in the 1950s, it meant long overdue social change. They even had a new name for themselves, one imported from America. They were called teenagers now.

WITH the stroke of a pen Eamon de Valera had relieved Barry of any uncertainty. The introduction of internment in the Republic was all the justification he needed to return to the struggle with a whole heart. The Irish government had abandoned the moral high ground staked out by Pearse and Connolly. Only keepers of the republican flame like Sinn Féin and the IRA could bring it back.

Under the circumstances, Barry did not expect to receive any coded assignments via the *United Irishman*. Republican activity would be at a near standstill until there was a wave of prisoner releases, or the few men still free could mobilise. While Barry waited he spent hours figuring out new timing mechanisms and methods for disguising mines. When the call came he would be ready.

Ursula was thinking ahead too. "Have they given you a pistol?" she asked her son. "A handgun's more convenient for self-defence than a rifle."

"I don't have a pistol."

"Then take mine. I'll feel better, knowing you have it. We won't be unarmed, there's always Gerry's shotgun."

Rather than try to explain his reasons for not carrying firearms, Barry accepted the pistol. He had not even told Séamus McCoy the whole story. That moment when he blew the face off another man was his alone to bear.

The Mauser went under his mattress with the Lee-Enfield.

IN September, President Eisenhower sent a thousand U.S. paratroopers to Little Rock, Arkansas, to enforce a federal court order granting black children the right to enter a public school formerly attended only by whites. Fifteen hundred demonstrators staged a furious protest beyond the military cordon, screaming, "Go home, niggers!" Seven segregationists were arrested. Nine black children successfully enrolled in Central High School.

Chapter Twelve

October 4, 1957

RUSSIANS FIRST INTO SPACE WITH SPUTNIK

Americans express determination to surpass Soviet achievement.

T HE Space Age has begun!" Barry cried as he burst into the kitchen. "This very minute there's a manmade satellite circling the earth five hundred miles above us."

Eileen looked up from her sewing. "Wherever did you hear such nonsense?"

"It's on the wireless right now, it's the biggest news story ever! And Ursula's missing it. When she gets back from her ICA meeting she'll be raging."

Barry ran out to look at the night sky. *Human beings have invaded the realm of the gods!*

Millions of people throughout the world were peering into the heavens that night, united in their desire to glimpse the tiny light streaking overhead.

T HE summer of 1957 had been excessively hot even by Texas standards. Drought and high temperatures continued into the autumn, so that by October not only the foliage but the people of Dallas were wilted. Henry Mooney felt the heat more acutely than usual. "I don't think I want any breakfast this morning," he told Isabella.

Following her mother's death, Isabella, the elder of his two daughters and widow of Michael Kavanagh, had given up her house in New York State and moved back to Dallas to care for her aged father. She tried to give the impression that she was making a great personal sacrifice, though in reality she was delighted. The Mooney house was much larger and infinitely more stylish than her rented bungalow. It also came complete with a Negro housekeeper called Pearl and a Negro cook called Opal. The widow Kavanagh never had been able to afford domestic help.

"Do you want Opal to boil an egg for you?" she asked Henry. "You have to eat something."

He shook his head. "Maybe later. The living room's the coolest place in the house, so I think I'll go in there and write a letter to Little Business. I owe her one. She's been so good about trying to cheer me up since the Cap'n died."

"Mmm," said Isabella. After an hour or so she put on a large-brimmed straw hat that had belonged to her mother, and found the pruning shears her father kept on the back porch. "I'm going to cut some of Dad's roses for the dinner table before the heat wilts them," she told Pearl. "Today would have been my parents' wedding anniversary so I want to do something special. Put the Irish linen on the table and set out Mother's best china. The Haviland," she added unnecessarily. Pearl had been working for the Mooneys for years and knew the contents of the china closet from top to bottom.

In the garden that was Henry Mooney's pride and joy, the atmosphere was breathless. Heat waves shimmered above the shrubbery. After a few minutes Isabella came back indoors. Handing the roses to Pearl to put into water, she went to her room to bathe her temples with cologne. Ella Mooney had always kept a bottle of cologne chilling in the refrigerator for that purpose.

It was lunchtime before Isabella realised that her father had not emerged from the living room.

She found Henry Mooney seated at the table between the front windows, slumped across the letter he had been writing to Ursula. Isabella's startled eyes registered only one sentence: "I am heartbroken that I won't be with the Cap'n on our anniversary."

But he would.

WHEN the telephone in the passage shrilled its double ring Ursula was halfway up the stairs. She turned and came back down. A few minutes later she appeared, ashen-faced, in the kitchen, where Eileen was still scrubbing the table. "Henry's gone," Ursula said in a stunned voice. "A heart attack. Bella said he was writing a letter to me at the time. She sounded reproachful, as if it was somehow my fault."

Eileen pressed clasped hands to her aproned bosom. "God have mercy on him! I know how much you loved him, we all loved him."

"Ella loved him the most," said Ursula. "And he adored her." She stood for a few moments trying to collect herself, then went to the foot of the stairs and called to Barry to come down.

"The funeral won't be until Friday," she told him. "Henry's daughter Henrietta—the family calls her Hank—lives in Colorado, and Henry had friends and business associates all over the country, so they want to allow time for everyone to get there. Hank's children are still small so she's leaving them at home, but I want you with me."

Barry was taken aback. *The Army might send for me at any time.* "Why me? All I remember about Henry Mooney is that he had a deep voice and wore both belt and braces."

Ursula said softly, "I remember everything about him. Even the smell of his shaving cream: it was cocoa butter."

The refusal Barry was contemplating died on his lips.

Gerry Ryan drove them to Shannon Airport in Ursula's old black Ford. They were accompanied by Eileen, who insisted on seeing them off. Before getting out of the car at the terminal Ursula pressed something into Eileen's hand. Barry did not notice; his attention was engaged by the scene before him.

Stacks of luggage, including luxuriously matched sets, were piled at kerbside. Newly arrived American tourists, pale with exhaustion but wearing bright green sweaters and cloth hats stitched with the slogan KISS ME I'M IRISH were queuing for taxicabs. On the tarmac a gleaming commercial airliner was being refuelled to make the return flight across three thousand miles of ocean.

Yet less than a mile away lived people who had no indoor toilets.

When they were standing in the queue at the check-in Ursula unexpectedly chuckled.

"What's funny?"

"I gave Eileen a present of some money. Not enough to buy the refrigerator she thinks she wants, but a fortune to her all the same. Now she's in a squandary."

"A quandary about how to squander the money," Barry interpreted. "You know as well as I do she'll just give it to the Church."

"I specified she must spend it on herself."

"I'll wager you half a crown she still has it when we get home."

Ursula shook her head. "Life is enough of a gamble. I never bet on anything else."

On board the aeroplane Barry insisted his mother have the window seat, though much of the fourteen-hour flight to New York would take place at night. *At least she'll have a view of the stars.*

He felt a great thrill when the plane roared down the runway and lifted into the air. *All that power under the control of a human being. A man like me. What was that line from Yeats? Oh yes. "Breaking the bonds of earth."*

As soon as they reached cruising altitude Ursula closed her eyes and leaned her head against the back of the seat. Throughout the long flight she rarely spoke. When the stewardess brought food on a tray, Ursula left hers untouched. Barry ate it as well as his own. After the cabin lights dimmed he could not tell if his mother was asleep or not; if not, she obviously preferred to be alone with her thoughts.

The plane landed briefly at Newfoundland for refuelling, and most of the passengers took advantage of the opportunity to disembark and walk around. Barry was certain his mother was asleep by then, yet he chose to stay on board with her.

Solicitude for Ursula was a new experience.

AFTER an eternity dominated by the exhausting thunder of the engines, they descended through layers of ragged grey cloud. The plane bumped and bounced. Then like a magic trick the clouds parted, and New York City lay spread out below them.

As they banked on final approach Barry leaned across his mother to stare at the fabled, unbelievable skyline of Manhattan. *Can that possibly be on the same planet as Brookeborough Barracks?*

Idlewild Airport was a revelation, with not one but nine terminals, each having its own distinctive design. Until he saw Idlewild Barry had never given a thought to architecture. The circular Pan American terminal, with its glass walls and huge disk for a roof, was a confident vision of the future. *I love America already!*

They had to wait for their connecting flight to Dallas. Leaving Ursula seated in a lounge area, Barry changed Irish money into American dollars that looked nothing like real money, then went in search of tea and scones.

A kaleidoscope of races in a mosaic of colours swirled through the terminal. Several people bumped into Barry but no one said "sorry." Barry could not help staring. The population of Ireland, north and south, was white, and, with the exception of those in the *Gaeltacht,** spoke English. And in the Republic everyone apologised, it was almost a national characteristic.

When he found a counter that sold food, the menu was chalked on a blackboard. Most of the items were unfamiliar; some seemed to be in a foreign language. *Prune Danish? Bagels?* At least tea was on the list. Barry thankfully ordered two cups. He was given stiff paper cups filled with hot water, and two teabags—unknown in Ireland—together with sugar in paper packets and two tiny plastic pots of milk. A metal container provided paper napkins, another first in his experience. Juggling his purchases on a flimsy tray made of grey

*Irish-speaking areas.

cardboard, he plunged back into the crowd. After a couple of minutes he realised he was turned around. He had no idea where he had left Ursula. *In spite of all the orientation training I've had!*

With trepidation—IRA Volunteers were wary of constables—Barry approached a uniformed policeman to ask for help. The man said, "Just off the plane from Ireland, are you?"

"I am."

"I thought I recognised the brogue. We'd like to go to Ireland sometime, me and the wife. Her mother's Irish. So is half the force in New York, come to think of it. You're gonna feel right at home here."

WHEN he found Ursula, Barry told her, "This place is like the Tower of Babel. As for the food, I bought what purports to be tea but I wouldn't swear to it. I think it's gone cold anyway. The woman at the counter didn't know what I meant by scones, she gave me something she called cookies." He held out a paper bag spotted with grease.

Ursula took a fat, golden-brown disk studded with bits of chocolate and nuts, and nibbled one small bite. "Sweet biscuits," she concluded. "Obviously the Americans speak a different English."

When Barry tried to open a container of milk he succeeded in pushing in the lid and sloshing the contents into his lap. He used the paper napkins to mop his trousers, finished off the cookies, and went back for another bag.

Neither of them drank the tea.

During the long flight from New York to Dallas, daylight through the small window revealed lines in Ursula's face that Barry had never noticed before. *When did she start to get old?* An appalling thought occurred to him: *Someday my mother's going to die. She's actually going to die.* It seemed impossible, yet he knew it was true. He had met death. Up close.

Death was inescapable reality.

The rifle . . . He pushed its image from his mind.

Rousing herself, Ursula began to reminisce about Henry Mooney. With obvious pride she related the highlights of his journalistic career in Ireland. "He did as much as any man could, without actually carrying a gun, to further the cause of republicanism," she told her son.

"But didn't he and Granda quarrel?" Barry said. "What was that all about?"

"It's not important, they made it up anyway. Papa and Henry were like brothers, you know."

"Brothers fight. Just look at the Civil War. And our own George and Gerry aren't speaking to each other half the time."

Ursula gave a wan smile. "Being related is no guarantee that people can get along."

Seizing the opportunity—his mother was buckled into her seat and could not evade him—Barry remarked, "You and Granda had a desperate row before I was born."

"Who told you that?"

To confess his source would be to reveal that he had found the notebooks; she might insist he give them to her. "Maybe Eileen said something about it, I don't remember."

Ursula's thin nostrils flared. "Pay no attention to anything she says. She loves to gossip; how many times have you heard her nattering away with the neighbours? What women like that don't know they make up."

"Then you tell me. Did you and Granda hate each other for a while?"

Ursula turned her head and looked out the window. "Hating is easy. It's loving that's hard."

IRONICALLY, in light of their conversation, the name of the Dallas airport was Love Field.

Their plane landed in late afternoon. Waiting at the arrivals gate was a tall, impeccably groomed brunette in a black dress. At her throat was a single strand of pearls. "That could only be Bella," Ursula said under her breath to Barry. "She has Henry's jaw."

In marked contrast to Bella's polished style was the little girl at her side. Her dark brown curls looked as if they had never been combed. She wore grubby jeans with torn knees, and scuffed penny loafers on otherwise bare feet. Dead-level eyebrows gave her childish face a strange fierceness.

Isabella Kavanagh greeted the Hallorans with the exact degree of warmth she deemed appropriate for meeting strangers. Then she put one hand in the small of the child's back and urged her forward. "This is my daughter Barbara. Say hello to the Hallorans, dear."

Barbara kept her mouth firmly closed. Her hazel eyes were hostile.

"She's only ten," Isabella apologised. "You know how they are at that age."

"I never had a ten-year-old daughter," said Ursula.

"I'm sure a son is equally difficult."

"Barry wasn't."

"Oh. Well . . . I mean . . . let's get your suitcases, then we'll go to the house. I have Dad's car outside."

The car waiting for them in the parking area was a gleaming four-door Chrysler sedan, larger than anyone drove in Ireland. "Ursula, you sit in front with me so we can get acquainted," Isabella directed. "The children can ride in the back."

Children! Barry made a great show of folding his lanky frame and long legs into the rear of the sedan. The car was stifling inside. Texas in October was hotter than summer in Ireland.

Before turning the key in the ignition, Isabella Kavanagh adjusted the rearview mirror to check her appearance. She blotted beads of perspiration from her upper lip with a lace-trimmed handkerchief that bore her mother's monogram: *ERM*. "I'll switch on the air conditioner in a few minutes," she assured her passengers. "The motor has to run for a while first."

Air conditioner?

The big car drove away from the airport with a self-satisfied hum and turned onto a road signposted MOCKINGBIRD LANE. The road bore no resemblance to any country lane Barry knew. Instead of being green, the fields on either side were an unrelieved shade of tan. No stone walls, no hedgerows. Just a flat expanse traversed by incredibly wide, impossibly smooth pavement beneath an unbelievably vast sky. Cloudless prairie sky with the blue baked out of it. In spite of the lateness of the hour, heat mirages shimmered on the road like pools of water, vanishing as the car drew near.

Barry leaned forward. "Ursula? Did you bring your camera?"

She glanced over her shoulder. "It's in my suitcase." Turning back to Henry's daughter, she said, "I remember you as a tiny girl, Bella, when your parents still lived in Dublin."

"Isabella, please. I detest nicknames of any sort. And I'm afraid I don't remember you. My father certainly did, though; he talked about you all the time."

As they drew nearer Dallas, country fields gave way to suburban neighbourhoods. In the larger towns of Ireland identical terraced houses huddled against one another, sharing common walls. American houses were individual in design, each standing free on its own rectangle of lawn. *Architecture expresses the character of the people,* Barry thought, feeling a sense of discovery.

Barbara bent forward to claw at her bare ankles. "I hate chiggers." Her voice was surprisingly deep for such a small girl.

"What are chiggers?" Barry asked.

"Bugs, of course. Teeny weeny red bugs that hide in the grass and jump on you. They're so little you can't see 'em, but they drive you crazy. Don't you have chiggers in Ireland?"

"I think not."

"You talk funny. Is that supposed to be an Irish accent?"

"It *is* an Irish accent."

"What's it like to live in a thatched cottage?"

"I don't live in a thatched cottage."

"You're a liar. Everybody in Ireland lives in thatched cottages because they're so poor."

The child was bringing out the worst in Barry. "We're not poor, we're wealthy," he claimed. "We have a fine farm and a big house with eight rooms." *Counting the scullery, that is.*

"Hunh." The hazel eyes were derisive. "If you're wealthy you can't be Irish. My grandfather was wealthy but he had to come to America to get that way. Is that what you're going to do?"

Barry leaned forward again. "Ursula . . ."

"I heard." Her shoulders shook with silent laughter.

The Chrysler's air-conditioning was beginning to take effect, producing a metallic smell and a clammy chill.

The houses they were passing grew visibly more prosperous. Larger, more lavish, and all with garages. *Does everyone here own an automobile?*

Like a tour guide, Isabella directed her passengers' attention to points of interest. "This is Highland Park, one of our better neighbourhoods. I had a number of friends here when I was a girl." A little farther on: "There's Southern Methodist University, where Hank took her degree."

"Did you go there too?" Barry asked.

"I got married," she replied stiffly.

When she gestured toward a modernistic building that she identified as the Dr Pepper Bottling Plant, Barry resisted the temptation to ask why anyone would put a doctor in a bottle.

They turned right onto Greenville Avenue, which took them past clusters of shops and more residential neighbourhoods. A velvet dusk falling. Street lights coming on. Barbara an uncomfortable presence beside Barry. Even his boundless energy was fading. His head nodded; jerked upright as the Chrysler turned again and yet again, eventually coming into a street lined with sycamore trees. Dark green in an increasing darkness.

"Here we are," Isabella announced. She braked in front of a symmetrically proportioned timber house framed by shrubbery. The steeply pitched roof extended to cover a columned porch across the front of the house. Someone had turned on the porch lights, casting a welcoming glow on cream-coloured walls.

"Mother wanted the house painted white like Mount Vernon, which would have been lovely," Isabella said, "but Dad said white wouldn't go with the Prairie Style. It's one of the few times he ever refused *her* anything."

"Mount Vernon was George Washington's house," Barbara piped up.

"I knew that," said Barry.

"How? I'll bet you don't know anything about America."

"I do so. Your grandfather gives—I mean gave—my mother a subscription to *Time* magazine every Christmas."

"Hunh." The child's tone implied that nothing Barry might say could possibly impress her.

A statuesque woman with skin the colour of mahogany came out onto the porch to meet them. "They been a lot of phone calls, Miz Kavanagh."

"Any from my sister?"

"Yes'm. She's still in Denver. They was some kind of mix-up about their flight but she thinks they'll be here late tonight. Probl'y. She says they'll take a cab from Love Field, but they'll phone you if they can't get one."

"Trust Hank to be disorganised," Isabella said. "She'd better find a cab, I'm not making that drive again. Bring the luggage inside, Pearl, and put it in their rooms."

Pearl gave a nod and started toward the car. Barry hurried to help her.

"There's no need," Isabella called after him. "That's what servants are for."

He went anyway.

Pearl rewarded him with a smile. A gold tooth glinted startlingly in the light from the porch and Barry realised that she was, in her own way, beautiful. "Miz Kavanagh won't like guests he'pin'," she said.

"My mother won't like it if I don't."

The smile broadened. "Yessir, Mist' Halloran."

It was the first time anyone had called him that.

Isabella ushered them into what she called the "living room." "I've told Opal to bring refreshments in here while Pearl unpacks for you."

"I had rather go straight to my room, if you don't mind," said Ursula. Her voice was hoarse with fatigue. "I really am . . ."

"Nonsense, you'll feel much better after a cold drink. Just make yourselves comfortable. Where is that girl? Opal! We're waiting!"

Too weary to argue, Ursula settled onto a couch. Barry was tempted by a cushiony armchair. It was like falling into a bog hole. He struggled out of the depths to perch warily on the edge. *A child could sit down in this and disappear forever.* He glanced hopefully toward Barbara, but she had flopped down on her stomach on the carpeted floor.

Prominently displayed against one wall was a cabinet with a panel of glass in the centre like the eye of a Cyclops. The room's seating was arranged to accommodate worshippers before an altar.

Barry was about to go over and take a closer look at the Cyclops when a short, plump woman entered the room, carrying tall glasses on a silver tray. Her skin was the same shade as the creamy brown beverage in the glasses.

Isabella said, "I do think iced coffee is so cooling, don't you?"

What the hell is iced coffee?

One swallow convinced Barry that Americans were mad. The drink was sickeningly sweet and so cold it paralysed his throat. Ursula, who must, he thought, be made of sterner stuff, sipped hers and politely said it was delicious.

Don't often catch her *in a lie. She must really be tired.*

Isabella gestured toward the silent Cyclops. "Dad had the first colour TV in the neighbourhood, you know. *The Dinah Shore Chevy Show* is going to be on in a few minutes, would you like to watch it?"

Barry had never seen a television programme; television was not yet available in the west of Ireland, although the owners of sets in Dublin were able to pick up BBC broadcasts from Belfast.[1] Barry had no idea what a Dinah Shore Chevy was. He longed to say yes, but a glance at Ursula's wan face dissuaded him. "I think we'd best make an early night of it, Isabella." To emphasise the point, he stood up and offered his hand to Ursula, though he was sure his mother could stand on her own.

Barbara crowed, "Mommy lets me stay up as long as I want to!"

When he wished Ursula good night at the door to her room, Barry remarked, "That's the most disagreeable child I ever saw."

"She's very like her mother, I suspect. Bella was a handful even as a toddler."

ISABELLA Kavanagh sat in front of her dressing table, removing her makeup with cold cream. "So that's the famous Ursula Halloran," she said to the image in the glass. "What's so special about her? She's not even pretty, but Dad thought she hung the sun and moon. I could never live up to her no matter how hard I tried."

And she had tried. After years of listening to stories of Ursula's daring exploits as an Irish republican, Isabella had married an Irish American with republican credentials himself. She had feigned interest in the tangled politics discussed night after night in her living room, she had turned a blind eye to men who came to the back door and whispered urgently to Michael but would not step into the light, she had endured frequent raids on their slender resources to help fund "the cause."

None of it had done her any good. Michael was dead and the bank account was empty and she had come home with her tail between her legs, only to find her father a shell of a man, his heart in the grave with his wife.

The dark eyes in the mirror burned with resentment. Isabella regretted the impulse that had caused her to telephone Ursula. It would have been easier and much less painful simply to send a copy of the obituary. But then she would never have met her rival for her father's affections.

Chapter Thirteen

W HEN Barry and Ursula entered the dining room for breakfast the next morning, they found Hank and her husband already there.

Henrietta Mooney Rice was a solid little woman, casually dressed, as genuine as her sister was artificial. At the sight of Ursula her whole face lit up. "You must be Little Business! Come here and let me hug you. You know, I've always felt as if we were sisters."

"I suppose I did too, Hank. Henry was like a second father to me, and I owe Ella a debt I can never repay."

"We've just finished our breakfast but I'm dying to get to know you better. We'll sit with you and have some more coffee."

John Rice, Hank's husband, was an amiable man who spoke with a slow drawl. While Opal served the Hallorans a daunting meal of ham and eggs, buttermilk biscuits and red-eye gravy and grits—*Grits?*—John and Barry found a common interest in sports. Barry was explaining the rules of hurling when Isabella entered the room. "John, I need you to go to with me to see the funeral director about some last-minute details. You don't mind if I borrow your husband, Hank?" Without waiting for an answer, she clamped a hand on John Rice's arm and drew him away.

The American way of death was alien to Barry. There was no removal of the remains, no Requiem Mass, no cortege following the coffin on foot for the last journey to the cemetery. Death was tidied away out of sight. Friends and family had no glimpse of the deceased until they arrived at the "funeral home." There, amidst a refrigerated hush and the overwhelming pungency of lilies, a waxen figure lay in a bronze coffin lined with white satin. The lid was open.

Ursula took one quick look and turned away. Barry noticed that her hands were trembling. He put his arm around her shoulders, something he had never done before.

After the funeral a large crowd gathered in the Mooney house. The living room was banked with flowers but there was no wake. No music, no drink except for coffee, no baked meats. Opal served cold sandwiches and sponge cake stacked in layers with filling between. Aside from a few words of sympathy to the family upon arrival, the guests talked about themselves and one another.

Only Hank and Ursula gave any outward appearance of grieving. Hank's eyes repeatedly filled with tears—"I'm puddling up again," she would say apologetically. Ursula, though dry-eyed, looked so heartbroken that several of Henry's business acquaintances mistook her for Isabella.

Barry stationed himself behind her chair, leaning against the wall with his arms folded. Offering her the silent comfort of his presence.

Eventually someone recalled that Henry Mooney had been born in Ireland. A sweet-faced woman gushed, "Oh, we know all about Ireland, we saw *The Quiet Man*. You certainly come from a wonderful place, Mrs. Halloran. Everyone is so happy-go-lucky."

A stout man with a strident voice disagreed. "You don't know zip, Thelma. There's war between the Catholics and the Protestants over there. Always has been, always will be."

Isabella spoke up. "Please don't, no one's interested anyway. The whole thing is so boring. My husband Michael called himself a republican but I . . ."

"You're a republican too, Mommy," Barbara insisted. "You voted for Eisenhower and Nixon."

"Don't interrupt, dear," said Isabella. A reprimand issued a dozen times a day, and as frequently ignored.

The man with the loud voice turned to Barry. "You're from over there, right? So you tell me. Why don't you guys stop fighting? Shake hands and be friends, that's what we'd do."

Barry slowly unfolded his arms and straightened up. Through some invisible chemistry he drew all eyes toward him. "After we won our War of Independence in 1921, Britain coerced us into signing a treaty that left six counties of Ireland under British rule," he said quietly. "Would the Americans have stopped fighting if the British had insisted on keeping New England after 1776?"

"That's different."

"Tell me how."

"It just is, that's all."

"Because this is America?" Barry asked politely.

"Well, yeah."

"Where do you get your information about Ireland?" Barry enquired. Still very polite.

"From TV and the newspapers, of course."

"Do they give much coverage to events over there?"

"Yeah, sure. I mean, when anything does happen, which isn't often. The Old World's as dead as a doornail if you ask me. But back in . . . February, I think it was; no, January . . . anyway, *The Dallas Morning News* reported on some IRA gangsters running amok in the north. They murdered a bunch of policemen in cold blood just for being Protestants."

"Gangsters. Cold blood." Barry's voice dropped lower. Became deadly soft. Ursula turned in her seat to give him a warning look. "Where did they get that story?" he asked.

"From the *London Times,* I guess."

"And you think it was an accurate picture, do you?"

The loud man was starting to sweat. Something about Barry made him nervous. "Yeah, sure. Ted Dealey wouldn't print anything in *The News* that wasn't true."

Ursula reached out and caught her son by the wrist. "I'm very tired, Barry. Would you take me to my room, please?"

He hesitated. She tightened her grip. "Now, please."

As soon as they were out of earshot Ursula hissed, "We are guests in this house and this country, and I expect you to behave accordingly. You won't do the cause any good by starting an argument."

"But . . ."

"Listen here to me, Barry, and remember what I say: All the words in the world won't change a closed mind."

Long after he had gone to bed Barry could still hear the self-righteous voice braying condemnation. *Is that what the Americans think of the IRA? That we're gangsters and murderers? Why should we care what they—or anyone—think of us? We have right on our side.*

That night Henry's daughters squabbled about the wording for his tombstone. It was the sort of family quarrel which made witnesses uncomfortable, so Ursula and Barry went outside to sit in the porch swing. A swing for honeysuckle-scented summer days. However, the autumn night was as warm as a summer day in Ireland, and the sky was emblazoned with the same stars. Here they were in a different configuration, but they were the same stars.

Ursula remarked, "I think a person should have only one word—aside from his name and dates—on his tombstone."

"What word?" Barry asked.

"The one that describes him best."

"What word for Henry, then?"

She thought for a moment. "Staunch."

The following morning Barry borrowed his mother's old Eastman Kodak and wandered around the neighbourhood taking pictures. Not of people, of houses. He was fascinated by the architectural details that made Texas so different from Ireland. Houses were built of brick or timber, with shingle roofs instead of slate. Deep porches sheltered the interiors from the glare of the sun. Sash windows set flush with the façade could be opened at top and bottom to facilitate the free circulation of air. *They would let the rain in,* Barry thought, *if it rains very much here. It doesn't look like it, though.*

Several times he went up to a house to take a closer look, noticing the small details. Observing the way they contributed to the whole.

HAD this been Ireland, Henry's family would have observed mourning for months. In America, life reasserted itself rapidly. Isabella proudly announced that she had a full week's programme of entertainment planned for the Hallorans, including a tour of Dallas, a visit to the world famous Mesquite Rodeo, a sailboat ride on White Rock Lake, and dinner in an authentic Mexican restaurant. They would also go shopping in a world-famous department store called Neiman-Marcus, and take a trip to the neighbouring city of Fort Worth for barbecue at the world-famous Big Apple Restaurant.

How can anything be world famous if we've never heard of it in Ireland?

Ursula demurred at Isabella's plan. "We only came for the funeral, this isn't meant to be a pleasure trip."

"Then I don't suppose you'd like to go to the symphony tomorrow afternoon either." Isabella sounded surprisingly relieved. "My mother was on the committee that brought Antal Dorati to Dallas, you know. He's a famous Polish conductor," she added patronisingly.

The steel returned to Ursula's spine. With one of the dazzling smiles she rarely displayed, she said, "We would love to go, Bella. That's too good an opportunity to miss, even though Dorati's not there anymore. He's conducting the Minneapolis Symphony now. And I think you'll find he was born in Hungary, not Poland."

Isabella's nonplussed expression delighted Hank. "Let's all go!" she cried. "We can take Barbara the way Muddie and Pop-Pop used to take us." She rolled mischievous eyes toward her sister. "You'd like that, wouldn't you, Bella?"

Isabella's father had often remarked upon how much Little Business loved classical music. As a result, Isabella loathed all forms of classical music. Now she could not think of an excuse for avoiding the symphony that did not sound as if she were denying her daughter access to culture.

"How nice," she said faintly.

Later Barry remarked to his mother, "That little girl has no more interest in the symphony than a pig does in politics. When I asked her if she likes music she said she loves Chuck Berry. She'll be bored to death, Ursula, and spoil it for the rest of us."

"You can put up with her for a little while longer, surely," Ursula said. "It's almost time for us to go home."

"Already?" Barry made no effort to hide his disappointment. "It seems like we just got here."

THE Dallas Symphony Orchestra was housed on the grounds of the State Fair of Texas, the largest of its kind in the country. *World famous, I'm sure,* Barry thought. As soon as they entered the gates Barbara begged her mother to let her ride the double Ferris wheel and the roller coaster, whose giant skeletons towered over the landscape.

"Not now, we're going to the symphony," Isabella said.

Barry would have liked to try the rides himself but he was one of the adults now, so he said nothing. However, Barbara would not let the subject drop. "I don't want to go to a stupid old symphony, I want to ride the rides!"

People were starting to look at them. "Not *now,* dear," Isabella reiterated. She threw an unfocussed, embarrassed smile in the general direction of the bystanders.

"Tomorrow, then. Let's come back tomorrow."

"We can't, tomorrow's for the coloureds."

"Coloureds?" Barry was puzzled. "Coloured whats?"

"Why, the darkies, of course." Isabella lowered her voice. "The nig . . . Negroes. They aren't allowed to attend the fair except on one certain day, and of course the rest of us don't go then."

Barry noticed a public drinking fountain nearby. Two drinking fountains. One bore a sign saying WHITE, and the other, COLORED.

Hank Rice saw the shocked expression on his face. "That's the way it is here," she told him. "In the south, at least."

"That's the way things are in Northern Ireland," he replied. "Except for 'colored' you could substitute 'Catholic.' "

It was her turn to look shocked.

Barbara complained all the way to the auditorium, where, to his chagrin, she was seated beside Barry. As the orchestra began tuning up she started to squirm, playing with her hair, fanning herself with her programme, and turning around to stare rudely at the people in the row behind her. Eventually the conductor arrived to a round of applause. The house lights dimmed. Hushed anticipation gave way to the eerie opening bars of Debussy's *Prelude to the Afternoon of a Faun.*

Barbara stopped wriggling in her seat. Barry glanced at her in time to see a rapt expression spread across her face. She sat bolt upright without saying a word, though occasionally she gave a sharp intake of breath. The orchestra followed Debussy with Berlioz's *Symphonie Fantastique*. By the time the programme concluded with the thunderous final chords of Ravel's *Bolero,* Barbara was lost in a world she had never dreamed existed.

Barry was so engrossed in watching her reactions that he hardly heard the music himself.

WHEN they returned to the Mooney house afterwards, Barry went to the kitchen for a glass of water. He took the opportunity to strike up a conversation with Pearl and Opal. Diffident at first, they could not long resist his engaging grin.

"By your names I assume you are sisters?" Barry asked.

Pearl laughed. "Nossir, but we're cousins. I got a sister named Sapphire and another one named Topaz, and Opal has a brother named Garnet. In our fambly we like to start the young'uns out with riches." She laughed again, flashing the gold tooth.

"We don't see many Negroes in Ireland, so I don't know much about your customs." Barry stopped, unsure what to say next.

"And you're curious," Pearl guessed. "Course you are. It's all right. I'm a curious-type woman myself. What you want to know?"

"I guess, well, do you have a good life here?" *Do you hate having to drink out of a special water fountain?*

"Our lives be just fine," Pearl assured him. "Miz Ella and Mist' Henry was always good to us."

"And Mrs. Kavanagh?"

The two women exchanged a veiled glance. "She all right," Opal said cautiously. "Once you get to know her."

"I've known her a long time," Pearl said. "Miz Ella brought an Irish housekeeper with her when she came to Dallas, a real nice white woman, but she died of the polio when Miss Isabella was in her teens. That's when Miz Ella hired me to help look after the girls. Miss Hank took to me right away but Miss Isabella never did. I reckon I was too different."

"An outsider?" Barry suggested.

Pearl was indignant. "I was born just 'round the corner on Grigsby Street!"

"So Negro families live in this neighbourhood too?"

"Yessir. Some. They's houses what have servants' quarters at the back for our people."

"And you're happy to live like that?"

"It's what we have," Opal said philosophically.

"But change is comin'," Pearl added. "It most surely is comin'. The Supreme

Court done ruled that it's illegal to make us sit at the back of the bus, and a Baptist preacher called Dr. King's startin' a group to fight for our civil rights."

Later that evening, when the two women were alone in the kitchen washing the dinner dishes, Barry heard them singing a powerful Negro spiritual filled with hope and joy.

THAT night a storm blew across east Texas. Sometime after midnight Barry was awakened by the perfume of rain. He went to the open window and stood greedily inhaling.

America was dynamic and exciting. But he was swept by an almost unbearable longing for the silky air of Ireland and that quiet circle of earth and trees on the west bank of the Shannon.

Ursula's right. It's time to go home.

The patter of raindrops sounded like applause.

BEFORE they left, Ursula asked Barry to take a photograph of herself and Henry's daughters together. "We three," she said.

"Henry's girls," Hank added. Isabella shot her an angry glance but said nothing.

At the last moment Barbara ran, uninvited, to stand in front of the women. She stuck out her tongue at Barry as he clicked the shutter.

Chapter Fourteen

URSULA bought a photograph album for the pictures taken in Texas. To add to them she turned her camera on family and friends, only to find that she had no gift for photographing people. She caught her subjects in awkward positions or, worse yet, cut off their heads or feet.

"There must be some secret to this that I don't understand," she complained to Barry. "You're better at it. I want you to take the camera and give me some nice pictures of Eileen and the Ryan brothers. Portraits, you know?"

He knew. Like Ned and Síle's.

Ursula was so pleased with the results that she bought a little pot of blue enamel and wrote "Barry's Photographs" on the cover of the album. It was kept prominently displayed in the parlour. From time to time Barry riffled through the pages, always surprised by the ability of a photograph to summon up a mood or a memory.

His favourite was the picture of Ursula with Hank and Isabella. Ursula, thin and tired but projecting the indomitable quality he knew so well. Hank wearing a warm, unselfconscious smile; the face of an honest woman. Rigidly posed Isabella, holding her head at a studied angle.

And Barbara Kavanagh, arrogantly thrusting herself into the centre.

AS the autumn of 1957 passed into winter, the republican movement began to recover. The IRA reopened operations in the north. The opportunity for a devastating strike followed by swift capitulation on the part of the British had been lost, if it ever existed. There remained only the slow, dogged process of guerrilla warfare. Ambush, sabotage, and subversion. Blow up bridges and railways. Cut communications. Undermine morale.

Early in 1958, Barry began receiving assignments hidden in the pages of the *United Irishman*. That spring he was often away from the farm. Although he went about his business with an air of nonchalance when others were watching, every time he put a bomb together his mouth went dry and he had butterflies in his stomach.

The thrill of danger was addictive.

While Barry was away on one of his assignments, listeners to an RTE broadcast were informed, "There are over five thousand drive-in movie theatres in the United States."

"What in the name of all the saints is a drive-in movie theatre?" one of Eileen's friends wondered as the two women were gossiping over cups of tea.

"An Occasion of Sin," Eileen retorted.

NINETEEN fifty-eight saw the naming of a new pope and a new era in the history of the Roman Catholic Church. Fresh thinking and an openness to change were the watchwords of John Paul XXIII. When he convoked the second Vatican Council, he demonstrated an unprecedented willingness to make the ancient institution relevant to the modern world. No condemnations were to be issued from the pulpit; political hostilities were to be ignored; the Church must realise it was the servant and not the master.

IN the wake of the aborted border campaign the RUC had eliminated most of the republican safe houses in the Six Counties. Volunteers on active service relied on dugouts in isolated areas, where they slept on branches on the damp ground and ate inadequately if at all. If they were lucky, the constantly searching RUC did not discover them . . . though one dugout was destroyed when a cow fell through the roof.

The IRA had a few successes. A Catholic family with nine children was rescued by Volunteers after loyalists set fire to their cottage in County Tyrone. An RUC sergeant was killed by a booby trap in County Tyrone. Another died during an attack at Carrickbroad.

But there were also some spectacular failures. Four Volunteers were trying to put together a mine in a farmhouse at Edentubber when the gelignite exploded prematurely. The house was blown apart. All the Volunteers as well as the owner of the house died in the blast. It was the largest loss the IRA had suffered since the end of the Civil War—excluding the republicans who had been executed afterwards by the Free State government.

On the day of the Edentubber explosion the Army Convention was being held in a safe house in Dublin. The house was too small to hold more than the Army Council and voting delegates. News of the disaster intensified their de-

termination to make sure that no republican lives were lost in vain. It was decided to step up the fund-raising campaign among Irish Americans. Contributions from organisations such as the Red Branch Knights of San Francisco soon
enabled the IRA to open more training camps in the south.

THE circulation of the *United Irishman* climbed toward 120,000—at home
and abroad.

HE was good. He was very, very good. A number of Volunteers had died in
accidents with explosives, but Barry Halloran made no mistakes. Officers began
notifying GHQ, "We want Halloran for this one."

The Army obtained most of its gelignite through raids on quarries and construction sites in the Republic, giving strength to the government's claim that
the IRA was a threat to the peace and security of the nation. When additional
guards were hired, gelignite supplies slowed to a trickle.

Barry Halloran considered the shortage a challenge to his ingenuity. If one
knew how, any number of everyday domestic materials could be used to make a
bomb. Salt, newspaper, weed killer, sugar, commercial fertiliser—the list was
almost endless. *It's damned satisfying to be able to create something out of nothing.*

One of Barry's innovations was the self-igniting petrol bomb. Strips of
newspaper were soaked in a sodium chloride solution and wrapped around a
glass bottle. As the paper dried it clung tightly to the bottle, which was filled
three-quarters of the way with petrol. A small amount of sulphuric acid was
added at the top. The "touch paper" did not ignite until the bottle hit something and broke. The bomb was much safer to throw than the notoriously
volatile Molotov cocktail.

IN August a Sinn Féin organiser was shot and killed by the Royal Ulster Constabulary—within the borders of the Republic. In another land, in another
time, this might have been taken as an act of war. But although Irish people
were outraged, the Dublin government made no formal protest to Stormont.

BARRY Halloran had grown into the strength promised by his large frame.
Physically he was a mass of contradictions. A rugged face with a gentle mouth.
His lean yet muscular body moved with the easy grace of a man in total physical control. The shoulders were as broad as a rugby player's; the long-fingered
hands might have belonged to a pianist.

Because his distinctive appearance might attract hostile attention, he taught himself the art of disguise. Much of his work was done under cover of darkness, so he learned to get by with little sleep. He was able to take short naps and wake up as refreshed as if he had been sleeping for hours.

He never shrank from a fistfight, that traditional testing ground of young manhood, and usually won. When not on active service he enjoyed downing a few pints in a pub, but it was a point of pride with him that no one ever saw him drunk. As for women, Barry attracted more than his share. He went only as far as a girl was willing and discouraged any talk of love. He did not want to run the risk of leaving a widow behind.

Men in a pack were capable of things that one alone could never do, and Army camaraderie was stronger than most family ties. But Barry deliberately kept an emotional distance from his fellow Volunteers. He did not reveal his inmost feelings to anyone, nor allow anyone to get close to him. He had learned his lesson with Feargal O'Hanlon. In the IRA death could come like a thief in the night.

Barry's sensitivity was a secret he shared with no one. If he felt more deeply than others, he showed it less.

He continued to pore over his grandfather's notebooks. In one of them Ned had written, "The IRA is sworn to restore the thirty-two-county Irish Republic, as proclaimed in 1916, to the people from whom it was so deceitfully taken. It is imperative that our own actions be morally justifiable."

Barry committed that last sentence to memory.

The next time one of his fellow Volunteers questioned his insistence on giving a warning for his bombs, he said, "If we're fighting in an honourable cause, we have to act honourably ourselves."

Soon the issuing of warnings became common practice.

IN September, Dave O'Connell and Rory Brady, who had been the IRA chief-of-staff during the border campaign, broke out of the supposedly escape-proof Curragh prison camp.

LATE in October, Barry recognised Rory Brady coming out of a shoe shop in Mullingar. Physically strong, highly cultured, and known for having a well-developed social conscience, he had graduated from college and trained to be a teacher. But that was not all there was to him. When he was only twenty-one years old Rory Brady had led a dozen men into the depot of the Royal Electrical and Mechanical Engineers in Berkshire, England, and stolen five tons of arms for the IRA.[1] The methods he used had become part of republican legend.

Brady's squad had sneaked up on the two guards on duty before dawn, surprising one in the act of cooking sausages and the other of writing poetry. "Bad poetry," Brady said later, with the authority of a man who appreciated good poetry. He then woke the other sixteen soldiers two at a time, made them strip below the waist, and lined them up with their fingertips pressed against the wall, their legs spread and their genitals exposed. No violence was needed; the men were all too aware of their vulnerability. They made no effort to stop the massive weapons theft.

According to rumour, Brady was now a member of the Army Council.

When he saw Barry looking at him he stared back for a long moment, then, with a nod of the head, indicated that they meet in the nearest laneway. Barry introduced himself; Brady gave his hand a hearty shake. "Of course! You were one of Seán Garland's men, were you not?"

"I was indeed."

"Dave O'Connell speaks highly of you. What brings you to Mullingar, Barry?"

"Travelling. From here to there. You know."

"I do indeed, I'm doing the same myself."

Although Barry was somewhat in awe of Rory Brady, the other man's ready smile put him at ease. Over pints in the nearest pub Barry found himself talking more than he had in weeks. When he mentioned that he had chosen to remain in the Army rather than going to university, Brady's beetling eyebrows drew into a frown. "That's too bad, the Army needs educated men."

"What use is a degree to a soldier?"

"Amongst other things, a third-level education teaches a man to think."

"I can think already," Barry retorted testily. Hoping to impress the other man, he led the conversation around to history, which was one area where he felt sure of his ground. "It's interesting to observe that in the eighteenth and nineteenth centuries many Protestants were Irish nationalists. Not just Robert Emmet and Wolfe Tone, but hundreds, perhaps even thousands, of others. There were even Presbyterian Fenians, because the Presbyterians were being persecuted by the English just as Catholics were."

"It's ironic," said Brady, "that the Presbyterians, who once were in the forefront of the struggle for Irish freedom, were so determined to remain in the United Kingdom in 1921 that they insisted on partition."

"They seem happy enough with it now," Barry said.

"Most of them are, because it's to their advantage. Your average northern Protestant is a pragmatist. Of course there are still some nationalists amongst them, but they don't dare stick their heads above the parapet.

"The unionists don't have things all their way, though. Partition let them hold on to a piece of the United Kingdom, but that doesn't make them 'British.' For the most part, their parents and grandparents and even great-grandparents were born in Ireland. If they go to London they expect to be welcomed with open arms, but instead people sneer at their accents and treat them like foreigners. As far as the English are concerned, they're Irish. Which proves that even the English get it right some of the time," he added with a laugh.

THE O/C of an IRA training camp in Tipperary sent for the Army's young explosives expert to teach his men how to build mines without blowing themselves up. After several days of intensive work Barry felt the need of some time off. He slung his pack over his shoulder and hitched a ride to Ballina.

Séamus McCoy was the exception to his rule about having close friends. Their relationship pre-dated his conscious decision to be a lone wolf and could not be set aside.

When Barry entered the Ballina pub the air was blue with cigarette smoke. Six or seven men sat at the bar, solemnly discussing the affairs of the world or staring into their drinks. In one corner two elderly farmers were arguing over a game of draughts. A little spotted dog sat in the middle of the sawdust-strewn floor, diligently licking his private parts. From behind the bar a large mirror reflected the life of the place with cracked and discoloured irony. On the wall beside the mirror an old hammer hung from a frayed rope.

Barry ordered a pint. After taking a deep swallow, he wiped his mouth on the back of his wrist and asked in a conversational tone, "Séamus McCoy been in here today?"

The bartender shook his bald head and began polishing glasses.

"How about upstairs? Would he be upstairs?"

"If he was here—and I'm not saying he is—then he might be upstairs. Or he might not. There's that possibility too."

"There is that possibility," Barry conceded. "I'm not here myself."

"Sure I haven't seen you," said the bartender.

Barry took his time about finishing his pint. He left by the front door and stood in the street, yawning, stretching himself, looking for all the world like a man with nothing on his mind.

The road was empty in both directions. The only people on the bridge were three schoolboys fishing with a chicken neck tied to a bit of string. Barry watched them for a minute or two, then turned and strolled around to the side of the pub. He climbed the stairs and rapped a signal on McCoy's door.

"Who's there?"

"*Me féin.*"*

*Me myself.

"Don't stand on ceremony then. Come through."

Barry found McCoy sitting at the table with an open book in front of him. Squinting up at Barry, he observed, "You're growing like a rumour, Seventeen. When d'ye plan to stop? This is a low ceiling."

Barry laughed. "Maybe I'll raise it for you."

"You've raised some other ceilings recently, I hear. An RUC barracks for one, when the men were not five hundred yards away on the parade ground. They came running back to find the whole place destroyed. Clever work, that. I wish I'd been there to see their faces."

Barry said modestly, "I was just doing my job."

"You're damned good at it. I'm proud of you."

The unexpected praise brought a lump to Barry's throat.

"You blew the locks on the Newry Canal, too, did you not?[2] That job had all the earmarks of a first-rate demolition expert. Rumour has it that *Saor Uladh** was responsible," McCoy went on, referring to one of several breakaway groups that had been formed by disaffected IRA men, "but Saor Uladh doesn't have an engineer of your calibre. Did GHQ loan you to them? In return for some gelignite, maybe? I heard they lifted a large amount from an arsenal in Tyrone."

Barry's eyes gleamed. "Good guess."

"What brings you to Ballina?"

"Just passing through on my way to Clare. My mother says she doesn't see enough of me."

McCoy smiled. "Every mother says that."

"Do you visit yours very often, Séamus?"

In a low voice, McCoy said, "I avoid graveyards."

"Sorry, I didn't know."

"Nothing to know. She was hanging out the washing in the yard one day when one of His Majesty's finest . . ." McCoy paused, lit a cigarette. Continued to stare at the match he held in his fingers. Fingers that began to tremble.

Barry cried, "Don't go on!" But the dam had burst. McCoy jumped up and began to pace the room, his feet beating a tattoo of rage on the plank floor. "The bloody bastard claimed it was self-defence. Self-defence my arse! Said she attacked him. My wee mother with her weak lungs and her bad back and her arms full of wet washing, she attacked a big husky soldier thirty years her junior and put him in fear of his life. The British Army gave him a promotion afterwards."

The cheerful mask had slipped and Barry saw the suffering man beneath.

"Let's go downstairs, Séamus," he said huskily. "It's my shout."

*Free Ulster.

That night they visited every pub in Ballina, then crossed the bridge to the pubs of Killaloe. On the way back they sang rebel songs, their voices floating out over the dark waters of the Shannon. Shortly before dawn McCoy tumbled face-first across his bed.

Barry fell asleep on the floor. His last waking thought was, *That's Séamus explained. And how many others?*

NED'S notebooks contained little military information because he had feared they might fall into the wrong hands. Sometimes a notation was nothing more than a comment on the weather. But the passages in code intrigued Barry; they appeared to be long lists. Familiarity with codes had become part of his life. After several false starts, he tried using the opening of the Proclamation of the Irish Republic for the key. The Proclamation his grandfather had made him learn by heart.

Barry's hunch proved correct—for the first five items. After that the key changed. *Oh, Granda, you were very careful.*

The lists consisted of names and addresses. The very first ones were Michael and Isabella Kavanagh, with an address in New York State. After their names was a single star and a minuscule dollar sign. The dollar sign was not repeated, but each subsequent name was followed by one to a dozen stars. *Isabella said her husband was a republican . . . these must describe financial transactions! Money raised in America for the IRA.*

URSULA made certain that Barry always left the farm with money in his pocket. He shared it freely with his fellow Volunteers, most of whom had none. Little was spent on himself. One of his few indulgences was a professional-quality camera he bought in Belfast while on his first assignment in the northern capital.

A pall of coal smoke sat atop the city like a dirty cap, but otherwise Belfast was an attractive place. Tidy, prosperous, with a wealth of handsome Victorian brickwork. Hoping to get some sense of the people, Barry attempted to strike up a conversation with a man who was sitting on a bench near the railroad station, feeding the pigeons. When the man heard Barry's accent he said, "I've never been to the south myself. I wouldn't understand the language."

"Most people in the Republic don't speak Irish, either," Barry told him.

"I don't mean Irish, I mean Latin. All the Catholics down there speak Latin," the pigeon feeder replied.

Barry tried to enlighten him but it was like talking to a stone. The man listened politely and made articulate responses, but obviously did not believe a word he said. At the end of their conversation the Belfast man believed exactly as he had in the beginning.

There's a mind like a steel trap—rusted shut, Barry said to himself. *Surely they aren't all like this?*

When he noticed a shop with cameras in the window, Barry went in. There was a wide assortment of equipment on display. Feeling that it might be a good idea to explain his accent, Barry said, "I heard one could buy the latest equipment here, that's what brought me to Belfast."

"You won't find anything half as good in Dublin," the clerk replied smugly.

Eventually Barry settled on a 35-mm Leica M2. "Brand new on the market," the clerk claimed.

"Is there an instruction booklet with it?"

"You'd need one," said the clerk. He might have meant to be helpful; he might have meant to be insulting. Barry paid for the camera and left, feeling vaguely uncomfortable.

After reading the instruction booklet and acquainting himself with the workings of the Leica, he set out to capture the character of Belfast on film. His intention was to photograph a few ordinary citizens going about their daily business in the heart of the city. It proved harder than he anticipated. When he asked permission of his prospective subjects, as soon as they heard his accent most were reluctant to talk with him. It was as if a wall came down.

At least I can photograph the architecture. Buildings have no politics.

Barry spent the rest of the day wandering wherever his feet would take him. Residential areas in Protestant neighbourhoods were well laid out, with solidly built, attractive houses. The bustling self-importance of the commercial areas spoke volumes about the nature of the city.

Although Catholics and Protestants lived in separate areas, there were no sharp lines of demarcation and the children of both religions played together in the streets. But in Catholic neighbourhoods many houses were dilapidated and some of the shops were boarded up.

Graffiti on a brick wall provocatively close to a Catholic church warned, "Rebels Beware. To hell with popery. Where popery reigns poverty remains. Down with IRA Scum!"

Barry recalled a quote from Winston Churchill which Ned Halloran had included in one of his notebooks: "Arm yourselves and be ye men of valour and be in readiness for the conflict, for it is better for us to perish in battle than to look upon the outrage of our nation and our altars."[3]

Under that quote Ned had written, "What Irishman can hear those words without thinking of Ireland?"

.   .   .

RISING from the Harland and Wolf shipyard that had built the *Titanic,* two giant cranes, known as Samson and Goliath, dominated the skyline, a perfect symbol of the British industrial power that sustained the Protestant north. Barry walked back and forth, photographing the cranes from a number of different angles. After a while he had the eerie sensation that they were watching him. And his feet were beginning to hurt. *Belfast has too much pavement.*

Although it was in a Protestant neighbourhood, Dempsey's Bar in Donegall Street looked inviting. A real working man's pub, a self-contained world. Sliding onto a bar stool, Barry ordered a whiskey, "Bushmills, please," since this was the north. This did not seem the sort of pub where he could take out a book of poems and have a quiet read, but the men he saw around him looked no different from men he might see in any pub in the Republic. The accents were different but they talked about the same things: sports, politics, and women, in that order.

Ballroom dancing was very popular in Belfast. Two men sitting near Barry were engaged in a lively debate about the relative merits of The Plaza in Chichester Street and the Floral Hall at Bellevue. As he listened to them Barry imagined himself walking into a ballroom in the company of some pretty Belfast girl; a girl who wouldn't care about his accent any more than he objected to hers, or to the regional accents of Cork or Kerry or Donegal. They were, after all, one people.

Then he overheard someone else make a vicious remark about "the filthy Taigs," and Barry's innocent dream died.

The following day he planted three separate explosive charges, timed to go off simultaneously, on the outskirts of the city. Telephone connections between Belfast and Armagh city were disrupted for the better part of a week. The RUC scoured the area for the saboteur but found no trace of him, though he sauntered past several search parties.

Evading the enemy had become a game. On assignment Barry customarily wore a threadbare coat and shabby trousers whose cut identified him as "up from the country." The garments were lined with expensive suiting material, a complicated alteration made by Eileen to Barry's specifications. When he turned his clothes inside out he became a city man in a striped navy suit. In his pockets he carried little wads of cotton to stuff into his cheeks, and a tin of brown shoe polish to extinguish his bright hair. He could not make himself shorter, but by curling his shoulders forward and bending his knees slightly he gave the impression of being a smaller man.

Barry made no effort to hide his natural grace. He was unaware that he moved with the controlled muscularity of a cat.

He refused to cower in the shadows. Hiding in plain sight gave him a better opinion of himself. If anyone questioned him, now that he had the camera he could claim he was a photographer who had come north looking for subjects. It was at least partly true. The camera was becoming an addiction. F-stops, depth of field—he even loved the language.

Society was a collage of misrepresentation. Devious human beings created multiple façades to mislead the multitudes. Only the camera was not deceived.

Chapter Fifteen

---·◦⟨∞⟩◦·---

IN March of 1959 the internment camp on the Curragh, which had become a
covert university in republicanism and military tactics, was officially closed. Éamonn Thomas was among the last seven republican prisoners to be released.
The closure of the camp did not mark an end to the Irish government's campaign against the IRA. Republicans still could be arrested and charged under
the Offences Against the State Act.

Meanwhile the Stormont government continued to arrest those whom it perceived to be a threat to the Union. The most notorious of the northern facilities
for incarcerating republicans was Her Majesty's Prison, the Maze. Originally
known as Long Kesh, the Maze was built on the site of a World War Two air-
field some eight miles from Belfast. The prison was claimed to be escape-proof.

"You could find a way to blow it open," several Volunteers suggested to
Barry Halloran. He was flattered. *Maybe I could. If I was given the assignment.*

However, there were some assignments he no longer would take.

Barry continued to plant mines on railways and bridges but refused to booby-trap buildings. There was a difference. A Jesuitical difference, perhaps, but a difference all the same.

The first time he wrote "no" on a coded slip and sent it back to GHQ, he fully expected to be thrown out of the Army. That night he went down on his knees beside his bed and tried to petition God, but he could not formulate the words. At last he gave up and crawled into bed, trusting God to know what was in his heart.

The next issue of the *United Irishman* held no message for him.

He did not know that Séamus McCoy had been called up to Dublin specifically to discuss "the little problem with Halloran." In a safe house on Serpentine Avenue, McCoy explained to members of the Army Council, "Halloran saw two good friends shot to death right in front of him at Brookeborough. It left him a wee bit squeamish. He's a damned good man, though, and too valuable to lose. Give him time and he'll get over it."

"He's got under your skin, hasn't he?"

"I'll probably never have a son," McCoy said. "I'm married to the Army and that's how it is. But if I did have a son, I'd want him to be Barry Halloran."

THE next issue of the *United Irishman* contained seven assignments for Barry.

PROSECUTING the war required flexibility. Different areas presented different problems. On open ground, sniper locations were too vulnerable, while the RUC avoided areas that might harbour an ambush. Blowing up a road was difficult because the constables were suspicious of any strange object near a roadway.

Barry thrived on challenge.

A crossroads on a route that carried a lot of military traffic was deemed a prime target. The site was very exposed, with no nearby trees or bushes. Under cover of darkness Barry took a milk can which had been sawn in half, filled it two-thirds with gelignite, and buried it deep in the drainage slope. The wires were hidden in the grass. Next morning an active service unit watched from a distance. They allowed civilian traffic to pass unharmed. When an RUC patrol came along they hit the detonator. The resultant explosion funnelled back into the roadbed, overturning the patrol car. The badly damaged road was impassable for days.

ON June 24, 1959, Séan Lemass became leader of Fianna Fáil and taoiseach of the Republic. Lemass was a decisive man with a keen mind. In 1952, while serving as minister for industry and commerce under de Valera, he had suffered from ill health and Frank Aiken had to deputise for him. De Valera had urged Lemass to spend the time learning Irish. Instead he had begged the department of finance to send him books on economics.

As taoiseach, Lemass immediately set about promoting industrialisation in what was still largely a rural economy. Extensive road building and the encouragement of foreign investment became high priorities. Irish Steel, the Shannon Free Airport Development Company, and Bord na Mona, which was supplying fuel to meet industrial expansion, received massive support from the Lemass government. Soon the mood of despondency which had characterised the Republic began to lift.

The Irish Times wrote, "If Mr. de Valera is the architect of modern Ireland, then Mr. Lemass is indisputably the engineer, the contractor, and the foreman, rolled into one."[1]

The new taoiseach was not without his critics. There was no doubt about his patriotic credentials—Lemass had fought the British from the roof of the GPO during 1916—but his vision was unremittingly fixed on the future. He had no time for the rhetoric of revival, including the revival of the Irish language. Those who were passionately committed to the Ireland imagined by Pádraic Pearse were horrified.

Meanwhile in Northern Ireland the war went on, month after month. Casualties were mounting on both sides. Stormont remained unalterably dedicated to maintaining a Protestant state for a Protestant people. The IRA remained unalterably opposed to the partition of Ireland and the oppression of Catholics in the Six Counties. The government of the Republic remained unalterably opposed to the existence of the IRA.

IN a college debate in Northern Ireland, a young working-class Catholic called John Hume argued in favour of Ireland joining the Common Market. Such a move would, he claimed, eventually make the border irrelevant.[2]

IN August a racist mob besieged Central High School in Little Rock, Arkansas, trying to prevent two black students from attending school. Barry saw the event depicted in the newsreels: stark black-and-white images of black and white people. Defying a federal court order, Arkansas Governor Orval Faubus told the protestors, "I am with you all the way."

Barry shook his head. *It could just as easily have happened in Texas, or anywhere in the deep south. Or even in another country. What is there about people that makes them hate so much?*

· · ·

WHEN Barry returned to the farm in September he found his mother in a near fury. "That wretched man's going to destroy all we fought for!" she cried.

"What man?"

"Lemass, of course! Don't you read the papers anymore?"

"What specifically are you complaining about?"

"He's picked up right where de Valera left off, attacking the IRA."

"To be fair, Ursula, Fianna Fáil's been attacking the IRA for a long time. It's because they recognise Sinn Féin as their rival, much more so than Fine Gael or any other party. Sinn Féin is the legitimate republican party, no matter how much Fianna Fáil claims to be. It's all politics, really."

"It's all Civil War politics," Ursula said bitterly.

"War is the failure of politics."

"Where did you hear that?"

Barry did not meet her eyes. "It's a well-known adage."

Actually he had read it in one of Ned's notebooks.

As time passed, Barry was aware of the odds mounting against him. He was a soldier. Sooner or later, in spite of his best intentions, he might find himself in a position where he must fight for his life or die.

He was not a man to die willingly. He loved life too much.

Loved everything about it, even the lonely times. Perhaps especially the lonely times. Watching in awe as the sun rose over the Irish Sea, staining the silver water with crimson. Wandering at twilight through the Silent Valley while the birds sang their sleepy good-nights to God. Pausing in some tiny village along the Shannon where time had stopped generations earlier and just *being* there. Part of the little shabby houses and the ribbon of road.

Taking photographs to capture one moment out of eternity.

Or trudging down the lane toward the Halloran farmhouse with his mouth already watering at the thought of Eileen's scones hot from the oven. He walked rather than ran to stretch out the delicious moments of anticipation.

Sometimes anticipation could be better than the real thing.

HE saved Ned Halloran's notebooks until long after everyone else had gone to bed. Only then did he turn the pages and hear his grandfather's voice again. To Barry that voice had become a precious link to an Ireland that was slipping away; the Ireland he was willing to die for, but not to kill for.

He reread some entries again and again. Unfamiliar passages were kept for future delectation, like sweets at the end of a meal.

In the autumn of 1959 he read one that disturbed him greatly.

"After Síle died I went mad for several years," Ned had written. "I did not know I was mad. My reality was as real to me as a sane man's is to him. I cannot say what made me well again, only that it happened gradually. My return to sanity was made up of small things.

"Is killing a fellow human being a sign of madness? I most certainly killed men while I was of unsound mind, yet I also killed men before Síle's death, when I was, I believe, sane. And was, I believe, fighting in a just cause. Was the man who killed Síle insane? Or was he sane when he drove his bayonet into her stomach? Did he think he was acting in a just cause?"

That night the terrible Brookeborough nightmare Barry thought he had escaped returned. Except this time it was not the face of the RUC man he saw but his own, glaring at him down the barrel of the rifle. He watched incredulously as the other Barry's finger tightened on the trigger. Worse still, he *felt* the shock as the bullet struck him.

Then he was not the RUC man but Feargal O'Hanlon with the bullets tearing into his body. He was Seán South, he was Paddy O'Regan. He was . . .

A nameless person on a nameless street, walking along minding his own business. Suddenly there was a violent explosion and he was thrown to the ground. Debris rained around him. Looking down at himself, he saw that his body was blown apart. After a moment of absolute disbelief he felt terrible pain . . . and knew that he was dying.

Barry awoke rigid with horror.

WHEN the latest issue of the *United Irishman* arrived he took it to his room without opening it and sat on the bed for a long time, holding the little monthly in his hand. *If I don't look I won't have to . . .*

He flung open the magazine like an act of defiance. Fifteen slips of paper fluttered to the floor.

ON the last day of January, 1960, Senator John Fitzgerald Kennedy of Massachusetts announced his intention to run for the presidency of the United States. He was young and wealthy—and an Irish American Catholic.

Kennedy immediately caught the imagination of the Irish people.

HER name was Claire MacNamara and she was exceptionally pretty.

On a blustery March day Barry found himself in Athlone on his way home from the north. He decided to have a hot meal at the hotel before continuing his journey. As he walked along the high street a customer emerging from a sweets shop allowed a mouth-watering fragrance to escape. On impulse, Barry went in.

And there she was, behind the counter. Her skin was very white; her lips were full and red. When she asked the usual shopkeeper's question, "Are you all right there?" she spoke with a lilting Cork accent.

A creamy girl, a silk-and-lace sort of girl. "I am. I mean I will be. As soon as I make up my mind."

"About which sweets to buy?"

"About which sweets to buy," he echoed, watching the curving fullness of her lips. "What brings a girl from Cork to County Westmeath?"

Casual conversation did not come easily to her, but there was something about this young man she could not resist. "How did you know I'm from Cork?"

He smiled. "Just a guess. Forgive me, I shouldn't have asked such a personal question. We haven't even been introduced." He thrust out his hand. "I'm Finbar Halloran. And you are Miss . . . ?"

She lowered her eyes. Her eyelids, Barry observed, were moist. He wondered what it would be like to kiss them. "MacNamara."

"MacNamara's a County Clare name."

"My father's people came from Clare originally," she said. "I suspect that's why I was called Claire. I was the runt of the litter and my parents had run out of names by the time they came to me." When she laughed, her laugh was the most beautiful Barry had ever heard. It rippled; it chimed.

She broke off with a delicate little cough and charmingly covered her mouth with her hand.

If she were mine I'd dress her in silk and lace. "You were reared in Cork?"

"In a house that used to belong to my grandparents. It's at the very top of the hill." She sounded homesick.

Barry had a sudden, vivid image of her standing on a hill with her frock moulded against her slender body by the wind. "What brought you to Athlone, Miss MacNamara?"

"One of my father's sisters was married to the man who owned this shop. He died last autumn and she's still in mourning. They have no children to take over the shop, so I was sent to help out until my aunt decides what she wants to do."

"What a coincidence!" Barry exclaimed with an enthusiasm the circumstances did not warrant. "I'm on my way home for my aunt's sake. Well, not really my aunt, she's my mother's aunt, but she's old and she hasn't been well. I'd like to take her some chocolates."

"How kind," the girl murmured. Raising her eyes. Meeting his full force. It was like an electric shock.

Barry purchased the most expensive chocolates on offer. He bought a large assortment of boiled sweets, two pounds of the toffee known as "yellow man," and various other confections. He loathed liquorice but spent long minutes trying to decide between the red and the black. Taking an inordinate amount of time making his selections allowed him to linger in the shop until it closed. By

then he and the lovely shopkeeper were on a first-name basis. When Barry offered to walk Claire home, a delicate blush rose up the slender column of her
throat and flooded across her cheeks.

She's adorable, thought Barry.

"It's only fair to warn you that my aunt lives three miles out the Ballinasloe
road."

"I walk all the time," Barry assured her. "Three miles is nothing to me."

The dying day was turning cold. As they stepped outside, he whipped off
his scarf and wrapped it around her neck. Claire gave a delicious little shiver.
The wool was still warm from his skin.

Peeping through net curtains, Miriam MacNamara Fogarty watched them
come up the road. "Now who's that young man?" She had talked to herself ever
since the late Declan Fogarty stopped listening to her early in their married life.
"Like bees around the jam jar, young men are." A cluck of the tongue. "And
would you look at the clothes on her, you can see her legs almost to the knee. In
my day the only one who saw a woman's ankles was her husband." A disapproving shake of the head. "I'd best let her hems down straightaway."

MIRIAM opened the door and stepped outside so they could see her waiting.
"You took your time," she accused. Wrapped in a dark shawl, she loomed in
front of them like a boulder in their path.

Claire went pink again.

I think I'm in love.

"I'm only after closing the shop, Aunt Miriam. This was my last customer, so
he offered to walk me home."

Miriam's face pleated into the familiar folds of a deep frown. "Just who is *he?*"

"Oh, I'm sorry. Aunt Miriam, this is Finbar Halloran."

Barry whipped off his cap and tucked it under his arm.

"And who's Finbar Halloran when he's at home?" the older woman demanded to know.

"I'm a photographer, Mrs. Fogarty. I live on the family farm, but I travel
around the country taking pictures."

"Thank you for your courtesy to my niece, Mr. Halloran. Now if you'll excuse us . . ." Interposing her bulk between Claire and Barry, Miriam took the
girl by the elbow and steered her toward the house.

At the door Claire turned and looked back. "Will I see you again?"

"I'll be in Athlone for several days," he decided on the spur of the moment.
"I have lots of things to photograph."

"Hmmmph," said Miriam Fogarty. She drew her niece into the house and
slammed the door.

Barry was waiting for Claire the next morning when she opened the shop.

He had been afraid her aunt might come with her, but she was alone. "Aunt Miriam doesn't leave the house yet," Claire explained.

"She came outside last night."

"Just onto the path; she won't come as far as the road. What would the neighbours think?"

Barry laughed. "'What would the neighbours think?' is an Irish obsession. My mother's the only woman I know who doesn't care."

"Does she not? That hardly seems possible."

"You don't know my mother. Ursula specialises in the impossible."

Since he could hardly spend the entire day in the shop, Barry wandered around Athlone. He had been there on several occasions but never explored it through the eye of the camera. Like all Irish towns, Athlone was scarred by long poverty. The first vestiges of change were creeping in, however. There were more motorcars in the streets than a year ago, and several abandoned shops were reopening.

Barry devoted part of the morning to photographing, from every angle, the bridge that spanned the Shannon. He found great beauty in its worn stones and graceful arches; in the lichens that clung to the mortar; in the pair of swans who, as indifferent to the weather as himself and Claire, sailed along the river's surface, admiring their mirrored images.

As they were sharing a lunch of brown bread and egg salad in the shop, Barry told Claire, "Speaking of coincidences, my middle name is Lewis. While I was exploring Athlone Bridge I learned about a legend concerning a name-sake of mine."

She clasped her hands together in a curiously childlike gesture. "Oh, do tell me!"

"There's an inscription carved on a stone tablet under one of the arches, re-lating to a man called Peter Lewys. He's said to have been an English monk who converted to Protestantism. He was sent by Sir Henry Sidney to supervise the building of the original bridge during the reign of Queen Elizabeth. Mind you, at that time all the rats in Ireland were still Catholic."

Barry had expected Claire to laugh. Instead she was watching him wide-eyed, totally credulous.

He began illustrating the story with gestures and grimaces. "An old Irish rat resolved to punish Lewys for being a turncoat and set out to haunt him. If he was trying to eat, it jumped on the table and dragged its long tail through his food. At night it crept onto his pillow and breathed its foul breath into his nos-trils until he woke up."

Claire gave a little shriek of revulsion.

"Lewys was invited to preach before a large congregation in St. Mary's, so the rat placed itself directly in his line of vision and mocked him with its glit-tering eyes. At last Lewys could stand no more. He snatched a soldier's pistol and tried to shoot his tormentor. But before he could fire, the clever rat leapt onto the pistol and gave the man's thumb such a savage bite that he died of lockjaw."[3]

"Oh, Barry, did he really?"

"I told you, it's a legend. But . . ." he lowered his voice, "I personally believe there's a seed of truth in every legend."

"I don't know any legends."

"Surely you've heard of Cuchullain, or Fionn Mac Cumhaill?"

"They were pagans," she said with distaste.

He gave her a pitying look. "Is that what your priest told you? I'm sure they were, but we were all pagans at one time. It's part of our history, Claire, part of what we are. And some of it was wonderful entirely. Let me tell you . . ."

He began spinning out stories he had known since childhood, recounting the great tales of heroes that were embedded in folk memory. Soon Claire was as caught up in them as Barry was. When customers came into the shop she tore herself away long enough to serve them, but almost shoved them out the door so that she could return to Barry. She was a wonderful audience, absorbing every word like blotting paper.

When he was with Claire, Barry could forget the terrible pictures imprinted on his brain. In her blue eyes the world was born fresh and new.

Chapter Sixteen

———⋅❦⋅———

MIRIAM Fogarty thoroughly disapproved of her niece's burgeoning friendship with the tall young man. It was not that she disliked Barry. She simply disliked the idea of Claire marrying anybody.

Marriage was the end of everything.

The man she had married was the proverbial "street angel, house devil." His many male friends had known him as a jolly, generous individual, a regular attendee of Mass who would always loan a pal money or stand the bar to a round of drinks.

When his wife went to the market, she often wore an old felt cloche pulled down almost to her cheeks. The deep brim had helped to hide the bruises on her face.

A drunken husband who beat his wife was all too common amongst Miriam's acquaintances, but for most of the women there were compensations. God had not seen fit to bless her with the children she longed for, however. After Mr. Fogarty died she had only nieces and nephews to knit mufflers for at Christmas. The arrival of Claire on her doorstep had been the first happy event in years.

She was not about to surrender the girl to a fate like her own.

BARRY spent several days in Athlone. He waited at the shop every morning for Claire, but when the first customer appeared he made himself scarce. In this way he became well acquainted with the laneways of the town.

They all led back to Claire.

She was a quiet girl, too shy to say much. Barry, who had schooled himself to be quiet, was forced to carry the bulk of the conversation while she listened with flattering attention. He never mentioned the Army. Instead he talked about growing up on the farm, about his mother and Eileen and the Ryan brothers, about horses and cows and boyish exploits. When he described his trip to America, Claire was fascinated. From the questions she asked, Barry realised that her knowledge of America was even less than the Americans' knowledge of Ireland.

He walked the girl home every evening, bravely confronting the frozen face of the aunt on the doorstep. Then he went back to the Prince of Wales Hotel to spend a restless night. Tossing and turning. Trying not to think about Claire *that way* and inevitably thinking about Claire *that way,* until desire became a torment. Against the demands of his body he had little defence. The heat that enflamed his groin spread upward and outward until it reached his brain and usurped all thought. Demanding relief.

HOWEVER, Claire was a nice girl, a devout Catholic girl, with all that implied. Nothing short of marriage would unlock her virginity. And Barry could not imagine ever wanting anyone else.

In April I'll be twenty-one, and someday I'll inherit the farm. But until then . . . I'd need something else to offer a wife. To offer Claire if she'll have me.

Suppose she won't?

A girl would be crazy to marry me, given the life I live. He had not yet told her about being a Volunteer; there never seemed to be the right moment.

She's from the Rebel County but that doesn't mean she's a republican. Maybe her people are Fine Gael. Maybe they hate republicans. She might ask me to give up the Army.

Or suppose she accepts my proposal but Ursula doesn't like her? They certainly have nothing in common. Where would we live if not on the farm? I'd have to buy a place for us, and that would mean asking Ursula for help. She'd give me the rough side of her tongue, but would she give me the money?

His biggest problem had been to avoid killing while remaining true to the oath he had taken. Then he had wandered into a shop in Athlone . . . and found a whole new set of problems. Sleepless nights, vivid imaginings. While he grappled with them the fire within him raged and burned.

AT last he had to tell Claire, "I have to go home, I've put it off as long as I can. It'll only be for a few days, though. I promise I'll be back soon."

"To take more photographs?" she asked innocently.

Barry cupped her chin in his hand and tilted her face up toward his. It was the first time he had touched her. "You know that's not the reason, Claire."

The sudden blush and the lowered eyelids were already familiar. And inexpressibly dear. "Is it not?"

"No."

"I'd best kiss you good-bye, then," she said. Standing on tiptoe, she brushed his cheek with her lips.

BARRY made his way to the farm with a light heart, hitching rides most of the time, but walking in between. His feet not touching the ground. He could not say if it rained or the sun shone. He whistled, he hummed. He even touched his cap to a passing garda patrol car.

The *United Irishman* was waiting for him when he got home. A veritable blizzard of notes fell out when he riffled through the pages.

Barry spent the evening composing a letter to Claire. Revising, crossing out, starting again. And again. The words simply would not come right. He sounded either too stiff or, when he went the other way, too soppy. Before he settled on a final draft the floor was littered with paper snowballs.

"My very dear Claire,

"I'm sorry to tell you that I can't come back to Athlone right away. For the next few weeks I shall be fully occupied with business." He did not specify the nature of the business. "I hope you're as disappointed as I am. Just know that you are very much in my thoughts, and you will see me again soon. In the meantime we can write to each other. No matter where I am, my postal address will be the farm."

He was eager to receive a letter from her. Perhaps on paper Claire would be able to express feelings she had been too shy to say to his face.

I wonder what sort of letters Síle wrote to Ned Halloran.

That night Barry dreamed not of Claire but of a woman with slanted eyes and a voluptuous mouth.

ON active service somewhere in Northern Ireland, Barry Halloran caught himself looking at his hands. Really looking at them. He always watched his hands when he was working with explosives, aware that the slightest mistake could be fatal, but now he observed them as if for the first time. Long, nimble fingers bent a tiny wire and fitted it into place with a precision that bordered on artistry. Those fingers could accomplish anything he chose. With training they could even design buildings.

Instead . . .

"Do you have any idea what a bomb can do?" Ursula had asked.

His gorge rose as his imagination presented him with explicit images of ordinary men and women . . . and pretty girls . . . and soldiers and constables and even loyalist thugs who might be caught up in the dreadful result of his work.

The nameless man on the nameless street of his nightmare.

"Do you have any idea what a bomb can do?" Ursula had asked. "Your own father . . ."

TWILIGHT. His mother just coming out of the milking parlour. Wearing an old red jumper and corduroy trousers too large for her slight frame, and raking her fingers through her short hair. When she saw him Ursula smiled the rare and dazzling smile that made her beautiful. "Barry! What a pleasant surprise."

"There's something I have to ask you."

"Certainly. But next week's your birthday, can you stay until then? I don't have a present for you yet but twenty-one's a milestone. Perhaps there's something special you'd like?"

"The answer to my question."

"Of course."

"I mean it, Ursula. No evasions."

She narrowed her eyes. "You're serious, aren't you?"

"More serious than I've ever been in my life."

"Shall we go in the house and talk?"

"Afterwards. First answer me. Here and now."

Ursula knew that unyielding tone. She gave a slight sigh. "Very well, what do you want to know?"

"Was my father killed by a bomb?"

She stared at him.

"Just yes or no, Ursula. Was he?"

"Yes," she whispered. "A German bomb that was dropped on Dublin's North Strand during World War Two."

There was so much pain in her eyes that Barry asked no more questions.

But as they were having dinner he reached across the bowl of roasted potatoes and covered her hand with his. "There is a special present you can give me for my birthday, Ursula. I'd like to go to Trinity."

She blinked. "Sorry? I'm not sure I heard you."

"I said I'd like to go to Trinity."

"What about the Army? I thought being a Volunteer was so important to you."

"It is important to me; I have no intention of resigning. But I've been told by someone I respect that the Army needs educated men, so I'm asking you to help me go to university."

Ursula's beautiful smile returned like a rainbow after a storm.

Next morning as soon as the milking was done she wrote to the registrar of Trinity College Dublin, requesting an admissions application. The oldest university in Ireland, Trinity had been founded by Queen Elizabeth in 1591. Until 1873 the school was limited to members of the "established Church," i.e., Anglicans. In that year religious requirements officially were dropped. The majority of the student body were still Protestants of various denominations. However, there also were some Jewish students, a few agnostics, and a small number of Roman Catholics—mostly the sons and daughters of landowners and professional people.

Yet Trinity remained fixed in Irish minds as a bastion of the old Ascendancy.

When the long brown envelope arrived Ursula opened it herself. She hung over Barry's shoulder while he read the application form. "Are you planning to ride on the crossbar of my bicycle when I take this to the post office?" he snapped.

She drew back. "There's no need to be sarcastic, I was merely interested."

Barry carried the prospectus to his room where he could pore over it in peace. *If I'm doing the studying, I'm going to choose what I study.* He spent a long time reading the array of courses, imagining himself taking almost every one. So many possibilities! More than a man could learn in a lifetime. It was an embarrassment of riches.

He completed the application in every detail before approaching his mother for the cheque which must accompany it. "Are you sure you got everything right?" she enquired. "Would you not like me to look it over before you send it off?"

"I've checked it twice and it's fine. But thanks for your offer of help." Barry smiled to take the sting out of his rebuff.

When the reply to his application arrived Barry made certain to get to it first. With thumping heart, he read that he was to present himself at Trinity the following week for interviews. *Now it begins! Now the rest of my life truly begins!*

Ursula purchased two train tickets to Dublin. Barry objected. "You're the most independent person I know," he told her. "Why deny me the same privilege?"

"This has nothing to do with independence. In Ireland everything comes down to a matter of who you know, and I have some connections in Dublin which might be useful. If I go with you I can introduce you to them. There's no harm in having references from a few prominent people."

They caught the early train to Dublin, arriving in a sudden rainstorm that abated as quickly as it began. The shabby old city, having survived a thousand years and innumerable power struggles, glistened with a misty glamour and smelled of the river. Ursula took Barry to a small hotel off Dame Street, her usual accommodation when visiting Dublin.

While they were settling in Ursula kept up a running monologue. "Don't mention the IRA, and there's no need to make any reference to your grandfather, either. You come from a strong farming family and that's all they need to know. I doubt if anyone will be so ill-bred as to enquire about your politics, but if they do, plead indifference. It's a common enough attitude these days."

Barry was not expected at Trinity until the following morning. Ursula devoted the rest of the day to visiting old friends and introducing her son to men and women whose names he knew only from the history books. She also called on several politicians who remembered her from her time with Radio Éireann. The name of Halloran opened many doors, Barry observed. But it slammed others. The divide left by the Civil War was as deep as ever.

WHEN he approached Trinity for the first time Barry half expected to be refused entry. Through those gates passed fresh young scholars and mature intellectuals. *I don't belong in either category. I've fought in a war and killed a man.*

His head came up; he strode forward. A brief moment under the shadow of the archway, and he was inside.

A helpful undergraduate gave Barry directions to his first interview. Her hair was white blond; her accent, she explained, was Finnish, and her name unpronounceable. But she did not seem like an outsider. She was clearly at home here.

The classical beauty of the college took Barry by surprise. As he picked his way over the cobblestones he feasted his eyes on one magnificent Georgian structure after another. The College Chapel, the Examination Hall, the Old Library . . . Barry Halloran was falling in love again.

The atmosphere of Trinity was unlike anything in his experience. In spite of hundreds of people constantly moving about the campus, there was an overlay of academic serenity that affected Barry's troubled spirit like a soothing balm. He had arrived feeling like a fraud. At the end of the day he left seduced; seduced by ancient tradition and modern opportunity.

Ursula was waiting anxiously at the hotel. "How did it go?" she asked before he even took off his coat. "Did you give them your letters of reference? Did you make a good impression?"

"Not too bad, I think. Everyone was courteous to me and one or two were quite encouraging about my prospects."

"You never told me, what courses will you sign up for?"

"It's academic until I'm accepted." He smiled at his pun.

"I think you should concentrate on history and the classics. That would prepare you for a career in teaching and teachers can always find work."

Why doesn't she ask me what I want?

"But you're right of course," Ursula went on. "The important thing is to be accepted."

"It isn't a foregone conclusion," Barry warned.

"You will be. I know it."

BEFORE they returned to Clare, Ursula took her son on a tour of "her" Dublin. Although she did not notice, he paid particular attention to the architecture. The city's elegant Georgian heritage, which represented British imperialism in many minds, had fallen into decay. Many of the spacious red brick houses had been carved into multi-family tenements in the last century and were falling down from neglect.

Busáras, the central bus station, was a different story. The first of Dublin's post-war buildings, Busáras with its cantilevered canopy to protect the buses had won major architectural awards and excited considerable controversy. Barry loved it on sight.

His mother was more interested in places connected with the Easter Rising. At the foot of the Mount Street Bridge she told her son, "Papa fought here." She stood for a while with her head cocked to one side, as if she could hear the British troops marching up the Northumberland Road. "Papa and Mama dodged British bullets here," she said at the Ha'penny Bridge.

At the General Post Office in O'Connell Street, Barry pressed his fingers into the bullet holes that still scarred the columns of the portico. But his eyes kept straying to Nelson's Pillar, only a few yards away.

The Pillar, erected three years after the Battle of Trafalgar, dominated Dublin's central thoroughfare. It consisted of a massive base of Portland stone supporting a fluted granite column in the Doric style, surmounted by a cylindrical plinth and a thirteen-foot-tall statue of Vice-Admiral Lord Horatio Nelson.

The Pillar was by far the highest structure in the street, towering over even the GPO. A landmark that could be seen for miles, it was the main terminus for public transport. As if Nelson were the heart of Dublin, tram lines radiated from his monument like arteries.

For sixpence one could enter the base and climb an internal staircase of 168 steps to an observation platform below the statue. This provided an unparalleled view of the city. A decorative iron railing had been heightened by an addition after an ex-soldier committed suicide in 1917[1] by leaping from the platform.

Nelson's Pillar appeared on almost every postcard of Dublin. For generations it had been the unofficial symbol of Ireland's capital.

Barry had to tilt his head far back to look up at the statue. Imperious and aloof, Lord Nelson was staring with eyes of stone across a city he had never visited in life.

Monumental architecture at its most arrogant, thought Barry.

Ursula said, "That monstrosity should have been knocked down ages ago. It's an insult to all those who died trying to win our freedom from England."

Barry sometimes enjoyed taking an opposite point of view, just to watch his mother rise to the bait. "To be fair," he said now, "as an island we're dependent on sea trade and Nelson rescued the international shipping routes by defeating Napoleon. Some might say he did Ireland a favour."

"To be fair," she mimicked, "Nelson was part and parcel of England's desire to rule the world. One of the Volunteers on the roof of the GPO during Easter

Week nicked his nose with a well-placed rifle shot. I consider that lad more of a hero than the swaggering admiral ever was."

"Would you not admit that's a rather prejudiced view?"

"I *am* prejudiced. On behalf of my country, my native land. And so should you be, Barry."

"Prejudiced on behalf of Switzerland, you mean?" he asked mischievously.

"Of course not! You're Irish, blood and bone."

"But I was born in Switzerland, and thanks to you I have a Swiss passport."

"I went to a lot of trouble to get that for you, young man. During World War Two a Swiss passport was worth its weight in gold."

"Surely you don't believe there could be another war? I thought the atom bomb made that unthinkable."

"World War One was supposed to be the war to end all wars," Ursula replied grimly.

AT the farm a letter was waiting for Barry. "I apologise for taking so long to reply," Claire had written in a schoolgirl's carefully formed script. "I had the most awful cold that went on and on. Aunt Miriam hovered over me like a mother hen. She kept me in bed for ages. She is a bit of a tyrant and I confess I am a little afraid of her. She has my best interests at heart, though. I hope your business will bring you back to Athlone sooner rather than later. I am longing for someone my own age to talk to."

Someone my own age to talk to? Barry was disappointed by her choice of words. The letter was less affectionate than he had hoped. *Perhaps she doesn't understand how I feel about her. Perhaps she needs more encouragement.*

He took up pen and paper to tell her of his plans: "I've decided to go back to school and get a university degree. I plan to have a career that will enable me to support a wife and family and . . ."

Barry halted the impulsive flow of words and wadded the paper into a ball. *It's too soon,* he warned himself. *I might frighten her.* He started over, filling page after page with cheerful chat and amusing anecdotes. Keeping it light. Keeping it charming. With just a few fond little phrases tucked here and there, so she would understand he was more than just a friend.

Then he went to Ennis to buy a gift to accompany the letter.

Barry visited shop after shop, seeking the perfect present. It was not as easy as he had thought. Clothing, he concluded, might be too intimate—especially as he did not know her sizes. A piece of jewellery might be presumptuous. A book? He did not know if Claire even liked to read. They had never discussed books. If she did like to read, what books did she enjoy? He could not send a mystery to a girl who loved romances. Or vice versa.

He finally decided a scarf would be safest. But what colour?

Red, perhaps. Like her lips.

This necessitated a fresh search. There were so many shades of red! At last Barry found a pretty square of crimson silk, darker and richer than flamboyant scarlet. The salesgirl assured him it would be perfect.

As Barry was wrapping the little package he thought, *If it's that hard to find the right gift for a girl who's still just a friend, how hard will it be to please a wife?*

In June the Army Convention would be held in Dublin. Séamus McCoy planned to go, he told Barry when they met for a pint. "They're going to try to rent a hall so there'll be enough room for ordinary Volunteers to attend. That's real democracy for you, Seventeen. Of course it also means there's more opportunity for disagreement. Not everybody's happy about the way things are going.

"Finances are worse than ever," McCoy confided, coughing through cigarette smoke. "If the border campaign had gone better the Americans would be rowing in with buckets of money, but now they don't want to know us. Thank God I know we're going to win in the end. Otherwise I'd be worried."

When Barry got home a letter from Trinity was waiting. Ursula was out riding and had not seen it yet. Barry tore the envelope open so hastily that he almost ripped the headed notepaper inside.

"Dear Mr. Halloran,

"Please present yourself at Trinity College Dublin on the date given below, prepared to sit your entrance examination. We wish you every success."

Chapter Seventeen

—⁂—

OVER his mother's objections, this time Barry would travel to Dublin alone. "Don't be making a holy show of me," he told her. "I'm too old to go everywhere with my mammy." The skin tightened around his eyes, warning Ursula not to argue.

THE entrance examination was difficult, though not more difficult than Barry expected. After he finished and turned it in, he was ready to put the next step of his plan into action.

The General Headquarters of the Irish Republican Army currently was located in a private house in an upper-middle-class neighbourhood. The well-dressed woman who responded to Barry's knock opened the door only halfway. "May I help you?" she enquired in an impeccable English accent. Thrown off guard, Barry hesitated before answering. "I'm looking for Éamonn Thomas."

"There's no one here by that name. Are you sure you have it right?"

Undaunted, Barry said, "I called 'round to the *United Irishman* office but it was closed, so I thought Mr. Thomas might be here. If he is, please tell him one of his subscribers, Barry Halloran, would like to speak with him."

The woman took a step backwards and closed the door. After a minute or two a man in his shirtsleeves came trotting around the side of the house. A lively little man with exceptionally bright grey eyes and a merry, elfin smile. He was ten or twelve years older than Barry. A lingering trace of prison pallor made him look older still. Behind the bright eyes were memories of pain.

"It's about time you came to Dublin!" Éamonn Thomas cried with genuine delight. "Inside with you now, and meet some of the other lads."

This time the door opened wide. In what miraculously had become an impeccable Irish accent, the same woman said, *"Failte isteach."**

Including Éamonn Thomas, three members of the Army Council were at headquarters that day. When Barry followed Thomas into the kitchen, Rory Brady and a middle-aged man whom Barry did not know were sitting at the table. "... But the Belfast republicans are only interested in protecting the Catholics from the RUC and the B-Specials," the middle-aged man was saying. "They don't have any commitment to a united Ireland."

Éamonn Thomas cleared his throat. "Look who's here."

"I know Volunteer Halloran already," Brady said, jumping to his feet with a broad smile. "He was one of Seán Garland's lads, a graduate of the Brookeborough School of Hard Knocks."

The other man was sturdily built, with thick, wavy hair turning grey. Putting down his cigarette, he extended his hand across the table to Barry. "Cathal Goulding. Éamonn and Rory and I are graduates of the Curragh Camp division of that same school." Goulding spoke with the rapid-fire cadence of a machine gun. "Curragh Camp was a great place. No privacy at all and nothing to sleep on but wooden pallets. People tried for years to get me out of there but I just wouldn't leave. Where else could a fellow get free food and board and spend all his time with friends of a like mind?"

"Sounds brilliant," said Barry. "I'd like to go there myself, but I heard it was closed."

"Unfortunately," Goulding replied. "What a tragic loss for us all."

Éamonn Thomas chuckled at the deadpan exchange. "Cathal joined the IRA long before you were born, Barry. He's a hard man and no mistake. Claims to be a house painter but I never caught him at it. His father fought in the Easter Rising and his grandfather was one of the great old Fenians."

"Sure don't we all come from republican backgrounds?" said Goulding. "It's in the blood." He reached into his pocket for another cigarette.

Rory Brady remarked, "You smoke too much, Cathal, it's bad for your ulcer. You should put some food in your belly instead."

"I'd as soon die of a bleeding ulcer as a bullet. At least I got the ulcer from my own government." With a wink in Barry's direction, Goulding added, "A little memento of my treatment in Curragh Camp. Great fun, that. Just think what you missed, Halloran."

"I'm despondent."

This time everyone laughed.

"I assume you came looking for me for a reason?" Thomas asked Barry.

Before answering, Barry swept his eyes around the table.

*Welcome in.

Three ordinary men. If you passed them on the street you wouldn't notice them. Yet they're the Army, the only hope we have of getting our country back the way it was supposed to be.

Heroes.

He drew a deep breath. What he was about to do would require a great deal of courage. "I want to go off active service."

Thomas looked surprised. The other two kept their feelings, whatever they might be, well hidden.

"Have you discussed this with Séamus McCoy?" Thomas asked.

"I have not, sir. I thought it would be best to come directly to you."

"Because McCoy might talk you out of it first?"

"He might try, but my mind's made up."

"You want to resign from the Army, is that it?" Goulding asked. There was no warmth in his voice now.

"Not at all. When I took the oath I meant it and I still do. But . . ."

They waited, sitting perfectly still. Men who had waited all their lives for something. Men who were determined to make it happen.

"I've too much imagination for a soldier," Barry said. "I can imagine what a man feels when I shoot him."

"We all can," Goulding told him. "Some of us from experience. Is this your way of telling us you're afraid?"

Éamonn Thomas had been watching Barry's face intently. "I don't think he's afraid, not any more than is good for him, anyway. No man could work with explosives the way he does and be a coward. It's something else, isn't it?"

Barry nodded. "I'm given this a lot of thought, and . . ." He met Rory Brady's eyes. "You once told me the Army needs educated men. I've applied to Trinity and taken my entrance exam. I don't know the outcome yet, but I'm reasonably hopeful of becoming a resident undergraduate there."

*"Go raibh mile maith agat, Ruairi,"** Goulding said to Brady. "You've lost us a damned good explosives man."

"I didn't expect he'd do this."

"You misunderstand, I don't want to resign from the Army!" Barry cried. "If I'm accepted at Trinity I won't be available for active service, but surely you can find something else for me to do. In whatever spare time I have," he added rather lamely.

"This is the Army we're talking about," said Brady. "If a man can't—or won't—fight, what good is he to us?"

"But you told me . . ."

Brady ignored the interruption. "We've never enough men in the field as it is."

*Thanks very much, Rory.

"There are other ways to serve the cause," Thomas suggested.

"Politics? Politics was highjacked by the Free Staters long ago, Éamonn," Brady said. "Fianna Fáil claims to be the republican party but they're just as bad as the others, they haven't the bottle to drive the British off this island once and for all. As for Sinn Féin, even you would have to admit they're so marginalised they have no power. Things have changed since the days when they provided the only government we had. The gun and the bomb, that's your only man now.

"Listen here, Barry. I told you that an education was important and it is. Someday we may be able to afford the luxury of seeing that every Irish child who wants one is offered a place in university. We're a long way from there right now, though. There are Irish children in the north who can't even get a primary education. Lemass has his hands full trying to create a viable economy; he's not worried about what's happening up there. But until that problem's solved and this island's reunited, all our futures have to be postponed."

"I don't want my future postponed! I want to go to university and be part of the Army too."

Cathal Goulding said, "You don't know when you're beaten, do you?"

The expression in Barry's eyes changed dramatically. It was like looking at a different man. A man who, if pushed hard enough, could explode like one of his bombs. "I'm not beaten."

"We can't afford to lose this fellow," Éamonn Thomas told the other two. "Let's approach this from a different angle. Tell us, Barry: What do you want to study at Trinity?"

"History. And the classics—for my grandfather as much as for any other reason. He studied the classics with Pádraic Pearse. "*There I go boasting again. Careful, Halloran!*" But I'll also take courses toward a career in architecture. That's what I really want. The last time I was in Dublin I was impressed by the bus terminal that Michael Scott designed a few years ago, and—"

"The Army doesn't need a new bus terminal," Brady snapped.

In a kindlier tone, Thomas said, "What else interests you?"

"Well, I like photography. I don't see myself making a career of it, though."

"Photography!" Thomas beamed. "The very thing. We're having an uphill fight to win back support for the cause. Most people have forgot about Northern Ireland, they have problems of their own. But you know your way around the north, Barry. You could cross the border from time to time—on the odd weekend, say—and take photographs that would wake them up again. You know what I mean?"

Barry knew. Images of the sort that would remain with him forever.

Too frightened to cry, a little girl with the eyes of a wounded deer watching arson destroy the only home she had ever known. The fire brigade would never come. Her parents would have to seek shelter for their family with their own parents—in a cramped one-roomed flat. As they retreated up the road hugging their few belongings, a sectarian mob taunted them.

A frail old man being frog-marched out of a tenement to be thrown into jail on the word of an Orangeman. When Barry enquired what the charge was, he was warned to mind his own business "or we'll take you for good measure, Paddy!" The man's wife, who was badly crippled with arthritis, hobbled after them, protesting that her husband was blind. The constables ignored her.

A woman sitting on a kerbstone with her head in her hands. When Barry approached she looked up in sudden terror. She had been pretty before someone smashed her nose. Her upper lip was still smeared with dried blood. "Who did this to you?" Barry had asked as he crouched beside her. But he knew without asking. A favourite pastime for a certain type of loyalist was to sally into a Catholic neighbourhood and force himself on one of the women. If his victim tried to resist she was beaten.

Such scenes occurred over and over again, year after year. No one in authority did anything to stop it. The Royal Ulster Constabulary was content to stand aside and let any sort of abuse be perpetrated upon Catholics. Meanwhile, Britain, whose "province" Northern Ireland was, turned a blind eye to the suffering of over 40 percent of the population.

"I know exactly what you want," Barry told Thomas. "I've seen it for myself. What the eye can see, the camera can record."

Cathal Goulding looked dubious. "Who's going to fund this little exercise? Cameras, film, all that class of thing. Our treasury's skint."

Before cost could become an issue Barry said hastily, "I have a good camera already and I'll pay my own expenses."

"Another question: Supposing they turn out the way you want, what are you going to do with the photographs, Éamonn? The *United Irishman*'s not equipped to publish them."

"What about *An Phoblacht**?" asked Barry, referring to a weekly IRA newsletter that had been sporadically published in the twenties and thirties. There were numerous copies amongst Ursula's collection of republican periodicals.

"Dead and gone, more's the pity," Thomas said.

"Could we not sell photographs abroad?"

Rory Brady brightened. "Now there's an idea. We could do something along the lines of the Irish News Agency that Seán MacBride established while he was minister for external affairs. He told the Dáil the agency's primary purpose was to gather news for export, but what he really envisioned was a propaganda agency to counter the unfavourable propaganda about Ireland the British were putting out."

*The Republic.

"I don't want to play the devil's advocate here," said Goulding, "but bear in mind that things didn't work out the way Seán hoped. His original plan was to operate the agency as a co-op supported by the Irish press in return for furnishing them with material. For a while everybody who was anybody wrote for him, even Brendan Behan—that was before *Borstal Boy* made Behan famous and he started swanning off to America. But the agency couldn't get enough support from the Irish newspapers. They saw it as competition for them; they were selling material abroad too. Seán had to turn the whole thing over to the government just to stay afloat. When the government decided to cut expenses a couple of years ago, they closed down the agency and that was that."

Thomas said, "We can do it differently, we'll keep tight control ourselves."

Barry leaned forward with his elbows on the table. His words tumbled out almost as rapidly as Goulding's. "If we can get our photographs into some newspapers and magazines in America they might pay off. I know contacts in the States who used to be big contributors to the IRA. If they can see what's happening now they might come on board again."

"Who? How do you know them?"

Barry had no intention of revealing Ned Halloran's notebooks. They were his secret asset. "Let's just say my information comes from an impeccable source."

The three Army men exchanged glances.

Barry looked from one to another, finding no clue as to their thoughts.

At last Cathal Goulding nodded. "*Sin sin,*"* he said. "We have a deal."

---

*That's that (pronounced shin-shin).

Chapter Eighteen

WAITING to learn the result of his entrance exam was excruciating. Days dragged by as if their feet were stuck in the mud. With every one, Barry felt a modicum of his self-confidence drain away. In the back of his mind—and sometimes, particularly at night, in the forefront of his mind—he was always conscious of Claire MacNamara.

There had been no letter from her since he sent the scarf. Had the gift offended her? Was it too expensive? Not expensive enough? Did she think he was trying to pressure her?

ON the thirteenth of July the radio newsreader reported, "At an Orange Order demonstration yesterday the Ulster Unionist MP Brian Faulkner said, 'We in the Unionist Party are perforce defending ourselves against the Roman Catholic hierarchy. Until the hierarchy renounces its influence in politics, the Orange Order cannot renounce its influence in the Unionist Party.' "[1]

"I hate to admit it," Barry told his mother, "but that sounds reasonable to me."

"It is reasonable. I would rather pull out my fingernails with pliers than agree with Brian Faulkner, but the attitude of the Church continues to make any hope of reuniting this country laughable. Why would northern Protestants want to be part of a society with no divorce, no contraception, and a constitution that hands control of the state to the priests on a silver platter?"

"Now, Ursula, it's not quite that bad."

"Is it not?" Her voice was bitter. "You aren't a woman."

WE are pleased to inform Finbar Lewis Halloran that he has been accepted as a resident undergraduate of Trinity College Dublin, commencing with the autumn term."

THE road to Athlone seemed a lot longer than Barry remembered. He hitched a ride that took him to the outskirts of the town but had to walk the rest of the way. Not walk. Run.

Brushing past people on the footpath, Barry sprinted the last few yards to the sweets shop. Skidded to a halt. Stared in disbelief.

The shop was boarded up.

He was looking at an absolute impossibility. In Barry's imagination he already had entered the shop, been warmly welcomed—perhaps even kissed—by a girl too beautiful to be real, proposed marriage to her and been accepted and set up practice as an architect and . . .

The shop was boarded up.

He burst into the newsagency next door. "Where's Miss MacNamara?"

"The girl in the sweets shop? We haven't seen her since it closed."

"When was that?"

"A few weeks ago now."

"What happened? Is it for sale?"

"I doubt it, not many are buying shops these days. Do you . . ."

But Barry was out the door and running again.

By the time he reached the aunt's cottage on the Ballinasloe road his heart was pounding painfully.

The cottage windows were tightly shuttered and there was a padlock on the door. Weeds were already springing up along the front path. Barry bent over and braced his hands on his knees while he caught his breath, then walked all the way around the house. It was as tightly shut as a clam.

In response to Barry's urgent knock at the nearest house an elderly man peered out. "Mrs. Fogarty's not there anymore," he mumbled between toothless gums.

"What happened?"

"She went away."

I can see that for myself, you old fool. "What about her niece? Claire?"

"She took the girl with her."

"Do you know why they left?"

The old man scratched his whiskery jaw. "A great woman for keeping herself to herself, Miriam Fogarty. But what I think is, the niece was ill." His voice dropped to a confidential whisper. "You know."

"I *don't* know. Tell me, for God's sake!"

"TB, that's what I think."

Barry shuddered.

Countries with more resources were well on their way to conquering tuberculosis, but in Ireland the very word still struck panic. Families went to desperate lengths to conceal its presence. Sufferers were often banished from home completely, hidden away to cough out their lives in a sanatorium.

Was it possible that Claire could have TB? Barry searched his memory for clues. The white skin, the red lips, the frequent cough . . . His heart sank.

"Do you know where they went?" he asked.

"I'd say she's after taking the girl home."

"Are you certain?"

"I am not certain. But that's what I'd do, take her back to her mammy."

Was I too besotted to think straight? Why didn't I ask more about her parents— such as their names and address?

All he had was Claire's remark about a house "at the very top of the hill." Cork was a city of hills. Or did she even mean Cork city? Cork was a county, too. And most of it hilly.

She could be anywhere.

At the local post office Barry was told that Mrs. Fogarty had left no forwarding address. The telephone office was able to provide a phone book for County Cork which revealed a daunting number of MacNamaras. "Of course they may not have a telephone at all," the office manager pointed out. "Many people don't."

If the neighbour was right in his surmise, possibly Claire was in a sanatorium by now. Which one? How could he find out? Such places had a policy of strict confidentiality.

Barry spent two long, fruitless days in Athlone, seeking some clue to Claire's whereabouts. But she had vanished without a trace.

Why didn't she write and tell me she was going away? She has my postal address.

Maybe she does have TB and was ashamed to tell me. But I wouldn't mind about that, I'd wait for her until she is well, no matter how long it takes.

He rather liked the image of himself as a faithful swain, patiently waiting for the girl he loved. But realistically he would rather have her whole and healthy and in his arms.

I'll just have to find her, that's all. If she is ill we'll deal with it.

When he returned to the farm, Ursula took one look at his long face and thought he had been wounded. He assured her that no such thing had happened. "I'm just tired, that's all."

"It's more than that surely."

"Leave it, Ursula." He gave her That Look.

URSULA closed the account book and massaged the bridge of her nose with thumb and forefinger. Her eyes felt grainy. There was a nagging pain in the small of her back, reminding her that she was not as young as she used to be.

She had been going over the figures for hours but they did not improve. Although the dairy business had done well enough in the past year, horse sales, upon which all extra expenditure was predicated, were disappointing. Not many in Ireland had the money to buy good horses. Foreign purchasers were few and far between. Sending Barry to university was going to be expensive, and he indicated that he would need a substantial amount of pocket money as well: "Everything costs more in Dublin." Meanwhile, Eileen had resumed grumbling about the lack of a refrigerator.

Ursula suspected that the older woman was letting the cream go sour on purpose.

She pushed the account book aside and stared bleakly out the window. Too much rain; crops were rotting in the fields. They would have to buy in feed again this winter. And George insisted that the tractor needed an overhaul. "Lucky me," Ursula said to the empty room. "I'm an independent Irishwoman."

FOR the weeks remaining until he went up to Dublin, Barry seemed closed in, lost in his thoughts. It was no use trying to get him to talk. When Ursula asked what he was thinking about he said, "Nothing much."

"I doubt that. Have you changed your mind about going to university?"

"I haven't changed my mind."

"What's wrong, then?"

"Nothing."

The night before Barry left for Dublin, Ursula went to his room. "Are you ready?"

"Almost, though I still need to clean my bicycle. I'm going to take it with me on the train so I'll have my own transportation in the city." Ned's notebooks were already safely out of sight in the bottom of Barry's suitcase. As his mother watched, he tucked a small chunk of limestone into the case amongst his folded shirts.

"Why are you taking a piece of rock? There are plenty of stones in Dublin."

"But this one's a part of the farm, Ursula. Do you never save mementoes?"

"I'm not that sentimental. Except for . . . well, the programme from the Eucharistic Congress in 1932, I kept that. And a rose pressed in a book."

"Did my father give you the rose?" Barry asked, ever hopeful of a clue.

"Hardly. It fell from the countess's coffin during her funeral procession."

"What countess?"

"Markievicz."

"You went to her funeral? You never told me."

"There's lots of things I've never told you."

Barry slammed down the lid of his suitcase with more force than necessary. "That, Ursula, is a profound understatement."

HE was assigned a room in the Rubrics, Trinity's oldest surviving building. Dating from the start of the eighteenth century, it was built of red brick with quaintly dramatic Dutch gables which had been added in the 1890s. Barry was delighted to take up residence in such an architectural gem. *It's streets ahead of sleeping in a muddy dugout in Fermanagh.*

When Barry arrived his roommate was already in the room, busily usurping all the drawers in the one and only chest by stuffing clothing into them. When the door opened he looked up. A beanpole of a man, slightly above medium height, with a cowlick, an exceptionally prominent Adam's apple, and bad skin.

Poor fellow looks like a plucked chicken. "I believe half those drawers are mine," Barry drawled.

"I was under the impression that I could use whatever I needed." The voice was high-pitched and slightly nasal.

"Only until I arrived," said Barry. He stood framed in the doorway, letting his new roommate have a good look at him. He had learned that there were certain situations in which his size and physical presence were enough to win a point. Before the silence could grow uncomfortable, he smiled and held out his hand. "I'm Finbar Halloran. Barry."

"Gilbert Fitzmaurice. Gilbert," the other stressed. Ignoring Barry's outstretched hand, he began taking some of his clothing from the drawers. "Obviously there's been a misunderstanding."

"Forget it," said Barry. "Where are you from, Gilbert?"

"Waterford."

"I'm from Clare myself."

"A country boy, I suppose." The tone was condescending. From Gilbert's accent, Barry could not tell just where he belonged in the complex fabric of Protestant social stratification that was a holdover from the nineteenth century in Ireland. It ran in descending order from the aristocratic Anglo-Irish grandees known as the Ascendancy to low-caste tradesmen and farmers who were no better off than their Catholic neighbours.

Lifting his chin, Barry said proudly, "I'm country born and bred and a Catholic as well. I'm twenty-one years old, six foot four in my bare feet, ride horses, speak Irish, read Latin, and have a lot of Shakespeare off by heart. I'm a good amateur boxer and hope to become a good architect. What about you?" he finished with a disarming smile.

Gilbert hesitated. "I'll, uh, be called to the bar."

"How can you be so sure? You're still an undergraduate, aren't you?"

"My father's a barrister and his father before him. We've never done anything else."

Barry lifted an eyebrow. "All the way back to Adam, eh? Did one of your ancestors defend the snake?"

Gilbert looked blank. "What snake?"

Jesus Mary and Joseph, I've drawn a roommate with no sense of humour.

Undergraduate life at Trinity was Spartan by the standards of its more affluent students, who comprised the majority. Classrooms were poorly heated and badly ventilated. Sprinting across the campus in a cold rain from one class to the next resulted in an endless round of head colds, which were passed from student to student. In the Rubrics the lights were turned off at eleven o'clock sharp, requiring anyone who wanted to read to use an electric torch.

During the first few weeks Barry rarely ventured outside the high college railings with their embossed coats of arms. One exception was a visit to the nearest bank to open an account. "Money will be sent from Clare every month to lodge in my account," he explained, "and I'll withdraw it as needed."

The banker was used to dealing with students from the university. "I'm afraid we cannot extend overdraft privileges until you've been with us for twelve months, Mr. Halloran," he said with practiced regret. "But should you find yourself in difficulties in the meantime . . ." He left the sentence unfinished. This young man might be a person of importance someday.

ALTHOUGH Barry wanted to enter fully into university life, his habit of reticence was hard to break. At first he stayed in the social background, merely observing.

Amongst the students at Trinity was a type of person he had never met before. Pompous, self-absorbed, and invariably Ascendancy, they seemed unable to have a normal conversation. Every sentence contained at least one reference to a famous person with whom they claimed a "close connection." Playing polo with the duke of this and cricket with the earl of that. Dining with the famous author of something else.

Barry's eyes glazed over. *I should hate to be nothing more than a list of celebrities.*

He quickly learned to recognise the inveterate name-droppers and avoid them. It was better to keep himself to himself. A lone wolf who stood out in the crowd by the fact of his singularity.

One day he happened to pick up a copy of the *Trinity News,* the in-house newsletter staffed by journalism students. The paper was an exuberant mixture of campus gossip, thoughtful editorialising, and crass schoolboy humour, with a leavening of genuine wit. Barry enjoyed it so much that he made a point of meeting the students responsible. He liked every one of them. Arrogant and articulate, they openly discussed the subjects that interested him most. Politics and power, sports and science. And sex.

Trinity's fledgling journalists paid scant attention to the repressive Archbishop McQuaid.

Soon Barry was sitting with them in the dining hall or buying his share of drinks in the nearest pub. It was not quite the same as the Army, but at least he had people to talk with.

Unfortunately, Barry had no choice in the matter of his roommate. Gilbert Fitzmaurice was not a name-dropper simply because he was interested in no one but himself. He could twist any conversational topic until he was at the centre. No one else inhabited his universe.

Barry learned this the first time he left the room they shared, telling Gilbert, "If anybody's looking for me I'll be in the library." Someone did come looking for Barry, and was bluntly informed, "I have no idea where he is."

After that experience Barry was polite to his roommate but otherwise ignored him. Gilbert did not notice. Whenever Barry was within earshot he bombarded him with unsolicited monologues about the life, times, and troubles of Gilbert Fitzmaurice. In self-defence, Barry developed selective deafness to the sound of his roommate's voice.

"It's like living next door to a barking dog," he said to Dennis Cassidy, one of the journalism students. "After a while you don't hear him anymore."

BARRY was often the first one into a lecture hall and the last to leave. His thirsty mind soaked up information like blotting paper. While studying he was too preoccupied to brood over Claire. Yet when he was hurrying across the New Square he might glimpse a girl who reminded him of her in some way, and the pain would come flooding back.

He continued to search for her as best he could. He sent letters to every sanatorium in the country, but his enquiries were fruitless. Eventually he was forced to conclude that Claire had never shared his feelings. Perhaps their romance had been all in his mind. Otherwise she would have found a way to stay in touch.

Lesson learned. I won't put myself in that position again.

THE camera was Barry's constant companion. He took numerous photographs of Trinity, then extended his field to include the surrounding city. Bicycling as far north as Swords and as far south as Dalkey in search of subjects, he discovered an unexpected bonus.

A tall young man with a camera in his hands was an irresistible magnet to women.

Outside a shop in Santry, Barry engaged in a bit of flirtatious banter with a particularly attractive girl who asked him to take her picture. When she said, "I'll give you my address if you promise to send me a copy," he wrote her address on the back of his hand.

The following day he bought an address book.

A new element was shoehorned into Barry's already crowded schedule. He was thankful for his inexhaustible energy. There were pretty girls and witty girls whom he arranged to meet under Clery's clock, the traditional Dublin trysting place, before taking them to the cinema or to Barry's Hotel for tea and scones. There were clever girls and studious girls—the blond Finn was one of the latter—whom he escorted to concerts or for walks in the rain.

But there would be no serious romance, no talk of love.

Whenever Gilbert Fitzmaurice saw Barry with a girl, he made the same remark: "I wouldn't use her for practice." His repertoire of comments was severely limited. Barry could predict what he would say on any occasion because it never varied. Gilbert was, he decided, the most boring person he had ever met.

How can a man who has nothing original to say become a barrister?

The camera was Barry's bridge between disparate worlds. The university, with its hierarchical society and introspective concerns, was one. He enjoyed his time in the library or on the hockey field, where his strength and speed were a great asset. In the golden days of youth, he was, to all appearances, a carefree young man amongst his peers. His letters to Ursula were filled with collegiate anecdotes.

That was the weekday world. Weekends found Barry on his way north with his camera in a rucksack. He did not mention these journeys to Ursula. Nor did he take Ned's notebooks with him. He took them to his bank to be put in safekeeping while he was away.

He carried his Swiss passport in case there was a problem at the border, but he was never seriously questioned. His cover story, that he was a graduate student on his way from Trinity to Queen's University in Belfast to do research, was accepted. He wore a suit and tie and was well spoken, a confident young man of obvious good breeding.

Once Barry was across the border his persona changed. GHQ had equipped him with a set of documents—driver's licence, hotel bills, library card, personal letters, and so forth—that identified him as Finbar Lewis, freelance photojournalist. There was even a passport in that name, though he had been warned it might not stand up to close scrutiny.

Dressed in an old tweed jacket and faded blue jeans, with darkened hair and the Leica on a leather strap around his neck, Barry Halloran became someone else.

Photojournalist. The word suggested a raffish glamour.

Members of the fraternity ran the gamut from professional newsmen who studied photography to augment their reportage, to the amateur with a camera who obtained a lucky shot, sprang to public attention, then settled down to learn his craft in earnest. The twentieth century was littered with photographic milestones. The last pictures of the *Titanic,* whose loss marked the end of an era; mud-caked, half-frozen soldiers in the trenches of World War One; the terrible mushroom cloud that ended World War Two. Photojournalism was giving mankind an unprecedented picture of itself.

WHEN Barry took his first rolls of exposed film back to Dublin he had waited anxiously for the developed prints. They were disappointing. Sharp images, cleverly composed, but just snapshots. He studied them for a long time, trying to decide what was wrong.

I'm only pretending to be a photojournalist. A professional would have shown not only the people of the Six Counties, but also found a way to show the unionist mindset that shapes and controls them.

He could not accept failure. *I've been viewing the unionists from the outside, that's the problem. Seeing them only as the enemy makes them one-dimensional— like these pictures. I have to get inside them, know what makes them tick. If I can imagine how a man feels when he's blown apart by a bomb, surely I can imagine what it's like to be a northern Protestant.*

Barry wandered down to Stephen's Green to sit on a bench and think. He could always think better in the fresh air. A parade of people passed before him. Courting couples, businessmen cutting across the park to save time between appointments, children running and shouting, women carrying bread to feed the ducks. Barry did not see them. In his mind's eye he was somewhere else, trying to think like a totally different man.

Northern Ireland was born in a crisis, he reminded himself, *and fear has dominated the province ever since. Sectarianism breeds fear. But Catholics aren't the only ones who're afraid. The Protestants claim they're living in a state of siege themselves.*

Are they?

He stared unseeing at the nearby pond, where a pair of swans were competing with the ducks for crusts of bread.

The Roman Catholic Church forbade contraception. Devout Catholics tended to have much larger families than Protestants.

Enshrined in the Anglo-Irish Treaty was a promise that Northern Ireland would remain part of Britain only as long as the majority wanted.

The Protestants are waking up to the fact that within a matter of decades they will become the minority. If there's a united Ireland, they're terrified they will be treated the same way they've treated the Catholics.

．　　．　　．

THE next time Barry was in Belfast he sought out a run-down Catholic church at the edge of a Protestant neighbourhood. A number of residents walked past the church every day. Barry waited until the unconscious expression on the face of a passerby revealed not only loathing but deep-seated fear.

Then he had his picture.

Chapter Nineteen

———•⟨∞⟩•———

November 9, 1960

JOHN F. KENNEDY ELECTED PRESIDENT OF THE UNITED STATES

Defeats Richard Nixon by narrow margin. Will become America's first Roman Catholic president.

CRACKS were appearing in the monolithic face of Northern Ireland. The industrial economy that brought prosperity to the north had been declining since the end of World War Two. The death blow came in 1960. Harland and Wolf, no longer contracted to build either great battleships or luxury transatlantic liners, laid off thirteen thousand workers, almost all of them Protestant, and warned of still more layoffs in the future. Other heavy industry followed suit, together with countless peripheral support businesses.

Working-class Protestants in cities and towns all across the north saw their quality of life diminish drastically. Within a few short years Protestants on the Shankill Road in Belfast would be suffering the same poverty as their Catholic neighbours on the Falls Road.

Meanwhile, moderate elements in the government had begun to allow an improvement in the educational system. A new, better-educated Catholic middle class was starting to develop. The possibility of a seismic shift in the social structure of Northern Ireland was disquieting to many.

THE Army hoped to take advantage of the situation, but GHQ kept receiving bad news. Resources were declining. There were too many arrests and too many resignations. November brought a double dose of disaster. On the fourth Seán Garland was arrested in Belfast, and on the night of the tenth a party including Dave O'Connell was intercepted by a laundry van near the village of Arboe. A group of men in civilian clothes jumped out and opened fire on the Volunteers. O'Connell was hit six times: in the chest, shoulder, stomach, groin, and both hands.

Miraculously he survived, but he lost a lung and would never be the same.

TRINITY was almost deserted during the holiday season, its life at low ebb. Barry telephoned Ursula to tell her he had too much studying to do and could not come home for Christmas. The truth was, he wanted to be left alone to do some thinking about himself and the direction his life was taking.

He loved the Army. But taking propaganda photographs was not the same as being on active service. He was planning for a career in architecture, which he also loved. But he was posing as a photojournalist.

On top of the locker beside his bed in the Rubrics he kept the small piece of limestone he had brought from the farm. When he woke in the morning his eyes went to it first, even before he looked at the clock.

The stone was solid. Uncompromising.

IN the new year rumours of dissension within the ranks of the IRA increased. The old guard was being seriously challenged by younger men. Those who believed that only physical force could restore a united Ireland were opposed by those who thought that playing the political game might yield more positive results in the long run.

"Exactly what is the relationship between Sinn Féin and the IRA?" Barry asked Éamonn Thomas when he delivered his latest photographs.

Leaning back in his chair, Thomas laced his fingers behind his head. "That's a good question. They're two separate organisations, but the Army needs Sinn Féin and Sinn Féin needs the Army—for now.

"Arthur Griffith founded Sinn Féin as a purely political party, the most nationalist of all the parties, but peaceful. Griffith was totally opposed to using physical force to achieve political goals. But after the Free State came into being, the republicans realised that they needed a political voice to oppose a government that was still dominated by British influence. So the 1949 Army Convention passed a resolution urging Volunteers to enlist in Sinn Féin.[1] Few of the senior IRA figures had any interest in politics, they were men of action, but they saw no contradiction between the two organisations.

"Their plan was to take over Sinn Féin and turn it into the civilian wing of the IRA, but," Thomas gave an unexpected chuckle, "they discovered that Sinn Féin's ideals weren't so easily subsumed. A number of Volunteers had only joined the IRA 'for the *craic*.'* The party's influence turned them into deeply dedicated men. Sinn Féin's educational programme exposed them to the high-minded principles of Pearse and the pragmatic socialism of Connolly and they absorbed it like blotting paper. Cathal Goulding is a good example.

"By the time Cathal and I were released from Curragh Camp, younger men with more radical ideas were running the Army. Confrontation was inevitable. There was no real split in the Army, but what you might call a 'splintering' around the edges, with several breakaway groups forming under their own leaders. One or two cooperate with the Army from time to time, though most of the mainstream consider them as heretics to the principles of republicanism. Both sides believe they're right, of course."

"That's not uncommon on this island," said Barry.

"Are you interested in politics yourself?"

"Not at all, I'm Army."

Thomas smiled his merry smile. "It's possible to be both. Many of us are."

SOMETIMES Barry went north on the train, being careful to ride in the first-class car. Those passengers were never questioned at the border. Sometimes he hitchhiked, in which case he made certain that he was on an unapproved road. Border guards on the approved roads were more thorough when it came to examining documents.

With every trip Barry's confidence increased.

As time went by he made less effort to change his appearance. Belfast was becoming familiar territory. Sinn Féin had a presence in the north. Known as "Republican Clubs," the party provided a focus for republicans and nationalists in towns throughout the Six Counties. Barry had only to make himself known to be directed to safe accommodations.

He slept in Catholic houses—but he drank in Protestant bars. His face was familiar in corner shops in both neighbourhoods. He read the pro-Unionist *Belfast Telegraph* and the pro-Nationalist *Irish News*. He could, and did, talk knowledgeably about current events to anyone he met—adjusting his point of view to fit the situation. The only way to get the pictures he wanted was to blend in.

He had two cameras now. The second was a used Nikon he had bought in a Dublin pawn shop. From the same source he had acquired a folding tripod. The quality of his photographs was improving. Éamonn Thomas sold half a dozen of the best to a news agency in Chicago.

· · ·

*Conversation; chat.

NINETEEN sixty-one was the Patrician Year, commemorating Ireland's patron saint. As a guest celebrant in Dublin, Bishop Fulton J. Sheen from America praised "the passionate chastity of the Irish male."

BARRY took most of his pictures in Belfast's Catholic enclaves such as New Lodge, Short Strand, and the Lower Falls Road. But relying on his size to discourage possible troublemakers, he also ventured into the Shankill Road.

Sometimes his size was not enough. One afternoon he rounded a corner and found himself facing four would-be toughs who walked with their legs wide apart as if their balls were too big. "Howya doin', Taig?" their leader asked with a totally insincere grin—thus proving that he knew a Catholic when he saw one. Or maybe it was a lucky guess. Religion was not really an issue. These four just wanted action and one man alone looked like a soft target.

Barry Halloran surprised them by baring his teeth in a savage grin. In that instant he changed from a photographer going about his business to a warrior going about *his* business. He did not even have to think about it, the skills were simply there. One long stride and his back was against a wall. In the same movement he let his camera bag slide to the ground. As the first man swung at him he waited until the ultimate moment, then ducked so swiftly that his assailant had no time to pull the punch and drove his fist into a brick wall. There was an audible sound of knuckles breaking and a howl of pain.

The other three lunged forward with no plan of action other than mindless attack. Barry danced to one side, spun around, and gave one man a blow over the ear that sent him reeling. As an extension of the same movement Barry ducked again and drove his skull into the midsection of another. The man let out a mighty "oooof" as the air rushed out of his lungs, and sat down hard on the pavement.

The third assailant received a kick to his kneecap that made him stagger, then Barry brought a powerful blow up from his hip to the point of the man's jaw. When he felt the head snap backwards he was afraid he had broken the fellow's neck. To Barry's relief, his victim remained upright long enough to reassure him that his neck was still intact, then fell like a timbered tree.

The whole fight lasted less than a minute.

Not even breathing hard, Barry reclaimed his camera bag and walked away. It was a point of pride not to look back to see if they were following him.

They were not.

THE Shankill Road, which styled itself the Heartland of Loyalist Ulster, hated Roman Catholics, otherwise known as Fenians, Papists, Taigs. Drummed into the citizenry since birth was the unshakeable conviction that all Catholics were heretics sworn to the destruction of Protestantism. To kill a Catholic was to kill not a fellow human being but a member of a lower species.

Yet the poor Protestant neighbourhoods around the Shankill were physically indistinguishable from the poor Catholic neighbourhoods around the Falls Road. The only difference to be seen was the ubiquitous Union Jack. The British flag flew from scores of windows and was painted on numerous walls.

By identifying himself as a photojournalist Barry was able to take pictures of several prominent loyalists. One proudly posed with a rifle cradled in his arms. "Yer gonna put me in the newspapers, right?"

Barry recalled the pride he had felt at the idea of being a sniper. With his grandfather's rifle.

That was a million years ago.

One of Barry's favourite photographs showed a slim youth and a pretty girl gazing into each other's eyes, oblivious to the world around them. The boy's open-necked shirt revealed a Cross on a chain around his neck. She wore a rayon headscarf printed with the Union Jack. In the background a man who might have been the father of either one was striding angrily toward them, waving a clenched fist.

Barry captioned the picture "Romeo and Juliet, Belfast, 1961."

LEFT to their own devices, the two communities, Protestant and Catholic, made tentative efforts toward integration. They had almost everything in common but their religions. Yet both religions contained secret societies which worked constantly to discourage any rapport with "the other side." Catholic and Protestant were kept apart by force if necessary.[2]

Politicians who had built their careers on bigotry were the only beneficiaries.

THE more time he spent in the north, the more difficult Barry found it to return to Trinity. The university seemed an artificial world where people lived greenhouse lives. Reality was sometimes brutal but that did not lessen its fascination. Barry was obsessed with the desire to show others what he had discovered: that nothing was as simple as it appeared from the outside.

Éamonn Thomas was selling more and more of Barry's photographs. It was being done quietly, attracting no attention in Ireland, but foreign news agencies were increasingly interested in the work of "Finbar Lewis." "Looks like the republican publicity bureau is up and running again," Thomas remarked to Goulding.

. . .

ON the twelfth of April, 1961, the Soviet Union put the first man into space. Twenty-seven-year-old Major Yuri Gagarin orbited the earth during a flight lasting 108 minutes, and returned safely. Elements of the American press were scathing in their denunciation of Russia for risking a man's life with what must be inferior technology.

On the fifteenth of May, Alan B. Shepherd, Jr., became the first American in space, with a fifteen-minute sub-orbital flight.

AS Barry's first year at university ended he was summoned to GHQ. "The campaign in the north doesn't seem to be going anywhere," Cathal Goulding told him. "But we have a plan to turn that around. We're going to cut a nationalist enclave out of the rest of Northern Ireland by blowing some strategically located bridges in County Fermanagh.[3] Are you up for it?"

When Barry hesitated, Goulding added shrewdly, "You're the best we have. Without you, we don't have a chance."

Barry flung back his head. Flame leapt in his eyes. "Then I'm up for it."

A room in a Dublin safe house was arranged for him while he waited for orders. When they came they were disappointing. The mission was off. "Our scouts report a number of patrols throughout the area." Goulding told Barry. He sounded bitterly disappointed. "There's been so much RUC activity along the border lately . . . well, we thought we had a chance, but maybe not. We hardly have enough locals to help us anyway, most of them are in prison. Forget about it for now, Barry. Maybe later."

Maybe later. Everything's "maybe later."

But there is something I can do now.

He paid only a brief visit to the farm before heading north again. This time he left Ned Halloran's notebooks in a bank vault in Ennis.

His destination was Derry, which he remembered from his early days in the Army. He arrived in Derry on a fine afternoon in early summer. The sky was swept free of clouds by a fresh wind. Sun-kissed light percolated through narrow streets where laughing children played the games of children.

From the moment he arrived, Barry was taking photographs.

Derry was situated in a valley traversed by the River Foyle and surrounded by gentle hills. Once, those hills had been mantled by oak trees, part of the primordial forest which had been destroyed during the Elizabethan conquest. To the north of the city glimmered the broad waters of Lough Foyle. The lake narrowed dramatically at the head, providing protection from the often violent sea off the northern coast.

"Derry" was derived from the ancient Irish word *daire,* meaning oak; a name the Irish continued to use although the city officially had been renamed Londonderry by the English. As a result of this Derry/Londonderry identity, the town was also known as "Stroke City." The nickname reflected its dual nature in more ways than one. Derry lay within County Londonderry, one of the Six, but a short distance out the Buncrana Road was County Donegal—in the Republic. Donegal considered itself as outside both the Six and the Twenty-Six. Although the people were emotionally committed to the Republic, they found much to admire in Northern Ireland. They abhorred sectarianism but appreciated the straightforward honesty of ordinary Protestants.

Like Belfast, Derry was a city divided. But in Derry the majority was Catholic. Unionist landowners and politicians made certain the Catholics never forgot they were inferior. They were contained in virtual ghettos, encircled by Protestants like thirteenth-century Marcher lords holding back the Welsh tide.

The Bogside district, which lay just below and to the west of the ancient walled city of Derry, covered nine hundred acres and was occupied by more than twenty-five thousand Catholics—half the total population of "Londonderry." Although there were some newly constructed flats, for the most part the Bogside and the nearby Creggan district, also Catholic, consisted of slums and tenements; substandard rental accommodations for people who could never hope to own their own homes.

If they did not own their homes, they could not vote in local elections.

In the Bogside, Barry chatted with unemployed men on street corners and women on their front stoops. Their humour was wry and irreverent, but there was a sweetness, a gentleness, about them in spite of generations of hardship. *They deserve better than this. God knows, they deserve better than this.*

Toward evening Barry was walking along Eastway Road in the direction of the Creggan when he heard someone shout his name—his real name—and turned around in surprise.

URSULA returned the snaffle bridle to its peg and massaged her shoulder, wincing as her fingers encountered a particularly sore spot. *Damn it to hell,* she thought resentfully. Her back, her knees, even her neck were often stiff in the morning, she who had been so agile. The right shoulder was the worst, though, a deep pervasive ache that robbed her arm and hand of strength.

The two young geldings were the best horses produced on the farm in years. With their powerful hindquarters and bold way of moving, they would appeal to wealthy Americans looking for show-quality hunter prospects. If she could have them schooling over low rails by the time of the Royal Dublin Horse Show, perhaps she could sell them both for high prices.

The geldings had been backed in the spring and accepted the saddle without major resistance, but they needed a lot of roadwork to muscle them up. More than that, neither one had much of a mouth yet. She would have to spend long hours in the saddle, fingering the reins with consummate skill, giving and taking and giving again, making constant microscopic adjustments of pressure until each horse understood the telegraphy she was transmitting. Somewhere along the way—because they were young and strong and full of life—one or both would rebel. If they did not have enough spirit to challenge her authority they would not have enough heart for a long day's hunting.

There had been a time when Ursula exulted in the feel of a young horse coiled like a spring beneath her. Matching her skill against his will. Using a subtle combination of strength and guile to convince the animal that resistance was useless. Then praising, rewarding, demonstrating the fun they could have together as long as the horse was obedient.

Such training required that the rider be in top physical condition. A horse could detect the slightest weakness and take advantage.

Ursula rubbed her shoulder again.

There was no one else she could entrust with the two geldings. Their quality demanded a talented trainer, something more than a local farm lad who would be willing to trot them down the road. *If only Barry were home . . .*

He was not as gifted with horses as Ursula, but under her expert eye he could have done the work. Instead she had just spent half an hour on the chestnut gelding, trying to convince him that she was in charge. But he knew better. He kept flicking an ear back toward her as if to read her mood, then setting himself against her hands. There was not enough strength in them to hold him. She had given up and turned him out into the paddock rather than risk an all-out battle that she was destined to lose.

Slowly she trudged back to the house.

Perhaps the shoulder would be better tomorrow.

As consciousness returned Barry received messages of distress from the outposts of his body. His mind was adrift with pain. With a deliberate effort he plunged back into the dark pit, and escape.

When he next opened his eyes he saw a balding man with the furrowed face of a bloodhound leaning over him. "How're you feeling then?"

"Fine as feathers," Barry croaked in a voice he did not recognise as his own. When he tried to sit up, fire shot along his leg and exploded in his chest.

The man eased him back down onto the bed. "You'll not be going anywhere for a while. Just lie still, you're safe enough for now."

Split lips and an aching jaw made it an effort to speak. "What happened?"

"I was hoping you could tell me. I found you lying all in a heap in a doorway. At first I thought you were dead, but when you groaned I brought you straight here, I couldn't leave you in the street. A job I had of it too; you're a mountain, you are."

"Where are we?"

"My house. It's only a stone's throw from where I found you."

Focussing on the man bending over him, Barry saw a clerical collar. "You're a priest?"

"I am a priest. Father Aloysius at your service." The man smiled, causing his face to fall into still more pleats. "From your accent, I'd say you're from the south."

"County Clare." Barry closed his eyes for a moment.

"Clare. And your name is . . . ?"

My name is . . . A cognitive struggle. "Finbar. Finbar Lewis."

"Shall I fetch a doctor, Finbar? Or would you rather go to hospital?"

"No hospital," Barry said quickly. *Helpless in a hospital in Northern Ireland? No way.* "How bad am I hurt?"

"I think you have some broken ribs, there's an almighty lump on the side of your head, and your left leg looks like it's smashed."

"Jaysus." A momentary nausea racked Barry. "It feels like that too. Plus there's a terrible pain in my back."

"Do you want me to have a look?"

"Please."

Father Aloysius eased Barry onto his side and pulled his clothing out of the way. Even the slightest movement hurt, but Barry gritted his teeth and made no sound.

"Almost the whole of your back is black and purple," the priest reported. "And there are some marks . . . you've been kicked in the kidneys by someone wearing steel-toed shoes, I've seen it before. They probably knocked you in the head, then battered you as you lay on the ground. It looks like you put up a fight before you went down, though. Your knuckles are badly bruised. All in all, I'd say you're lucky to be alive. A weaker man might have died from a beating like this."

Barry's stunned mind was beginning to work in fits and starts. He recalled hearing his name—*My real name!*—and then several men—half a dozen, maybe seven, not wearing uniforms—came running toward him. *B-Specials?* The nausea was growing worse. *I fought back.* He held on to that small consolation. *I fought back!* In his mouth there was a taste of blood. "Perhaps you'd best fetch a doctor," he whispered to the priest.

"Will you be all right if I leave you alone for a few minutes? My housekeeper's away for a couple of days, but I'll lock the door and be back as soon as I can."

"Thanks," Barry murmured as the darkness engulfed him.

The next time he opened his eyes two men were bending over him. One was the priest; the other was a stubby little man with a nose empurpled by broken veins. "Back with us, are you?" he asked in a curiously lifeless voice. His teeth were bad and his lustreless eyes looked like dirty marbles.

Barry felt an immediate aversion for him.

Father Aloysius said, "This man's a GP. He's come to help you."

"I don't need help. Just let me rest awhile and I'll . . ."

"You'll do nothing," said the doctor, "until we see to your injuries. John— Father Aloysius—tells me you don't want to go to hospital. Is that right?"

"Right."

"Listen to sense, young man. You may be concussed and you definitely have a couple of broken ribs. The leg's the worst, that's a compound fracture. We could set it here, I suppose; John could help me. But you'd be much better off in hospital where—"

"No hospital," Barry growled through clenched teeth. "I mean it." He glared at the doctor.

"All right," the man said reluctantly, "but you may regret it. There are fractures both above and below the knee. A shard of bone's actually pierced your trousers. Looks like they beat you with clubs—or an iron bar. I can't think how they missed shattering the kneecap. Maybe there was so much blood, they thought they had."

Barry made another desperate effort to get up. The two men gently pushed him back down. "None of that now."

How do I know this man's a doctor? I have only the priest's word for it, but is Father Aloysius really a priest? Wearing a dog collar doesn't prove anything. I could buy clerical garb myself. Barry's head was swimming. There was a maddening buzzing in his ears.

During the ordeal of straightening the bones and setting the leg, he fought with all his strength to remain conscious. At last the doctor stepped back and mopped his forehead. "Now don't move until that plaster hardens, young man. I believe there's some ligament damage, but I'm hopeful it will heal itself along with the bone. We're not out of the woods yet, though. With an injury like yours there's always a chance of infection. There's also a possibility that the blood could form a pool in your calf muscle, in which case we'd have no option but to put you in hospital. You could lose your leg."

"I love good news," Barry croaked.

Damn it all. Damn it all to hell. Damn them all to hell.

Much of his body was now either bandaged or encased in plaster. His head was swathed in gauze with only his eyes showing.

"Your own mother wouldn't know you," Father Aloysius told him.

My own mother. God, I can't let her see me like this. "I can't stay here, Father. People are expecting me."

"And where would that be? Clare?"

"No." *Whatever you say, say nothing.*

"You'll not be fit to travel for a while, I'm afraid," the priest said. "But you're welcome to stay here as long as needs be."

What if he knows the men who attacked me? What if he's only waiting to turn me over to them? "I don't want to be any trouble."

"Ministering to the sick is part of my work, and anyway May Coogan—she's my housekeeper—will be back soon. She's good at nursing. Meanwhile, do you want me to send word to your family?"

"I don't have any family." *What a fool I was not to tell someone where I was going.*

"What about the people who're expecting you?"

"Just acquaintances. Not important." Barry closed his eyes. With a sense of relief he heard the two men leave the room.

Several times during the night Father Aloysius brought a bucket into which Barry pissed a stream of what looked like pure blood. The doctor was there first thing next morning to check on his condition. "How're you feeling now?"

Barry's head was pounding and his entire body hurt more than he would have thought possible. "I'm wonderful entirely," he said. "How long until my leg heals?"

"If nothing goes wrong? The bones will take twelve weeks to mend if you're lucky and there are no complications. It may be a year before you can walk normally, though—if you ever do. I believe I mentioned the possibility of ligament damage, and there's bound to be some muscle atrophy."

For another day and night it was impossible to concentrate on anything but fighting the pain. The doctor left tablets for him, but Barry was unwilling to take anything which might further dull his mind. *Something's gone terribly wrong. Someone identified me.* He would think about it when his brain was clearer. In the meantime he dare not make himself any more vulnerable than he already was.

At least one worry was lessened when Father Aloysius's housekeeper returned from visiting her mother in Cookstown. A thin woman with lank hair but brilliant blue eyes, May Coogan assured Barry that the priest was exactly who he said he was. "I've kept house for himself since he was assigned to this parish, and you won't find a man with a better heart anywhere. You're not the first stray he's taken in off the street, you know. What happened to you? Were you robbed?"

"I had a wallet in my coat pocket and a black hold-all with two cameras in it. Did Father Aloysius find them?"

She shook her head. "He said he looked for a wallet with your name in, but there was none on you. I'll ask him about the bag, but he never mentioned it to me."

Barry had been stripped not only of his cameras but of anything identifying him as Finbar Lewis.

They called me Barry Halloran.

It might have been Special Branch; it might have been the RUC. Either way, they had known who he was. The only answer was an informer. In Belfast he was Finbar Lewis, but one of the safe houses where he stayed had demanded verification of his true identity. His description could have spread through the Six Counties as quickly as a telephone call. *And I made it easy for them by being careless.*

As his convalescence continued, so did the sleepless nights. Nights when he kept the pain at bay through sheer willpower. Father Aloysius always seemed to know, and often came in to sit by his bed. The two would talk for hours, with Barry concentrating ferociously on every word to avoid thinking about his body.

He revealed something of himself during those long pre-dawn conversations, though he was careful never to give too much away. He admitted to being "an Irish republican" without ever once saying he was a Volunteer. He talked more about his time at Trinity and his interest in photography.

"You'll be taking photographs again one of these days," Father Aloysius assured him. "You don't need two good legs to use a camera."

"No, but it would help. I have to be able to get to the subjects."

"Of course you do; I wasn't thinking. I'll say a prayer every day for your total recovery, my son."

Barry was grateful to the priest. He even liked him. But although he called him "Father" he could not accept him as someone holy. Ursula Halloran's opinion of priests had insinuated itself into her son's subconscious like a worm into an apple.

Still, he would be sorry to say good-bye. The shabby little house, the kindly priest, the solicitous housekeeper who learned to make tea as strong as he liked it—even the floral pattern of the wallpaper in his room—had become familiar and comforting.

Chapter Twenty

THE young man sat stiffly upright on his seat. Occasionally the jolting of the train made him wince. His left leg in its plaster cast protruded far into the aisle. Every time someone edged past the obstacle he offered a low-voiced apology. After the train crossed the border into the Republic he unwrapped the bandages from his head. Without them he felt strangely naked, but more like himself again.

The money to buy his train ticket had been loaned to him by the doctor with the dead voice and lustreless eyes. His name, Barry had learned, was Terence Roche. He and Father Aloysius had been schoolboys together in the Bogside. In spite of his repellent appearance Terry Roche was kind and caring. *And I'm a damned poor judge of character,* Barry told himself reproachfully.

Roche had visited Barry several times a day. When he learned that his patient had lost his money, he said, "Don't worry about paying me. You have enough on your plate."

Making conversation while his dressings were being changed, Barry had asked Roche which hospital he used. The man replied, "I don't have privileges in any of them."

"Are you not a qualified doctor?"

"Oh yes, I'm fully qualified, I can show you my certificates. But I'm a Catholic."

"There must be some Catholic doctors in the hospitals here."

"A few," Roche conceded. "If they're willing to kowtow to the authorities and limit their patients to Catholics only."

"That's ridiculous."

"You think so? For us it's normal. My father trained as a telephonist and got himself appointed to Stormont, but when the minister for home affairs learned there was a Catholic on the switchboard, he refused to use the telephone for government business. My father had to be transferred."[1]

In spite of the care he was receiving, as soon as the pain was bearable Barry announced that he was going to leave.

"I strongly advise against it," Roche said, "until you're much farther along in the healing process. You could do irreversible damage to your leg. You have an iron constitution, but that doesn't mean you can disregard something so serious."

Barry was adamant. There was only one place he wanted to be right now, only one person he wanted to see.

At his insistence the doctor had put a metal fitting on the bottom of his cast to make it a "walking cast"—"This doesn't mean you can put any weight on that leg, though, so don't try,"—and equipped Barry with a pair of crutches. His ribs remained tightly bound.

A fortnight later Barry was on his way back to the Republic. He had no intention of going to the farm. Seeing him in his current condition would give his mother all the ammunition she needed. Tucked away in his bed upstairs, closely watched by Ursula and fussed over by Eileen, he would be trapped.

Prison would almost be preferable. What did Cathal Goulding say about the Curragh? Oh yes. "Where else could a fellow spend all his time with friends of a like mind?"

No girls, of course. But if Mam had me under her eye every minute there would be damned little opportunity for girls anyway.

THE pub in Ballina had not changed appreciably in decades and would not change for decades more. The air was still blue with cigarette smoke. What appeared to be the same six or seven men sat at the bar, discussing the affairs of the world or staring into their drinks. The floor was covered with more or less the same sawdust. The old hammer still hung from its frayed rope. With his back to the bar, the bald-headed man was wiping the discoloured mirror.

"Séamus McCoy been in here today?"

"Never heard of him," the bald man said without turning around.

"Would he be upstairs, d'ye think?"

"I told you," the bartender said truculently as he turned around, "I never . . ." He paused. Looked hard at the tall, haggard man leaning heavily on crutches, with one leg in a cast almost to the groin. "Is it yourself?"

Barry gave a rueful smile. "I'm not sure."

"Neither am I," the bartender retorted. "But I can tell you there's no one upstairs. If you want to wait, he might come in later. Sit over there and I'll bring your drink down to you. A pint, isn't it?"

Barry leaned his crutches against a table and gratefully eased himself onto a chair. When the pint with its creamy head was set on the table in front of him he took out the last coins he had. The bartender refused them: "Your money's no good here."

"Thanks." Barry left the coins on the table anyway.

His whole body ached. The effort to hitch a ride from Limerick to Ballina had exhausted what little remained of his strength. He looked longingly at the sawdust-strewn floor, wondering what the bartender would say if he just lay down.

Then the door opened and Séamus McCoy came in.

His reaction to Barry's appearance was the same as the bartender's.

Without asking any questions, he put Barry's arm across his shoulders and half carried the larger man to the room upstairs. Only when the door was closed and bolted behind them did McCoy ask, "What in God's name happened to you?"

Barry told him as best he could.

"And you've no idea who attacked you?"

"Only a hunch. I think it might be Special Branch."

"When I learned what you were doing, I confess I was none too happy about it. I told 'em as much at GHQ. They were taking a chance letting you go back across the border alone."

"They thought it was worth the risk."

"I'm not saying it wasn't. We've all risked as much and more. The question is, What to do with you now?"

Barry had been asking himself the same question. "I was hoping you could suggest someplace where I can lie low until I've healed."

"Will you not go home?"

"That's the last place I want to be now. I have my own reasons, but there's also the risk of bringing trouble down on my mother."

"Aye." McCoy gave him a mock-angry scowl. "Apparently you don't mind bringing trouble to me."

Barry smiled; his ribs hurt too much to laugh. "I knew you could handle it." He felt an almost overwhelming sense of relief. He was back with Séamus McCoy. He was safe.

McCoy made the necessary arrangements. Before sundown Barry was ensconced in a house on the Killaloe side of the river, the home of a republican called Reddan. A doctor of the same persuasion had been to see him and pronounced him in good shape for the shape he was in, which was pretty bad. "We'll have the tape off your ribs as soon as they've had a chance to mend, but you're going to wear a cast for a while. If you were up in Dublin they'd put pins in that leg, but we don't have the facilities to do that down here. A good rest and plenty of nourishing food will do you a power of good, though. We can trust Mrs. Reddan to take care of you on that score."

McCoy promised to tell Éamonn Thomas where Barry was and what had happened to him. "I can get in touch with your mother, too."

"Let it be for now; I don't have to report to her. All I want at the moment is a newspaper to read and a large tin of aspirin."

ON the first of August, 1961, the Republic of Ireland applied for membership in the European Economic Community—the EEC.

On August thirteenth the last gap in the border between East and West was firmly closed: The Berlin Wall was erected.

In Ireland the partition between north and south remained firmly in place. The level of violence in the north had receded; or perhaps it simply was no longer news. But the conditions which fostered violence remained. "Sectarianism and injustice don't create peace, and peace is more than an absence of violence," as Barry remarked to Séamus McCoy.

THERE was no question of Barry's returning to university in the autumn. The doctor had taken him to Limerick for X-rays, which revealed that the damage to his leg had been extensive. He would require a protracted convalescence.

"I'll be going back to university as soon as possible," Barry told McCoy. "In the meantime I'll write to Trinity and explain that I've been injured; they don't need to know how. If I write a letter to my mother, can you arrange for it to be posted from Dublin? I want her to believe everything's normal."

"Think you can fool her?"

"People who can fool Ursula Halloran are few and far between, but I'm going to give it a damned good try. At least the big horse show at the RDS is over, so she won't have any reason to go up to Dublin for a while."

Barry's letter was carefully worded. He apologised for not having been home recently, and gave the impression that he was returning to Trinity immediately without actually saying so. He concluded the letter with a request: "Please lodge additional money to my Dublin bank account. I don't know where it all goes, but the city is twice as expensive as the country."

Ned Halloran's notebooks were still in safekeeping in the Ennis bank.

AT the September meeting of the Irish Countrywomen's Association, Ursula Halloran was one of the few who was not delighted by the possibility of Ireland's joining the EEC. "It would mean so much more money for farmers!" other women enthused. Ursula, however, was sceptical. "If you believe the politicians. But have we not learned the hard way that one cannot believe the politicians?"

"Oh, you—you're just a begrudger. You have plenty of money already."

"Indeed," Ursula said dully. "Plenty of money."

HOW did you feel the first time you were arrested, Séamus?"

"Bloody stupid and that's a fact. It was my own fault. I'd been to a friend's wake earlier in the day and I didn't keep a sharp lookout the way I usually do. The RUC drove right up beside me on the road as I was walking home, and before I knew what happened I heard the cell door slam behind me."

"How were you identified?" Barry wanted to know. "Were there constables at the wake?"

"Not a sinner. The corpse wasn't even a republican. Or a man, come to that. It was . . ." McCoy paused, coughed. "A girl I used to know."

"Oh," said Barry.

The two men were sitting in the kitchen of the Reddans' modest house beside the Shannon. Less than a half mile away was the ring fort with its crown of oak and beech trees. Barry had promised himself that as soon as the cast came off his leg, he would return there and explore the place fully. Although it could not be seen from any window of the bungalow, he could feel its presence. Calling him.

Mrs. Reddan was a cheerful woman with a shelf-like bosom. Her husband owned a pub in the village. Their seven grown children all lived within walking distance, and a caper of grandchildren rollicked through their house like rowdy puppies. The household also included a tabby cat who produced two litters of kittens every year. Peg Reddan took everything in her stride. Including an unexpected boarder.

"At least that's what we'll tell them as don't mind their own business," she said to Séamus McCoy. "The lad's a Volunteer; he don't have to pay me anything. There's always food in the larder here, one more mouth won't make any difference."

"You're a good woman, Peg."

She blushed like a schoolgirl.

Margaret Reddan had been born and raised in East Clare, married a distant cousin also named Reddan, and considered a trip to Limerick an exotic journey. But she knew everything about her home place. During Barry's convalescence she regaled him, over endless cups of tea, with local history.

"Ye were asking about that place on the river, the old fort? It's been there a thousand years or more. Brian Bóru was born there."

Brian Bóru. The splendid myths and legends which Barry had learned at Ned Halloran's knee came rushing back. What thrilling games Cuchullain and Fionn Mac Cumhaill had inspired, using a broomstick for a spear and a helmet fashioned from an old milk bucket! Brian Bóru was no myth, however; he was the real life, flesh-and-blood tenth-century king who had been the only man ever to achieve, however briefly, a united Ireland.

And to think he started here. A wave of passion swept through Barry; a desire to do great things himself, to lead armies into noble battle and restore Pearse's shining republic to what it should have been all along.

BUT he had met reality face-to-face. The past was just that: long ago and lost. Neither Ireland nor the twentieth century was simple. Barry could have wept with frustration.

Time weighed heavily on him. After he had read Mrs. Reddan's Catholic periodicals and back issues of *Ireland's Own,* he asked one of her sons to bring him books from the library.

"What are you interested in?"

"Everything," Barry assured him.

He returned with an assortment of the bland material which Church and State approved for public consumption. Amongst them was one gem: *Twenty Years A'Growing,* by Maurice O'Sullivan, the autobiography of a man who had grown up in the Blasket Islands.

From the first page Barry was transported to the lost world of Gaelic Ireland and a way of life that had vanished as recently as 1953, when the last person living on the Blaskets was removed by government order and taken to live on the Irish mainland, on the theory they would be "better off." Thus had ended the long saga of human habitation in one of the most beautiful places on earth.

O'Sullivan's book was written in the muscular yet lyrical vernacular of the peasantry. Men and women who, over many generations, had eked out a living on the Blaskets. Fishing the dangerous sea. Raising sheep on the stony soil. Elsewhere the blessings and banes of the modern age—electric light and radio and the atomic bomb—appeared, but on the Blaskets life had remained at its most elemental level. What kept people on the islands was a feeling for the land which transcended buried ancestral bones.

ON the day the cast came off Barry was horrified to see how shrunken his leg was. It looked like the diseased limb of a spindly tree, covered with a "moss" of crinkly, surprisingly grey hair.

The rest of his body was strong again, thanks to Peg Reddan's cooking, but he doubted that the pitiful leg would be able to bear his weight. He insisted on being left alone to attempt a few faltering steps.

"If ye fall down there'll be no one to pick you up," Peg warned.

"I'll pick myself up."

Three days later, and leaning heavily on his crutches, he made the journey on foot from the Reddan house to the ring fort beside the Shannon.

The path to the ancient ruin was badly overgrown. Barry used one of his crutches to beat aside the brambles. Once or twice he slipped on the muddy path. *If I fall down here it'll be the very devil to get up again.* At last he made it safely and stood, breathing hard, at the entrance: a gap in the ivy-clad embankment.

Above his head, oak and beech flaunted their autumn leaves like ragged banners. Nettles had invaded the deep bowl of the ring fort, replacing summer's wild roses. Beyond a phalanx of reeds in the shallows the river sang.

Barry drew a deep, satisfied breath. *I belong here.*

That's what the islanders must have felt on the Blaskets. How agonising for them to have to leave.

When we have a united Ireland, will the unionists choose to go to Britain? I doubt it. This is their land too. They belong here.

Chapter Twenty-one

IN December of 1961, television—the greatest revolutionary force to hit Ireland since the arrival of Christianity—was launched in the Republic. Combined with the national radio service, it was known as Radio Telefís Éireann, or RTE. The people were assured that television brought unprecedented opportunities for education and culture. Urging the national service to provide only "good, true, and beautiful programmes," President Eamon de Valera said, "I for one will find it hard to believe that a person who views the grandeur of the heavens, or the wonders of this marvellous, mysterious world, will not find more pleasure in that than in viewing some squalid, domestic brawl or a street quarrel."[1]

HOW do you feel about going back to the north?" Séamus McCoy asked Barry.

"Are you asking for yourself, or for GHQ?"

"Headquarters," McCoy admitted, squinting through his cigarette smoke.

"I'll go back if they want me. I'd be happier, though, if I knew who I could trust once I get there," Barry said.

"You were warned about this from the very beginning, Seventeen. I know because I warned you. Paid informers are the British way. Someone in Derry grassed you, that's obvious. I don't think it was the RUC who attacked you, though, because they'd have hauled you off to jail first, then beat you senseless in private. You might have died, men have before. It's always claimed they were prisoners trying to escape. As things are, at least you're alive. Maybe you should be satisfied with that."

"Are you trying to tell me GHQ doesn't want me to go back? But I have to,

Séamus. I can't . . . I can't give up just because I got hurt. What I'm doi
portant, you believe that and I do too. I accept that my own stupidit
what happened and I'll be more careful next time. I'll buy another camera
and . . ."

"Face facts," said McCoy. "You're still limping a lot, you're going to need
crutches for a while yet."

"I'm sound enough to go back to Trinity. I'll be travelling up to Dublin next
week."

"It's one thing to sit in a classroom and another to duck and dodge in hostile
territory. I had to tell headquarters that in my opinion, you're not able for it."

"You had no right to do that, Séamus." The lightning change; the suddenly
icy eyes. "I can speak for myself. I know what I'm able for."

"And I know there's a streak of recklessness in you that could get you killed.
If you don't care about saving your own neck, I do." It was as close as McCoy
could come to an admission of affection. "There are other ways you can work
for the Army, Barry. Did you once tell Cathal Goulding that you have contacts
in the States who used to be big contributors to the IRA?"

"I might have done," Barry said guardedly. "But you know me, sometimes I
boast a bit."

"If it was just a boast, *sin a bhfuil*.* But if you do have such contacts . . . well,
the Army's in desperate need of funds. Everything's going all to hell without
money. Éamonn Thomas has sold a few of your photographs but that's only a
drop in the bucket. If you were to contact the people you referred to, and reac-
tivate their interest in the republican cause . . ." McCoy stopped. Let the words
hang in space.

*Granda's notebooks are still in the bank in Ennis. If I call in for them someone's
bound to tell Mam I'm in the area. If I go in disguise to protect my identity, the
bank won't release them to me. Damn!* "I'll see what I can do, Séamus," said
Barry. "But I warn you, it'll take time."

HE returned to Dublin to prepare for the start of the spring term. At Trinity
some mail was being held for him, consisting entirely of unpleasant letters
from his mother. She demanded to know why he had not come home for
Christmas. Then she insisted that he must come home at Easter. He ignored
them. *An Irish solution to an Irish problem,* Barry told himself. *Ignore anything
long enough and it will go away.*

He was determined that she never see him limping.

Reinserting himself into university life was awkward. He had fallen behind

*That's all.

in his studies and had to avoid numerous questions about his injury. In a short span of time some of the people he had known were gone and a new spate of undergraduates had arrived. To his surprise, however, his old room in the Rubrics was available. "We had to reassign it when you notified us you would not be here in the autumn," Barry was told, "but the chap we put in has asked to be moved. It seems he can't get along with Mr. Fitzmaurice."

Barry gave a slight smile. "Not everyone's cup of tea, Mr. Fitzmaurice. But I'll take the room."

When he entered, Gilbert was lying on the bed reading. He looked up but never seemed to notice that Barry was using a cane, much less to comment on it. "Thank God you're back, Halloran. The last fellow who was in here was a total bore. He never listened to a word I said."

"Astonishing."

"Isn't it?" Gilbert went back to his book.

The next day Barry went to the bank. From the moment he entered the building his limp was acute. At the front desk he asked for the official who had arranged his account.

The man's eyes widened in sympathy when he saw the cane. Barry said, "I've had rather a nasty accident and I'm not able to travel, but I have some things in safekeeping in Ennis which I really do need. I was wondering . . ."

"If we might handle that for you, Mr. Halloran?" The banker arranged his features in an amiable smile. Barry had caused no problems, which was more than one could say for many university students. "I believe we can oblige you. Give me the information and a signed letter in your own hand, authorising your bank in Ennis to release the material to us. We'll have them send it here by courier."

Barry was relieved. "I wasn't sure it was possible. I know that banks have strict rules."

"This is Ireland, Mr. Halloran. Something can always be arranged, even with a bank. Now . . . may we expect the lodgements to your account to continue?"

A few days later Barry visited the bank to collect a parcel wrapped in brown paper and tied with strong twine. His name was scrawled across the paper seals. At a stationer's in Nassau Street he bought a metal strongbox advertised as fireproof. The box would just fit beneath his bed in the Rubrics.

Gilbert Fitzmaurice had many faults, but his self-absorption was so intense that he would never bother to go through anyone else's things.

Dear Ursula,

When I entered university I hoped to become an architect. But architecture does not seem very relevant in today's Ireland. Your friend Henry Mooney was a newspaperman in Ireland before he emigrated, and most of my friends here, the people I enjoy talking to and being with, are journalism students. So I have decided to enter the field of photojournalism.

I could apprentice myself to a local photographer, then apply for a staff job on one of the newspapers. That's how some men do it. But I already know how to use a camera and besides, I want to work freelance. Independence is important to me. What I really need is a degree in journalism from Trinity. That would be the best possible foundation I could have before launching myself on the unsuspecting world.

Unfortunately there would be quite a few additional expenses involved in changing courses. But I have been giving this a lot of thought, Ursula, and am convinced it would be right for me. I hope you will agree.

Barry waited apprehensively for Ursula's reply. If she disapproved of this latest step—which he had tried to ameliorate by the reference to Henry Mooney—she might cut off his money.

Her response when it came was not what her son had expected.

"I support whatever decision you make, and will arrange for additional funds to be sent to your Dublin bank at once."

He would never know how painful it was for his mother to write those words. She was accepting that he was his own man; it was the final cutting of the cord.

Barry celebrated by buying a new camera. Not as fine as the lost Leica, but serviceable.

IN journalism he found his metier. But he was still a Volunteer; he never thought of himself any other way.

Throughout the spring he worked on decoding the names and addresses in Ned's notebooks. After the first five it was very difficult. Ned had changed the key again and again, according to no pattern Barry could discover. Grimly determined, he kept working his way through. There were hundreds of names. Even if many of them were no longer still alive, there would surely be some who could be re-enrolled in the cause.

Late at night, when most people in the Rubrics were asleep, Barry sat at the small desk in his room with a notebook open in front of him.

"Turn that feckin' light off," Gilbert Fitzmaurice snarled. "Don't you know I need my rest?"

There was more work to be done than just decoding. Barry tried out a dozen different draft letters, trying to find just the right words to encourage the recipient to renew support for the IRA. When Barry finally had a draft he liked he took it to Éamonn Thomas. Thomas tore it apart. "Start over and don't sound so posh. Talk to them like real people. Remember that we need every shilling we can lay hands on. We're all trying to raise funds, but if we don't get a lot more money soon, we may have to disarm altogether and wait for better times."

Barry revised and rewrote the draft letter until Thomas was satisfied. He described in graphic detail the situation in the north. A small assortment of telling photographs would be included. Thomas would rent a post office box in a Dublin suburb to receive the replies. "I only hope they come in time to make a difference," he said gloomily.

"Do you think they'd have more impact if I wrote them longhand?"

"It couldn't hurt. People like the personal touch."

Barry added the task to his workload. Less sleep, bleary eyes, a cramped hand. *But it doesn't matter, I'm doing it for the Army.*

The first off-campus assignment for the new journalism students was to attend a press conference. Dr. Conor Cruise O'Brien, an Irish politician seconded to the United Nations, had provoked a storm of controversy when he ordered UN forces in Katanga to suppress the province's cessation from the Congo. In December of 1961 Dr. O'Brien had been released from United Nations service in circumstances that remained unclear. He claimed to have resigned; the UN said his removal had been requested by the Irish government. Dr. O'Brien had not returned to Ireland, but a statement purporting to clarify the matter was going to be read from the steps of Leinster House.

It was only a short stroll from Trinity to Leinster House, the seat of government in Dublin. Barry walked in company with Dennis Cassidy and another first-year journalism student, Alice Green. Cassidy was a dark, sturdily built young man; one of the small minority of Catholics at the college. Barry suspected Cassidy also had republican leanings, though they had never discussed politics. He was wary of bringing up the subject for fear of revealing too much about himself.

Both men were mildly infatuated with Alice, a plump blonde with creamy skin and an infectious giggle. On the way to Leinster House she walked between Barry and Dennis, linking their arms with hers. "Did you know," she said, "that Dr. O'Brien's getting a divorce so he can marry some woman who went with him to the Congo? She was part of the Irish delegation to the UN, but she resigned when he was fired."

"That's just gossip," Dennis told her. "Besides, we don't know that he was fired. 'Speculation is not journalism,' remember?"

Alice giggled. "But it's ever so much more fun. Imagine the staid old Irish running amok in a hot climate."

Barry glanced down at the girl. "Do you ever think of running amok?"

"Why, Mr. Halloran. Whatever are you suggesting?"

"What would you like me to suggest?"

"Hold on there, Barry," Dennis interrupted. "Are you propositioning my girl right under my nose?"

"She's not under your nose, she's on my right arm. And I don't hear her complaining."

Alice looked from one to the other. Barry was imposingly tall and undeniably handsome. Although he was self-conscious about his limp, she did not mind. She thought the cane he carried made him look rather distinguished. But Alice doubted that any man who looked like Barry Halloran would be receptive to her charms. Women probably threw themselves at him all the time.

She turned to Dennis, who was just an ordinary man. An attainable man. "Am I your girl?" she asked sweetly.

Dennis squeezed the little hand tucked into the bend of his arm. "You'd better be. I have plans for you."

Barry looked away. *Why would any girl prefer me to a man with two good legs?* He told no one at Trinity the true cause of his limp, giving instead the impression that his leg had been broken in a riding accident. "My mother raises horses, you know, and I ride the young colts for her."

In spite of the good care he had received during his time in Killaloe, Dr. Roche's warning had proved accurate. Barry's leg had not healed well. He was beginning to worry that the limp might be permanent. When he mentioned this to Dennis Cassidy, the other man assured him, "You're trying to rush things, that's all. Trust me, your limp is minuscule."

"It seems majuscule to me," Barry said, trying to laugh.

The injury had changed everything. No longer did he play hockey, or go for long walks in the rain with pretty girls. Since returning to university Barry had not spent any time alone with a girl. He did not want their pity any more than he wanted it from his mother.

When he thought about Claire MacNamara—and he still did think about her, more often than he liked—he schooled himself to feel angry rather than sorrowful. She had let him down by failing to keep in touch. As long as he could hold on to that feeling it kept the pain of rejection at bay.

Barry had his studies to keep him occupied and, more important, he had his mission. The letters to America. The precious notebooks. And he had friends. Friends like Dennis and Alice were safe; nothing was going to happen to them.

On the twenty-sixth of February, 1962, the IRA issued the following formal statement:

To the Irish people.
The leadership of the resistance has ordered the termination of the Campaign of Resistance to British Occupation launched on December 12, 1956. Instructions issued to Volunteers of the Active Service Units and of local Units in the occupied area have now been carried out. All arms and other material have been dumped and all full-time active service Volunteers have been withdrawn.

The decision to end the Resistance Campaign has been taken in view of the general situation. Foremost among the factors motivating this course of action has been the attitude of the general public whose minds have been deliberately distracted from the supreme issue facing the Irish people—the unity and freedom of Ireland.

The Irish Resistance Movement renews its pledge of eternal hostility to the British Forces of Occupation in Ireland. It calls on the Irish people for increased support and looks forward with confidence to the final and victorious phase of the struggle for the full freedom of Ireland.[2]

Barry read the statement published in the papers with a sinking heart. *All those years of planning and work and sacrifice; of death and hope. The guns dumped, the Volunteers going back to private life, and Ireland still divided. It doesn't seem possible.*

He went to Éamonn Thomas. "Is this really true? If so, what will become of the Army?"

"Didn't you read the last paragraph of that statement? Don't you worry, as long as part of this country's occupied by a foreign power, there'll be a reason for the IRA. And the IRA will always need good publicity, so there'll be a place for you too."

"Have there been any replies to my letters, Éamonn?"

"Not a sausage, but it's early days still. If some money does come in we'll hold it for the future. There will be a future, you know."

AT the end of the spring term Barry had to face the prospect of returning to the farm. He could not stay at Trinity through the long hiatus from July to October; the campus would be taken over by private study groups and visiting academics. Nor would he be going north with his cameras. And he felt sure that Ursula would not be willing to fund rented digs in Dublin. He could just hear her: "You have a perfectly good home right here on the farm."

Barry hated the power that money, or the lack of it, could exert. He resolved to become self-sufficient as soon as possible.

The train ride from Dublin to Clare was not as uncomfortable as his last train journey had been. Barry put his cane in the overhead rack, and gazed out the window at rural Ireland. Beneath a blue summer sky blue barrels of poison waited to be sprayed on the potato drills, a modern preventative for the blight that had destroyed the last vestiges of ancient Ireland.

As Barry entered the Halloran farmhouse—through the front door, like a stranger—he glanced into the parlour on his left and saw a television set next to the wireless.

"I'm home!" he called. There was no answer. He called again, more loudly. "Is anyone here?"

He slammed the door behind him.

The sound echoed through the house like a closing lid echoing inside the coffin.

Chapter Twenty-two

BARRY stood perfectly still, every sense alert.

In living memory he had not known the big old farmhouse to be so quiet. Usually it hummed with the invisible currents of human habitation. Today the air was dead.

A dozen possible scenarios flashed through his brain in quick succession. The worst was that loyalists—*the faceless Enemy*—had learned where he lived and staged a reprisal against his family. Ursula and Eileen might be lying upstairs murdered in their beds.

Don't be silly, Barry admonished his pounding heart. *The loyalists don't attack people in the Republic, they find quite enough prey on their own side of the border.*

Nevertheless he made a thorough search of the house, moving as quietly as he could from room to room. Ursula could be out anywhere, of course. Riding, supervising the hired men, shopping in town. Eileen's absence was harder to explain. She hardly ever left the house except to go to Mass—*except it isn't time for Mass*—or to gossip in the kitchen of a neighbouring farm. At this hour she should be in the kitchen, preparing dinner for George and Gerry.

Barry returned to the kitchen. The first time he had been looking for Eileen and had seen nothing else. This time he noticed a gleaming new refrigerator standing against the wall, purring to itself with domestic satisfaction.

"She never got to see it," a voice remarked behind Barry.

He whirled around. Clothes caked with manure, George Ryan stood in the doorway.

Eileen would never let him in the house in that condition. "She who? Eileen? Where is she? And where's my mother?"

"At Ennis General."

Barry's stomach clenched. "What's happened to Ursula?"

Nothing. She's staying with Mrs. Mulvaney because the doctors don't expect her to last 'til nightfall."

It isn't Mam. Thank God. "What happened to her?"

"Massive stroke, they say. She fell like you'd chop down an old apple tree. Yesterday morning, that was; about an hour before they delivered that contraption over there. It was to be a surprise for Mrs. Mulvaney but she never got to see it."

URSULA notified Eileen's far-flung children by telephone. Her married daughters, who lived elsewhere in Ireland, promised to make their way to the farm as soon as they could. Her sons in Australia had good jobs, but said they could not possibly come . . . unless perhaps Ursula would pay the air fare?

She did not take the bait. She would be paying for the hospital and the funeral and the gravestone. Her account books, which had been precariously balanced for some time, were about to go into the red.

The funeral was one of the largest held in Ennis that year. Barry was astonished at how many people turned out to mourn his great-aunt. Only a fraction of them could have known her personally, but everyone knew who Ursula Halloran was. Besides, as Gerry Ryan remarked to Barry, "We all love a good funeral."

Eileen was buried with her rosary beads laced through her fingers. Ursula placed half a dozen of her favourite holy pictures in the coffin with her. "It's what she would want."

Later she burned the rest.

URSULA and Barry did not have a real conversation until a few days after the funeral, when everyone had gone home and they had the house to themselves.

Ursula looked wan and tired as she attempted to prepare breakfast. "I think you're supposed to start the rashers in a cold skillet," Barry told his mother. "And crack the eggs into a bowl first before you slide them into the pan. That way you won't break the yolks."

Gratefully, she stepped aside and let him take over. "Where'd you learn to cook?"

"I've been on my own for quite a while now, remember?"

"And by the looks of you, it hasn't been easy. Why are you using a cane? What happened to your leg?"

"Broke it. Here, you can slice the bread."

"*You broke your leg?* And you never told me?"

"What could you do about it? You're no doctor. It's healing now anyway. Make those slices thinner, will you? They'll never toast through otherwise."

Exasperated, Ursula brandished the knife and pretended to threaten him with it. "When and how did you break your leg and what else have you kept from me? Speak up now!"

"Last summer. Taking photographs."

She looked at him in disbelief. "That's preposterous."

"It's true."

"I thought you were visiting friends last summer."

"Is this a formal interrogation, Ursula?"

"I have a right to be concerned about my own son."

"And I have a right to my own life," he countered.

Her eyes narrowed. "You were with The Boys, were you not? That's how you got hurt?"

He said with perfect truth, "I haven't been on active service since I entered university."

"Then how . . . Never mind. If you don't want to tell me I shan't insist."

"Thank you." Barry offered a placating smile. He would not give in, though. Could not let her dig and dig into him the way she had when he was a child. It was a matter of principle.

In silence, she finished slicing the bread.

In silence, he cooked the rashers and eggs.

When they were sitting at the table he noticed her eyes slide past him and fix on the refrigerator. "That's all she wanted," Ursula said in a low voice. "With ice cubes. Why did I wait so long?"

THE Irish people were not prepared for the images of radically different ways of life that were beginning to appear on their television screens. Nineteen sixty-two saw the introduction of a new Saturday-night programme on Telefís Éireann. *The Late Late Show* was presented by Gay Byrne, who had a more than passing resemblance to the popular image of a leprechaun, and from its inception both shocked and delighted its audience with an unfailingly iconoclastic approach.

In July, Barry and Ursula watched the first programme together. A sort of armed truce existed between them that summer. They could discuss a television programme objectively, but they could not talk about anything personal. Barry was unwilling to give his mother access to his private life. After all, she never discussed hers, nor told anyone anything about her financial situation.

We Hallorans play our cards close to our vests, Barry thought, remembering Gerry Ryan's words so long ago.

Long silences were commonplace at the kitchen table.

Once, when the figures in the account book had given her another sleepless night, Ursula tried a trial balloon. "I don't suppose you can ride a horse now, not with your leg."

ᴗarry grinned. "I wouldn't care to ride without it."

"I'm serious. Can you still ride, do you think? If I put you on one of the young horses would you be able for him?"

The grin vanished. "Not yet. Someday, of course. But not yet."

BARRY'S thoughts drifted like autumn leaves across the landscape. Summer was drawing to a close and soon he would return to university. *Thank God.* There was a stiffness in the atmosphere of the house which had never been there before. Barry wondered if all adult children were as alienated from their parents as he felt. He would have preferred a more open relationship with Ursula but it did not seem possible. *She's Ned Halloran's daughter after all; Ned of the notebooks and the secrecy.*

And I'm his grandson.

He was still decoding names and writing letters which he surreptitiously gave to Gerry Ryan to post from Ennis. He looked forward to returning to Dublin and learning the extent of his success so far. There had to be some success. What he was doing had to be of value to the Army.

When he could get away without Ursula seeing him, Barry went to a far corner of the farm and practiced walking without the cane. Forcing his muscles to normalcy. Up hill and down. Clambering over rocks. Jogging. Then running, which was agonising at first.

With clenched jaw and impassive expression, he willed himself to ignore the pain.

Ignore anything long enough and it will go away.

WHEN Barry next walked through the front gateway at Trinity College he did not limp.

As soon as he was settled in, he went to see Éamonn Thomas. "We've had some replies to your letters," Thomas said, though he did not seem as happy about it as Barry would have expected. "Several of them included money."

"That's a good sign, isn't it? I knew we still had friends in the States. I'll write more letters, I'll . . ."

"I'm afraid that won't solve our problems, Barry. The Army Convention's this month, you know, and there's sure to be trouble. Remember what I told you about the divisions in the Army between the old guard—the Curragh Camp men—and the newer Volunteers?"

"I do remember."

"It was obvious that the northern campaign had run its course, but there was a lot of bitterness about the order to dump arms. Tom Gill, who's a close friend of mine, made a speech at the Wolfe Tone Commemoration. He insisted it was a step forward, not backwards,[1] but that didn't satisfy many of the active service crowd. There's not much to offer them right now, though."

Thomas began ticking off a litany of woes on his fingers. "The Army's in disarray and Sinn Féin's no better off. The *United Irishman* has rising debts and falling circulation. The National Graves Association's looking after our honoured dead, but what can we do for the living? Shag-all, that's what.

"The shortage of money is only a small problem compared to uncertainty about the future of the movement as a whole. I hate to have to say this, but I suppose you'd best put your letter-writing campaign on the long finger, Barry. I expect a lot of resignations at the upcoming Army Convention, and there's no predicting what will happen afterwards."

THE convention was held in a warehouse near the Dublin docks. When Barry arrived he found a sentry posted at every door. Defending the men who had sworn to defend the Republic. As the meeting progressed one Volunteer after another stood up to offer his resignation. Some said they could no longer tolerate inactivity. Others said they had had their fill of violence.

Most of the older generation had invested too much of themselves in the Army to imagine a future without it. But even amongst them there was dissension. When a delegate suggested that the IRA would receive unlimited support if it aligned itself with international communism, Éamonn Thomas leapt to his feet. "We fought the Brits long and hard for our religion. I won't hand it over to the communists!"

Many of those present, particularly the members of Éamonn's own Dublin brigade, applauded.

A few minutes later Rory Brady announced that he was going back to County Roscommon to teach. Cathal Goulding remarked, "That's a long way for you to commute to Army Council meetings."

"I'm resigning from the council."

After a momentary silence Goulding said tightly, "I think you owe us an explanation, Rory."

"Let's just say I'm disillusioned. Besides, I'm tired of life on the run. Nobody's going to bother a schoolteacher in the wilds of Bally-go-backwards. I'm not leaving the Army altogether, but don't expect to see me in Dublin anymore."

With Brady's departure the makeup of the Army Council changed substantially. By the end of the convention Cathal Goulding was chief-of-staff of the IRA.

Barry queued up with the others to shake his hand. "Good luck, Cathal."

"I don't need luck. I need a bleedin' miracle."

Éamonn Thomas and Barry left the meeting together. "Why didn't you go for the leadership?" Barry asked his friend.

"Right now the Army needs a hard man with a forceful personality. Cathal answers to that description better than I do."

"You'd have a lot of followers, though. You're certainly popular in Dublin."

Thomas smiled. "Thanks for the vote of confidence. I'm glad you didn't resign, Barry."

"I never even thought of it."

"Whatever it takes, we have to keep the IRA alive," Thomas said earnestly. "Without the Army the republican movement would be just another Old Boys' Club, and southern Ireland would become little more than an annex of Britain in spite of our so-called independence.

"From what we saw tonight, I'm convinced there's danger of a total split in the IRA. So I'm thinking of standing for president of Sinn Féin. As president I could work to separate Sinn Féin from its Army connection and make it a strictly constitutional political party. That would let the Army remain intact, with Sinn Féin offering an acceptable alternative for republicans who're against using physical force."

"What a great idea," said Barry. "Who else knows about it?"

"No one—yet. I want to test the water and see if I can get enough support in the party before I announce. Party politics is a shifting bog at the best of times."

"Not straightforward like the Army?" Barry teased. Both men laughed.

The next time they met, Thomas was deeply depressed. "My friend Tom Gill refused to support me for the presidency," he told Barry, adding poetically, "so my dream's come to nothing. Sinn Féin will go on without me as its chief, I'll just be one of the Indians."

BARRY soon slipped back into the university routine. As if planning a military campaign, he began establishing a network of contacts in the field of journalism. He was careful, however, to avoid anyone connected with *The Irish Times*.

"Why discriminate against *The Times*?" Dennis Cassidy wondered.

"Their pro-British policy gets up my nose."

"Aha. Can it be that dear old conservative Trinity's harbouring a radical?"

I may not be a good judge of people, Barry thought, *but I'm damned if I'm willing to go through life mistrusting everybody.* "Would you call a republican a radical?"

"The Americans might," said Dennis. "Their current president's a Democrat."

"I mean an Irish republican."

"Oh." Pause. "Are you one?"

"I am. Definitely anti-Treaty." Barry could go that far; he did not have to mention the IRA.

"That's all right then," said Dennis Cassidy. "My family's republican too."

"I wondered. You never said anything."

"It would take more courage than I possess to stand up in the dining hall and shout, 'Throw out the unionists!'"

"You don't have to, Dennis. Remember the words of the Proclamation? 'The Republic guarantees religious and civil liberty, equal rights and equal opportunities to all its citizens, and declares its resolve to pursue the happiness and prosperity of the whole nation and of all its parts, cherishing all the children of the nation equally, and oblivious of the differences, carefully fostered by an alien government, which have divided a minority from the majority.'"

"Whew! If I was wearing a hat I'd take it off to you, Barry. I'm republican because my parents are, but I can't quote the Proclamation. Realistically, though—it's part of the past, would you not agree? Ireland's moved on since 1916."

ON December 3, 1962, an auction was held at Dromoland Castle in County Clare to sell off the contents of the castle. The ancestral home of Brian Bóru's descendants had been purchased by an American.

Chapter Twenty-three

$$\cdot \hspace{-2pt}\text{---}\hspace{-4pt}\triangleleft\!\infty\!\triangleright\hspace{-4pt}\text{---}\hspace{-2pt}\cdot$$

BARRY went home for Christmas. He could not bear to think of Ursula rattling around in that empty house by herself. Even the Ryan brothers had kin with whom they would go to Mass and have Christmas dinner.

He hitched a ride from the train station to the foot of the farm lane, but walked the rest of the way to the farmhouse with no trace of a limp. Occasionally—usually when he least expected it—his damaged leg gave way, but most of the time he could stride as briskly as anyone else.

Dropping his suitcase at the door, he shouted, "I'm home!" This time he was not met with silence. Ursula came running down the stairs like a young girl to meet him. "Now it will truly be Christmas!"

Barry's present for his mother was an antique print of a famous racehorse called Nestor. When Ursula unwrapped her gift on Christmas Eve, a proudly lifted head and a pair of huge liquid eyes looked out at her from a gilded oval frame. An unconquerable spirit glowed in those eyes. "It's the spitting image of *Saoirse!*" she gasped.

She rarely spoke of the horse she had named Freedom, her favourite mount for many years. All Barry knew was that Saoirse was buried somewhere on the farm.

Ursula was unable to say anything else for a while. She just sat looking at the picture. At last, however, she handed a package to her son. "Here, open your present. It's a little something I bought for you at the auction at Dromoland. Papa's father used to work for the O'Briens and they were very good to him, so this is a memento of sorts."

The present was a steel engraving of a tree-crowned promontory viewed from the River Shannon. Beal Bóru.

Barry's heart leapt like a salmon rising from a deep pool. "How did you know, Ursula?"

"Know what?"

"How I feel about this place."

"I didn't know. How could I when you never tell me anything?"

She has to get the knife in, thought Barry. But nothing could spoil his delight in the gift. "Granda used to say you were fey, and I believe you are."

"Maybe we both are," she replied. "Maybe it's in the blood."

The atmosphere between them improved after that. They went to Mass together, kneeling side by side while the solemn splendour of the old miracle was celebrated once again. Barry knew, or thought he knew, that his mother no longer believed, but it was not important. The shared ritual was reassuring.

When Ursula drove Barry to the train station he promised to come home again at Easter.

ON Good Friday, 1963, the Reverend Martin Luther King, Jr., led a large march of protestors against segregation through the streets of Birmingham, Alabama, in direct defiance of the racist laws of the city.

The following day, Barry and Ursula watched the event rebroadcast on Irish television. The images on the small screen were in grainy black-and-white, yet they transmitted the intense excitement of the marchers; the sense that something momentous was happening.

Ursula was visibly moved. "They're having their own Easter Rising."

"Except they're not a military force," Barry pointed out, "they're just ordinary men and women. What we're seeing is a People's Revolt."

"None of the protesters was armed," the news presenter informed his audience. "Last year Dr. King paid a visit to India to study Mohandas Gandhi's philosophy of nonviolence, and yesterday that philosophy was demonstrated on the streets of Birmingham."

The camera panned to the ranks of grim-faced policemen lining the route of march. A close-up showed a holster on every belt and a gun in every holster. More than one man had his hand on the butt of his gun, ready to draw it as the marchers passed by, singing.

"Dr. King and some of his followers have been arrested," the presenter went on, "but they've made their point before the eyes of the world."

The eyes of the world. Watching through the lens of a camera!

Barry imagined himself behind a television camera, then discarded the idea. Television cameras were large and unwieldy and tethered by lengths of cable, and the scenes they shot were chosen by someone else. That would not suit Barry's temperament and he knew it.

He was eager to buy a still camera of a quality to replace the lost Leica. He planned to ask his mother for additional money before he left the farm, but on his last morning Ursula looked so grey and drained that he changed his mind.

"Would you not hire some additional men to help you?" he asked. "The Ryan brothers do all they can, but they're not young anymore." *And neither are you, Mam.*

"More men would cost money."

"Surely you can afford it."

"I can of course," she agreed almost too quickly. "If I wanted strangers about the place, which I don't. We're doing fine just as is."

Barry thought about offering to come home and help her himself, then discarded this idea too. *She'd be insulted. She'd think I was interfering in her business. We're getting along better now; leave it be.*

When the train pulled out of the station he looked back and saw her on the platform, waving good-bye—and wondered if he had made a mistake.

By the time Barry reached Dublin he had decided to join the ranks of university students who pored over adverts in the backs of newspapers and scoured the streets of Dublin looking for Help Wanted signs. A big, strong, able-bodied—*well, almost able-bodied*—young man should have little trouble finding work, Barry thought.

After several days he found early-morning employment as a trainee breakfast cook in the coffee shop at *Busáras,* the bus terminal designed by Michael Scott. The irony was not lost upon Barry, but his dreams of being an architect were like something from the remote past, an adolescent fantasy he had outgrown.

Like Claire MacNamara.

For some, the 1960s promised to be an era of hope and optimism. At last the economy was improving. Wages in a few areas were rising by as much as 25 percent. Irish fashion was a growth industry. Skirts were going up with the economy and there was a definite youth culture. Two lads in their twenties, Peter and Mark Keaveney, had opened a hairdressing salon in Grafton Street that was setting a new standard for contemporary style.

Alice Green worked on Saturdays in Switzer's Department Store. Dennis Cassidy was an usher in the Adelphi Cinema at night and on weekends. "Alice and I don't get to see much of each other these days outside of class," he confided to Barry, "but we're saving to get married, so it's worth it."

The times were not improving for everyone. Recently a tenement had collapsed in Dublin's inner city, killing two small children. Public housing was a disgrace, with both Church and State telling mothers that they could not get on a waiting list for housing unless they had at least five children. On the outskirts of the city impoverished families lived in rotting wooden caravans where they were prey to every known disease.

Barry did not need to go to Northern Ireland to find subjects. Wherever he went in Dublin he took his camera with him, trying to capture the city in one specific moment in time.

ON the third of June, 1963, one of the most popular popes in the history of the Roman Catholic Church died. The world mourned John XXIII, man of the people, genuine reformer, humble saint. In his will he bequeathed to the surviving members of his family less than twenty dollars each—which represented his entire personal fortune.

During John's papacy a thaw had begun in the relations between Catholics and Protestants in the north. A few unionist leaders had begun to discard sectarian slogans. Upon the death of the pope, Terence O'Neill, who had recently become prime minister of Northern Ireland, sent an unprecedented letter of condolence to the Catholic primate of Ireland. Protestant church leaders also expressed their condolences. The lord mayor of Belfast ordered the Union Jack flying over City Hall to be flown at half-mast.

One man chose to be mightily offended by these gestures of reconciliation. Ian Paisley was a fundamentalist preacher who had founded his own church, the Free Presbyterian. For years the Reverend Paisley had done his utmost to foment anti-Catholic prejudice. His thundering rhetoric appealed to the worst in a tiny minority of northern Protestants. In 1956 he reputedly was associated with the kidnapping and proselytising of a fifteen-year-old Catholic girl.[1] At a rally three years later he whipped his followers to such a frenzy that a mob attacked and destroyed a Catholic-owned chip shop on the Shankill Road.

In the death of Pope John, Paisley found an opportunity. At a meeting of the Ulster Protestants Association, a small group which he controlled, he called O'Neill and the Protestant church leaders "the Iscariots of Ulster," and assured his audience that Pope John, whom he described as a "Romish man of sin,"[2] was now suffering the torments of hell. Spellbound listeners were treated to vivid descriptions of the pope's skin crackling as the flames licked his body.

The mesmerising performance was talked about for weeks afterwards. Like a stone dropped into a pond, the ripple of Paisleyism extended outward in concentric circles.

Unfortunately for Terence O'Neill, his Ascendancy background played into their hands. In Northern Ireland, symbol triumphed over substance. Had O'Neill been able to articulate his moderate policies in a populist style he might have carried the majority with him. But he spoke with an upper-class English accent guaranteed to alienate him from working-class Protestants—Paisley's growing power base.

At a moment when some of the old wounds might have been healed, instead they were exacerbated.

A dozen or so loyalists, most of them ex-British army, regularly met in the

Standard Bar in the Shankill Road. Reacting to Ian Paisley's furious condemnation of Terence O'Neill's perceived "sell-out to the nationalists," they decided to form a new militia. Taking the name of an earlier organisation that had been wiped out during World War One in the Battle of the Somme, they called themselves the Ulster Volunteer Force.

ON the twenty-third of June, the Reverend Martin Luther King, Jr., led 125,000 people on a Freedom Walk in Detroit, Michigan.

ON the twenty-sixth, John F. Kennedy arrived in Ireland. For four days he travelled around the country, receiving a rapturous welcome everywhere. There was great excitement at Trinity over the American president's visit. He was young, too, and intelligent and charismatic and *Irish!*

Gilbert Fitzmaurice, who had vague connections with someone in government, was given two reserved seats in the visitors' gallery in Leinster House to hear Kennedy address Dáil Éireann. To Barry's surprise, Gilbert offered one of the seats to him.

"Do you mean it? You must have some friend who . . ."

"Do you want one or not?"

Barry did not need to be asked twice. *Maybe the poor wanker doesn't have any friends. Come to think of it, I've never see him with anyone.* "You're a good skin, Gilbert," he said. "I appreciate it."

Gilbert ducked his head. " 'S nothing at all. Don't mention it."

Why, he's embarrassed! I'll bet he's never done anyone a favour before.

Barry sat beside his roommate in the packed visitors' gallery. From his first words, John Kennedy had his audience in the palm of his hand. "Sure he's as Irish as the rest of us," someone whispered.

Kennedy remarked that if Ireland had been as prosperous a hundred years earlier, his great-grandfather might never have left. In that case he could be sitting amongst the members of the Dáil today. His listeners smiled and nodded to one another. Kennedy went on to say that if the current president of Ireland had never left Brooklyn, it might be de Valera standing before them making the speech.

There was a gale of appreciative laughter.

From his place in the gallery Barry caught his first glimpse of the legendary Eamon de Valera. The man whose portrait hung on many Irish walls beside that of the pope. The man his mother blamed for so much that had gone wrong in Ireland.

At eighty-one de Valera retained the towering height that made him instantly recognisable. His broad shoulders had borne the burdens of the nation longer than any other living man. He wore old-fashioned steel-rimmed spectacles and carried his head slightly tilted forward, in a permanent attitude of listening. His deeply furrowed features appeared mask-like in repose, perhaps due to his near blindness, but when he smiled at Kennedy's remarks he smiled with his whole face.

De Valera doesn't look arrogant and vindictive, thought Barry. *He looks like an old man who has survived a stormy life and come at last into safe harbour.*

WORKING the early-morning shift at Busáras meant rising in the dark and hurrying across the Liffey, then hurrying back to Trinity in time for his first class. Barry was thankful that he had schooled himself to get by with little sleep. As soon as he had enough money for a new camera he went shopping. The first camera store he approached had a sign in the window: ASSISTANT MANAGER NEEDED.

What do I know about managing a retail shop? Nothing at all. But I know how to learn.

Barry strode into the shop with an engaging smile and an aura of self-confidence. Within half an hour he had a new Leica and the promise of a job. *Assistant manager* was a glorified term for a salesclerk, but the position carried considerable responsibility because the only other person working in the shop was the owner—who was eager to spend more time off the premises. Barry would be in sole charge for much of every day.

He wrote to Ursula, "If you do not need me at home I shall stay in Dublin this summer. I have a very responsible job here as soon as the term is over, and have found a nice flat close-by."

In the kitchen of the farmhouse, Ursula read Barry's letter twice. "That's it then," she said to the empty room. The single cup of tea on the table, the solitary plate. "My eaglet has flown, and I'm glad." She swallowed hard. "For his sake, I'm glad."

Barry's new home was not actually a flat. It was a bedsit in a boardinghouse near Harold's Cross. Furnished with a couch that unfolded into a bed, the one room also contained a small dining table and chairs, a comfortable armchair, a writing desk, and a washbasin. A bay window overlooked the street.

The large, yellow brick boardinghouse had once been a private residence. Like its owner, the house had seen better days. Mr. Philpott, a small, bespectacled man with a raspy voice and fluttering hands, was the last in his line, inheritor of a piece of property that he could not keep without renting out rooms. He occupied a private apartment on the ground floor. There was no Mrs. Philpott.

"At the present time we have seven paying residents here," he told Barry. "I manage this property myself and insist that my boarders abide by the rules." He ticked these off on his fingers. "I only accept gainfully employed gentlemen.

There are to be no women in the rooms, ever. Sheets are changed every fortnight. Two fresh towels are provided at the same time. There is an extra charge for a three-course Sunday dinner if wanted. A resident may have one invited guest for that, if I am informed two days in advance." At this point he ducked his head and shyly confided, "I do all the cooking myself, you know. I make quite a decent Dublin Coddle." Then, crisp and businesslike again:"Now tell me, Mr. Halloran, will you be wanting one bath a week, or two?"

One week in the camera shop convinced Barry that the retail trade was not his life's calling. Eight hours a day, five and a half days a week, confined within the same four walls. People asking the same questions, complaining about the same problems, misunderstanding the precise instructions he gave so patiently.

The IRA was not alone in limbo. Barry had the same feeling.

Everything was so clear in the beginning. I became a Volunteer to help restore the Republic. Then I was planning to get married and become an architect and my life was more complicated, but I still thought I knew where it was going. Then architecture gave way to photojournalism and now I'm trying to sell cameras to people who want to take pictures of their grandchildren.

But I have to support myself, Barry argued with the voice in his head. *This isn't forever, it's just until . . . until what?*

As he left the camera shop one evening, he was so preoccupied that a girl walked across the footpath a few yards in front of him and disappeared down a laneway before he really noticed her. When her image registered in his mind's eye, it was too late. He sprinted after her, but she had disappeared.

Claire! Was it really you?

Barry systematically quartered and searched the area, going up one street and down the next, peering into shops, even knocking on the doors of houses to ask if a Miss MacNamara was there. Most people were polite, but all told him no.

It was dark by the time he returned, crestfallen, to his room.

I thought I'd forgotten her. But I haven't.

Living in a boardinghouse helped assuage his loneliness. There usually was lively conversation in the front parlour in the evenings, though it lacked the dimensions of an Army chin-wag. One of Barry's fellow boarders could be relied upon to get a debate going. As Philpott remarked, "He's a great argufier, that one. He may not always believe what he says himself, but he'll contradict you for the fun of it and then fight his corner passionately."

Barry laughed. "That just proves he's Irish."

The camera shop where he worked also sold radios and television sets. When he arrived each morning his first task was to turn on a television and adjust the picture. He lowered the volume so the sound was not distracting. Customers were most likely to buy the first model they saw "alive."

On the twenty-eighth of August the largest civil rights demonstration in history was held in Washington, D.C. Martin Luther King, Jr., addressed a quar-

ter of a million people from the steps of the Lincoln Memorial. Part of his televised speech was replayed in Ireland on the noon news broadcast the following
day. There were no customers in the camera shop just then, so Barry turned up
the volume.

"Let us not seek to satisfy our thirst for freedom by drinking from the cup
of bitterness and hatred," King urged the vast crowd.

A noble aspiration, thought Barry, *but is it possible? Isn't the result of oppression always bitterness and hatred?*

"We must forever conduct our struggle on the high plane of dignity and
discipline."

That was the intention of the Irish Republican Army, too. In the beginning.

"We must not allow our creative protest to degenerate into physical violence."

*Easy enough for you to say, Dr. King. You never had to deal with the Orange Or-
der and the RUC.*

"And as we walk, we must make the pledge that we shall always march
ahead. We cannot turn back."

No, Barry agreed. *We cannot turn back.* He was listening intently now,
caught up in the spell of brilliant oratory.

"I have a dream," King was saying, "that one day every valley shall be ex-
alted, every hill and mountain shall be made low."

Oh yes, Dr. King; we know about dreams in Ireland.

". . . Jews and Gentiles, Protestants and Catholics, will be able to join hands
and sing in the words of the old Negro spiritual . . ."

Barry felt the hair rise on the back of his neck. Intuitively, he knew what the
song would be. He had heard Pearl and Opal sing it in Dallas.

"Free at last! Free at last! Thank God Almighty, we're free at last!"

Chapter Twenty-four

THE meaning of King's speech slowly percolated through the consciousness of oppressed minorities everywhere—including the Catholics of Northern Ireland.

In homes and offices in the Republic, pictures of John Kennedy hung beside portraits of Pope John XXIII and Eamon de Valera.

In the north there was a brisk underground sale in photographs of Martin Luther King.

Two very disparate singers were topping the pop music charts: Elvis Presley and the Singing Nun.

So here you are, Seventeen!"

Barry turned to see Séamus McCoy standing in the doorway of the camera shop. "Séamus! How'd you find me?"

McCoy closed one eye and tapped the side of his nose. "Sure I have my sources. I'm up here for the day on Army business, and right now I'm hungry. Join me for a bite?"

"*Go mhaith, le do thoil,*"* Barry said. "I know several pubs that serve a decent lunch."

"A pub's fine. Let's go."

"It's a bit early to close the shop for lunch, but if you're willing to wait for a few minutes . . . ?"

McCoy gave Barry a mock salute. "*Ceart go leor.*"†

The few words in Irish were like a secret code between brothers. One rarely

*Yes, please.
†Right enough; okay.

heard Irish spoken in Dublin. The official language of Ireland still bore the stigma of the old bad days, of poverty and subservience. English, which had become permeated with Americanisms during the Second World War, was the language of success.

Over bowls of lamb stew McCoy told Barry, "It's hard to think of you as a camera salesman."

"For me too, Séamus, but it's only temporary. I'm going back to Trinity in the autumn. I may continue to work there on the weekends, though. I need the money."

"What about your photography?"

"There's not much happening now, at least not with the Army."

"Don't I know it?" McCoy pushed his plate away and lit a cigarette. "I can't come to terms with the way the republican movement's going, Seventeen. I'm military through and through, and there's a lot of men in the same boat. Army's our career. We don't have a fancy education, we can't be lawyers or businessmen. We do what we *can* do, what we're good at, and that's soldiering. Maybe it's hard for some people to understand, but I *like* soldiering. Getting involved with local government and staging sit-ins about overcrowded hospitals, that's not me. Hell, I hate hospitals."

Barry smiled sympathetically. "Selling cameras isn't me, Séamus. But maybe this new direction's not so bad. It owes more to James Connolly than Pádraic Pearse, but the ultimate goal of republicanism is to serve Ireland, is it not?"

McCoy replied with a grudging nod.

"Then perhaps it's time to take some new ideas on board, Séamus. How do you feel about passive resistance, for example?"

"It would never work against the British."

"It did work against the British, Séamus. Gandhi's methods played a large part in gaining India's independence in 1947."

McCoy squinted at the younger man. "I don't pretend to be a student of international politics, Seventeen, but I know one thing. The Brits may have granted India her freedom, but they also partitioned the country and created a situation that could be at least as bad as the one here in Ireland. Anywhere the British Empire's involved they leave a bloody mess behind."

AT the Sinn Féin *Ard Comhairle** that year members agreed to use the Irish versions of their names where possible, including on legal documents. Éamonn Thomas would be *Éamonn MacThomáis,* and Tom Gill, *Tomás MacGiolla.* The

*High Council.

practise was adopted by a number of Army men. Rory Brady became *Ruairí Ó Brádaigh*. Dave O'Connell, who was slowly recovering from his horrific wounds, became *Dáithí Ó Conaill*.

Finbar Lewis Halloran considered adopting the Irish for his own name. Finbar was easy. Lewis became *Lugaid*. But Halloran in Irish was *hAllmhuráin*; too daunting, Barry decided, for everyday use. In an Ireland rapidly forgetting its Gaelic past, he would have to waste hours spelling it for people.

He abandoned the idea.

One idea, or rather one dream, which he had not abandoned was Claire MacNamara. He went for days and weeks without ever thinking of her and then suddenly she would pop back into his mind again. Yet he was slowly coming to terms with the fact the she was out of his life. He recalled the old Irish saying, "What is for you will not pass by you." Claire had passed by. Like the Army's missed opportunities during the border campaign, she had come and gone.

Let go, Barry urged himself. *Learn how to let go and move on.*

But it was not easy.

WHEN he returned to his studies at Trinity in the autumn he continued to live in Harold's Cross. Having his own space was important to him; he needed quiet moments in which to dream. To Barry's surprise, Gilbert Fitzmaurice was unhappy about the arrangement. "I thought you were coming back to the Rubrics. What am I going to do now?"

"They'll assign someone else to the room," Barry assured him.

"I don't want anyone else. It took me long enough to get used to you. Why should I have to change?"

"This is nothing against you, Gilbert. My landlord's agreed to let me have a disused pantry as a darkroom and I've bought some equipment so I can develop my own pictures. I couldn't do that here."

"It wouldn't bother me," Fitzmaurice said in a hurt voice. "But please yourself, you always do anyway."

Later, Barry remarked to Alice Green, "I didn't expect Gilbert to be upset."

"He doesn't want to lose you, Barry." She gave a nervous giggle. "You're the sort of person that people naturally want to be with."

"Don't try your *plámás** on me," he said, smiling.

"But it's true." Alice leaned toward him with her heart in her eyes.

Barry drew back almost imperceptibly. "I'm . . . I'm a very private person, Alice," he said gently, hoping she would understand. "I don't make friends eas-

*Flattery.

ily, but I'm fond of you and Dennis. You are both my friends. The *pair* of you."

She deflated before his eyes. "Yes," she said. "The pair of us."

After that Alice kept a physical distance between herself and Barry when they met. Dennis, though puzzled by her behaviour, never questioned it. But the relationship between the three of them changed in some subtle way.

Barry retreated into his studies and his work. Every spare moment found him out with the camera, looking for subjects to photograph. One evening he was hanging up a series of prints to dry when Mr. Philpott opened the door of his darkroom and peered in. "Did you not want dinner, Mr. Halloran?"

"Sorry, I forgot all about it. I've been busy."

"May I have a look?"

"I didn't know you were interested in photography." Barry stepped aside to let his landlord enter the erstwhile pantry. Philpott studied each picture in turn, then said, "I've never seen anything so sad."

"Sad?"

"Lonely," Philpott amended. "Dreadfully. I know something about loneliness, you see."

Barry surveyed the photographs with a critical eye. A series of Dublin scenes. Rain gleaming on cobbles in a little crooked alley, a view from a tenement window showing an army of chimney pots stretching almost to the horizon, once-elegant Georgian doorways with broken fanlights, sycamore trees in O'Connell Street silhouetted against the sky. "I don't know what you're talking about," he told Philpott.

"Look again, man. Where's the people?"

Where's the people?

Suddenly Barry understood. The camera had revealed not Dublin, but himself.

God, how I miss the Army. The camaraderie, the sense of doing something important . . .

But there was no going back. The IRA had changed and was changing still, almost out of recognition.

What is there for a soldier in peacetime?

I could go to America and join Kennedy's Peace Corps, that's a different sort of army. It just shows you what a politician can accomplish.

Maybe politics does have value after all.

Throughout a rainy afternoon Barry's imagination transported him to distant corners of the world where again he worked shoulder to shoulder with volunteers. Skill and dedication making a difference.

By teatime he had abandoned the idea.

Ireland needs me too. As long as part of my country's occupied by a foreign power, there'll be a need for the IRA.

•   •   •

IF a young Irish lad got in trouble in the 1960s it was not unusual for a judge to tell him, "You can go to jail or you can go to England." Most of them opted for England, where they worked as labourers. Their parents dreaded receiving letters from them, fearing the neighbours would see the English postmark and rightly assume that the boy had been in trouble. But the journey across the Irish Sea was not all one-way.

On the seventh of November, 1963, four boys from Liverpool who called themselves the Beatles played to a packed house of rapt teenagers at the Adelphi Cinema in Dublin. Dennis Cassidy gave Barry a ticket. "This should be worth seeing," he promised. When Barry arrived at the theatre hundreds of ticketless fans were already gathered outside in Abbey Street. The St. John's Ambulance Brigade was parked nearby, waiting to carry away anyone who fainted from excess emotion.

Inside the theatre young girls stood on their seats and screamed with sheer excitement. The screams became a determined chant of "We Want the Beatles!" that lasted until a guitar sounded the first chords of "I Saw Her Standing There." The curtains drew back. And there they were. John Lennon on the right, George Harrison and Paul McCartney sharing one mike, and Ringo Starr on a raised dais with his drums. The audience went wild. *Yeah, yeah, yeah!*

Within days, Beatlemania had swept the country in a revolutionary wave. Barry photographed youngsters on the streets of Dublin looking as no young people had ever looked in Ireland before. Squeaky-clean pudding-bowl haircuts and tight suits. Music stores were swamped with demands for guitars. The bodhran was abandoned for the beat of a different drum. *Yeah, yeah, yeah!* Parents were alarmed. So was the Church.

It was a wonderful time to be young and optimistic.

Chapter Twenty-five

November 22, 1963

PRESIDENT KENNEDY ASSASSINATED

Kᴇɴɴᴇᴅʏ'ѕ assassination rocked Ireland, which had taken him to its heart. He might have been born in County Wexford, rather than being separated from the land of his forebears by three generations. To the Irish he was one of their own who went to America and made good, then came home again to share his success with them.

In one unimaginable moment they had been robbed of him.

In three unimaginable days live television reportage came of age.

Barry was as shocked, as disbelieving as everyone else. The fact that the president had been killed in Dallas made it worse. His memory ran reels of sunlit Dallas images, taunting him with their innocence.

In every church in Ireland prayers were said for the repose of the soul of John Kennedy. Barry spent the day of Kennedy's funeral glued to the television. The blind president of Ireland marched in the Kennedy funeral cortege beside the president of France. Two giants towering head and shoulders over prime ministers and kings and emperors.

De Valera and de Gaulle. Two old men, two survivors of terrible wars. Following one young man lying on a gun carriage with all his promise destroyed.

Does politics really mean anything after all? Barry wondered. *Or will violence always win?*

•   •   •

As 1963 drew to a close Lyndon Johnson was in the White House and Northern Ireland had a new prime minister, Terence O'Neill. Born in Country Antrim, O'Neill, who had served in the British army as a captain of the Irish Guards, would be heading a province in transition. Elements in the Protestant working class were increasingly restive. A new generation of Catholics was graduating from formerly Protestant strongholds like Queen's University. A new organisation, National Unity, was addressing the aspirations of the expanding Catholic middle class.

Pressures were building toward boiling point.

In January of 1964, Dr. Con McCluskey and his wife, Patricia, founded the Campaign for Social Justice in Dungannon, Northern Ireland. Their intention was to work within the system for an end to discrimination.

That spring Barry Halloran received his degree in journalism. Ursula Halloran attended the ceremony.

She had secretly come up to Dublin ahead of time to visit Mary O'Donnell's atelier at 43 Dawson Street. The young designer, who had trained with some of the greats of the world fashion industry, had greeted her new customer with genuine warmth. She made Ursula comfortable, gave her an excellent cup of tea, and proceeded to create an outfit exclusively for her, combining the best Irish fabric with the latest Paris style.

Being pampered was a luxury Ursula had experienced only once before, when she attended the Swiss finishing school. Since then her life had been one of intense practicality. Sitting in one of Mary O'Donnell's deeply cushioned armchairs, worrying about how much all this was going to cost, she found herself thinking wistfully of the girls she had known in Switzerland. Some of them had married successful European businessmen and were still being cosseted.

Barry could not take his eyes off his mother. The hairdressers at Peter Mark had burnished her hair to silver, while skilful makeup enhanced her dramatic features. Her fitted suit of heathery Donegal tweed was the epitome of elegance.

"You look amazing, Ursula," Barry said.

"The road not taken," she murmured.

"Sorry?"

"Nothing, just thinking aloud. Would you like to have a celebratory dinner at the Shelbourne?"

That evening she laughed and drank champagne and sparkled in the light of the chandeliers, and Barry saw the woman his mother might have been. The girl who went to a Swiss finishing school. The girl who had once loved and been loved.

Barry felt a stab of pain at the thought of the lost and faceless man who had fathered him. Who should be with them now. Who should be seeing her with the lights caught in her hair like stars. Who would have adored Ursula, as his son did in this moment.

She has had so much and lost so much, Barry thought with enhanced understanding. *Yet I've never heard her complain.*

He knew he would never ask her anything else about his father. If she had wanted him to know, she would have told him before now. To bring it up would be like tearing open a wound.

Claire MacNamara is a wound, he thought. *But I'm my mother's son and I'll recover.*

ALTHOUGH he was eager to get on with his life, Barry had developed a deep affection for the college. Walking through the gates for the last time was very hard. *I can always come back to visit,* he comforted himself. But it would never be the same.

Barry set about finding work. His classmates were, for the most part, smugly certain of employment. They were Trinity students, the privileged, the cream. Barry did not apply for any of the trainee reporter jobs that were on offer. Pictures still drew him more powerfully than words.

Let the camera tell the story.

As a freelancer he would not have the safety net of a regular salary. If he could not make a living with his photographs he could always go back to the camera shop, or apply to Ursula for help. But he knew he would do neither. He would stand or fall on his own.

Assembling a portfolio of his best eight-by-ten enlargements, he began calling on photo editors. After a discouraging day—they all professed to like his work, but no one bought anything—Barry happened to see Dennis Cassidy and Alice Green coming out of a jewellery store in Grafton Street. "We're after choosing our wedding rings," Dennis announced in high good humour, "and we're off to have a meal. Care to join us?"

Barry glanced quizzically at Alice. "Please do," she urged.

When they were comfortably settled in a booth in The Irish Steak House, Dennis told Barry, "The *Evening Press* has taken me on, and not at entry level, either. I'll be working on the city desk at first but I hope you'll see my byline one of these days. How are you doing?"

"Still knocking at doors," Barry admitted.

Dennis gave a sympathetic nod. "You might do better to go for a straight reporting job. Photography's chancy. You know the *Sunday Independent* recently gave up on their colour magazine."

"Just my luck. I had a series of pictures showing poverty in the north inner city that would have been perfect for the magazine format. It's harder to find subjects that will tempt the broadsheets."

Dennis snapped his fingers. "How about this, Barry? We just heard there'll be a big demonstration in County Mayo this coming weekend. Seventy cadets and instructors from the Royal Navy plan to spend their holiday there—in uniform, mind you—and the local republicans are dead against it. That should be right up your street."

Barry arrived in rural Mayo with little more than his camera equipment and a change of underwear. No newspaper had bothered to send a staff photographer to cover the story. In fact there was only one reporter, a middle-aged man from Castlebar who pumped Barry about job opportunities in Dublin.

This time Barry's photographs did not lack for people. People whose faces were suffused by the passion they felt. Glowering men marched with handmade placards reading, NO KINGS IN CONNACHT! ROYAL NAVY GO HOME! Matronly women and photogenic young girls swelled their ranks, carrying slogans of their own. A winsome lad togged out in a homemade imitation of a Royal Navy uniform stood, laughing, on an overturned cabbage crate, while his friends bombarded him with water bombs.

Barry lay on his belly on the earth and angled the camera upward, making the protestors seem like giants. Then he stood atop a farm wagon and photographed downward, shrinking them into pygmies. *It all depends on the point of view,* he thought as he took frame after frame. He returned to Dublin weary but with a sense of accomplishment.

Now comes the hard part.

If his career was going to go anywhere, he needed to break into one of the broadsheet papers. And *The Irish Times* was the most influential of them all. *It's easy to be idealistic when you're in college and the real world is on the other side of the walls,* Barry told himself. *Now that I'm back in the real world I can't afford to ignore The Times just because they're pro-British. Anyway, the paper's not as one-sided as it used to be. It's making an effort to be a truly national publication.[1] Mam used to work for Seán Lester at the League of Nations, and Lester is the father-in-law of Douglas Gageby, the new editor. Might that be enough to get my foot in the door?*

Dressed in his best suit and carrying his portfolio under his arm, Barry went to the editorial offices of *The Irish Times* in D'Olier Street. Shuttled from person to person, through sheer perseverance he finally managed to see Gageby—who recalled hearing his father-in-law speak fondly of Ursula Halloran.

On the strength of that memory Gageby agreed to look at Barry's pictures. He spread a dozen black-and-white prints out on his desk and bent over them, thoughtfully rubbing his chin.

Barry began sweating inside his good suit. *This is what it all comes down to. Making a breakthrough. Any way you can.*

After an interminable time, or so it seemed, Douglas Gageby gave a low whistle. "The final decision is up to the photo editor, Barry, but I think I can promise you we'll take something. And we'll be glad to look at anything else you care to bring us."

On an inside page of the next edition of *The Irish Times* two photographs from the Mayo protest were published side by side. In one the demonstrators looked like pygmies; in the other they were giants. There was no comment aside from an identification of the event. Readers were allowed to draw their own conclusions.

Within days Barry was contacted by five news agencies expressing interest in his work.

15 July, 1964

Dear Barry,

I have received the most amazing letter from Isabella Kavanagh. She and Barbara are going to Europe this summer. They plan to stop over in Ireland on their way to Milan, where Barbara will be assessed by a famous voice coach who specialises in working with opera singers. Isabella claims the girl has a remarkable singing voice. Isn't that a turn-up for the books?

They will be here for a few days in August, so if you can find a little time to come down to the farm I would appreciate it. I do not know how I am going to entertain those two on my own.

Barry was amused by the thought of Ursula playing hostess to Isabella Kavanagh in an old farmhouse in rural Clare. *I'd best take the camera with me. That will make quite a picture.*

He went down to the farm a day early to help his mother prepare for her guests. Since Eileen's death Ursula's housekeeping efforts had been desultory at best, but Barry entered a house that had been swept and dusted and scrubbed within an inch of its life. The beds were freshly made up with crisp linen and a wonderful aroma was wafting from the kitchen.

Barry rolled his eyes at his mother. "Don't tell me you're baking."

"Not at all; I asked one of Eileen's old friends to help me out. But she'll be away before the Kavanaghs arrive."

"You're going to let them think you've done everything yourself?"

"They can make whatever assumptions they like. I can't help what other people think."

. . .

THE Hallorans were late reaching the airport. Along the way, Ursula's ancient black Ford sat down in the middle of the road and refused to go any farther. "Are we out of petrol?" Barry enquired.

"Do you think I'm an eejit? Of course there's petrol, I filled the tank just the other . . ."

Barry leaned over and peered at the gauge. "It's sitting on empty, Ursula."

"It can't be."

With a sigh, Barry got out of the car and trudged off down the road to the nearest filling station.

When they pulled into the airport car park they saw two women waiting on the kerb outside the terminal. Ursula remarked, "Those clothes must have cost a few bob. Not to mention that mountain of matched luggage. I suspect Isabella spent her share of her father's fortune as soon as she got her hands on it."

She stepped out of the car and lifted one hand in a wave. "Isabella! Over here! Fetch their suitcases, Barry. Barry? Hurry now, don't stand there staring."

Barbara Kavanagh was no longer the unkempt child Barry remembered. At seventeen she was a woman. Like her mother she had a broad jaw, but Barry would never know whether she was beautiful or not. At first sight she imprinted herself so strongly on his mind that he would see her in just that way for the rest of his life. A very tall, suntanned young woman with an athletic figure. Hair like waves of bronze. Dark, dead-level eyebrows above hazel eyes that looked gold in the sunlight.

Tiger's eyes, thought Barry.

Barbara was looking at him with equal intensity. She remembered him as a grown-up—to a ten-year-old, anyone over sixteen was a grown-up—but she had not remembered that he could stand so absolutely still, so quiet at his centre. "Barry Halloran! Don't you know me?"

"I'm sorry, I just didn't recognise you for a moment."

Barbara laughed. "I'll take that as a compliment. People do tell me I've changed a bit."

"A bit," Barry conceded. While he stowed their suitcases in the boot of the car he could feel her eyes on him.

Once again Barry and Barbara rode together in the back seat. Barry tried to make conversation but could think of little to say. She was so totally different from his expectations.

In the front seat Isabella talked nonstop about her talented daughter. She gave the impression that the girl was the greatest singer anyone had ever heard, someone who would set the world of music on fire. Her boasts piled atop one another like too much sugar icing on a cake.

Barbara seemed content to stare out the window at the passing countryside.

When they turned into the lane leading to the farmhouse Barry was painfully conscious of the numerous potholes. He had never paid any attention to them before; they were simply part of the farm, like the sag in the roof of the house. Ursula put her effort into the things that mattered to her. The livestock were always in top condition.

Barbara turned toward Barry. "You told me you were wealthy and lived in a big house. That one isn't big at all."

"You remember something I said all those years ago?"

"I remember everything you said. I had a terrific crush on you."

Barry felt his ears redden. "You were just a little girl."

"Oh yes," she agreed. "But as I said before, I've changed."

That evening Ursula set the table with the fine china that was rarely taken from the cupboard. Atop each plate was a linen napkin folded into an elaborate flower shape. Barry was struck with admiration. *None of our neighbours would know how to do that. It must be something Mam learned when she was in Europe, and never forgot.* As he unfolded his napkin he saw his mother watching him. He gave her a tiny wink. A salute.

EXHAUSTED by their long flight, the Kavanaghs went to bed early. Afterwards Barry remarked, "Isabella hasn't changed very much, but the way she carries on about Barbara is cringe-making."

"She considers her daughter a fashion accessory," Ursula replied. Her eyes twinkled with merry malice. "Isabella loathes classical music, you know. Now she'll have to endure hour after hour of it. It's enough to restore one's faith in God."

IN Irish your name would be Bairbre," Barry said the following morning. At Ursula's suggestion he had taken Barbara out to look at the horses. With their arms folded on top of the paddock railing, they were watching the current year's crop of weanlings.

"Bairbre." She repeated the word, tasting the sound of Irish on her tongue.

"I could teach you a bit of Irish while you're here," Barry offered.

"Why on earth would I want to learn a dead language?"

"Irish isn't dead. It's—"

"Of course it's dead, everyone knows that. Besides, I'm studying Italian already, and I'll have to learn German and French too. That's enough."

"You won't need any of those languages unless you actually become an opera singer."

"Well I will, smarty pants! My grandfather left a trust fund for each of his grandchildren, and I'm going to use mine to get the best training there is. So there."

Her tone irritated Barry. Lifting one eyebrow, he drawled, "You think you have enough talent, do you?"

Instead of answering, Barbara turned around and leaned against the fence. She inhaled deeply several times. Then, surprising in its power, the voice of a mature woman rose through the strong column of her throat. Adalgisa's aria from *Norma* filled the air. *"Deh! Proteggimi, o Dio!"* The impassioned plea of a woman begging the gods to save her from a fatal love.

One of the colts in the paddock gave a violent snort and raced off across the grass.

If amber could sing, thought Barry, *it would sound like Barbara Kavanagh.* A rich contralto, so deep and dark a man could drown in it.

Or struggle as helplessly as a fly caught in amber.

BARBARA Kavanagh swept over Barry like a thunderstorm. The beauty of her voice bewitched him. Her personality annoyed him. "That girl constantly interrupts me," he complained to his mother, "and contradicts everything I say."

"She's just trying to take the mickey out of you."

"Well, she's succeeding. Sometimes it's all I can do to keep my temper."

"Ignore her," Ursula advised.

But it was impossible to ignore Barbara Kavanagh. She took centre stage as her natural right. Torn between amusement and exasperation, Barry said to her, "I'd like you to meet a fellow called Gilbert Fitzmaurice. You two were made for each other."

"Is he a friend of yours?"

"We were roommates at Trinity."

"I don't need to meet another boring old man, thank you very much."

"Old!" Barry was outraged. "He's the same age as me. Do you think I'm . . ." But she was walking away.

"I feel like I've been run over by a lorry," Barry told Ursula after they took the two women back to the airport. "Is that girl really only seventeen?"

"Seventeen going on thirty-five. Frightening, isn't she? What do you suppose she'll be like ten years from now?"

"I shudder to think," Barry replied.

When he returned to Dublin he bought a used gramophone in a pawn shop. "I'm very fond of music," he explained to his landlord. "Do you mind?"

"Not if you keep it low and don't play any of that jump-up-and-down music. The young ones like that sort of thing, but it gives me a headache."

Barry liked "jump-up-and-down music" too. But he spent his hard-earned money on classical music and operatic records.

IN spite of the inroads that popular music and television were making on the consciousness of the younger generation, sex in Catholic Ireland was still a taboo subject.

For Barry sex was a nagging constant, a distraction when he was working and a preoccupation when he was not. Either way he felt guilty. His logical mind told him there should be no guilt for a basic biological urge, but he could not help it. Some conditioning ran too deep.

That conditioning drove many young Irish men into the priesthood.

Barry never considered becoming a priest—Ursula's opinion of institutionalised religion had its own effect—but he no longer thought of marrying. A wife and the inevitable children would tie him down too much. *A freelancer needs to be free.*

Having a family would also place an intolerable strain on his finances. Although he was beginning to build a reputation, the assignments he received from the Dublin print media were not enough to support him. Most of his sales were self-generated, which meant he had to go out and find stories for his camera to tell. Sometimes he did not return to Harold's Cross for days.

But, as he said to Séamus McCoy, "*Bíonn gach tosach lag*. Every beginning is weak."

"And the endings too," McCoy replied.

"It's not like you to be so pessimistic."

"Look what's happened to the Army, Seventeen. The gun's on the shelf, full stop. I should be training a new company of recruits, and you should be blowing the hell out of roads and bridges in the north. Yet here I am in my room, reading the writings of James Connolly, and you're . . . What did you say brings you to Ballina?"

"I'm on my way to Foynes to see what's left of the facilities for amphibian aircraft. The flying boats were a vital link between Europe and America during World War Two, but I understand there's hardly anything left now. It might provide some dramatic photographs. You know the sort of thing: death of a dream, et cetera."

"Ireland's full of places where dreams died," said McCoy. "Everything from castles to linen mills. You think anyone would be interested in an old airport?"

"I hope so. I'm doing it on spec."

McCoy picked a shred of tobacco from his tongue and ground out his cigarette as if it were an enemy he lusted to break. "I'm living my life on spec," he said. "The hope that the Army'll be back in business one of these days. I envy you, Seventeen—having something else."

Barry spent a day in the small town of Foynes on the bank of the Shannon. There was an ineffable sadness about the place. The Monteagle Arms Hotel, which had been adapted as a control centre, still contained communications equipment. A rail link still ran toward the flying-boat basin. But rotting piers, deteriorating storage hangers, and rusting fuel tanks told the story of an era that had come and gone.

Barry stood at the edge of the river and gazed out across the reed-fringed water, toward the open sea. *The next parish is Boston.* He was swept by sudden yearning for America, where the air was electric with energy and dreams were still coming true.

America. Barbara Kavanagh.

Barry smiled to himself. "I hope your dream comes true, little girl." The smile expanded to a laugh. "God help anyone who gets in your way!"

The photos from Foynes generated a modicum of interest but no sales. Barry refused to be discouraged. He wrote an evocative article to accompany the pictures, recalling the exploits of the heroic pilots who had braved the Atlantic during the darkest days of the war. Going one step further, he suggested a museum devoted to that brief but important period in aviation history. He sent copies to the few aviation magazines in Britain, then began haunting the newsstands, looking for suitable publications farther afield.

Camera in hand, he scoured the Dublin area for subjects. He was developing an eye for what the market wanted. Human interest pictures. An impromptu football match on a grassy field, the young lads grimacing with effort while old men watched from the sidelines, their faces seamed with nostalgia. A lean-to in which a woman sat hunched on a three-legged stool, showing her small daughter how to milk the family cow. Every picture presented an image of Ireland in the 1960s. None depicted the underlying politics. There was no market for visual political commentary. Whatever was happening in the north, the south did not want to know.

Barry went out with a number of young women that autumn. He liked all of them, slept with one or two, committed himself to none. Sometimes he met friends from Trinity and they spent an evening together, but they were going their way and Barry was going his. His old lone-wolf habit had returned. On the day he sold the Foynes series to an American magazine Barry found himself sitting alone in a pub in Middle Abbey Street, staring into a pint of bitter that he really did not want. Leaving the drink untouched, he went home to listen to his newest acquisition, a recording of *Cavalleria Rusticana*. The role of Lucia was sung by a contralto whose name meant nothing to him, but he could lose himself in her voice.

. . .

IN Northern Ireland the staple industries continued to decline. Marine engineering and linen manufacture were particularly hard-hit. In spite of the efforts of Terence O'Neill's government, unemployment remained stubbornly high.

The IRA, north and south, seemed to be fading into oblivion. The only time republicanism came to public attention was when one of the splinter groups staged a bank robbery to gain funds. Quite a few were undertaken by these dissidents; only a small number were successful; several were farcical. On one occasion, the only weapon the gang possessed was an ancient revolver that literally fell apart as the ringleader was waving it at a bank clerk. The men fled the building amidst hoots of derision from bystanders.

Barry cut the article from the newspaper and posted it to Séamus McCoy, with, "This is embarrassing," written in the margin.

Under Cathal Goulding's leadership the Army, or what remained of it, had taken a decided turn to the left. Social issues were the order of the day. Instead of military drill, Volunteers marched shoulder to shoulder with trade unionists protesting unsafe labour practices.

"Joe Cahill's thoroughly disgusted," McCoy wrote to Barry, referring to one of the Army's stalwarts who had been a close friend of Goulding's since the early fifties, "and so am I. To add insult to injury, Éamonn Thomas has been voted off the Army Council. I don't know why. We're on the ash heap and Ireland's not a damned bit better off than it was in 1921. In fact it's worse. Now we haven't a hope in hell of getting our republic back."

Chapter Twenty-six

September 21, 1964

MALTA ATTAINS INDEPENDENCE WITHIN THE BRITISH COMMONWEALTH

Activists launch campaign for a Republic.

September 27, 1964

IAN PAISLEY OUTRAGED BY SIGHT OF IRISH FLAG

Using sledgehammers, the RUC has broken down the door of Sinn Féin's Belfast office on Divis Street and destroyed a small tricolour flag flying from the window. Rev. Paisley had vowed to destroy it himself if the police did not.

December 10, 1964

MARTIN LUTHER KING JR. AWARDED NOBEL PEACE PRIZE

Workers on behalf of civil rights around the world rejoice.

ON the fourteenth of January, 1965, Seán Lemass and Terence O'Neill had lunch together at Stormont. In a joint statement later that day the two claimed that neither political nor constitutional matters were discussed. Ian Paisley protested against the idea of any meeting whatsoever between the Irish taoiseach and the prime minister of Northern Ireland, but his protest came a day too late.

Ten days later Sir Winston Churchill, twice prime minister of Great Britain, died. The United Kingdom and the British Commonwealth were plunged into mourning. The world joined them in grief. No one would ever forget Churchill's defiant stand against Adolf Hitler.

The second of February was another historic day at Stormont. The Northern Ireland Nationalist Party became the official party of opposition. The government of the province was beginning to become more inclusive.

Upon learning that the archbishop of Canterbury was to fly to Rome to visit the pope, Ian Paisley caught the same aeroplane in order to stage a protest. When he arrived in Rome he was refused permission to leave the plane, however, and had to return to London.

In February, Roger Casement, hero of the Congo, former consul general to Rio de Janeiro, anti-colonialist and champion of human rights before his time, came home at last. Born in Dublin, Casement was brought up as a Protestant. Following family tradition he was also a unionist and a loyal servant of the Crown. In 1911 he was knighted by King George V for distinguished public service. Yet in 1916, and in spite of huge international protest, the British had hanged him as a traitor for his role in the Easter Rising.

Winston Churchill had always been adamant in his refusal to return Casement's body to Ireland. Harold Wilson's new Labour government wanted to put Anglo-Irish relations on a better footing for the sake of an upcoming trade agreement and the possibility of a European economic union. So on a bleak February afternoon, Roger Casement's remains were exhumed from the graveyard at Pentonville Prison. In the presence of a representative of the Irish government they were examined by a pathologist, formally identified, and put into a new coffin. The coffin was wrapped in an Irish flag and flown across the Irish Sea by Aer Lingus, the Irish national airline.

During the next five days Casement lay in state in the Church of the Sacred Heart, Arbour Hill Military Barracks,[1] while many thousands filed past the bier. Touching the flag-draped coffin with their fingertips. Breathing a prayer for the soul of a man whose courage was legendary.

Ursula Halloran wanted to go up to Dublin to pay her respects, but as she told Barry on the telephone, "I have three pregnant mares about to drop their foals any minute. If at least one of the foals is a colt, though, I'll name him Sir Roger!"

On the first of March a contingent of the Irish army accompanied the funeral procession as it wound its way to Glasnevin Cemetery. A huge crowd lined the route.

Although film was very expensive, Barry purchased two rolls for the event. Leaving his bicycle in a shop doorway, he joined the ten-deep throng gathered on O'Connell Street to see the funeral cortege. Since he could not wedge himself through the crowd he held his camera aloft and photographed the procession over people's heads. Then he ran to his bicycle and raced to Glasnevin.

Mam had Constance Markievicz but I'm here for Roger Casement.

The cemetery was crowded with dignitaries. Eamon de Valera had risen from a sickbed to deliver the funeral oration. Barry was so preoccupied with organising his shots that the solemnity of the moment escaped him. As the ceremony drew to a close he snapped a last picture of de Valera just to use up the roll. He did not realise what he had until he developed the film.

Amidst lengthening shadows, one ray of light gently caressed the old man's gaunt features like a promise of forgiveness. That iconographic image would outlive both the president of Ireland and his photographer.

NINETEEN sixty-five was a good year for Barry. His candid portrait of de Valera was reproduced in a dozen countries. By autumn he had a nonexclusive contract with an international news agency and was also employed as a stringer by a couple of American newspapers. The money involved would not make him wealthy, but it guaranteed he could pay his rent on time. He could take a woman to dinner at the Royal Hibernian Hotel instead of buying her a sandwich in Robert Roberts'.

NINTEEN sixty-six was the fiftieth anniversary of the Easter Rising. As the new year dawned, a veritable avalanche of radio and television programmes, lectures, books, plays, poems, and ballads about 1916 began to roll across Ireland.

In February commemorative souvenirs of the Rising began to appear in the shops. Barry's first purchase was a strikingly designed badge. Against a background of green, white and orange, Pádraic Pearse in Volunteer uniform stood in front of the GPO.

I was born forty years too late, Barry thought as he pinned the badge to his coat. *The war's over and we didn't win.*

That evening he called in to the Oval Bar in Middle Abbey Street, favourite watering hole of many Dublin journalists, for a hot whiskey. The pub was abuzz with talk about the upcoming celebrations. It sounded as if they were going to be a combination of the Fourth of July and Bastille Day, with the added attraction that some of the participants were still alive.

"How will you celebrate the jubilee, Lily?" a man at the next table asked the woman beside him. Barry had noticed her when he came in; a handsome, dark-haired woman with roving eyes.

"I'll tell you what I'd like to do," she said. "Out there in the middle of O'Connell Street, Admiral High-and-Mighty Nelson is still lording it over us. I'd knock him if I could. Blow him to smithereens!"

Her companion brayed with laughter.

Barry put down his drink.

The laughter swelled into a wave. Others joined in. "Knock the Pillar!" "Down with the admiral!"

Do it do it do it do it do it!

Barry stood up and left the bar.

"Please join me in Dublin for a picnic," he wrote to Séamus McCoy. "If you can persuade our friend Mickey from Limerick to come with you, so much the better. Ask him to bring some of that good jelly his wife makes, for the sandwiches."

Two days later Séamus McCoy arrived on Barry's doorstep with Mickey in tow. The Limerick man was carrying a suitcase. "I brought jelly for the picnic," he said.

"Good on you! How much?"

"There's enough gelignite in here to blow open a bank vault."

"Nobody has a picnic in a bank vault, Mickey. This party's going to be in the middle of O'Connell Street."

Séamus McCoy gave a low whistle. "You're coming out of retirement in a big way, Seventeen."

"One performance only, and I'll need some help. I want to blow up Nelson's Pillar . . ." Barry paused and took a deep breath, "without damaging anything else."

Mickey's jaw dropped. "You're daft."

"It can't be done," McCoy said flatly. "The Pillar's smack in the middle of the busiest street in Dublin, with buildings on all sides."

"There has to be a way, Séamus, and I'll tell you why. In 1916 British artillery demolished the centre of Dublin. I want to destroy nothing but the symbol they left behind. We must prove we're better than they were."

"You really mean to do this?"

"I really mean to."

McCoy turned to Mickey. "Is what he's suggesting remotely possible?"

"I can't say until I've had a look at the problem, but for a good engineer anything's possible, I suppose."

"Well then, let's do a reccy."

Barry gave McCoy a grateful smile.

The three men walked at a brisk pace from Harold's Cross to O'Connell Bridge, then slowed to a stroll. They paused frequently to admire the merchandise in shop windows in O'Connell Street, and debated the merits of various publications before buying an out-of-town newspaper at a kiosk. In this leisurely fashion, they at last came to the Pillar. As usual, there was a queue of people waiting for admission to the observation platform.

Barry and Séamus McCoy went into the GPO and bought postage stamps. When they came out they blended into the group of Dublin regulars who habitually lounged under the portico, commenting on everyone and everything that passed. McCoy lit a cigarette. Barry opened the newspaper he was carrying.

But though he scanned the *Cork Examiner* with a practiced eye, as usual there was no mention of anyone called Claire MacNamara.

Meanwhile, Mickey, gawking like a tourist, walked several times around the Pillar before stopping to chat with the guard at the entrance porch. The guard felt a proprietary interest in the monument and was happy to tell him all about it. He asked if Mickey wanted to buy a ticket for the observation platform. The Limerick man shook his head. "Afraid of heights, me. But I have to have something to tell the children. Just let me look in the door; seeing the inside of the column'll do me."

"I can't charge you for that," the guard said with a laugh. "Look all you like, then take home this little pamphlet about the Pillar for your family. They don't need to know you never made it to the top. It'll be our little secret."

Thanking the guard, Mickey put the small folder in his pocket. He ambled over to a fruit stand and bought an orange wrapped in tissue paper. After exchanging comments on the weather with the fruit vendor, he headed for the GPO, peeling the fruit as he walked. His mutilated hand was awkward; orange juice ran down his wrist and soaked his sleeve.

"There are several problems here, all difficult," Mickey said when they were back in Harold's Cross. "My first thought was to plant a bomb inside the column, but we can't because there's absolutely nothing in that shaft but smooth stone walls and the staircase. People going up the steps would notice any kind of foreign object attached to the walls.

"So the bomb has to be on the outside—but how do we place it without getting caught? That's a damned public location, you know. Then there's the question of just how much explosive we'd need to bring the Pillar down. Should it be powerful enough to include the base too? That's like a big stone tomb itself. As for avoiding any other damage . . ." He spread his hands palmsup in a tacit admission of defeat.

"Go on," said Barry. His face was expressionless but there was command in his voice.

Mickey sighed. "An explosive charge should be tailored for the object you want to blow up. But the statue and the column are made of different materials. Nelson and his plinth are carved of Portland stone. And plastered with bird shit, according to the guard. As for the column, people think it's Wicklow granite but it's actually only black limestone sheathed in granite."[2]

Barry looked thoughtful. "Would there be a join between the statue and the column?"

"A join?"

"Like a seam."

"Has to be."

Suddenly Barry leaned forward, his whole body electric with excitement. "Suppose we have two explosions in quick succession near the top of the Pillar. An initial blast to jolt the statue loose, followed by a larger one embedded in the column. We'll want a five-second delay on the second detonator and . . ."

"I don't understand," said McCoy.

But Mickey did. "That's brilliant! Because the statue's so much higher than anything else in the street, if it's not blocking the way . . ."

"The main explosion will go upwards as well as outwards," Barry finished. "It should demolish a large part of the column without touching the nearest buildings. And if we set off our bomb in the wee small hours we won't injure anyone, either. Except the hero of Trafalgar. We'll finish him once and for all." His voice was gleeful.

"Damn," McCoy breathed almost reverently. "Damn!"

Mickey was beginning to warm to the possibility. "If we can get it placed right—and that's a big 'if'—gelignite would take care of the column. But for his lordship we'd want a lifting explosive, something like ammonol. You ever hear of it, Séamus? It's a mixture of TNT, ammonium nitrate, and aluminium powder."

"Did you happen to bring any with you?"

"No, but a pal of mine here in Dublin should have enough."

"Is he trustworthy?" Barry wanted to know. "The last thing we need is an informer." The mere mention of the word made his left leg twinge.

"I've known this lad for donkey's years; he used to be in the Army."

Barry raised an eyebrow. "Used to be?"

"He left after sixty-two to join a more, er, active organisation. But don't worry about him informing. If anything, he and his crowd are more passionate republicans than any of ye."

"What will he want for the ammonol?"

"A place on the team, most likely. If there's really going to be a picnic."

Barry's eyes danced with mischief. "Oh there's going to be a picnic right enough. With beer, and jelly sandwiches, and . . . and boiled eggs. Welcome to Operation Humpty Dumpty."

FOUR men, including the provider of the ammonol, met in Barry's room to plan the details of the operation. Barry turned up the volume on his gramophone to keep anyone outside the room from overhearing them.

"We can't hear ourselves think with that going on," McCoy complained. "I like music as well as the next man, but I hate to hear women screeching."

Barry was indignant. "That's not screeching. It's Kathleen Ferrier singing 'What Is Life for Me without Thee?'"

"Well, she's making me nervous."

"If your nerves are that fragile," Barry retorted, "it's a good thing I'll be carrying the baby."

Chapter Twenty-seven

DUBLIN was still shaking itself awake when McCoy and the ammonol man, dressed in boilersuits, arrived at the Pillar. They brought a handcart loaded with equipment. Buckets and brooms and stiff brushes, hammers, chisels, towels, a small drill, even a folding ladder. "We're maintenance. From the Corpo," McCoy told the guard who had just come on duty. The cold air was making McCoy cough. The ammonol man stood to one side, chewing gum and looking bored.

"Sorry?"

"You know, Dublin Corporation. Y'want that article up there thoroughly cleaned or not? If not we can turn around and . . ."

"Stay right here!" cried the guard. "Just the other day I was telling a fellow that the pigeon shite on poor Lord Nelson is so thick it's turning to cement. The sightseers are complaining about it. In fact one lady said to me . . ."

"Just show us where the nearest water tap is," McCoy interrupted, "and hang out a sign saying the observation platform's closed. We don't want to get a mess all over the taxpayers' clothes, do we?"

It took several trips for the two men to carry all their equipment up the stairs. Then they set to work scrubbing the statue and chipping away encrusted pigeon droppings. The protruding platform hid much of what they were doing from the street below. When they crouched at the foot of the plinth, no one could see them drill a series of downwards boreholes into the column. Barry had drawn a diagram showing the angle required. Before they left the platform the men filled the boreholes with dust and dried pigeon shit, then tamped it flat with their feet. To the casual observer the holes would be invisible. People on the observation platform would be looking out at the city anyway.

Meanwhile, Barry and Mickey prepared the explosives. A small timer would be used to detonate sticks of ammonol which had been wrapped in paper the exact colour of Portland stone. Attached by wire to the timer was a second detonator with a five-second delay for the gelignite. "One *two!*" Mickey said, clapping his hands to illustrate. "Like dominoes falling."

ON the last day of February, Barry Halloran, wrapped in an overcoat and wearing a woollen cap pulled down over his ears, approached Nelson's Pillar. A bitterly cold wind had been blowing all day, discouraging the usual crowd of sightseers from attempting the observation platform. The guard on duty was cradling his hands in his armpits to keep them warm.

Barry nodded to him. The man touched the brim of his cap.

Referring to his bulging canvas hold-all, Barry said, "I have a lot of camera equipment and a tripod here. May I take them to the observation platform? The boss wants photographs for a new set of commemorative postcards."

"You don't want to go up now," the guard replied. "There's a right gale blowing up there. It'd strip the hair off a man's head."

"My head's covered."

"Would you not take your snapshots down here? Maybe show a man in uniform standing beside the Pillar to give an idea of its size?"

"I wish I could, but the boss insists on views looking out over the city."

The disappointed guard opened the gate and waved Barry inside. Halfway up the twisting staircase, his left leg betrayed him. He lurched heavily against the wall. When he recovered his balance he continued the climb, ignoring the pain.

On the observation platform he opened his hold-all and took out the explosives. With a long, narrow brush, he cleaned out the downwards boreholes below the plinth and packed them with pliable gelignite, then replaced a bit of the debris on top to hide the contents. The disguised ammonol was tucked into an aperture in the base of the statue, facing Henry Street.

The timer had been set to go off at 2:00 A.M.

BY the time Barry started back down the stairs the pain in his leg had eased. There was no one to see, but he was wearing the old, devil-may-care grin again.

The team of Operation Humpty Dumpty scattered to different places around the city. Alone in his room in Harold's Cross, Barry played his records for a while, then went to bed.

At two in the morning he tensed. Sat up. Every sense painfully alert.

He heard no distant explosion.

I'm probably too far away.

He fought against a powerful desire to go to O'Connell Street. He lay back down and put his head on the pillow, which felt like a rock to him. *How many hours until daylight?* At last he gave up the struggle and turned on the light. Selecting one of Ned's notebooks at random, he settled himself in the armchair to read.

Shortly after dawn Séamus McCoy pounded on Barry's door. "The Pillar's still standing," he announced in disgust. "I don't know what happened, but we'd best retrieve our stuff before someone finds it."

A different guard was on duty at the Pillar that morning. Barry repeated his story about postcard photographs. "I know it's a big favour to ask," he said, "but could you possibly keep anyone from coming up there while I'm working? Other people would distract me or even jiggle the tripod. You understand." He grinned engagingly. "I'll make up the missed ticket fees out of my own pocket." His slight nod and lifted eyebrows hinted that there might be a little something extra.

"I can give you ten minutes," the guard decided. "Will that do?"

"It'll have to."

The day was cold but as Barry climbed to the observation platform he was sweating. *Whatever went wrong, the explosives might still go off.*

In a ringing silence, he gingerly retrieved the components of the device and made his way back down the stairs. One very careful step at a time.

"Did you get some good pictures?" the guard asked.

"I can't be sure 'til I see how they develop."

Back in Harold's Cross, he and Mickey cautiously examined the device "Here's your trouble," said Mickey. "The feckin' wire on the timer's loose. Did you shake this thing, Halloran?"

Barry bridled. "You know better than that. It must have happened when I slipped on the stairs. I guess the hold-all hit the walls. It's just bad luck; we'll give it a few days and go again."

"You want me to carry the baby this time?"

"No way," Barry said emphatically.

There was a change of guards at the monument over the weekend. On the seventh of March, Barry, whose face was unknown to the new man, again made arrangements to take photographs undisturbed, then climbed the Pillar with his bag of equipment.

This time he did not return to Harold's Cross. After stowing his hold-all in a locker at Busáras, he bought a meal he was too excited to eat and wandered for hours around the city. Nightfall found him back at the bus station. He pulled his cap low, hiding most of his face, and slumped in a seat like someone waiting for a late bus. People came and went. No one paid any attention to him. From time to time he got up to stretch his legs and move to a different seat.

At last the station grew quiet. Only one other intending passenger remained, a man who had fallen asleep with his mouth open. He snored in a jerky, broken rhythm.

.   .   .

AT 1:32 in the morning the ammonol blew. Like a huge, startled bird, the petrified admiral lifted off his perch. Before Nelson could settle back down, the gelignite exploded. The blast reduced the statue to rubble that collapsed into the street, followed by two-thirds of the Pillar. Bits of the monument were scattered for hundreds of yards. A massive dust cloud arose, but there were no fatalities. No injuries.

No substantial damage to any other structure.

The team of Operation Humpty Dumpty was jubilant. It was the perfect prank, making them all schoolboys again. Making them all winners.

BY dawn the local urchins were scrambling through the rubble looking for souvenirs. But the best souvenir was long gone—taken by a very large woman swathed in a heavy shawl, the first person on the scene after the explosion. As the gardai arrived she was seen scurrying away, but no one challenged her. She was only a woman after all.

SHORTLY after noon Barry was in his room when his landlord knocked on his door. "There's a telephone call for you. Did you give this number to a woman?" Philpott's voice was clotted with disapproval.

"Only my mother. For emergencies."

When Barry picked up the telephone receiver in the hall, Ursula exclaimed, "Nelson's Pillar's been bombed! Have you heard yet? It was on the wireless first thing this morning!" She did not sound like anyone's mother, her son noted with amusement. In her excitement she sounded like a young girl. "The British Empire's crumbling to dust, Barry. Isn't it wonderful?"

Mr. Philpott had a different opinion. "Isn't it shocking? I don't know how anyone could commit such an appalling crime. It's obviously the work of mindless barbarians."

By that afternoon traders in Moore Street were selling genuine fragments of the Pillar. When their initial stock ran out they had no trouble resupplying. A short drive to the Dublin or Wicklow mountains provided enough pieces of granite to meet the demand.[1]

There was widespread public condemnation of the bombing, and a certain amount of private glee. The desecrated monument—quickly nicknamed "The Stump" by Dubliners—was an embarrassment to the government, who wanted it removed as soon as possible. They assigned the job to the Irish army.

Unfortunately, what remained of the Pillar was at street level. When the army blew it up, the explosion damaged buildings up and down O'Connell

Street. Every window was shattered, littering the broad boulevard with danger-ous shards of glass. The Dubliners were not slow to comment. "The govern-ment should have brought in the first lot to do the job proper," they said.

Although badly damaged, Admiral Nelson's head was not destroyed. Dublin Corporation reclaimed the head and put it in storage, in case an attempt was made in future to restore the famous landmark.

Speculation as to the identity of the bombers ran wild. Most people thought it was an IRA job—the Boys' way of celebrating the Rising. Irish army explo-sives experts said that the skill displayed pointed to the importation of French explosives experts. A northern evangelist told his congregation it was a light-ning strike, God's way of demonstrating his wrath on Catholics.

A number of people were brought in for questioning. None was from the ac-tual team involved. No one was ever charged.

Chapter Twenty-eight

THE spectacular success of Operation Humpty Dumpty lifted a great weight from Barry's shoulders. The Irish Republican Army had not reclaimed the Six Counties with all flags flying, as he had once imagined, but he had pitted his skill against the hated symbol of imperialism and brought it crashing down.

He was done with all forms of weaponry now. The secret, nagging impulse to violence which he had suppressed for so long was gone.

In the absence of the Pillar a new symbol was needed to represent Dublin. Barry began photographing the Ha'penny Bridge in every mood and light. Seen through the lens of his camera, the graceful old footbridge was as romantic as a Victorian valentine. Within a week he sold some of the pictures to a postcard company.

The money bought a glass dome atop a polished walnut base. It was the perfect place to display a stone nose that had once been nicked by a well-placed rifle shot.

THE official Easter Rising commemoration ceremonies began on the tenth of April. Barry telephoned Ursula to see if she was coming to Dublin for the occasion. "Some of the mares have yet to foal, so I can't leave," she told him. "Is that not the worst luck! Take pictures of everything for me, Barry. Be my eyes."

Vast crowds packed O'Connell Street on the morning of the tenth. Many of them had been there since before dawn. Wrapped in blankets, sharing family reminiscences and flasks of hot tea. When the signal was given, six hundred men and women, surviving veterans of the Easter Rising, took their places in the reviewing stand in front of the GPO. More than two thousand veterans of the War of Independence lined up facing them across the street.

Although Ireland professed to be outraged at the destruction of Nelson's Pillar, quite a few smiled at the empty space where the monument had stood.

The military parade that marched to the GPO from St. Stephen's Green included civilian contingents from as far away as America and Australia. Children of the Irish Diaspora had come home to help celebrate.

At noon the Proclamation of the Irish Republic rang out from loudspeakers, repeating the historic words of Pádraic Pearse fifty years before. The Irish flag was once again raised on the roof of the GPO. For a moment the tricolour clung to the flagpole; then it broke free and billowed above the crowd in a glory of green and white and orange.[1]

Barry Halloran felt a lump in his throat. *If I take no other photograph today, I'll have one of the flag flying over the GPO. For Ursula.*

Following a twenty-one-gun salute, President Eamon de Valera reviewed the parading Irish army. As the last units passed the reviewing stand a flight of jet aircraft swept overhead. The army band struck up the Irish national anthem:

Soldiers are we, whose lives are pledged to Ireland,
Some have come from a land beyond the wave,
Sworn to be free,
No more our ancient sireland
Shall shelter the despot or the slave.

The eleventh of April was Easter Monday.

With the exception of individual clerics, the Roman Catholic Church had vilified the rebels in 1916. Now it honoured them with religious ceremonies in every parish. A solemn Votive Mass in Dublin's Pro-Cathedral was attended by all the leaders of government as well as foreign ambassadors and the papal nuncio. Special places were reserved for relatives of the leaders of the Rising.

St. Patrick's Cathedral in Dublin hosted the largest Protestant commemoration. The service was conducted by the Anglican dean of St. Patrick's; the lesson at the ecumenical service was read by a Presbyterian minister and a captain from the Salvation Army, and prayers were recited by the chairman of the Dublin and District Methodist Church.

As Barry read in the papers, Jewish services of prayer and thanksgiving were held throughout the country. Robert Briscoe, the Jewish former lord mayor of Dublin, represented President de Valera at the Adelaide Road Synagogue in Dublin.

In Northern Ireland the archbishop of Armagh presided at a celebratory Solemn High Mass in St. Patrick's Cathedral, Armagh. The church was packed with Catholics, nationalists, and not a few Protestants.

Ian Paisley called a meeting of his followers in the Ulster Hall, where he gave thanks "for the defeat of the 1916 Rising."[2]

This was reported in the newspapers too.

ON the seventeenth of April another protest against the commemoration was held in Belfast. On this occasion Ian Paisley heaped praise on the Ulster Volunteer Force, which he had inspired.

The original UVF had been formed in January, 1913, to resist home rule for Ireland by force of arms. The threat posed by this powerful Protestant militia had led to the founding of the Irish National Volunteers the following November as a defensive measure. In 1916 the Irish National Volunteers fought the British under a new name bestowed on them by James Connolly: the Irish Republican Army.

Thus had the first UVF, in a cruel irony, given birth to the IRA.

BARRY Halloran took hundreds of photographs connected with the jubilee of the Rising. They sold quickly, both to Irish-oriented publications abroad and to local newspapers. Some of Barry's pictures excelled anything their staff photographers produced. He was now lodging more money in the bank than he was taking out.

Barry bought a sizeable banker's draft to send to Father Aloysius. "Please use this to pay Dr. Roche for his medical services when I was injured, and to repay the money he once loaned to me. The rest is for the benefit of your parish."

By return post he received a warm letter of thanks. "We think of you often and remember you in our prayers," the priest wrote. "Never forget you have friends in Derry."

After that Barry wrote fairly regularly to the priest. Father Aloysius always wrote back and told him what was happening in Derry. Since hardly any information from that quarter reached the south, Barry was grateful. *Ursula infected me with her passion for the news, and that's no bad thing.*

Trinity College, long the bastion of the Protestant Ascendancy, had a new but growing Republican Club[3] and its own observance of the Rising. Under the imprint of TCD Publishing Company, the current crop of journalism students produced a booklet entitled *1916–1966; What Has Happened?* Articles were contributed free of charge by professional men and academics. Copies of the booklet were distributed for sale locally.

One morning Barry stopped at his usual newsstand to buy his customary copy of the *Cork Examiner,* but at the last moment changed his mind. *Why bother? Move on, that's the secret.*

As he was about to walk away he noticed the new pamphlet and stopped to leaf through it. One essay in particular caught his attention. A writer from the Six Counties commented, "We in Ireland have found and are already using a common denominator for re-adjusting our society. We are experiencing acts of real leadership in fostering friendships regardless of geographical borders."[4]

Please God, thought Barry, *let it be true.*

A few days later he encountered Cathal Goulding in one of those accidental meetings so common in Dublin. The two men stood on the footpath for a while, talking of this and that. Barry casually mentioned the article.

"Real leadership?" said Goulding. "I wonder. I agree that a few things in the north are improving under O'Neill, but it's a bloody slow process while others are leading in a very different direction. Sectarianism is as bad as ever. In some areas it's even getting worse. It's damned hard to stand on the sidelines and do nothing."

"Of course it's hard," Barry agreed. "That's why . . ." He stopped himself abruptly. He longed to boast, but in the interests of their own safety the team of Operation Humpty Dumpty had agreed to take their secret to the grave.

". . . That's why I'd like to suggest something the Army could do," Barry extemporised.

"What are you talking about?"

"Are you aware of the civil rights marches Martin Luther King's held in the States? They require large numbers of volunteers who can remain nonviolent in the face of severe provocation. Well, our Volunteers have been rigorously trained in discipline and they know a thing or two about marching. They could stage peaceful protests on behalf of the Catholics in the north. Maybe shame Stormont into doing something."

Goulding scowled. "Stormont is beyond shame. Take gerrymandering. The northern government claims to be run on democratic principles but that's a load of bollocks, thanks to gerrymandering. The population of Derry is two-thirds Catholic, yet they have no voice in Stormont because the Unionist Party re-draws constituency boundaries to skew the elective process in its own favour. Does this embarrass the northern government? Not a bit of it; it's the way things are done. The way they've always been done."

"All the more reason to give the civil rights movement a try," Barry argued. "In the United States the demonstrations are forcing a change in the legislation, even in areas that were hopeless only a few years ago. Why not here?"

"You're living in Cloud-Cuckoo Land, boyo," said Goulding. "Northern Ireland's nothing like the States."

"How do you know something won't work until you give it a try?"

Goulding did not answer. But Barry saw his eyelids flicker.

ON May seventh a group of loyalists, including at least one member of the Ulster Volunteer Force, set fire to a house in the Shankill Road. The house was next door to a Catholic-owned bar. However, the occupant of the house, Matilda Gould, was a crippled seventy-seven-year-old Protestant widow.[5] Mrs. Gould was badly burned in the fire and had to be taken to hospital.

On the twenty-sixth of June, Peter Ward, who worked in the International Hotel in Belfast, accompanied three friends to the Malvern Arms in Malvern Street for a drink. Several members of the Ulster Volunteer Force were also in the bar. One of them identified Ward and his friends as Catholics. The UVF men followed the three when they left and opened fire on them outside. Two were seriously wounded. Peter Ward took a bullet to the heart.

Ward was the first fatality of what eventually would be known as The Troubles.

A day later John Patrick Scullion, a twenty-eight-year-old Catholic who lived with his elderly aunt and his blind father, was making his way home from a bar off the Falls Road. As he reached his front door a car sped by. A witness reported hearing the sound of gunfire; a bullet was later found in the street. Scullion managed to get into the house, then collapsed. Two anonymous telephone calls to the *Belfast Telegraph* claimed he had been shot by an extreme Protestant organisation. In hospital Scullion suffered several heart attacks and ultimately died from brain damage.

Terence O'Neill cut short his attendance at a commemoration of the Battle of the Somme, where the first Ulster Volunteer Force had been wiped out, to return to Belfast to ban the contemporary UVF. He described the organisation as "this evil thing in our midst using the sordid techniques of gangsterism."[6]

Seven weeks after being attacked in her home, Matilda Gould died of her burns.

Three men were given life sentences for the murder of Peter Ward.

JULY brought the Anglo-Irish Free Trade Agreement, which allowed for the gradual removal of protective tariffs between the U.K. and the Republic.

Northern Ireland reverberated with the strident chant of the demagogue, warning of a papist conspiracy. Warning too of the thousands of evil IRA gunmen he claimed were lurking in the shadows, plotting to destroy the lives, the homes, the very heritage of decent God-fearing Protestants.

The outlawed UVF began beefing up its arsenal.

IN August, Cathal Goulding, Tomás MacGiolla, and Roy Johnston, a Trinity lecturer and socialist in the Marxist mould, were amongst those attending a meeting at the home of a republican solicitor in Maghera, County Derry. People of differing religious outlooks and political philosophies came together to discuss ways of solving the north's sectarian problems. One of the ideas proposed was a nonviolent civil rights campaign modelled on that of the Reverend Martin Luther King, Jr.[7]

AT the Sinn Féin *Ard Fheis**, Éamonn MacThomáis put his name forward to become secretary. Afterwards Barry Halloran paid a visit to his friend to learn the outcome of the vote. Éamonn told him, "When the ballots arrived I discovered my name had been left off."

"You're not serious."

"He is serious," interjected Rosaleen MacThomáis, Éamonn's lovely young wife. "And I'm that upset about it too!" Her brown eyes snapped with anger. Barry was suddenly reminded that Eamon de Valera had described the female republicans of 1916 as "at once the boldest and the most unmanageable revolutionaries."[8]

Éamonn patted his wife's hand. "It's all right, *Roisín*."†

"It's not all right. Tell Barry what happened next."

"I complained to Cathal Goulding. Since Cathal has a reputation for ruthlessness, you can imagine my surprise when he said—very gently—'You have your fingers in so many pies, Éamonn. Your friends thought you were probably doing too much already.' In the kindest possible way, he was telling me I'd been purged without even knowing it."[9]

"I'm gobsmacked, Éamonn."

"So was I, at the time. I suppose I should have seen it coming when I was voted off the Army Council. But there were things going on that I couldn't stomach and I said so."

"Such as?"

"Robbing banks, for one. The dissidents have been doing it for a while; now some of our lads seem to think it's a good idea. But I ask you, Barry—how can we hope to create the republic we dreamt of on the proceeds of thievery?"

"Put that way, it sounds absurd."

"It is absurd. Men who break the law can't be trusted to make the law."

"Where does that leave the IRA? And you, for that matter?"

"I honestly don't know," Thomas said wearily. "The physical-force men were afraid I'd take the Dublin brigade in the opposite direction, so they got me off the Army Council. Now those who think like Cathal Goulding have denied me any power in Sinn Féin because I can't support their communist leanings. But I'm still a republican. I'll always be a republican."

"So will I," said Barry. *Whatever that means today.*

*Convention; literally "high festival."

†Little Rose.

.   .   .

WHEN Barry returned to Harold's Cross a letter was waiting for him. "It's from a woman," Philpott said. "The envelope smells of perfume."

"Thank you." Barry took the note and turned away.

Philpott followed him. "That doesn't look like your mother's handwriting, Mr. Halloran. I don't allow women here. You know that, don't you? You have to abide by the rules!"

Barry walked swiftly to his room, fighting back an impulse to hit the man.

October 5th
Dear Barry,
I'm in Dublin and I'm staying at the Russell Hotel. Please phone me. I'm dying to see you.

Yours ever,
Barbara Kavanagh

Chapter Twenty-nine

D O you want to make love to me?" Barbara asked.

Barry choked on his tea. "What?"

"I said do you want to make love to me?" Her eyes were bold with challenge.

Nothing in Barry's experience had prepared him for this moment. "Have you ever ... I mean ..."

"I was in Italy for two years, so what do you think? I went through those romantic Italian men like a hot knife through butter." Seeing his appalled expression, Barbara laughed.

B ARRY had telephoned the Russell with mixed feelings. Barbara Kavanagh made him uncomfortable, yet he found the prospect of meeting her again exciting.

He was not disappointed. Waiting at the front desk when she emerged from the lift, Barry saw the way every man in the hotel lobby turned to look at her. She ignored them. Fixing her golden eyes—*tiger's eyes!*—on Barry's, she walked straight across the lobby to him. "I'm so glad you're here!" She threw her arms around his neck and kissed him on either cheek.

Barry felt his ears burning. He was terribly, wonderfully aware of the other men staring at them.

"Of course I'm here," he said. "Your letter amounted to a command performance."

Two years had wrought a number of changes in the girl. She was by far the tallest woman in the hotel lobby; she did not have to stand on tiptoe to put her arms around his neck. Her bosom was fuller than Barry remembered, and her voice had taken on a husky quality.

He gently disentangled her arms and stepped back. Yet he could still feel the imprint of her body on his. "Would you care to sit down?" he asked politely. "They'll serve us tea right here if you like."

"I'd like something stronger."

"But you're only . . ."

"Nineteen years old, and I'd like a drink."

"I don't think they'd serve you anything alcoholic here."

"Then let's go somewhere else."

I'm not about to let her dictate to me. Nineteen years old indeed! Firmly taking Barbara by the elbow, Barry steered her toward two armchairs on either side of a small table. "I would like a cup of tea," he said emphatically. "You can have one with me, or not."

"Can we have some cookies too? Real cookies, not amaretti or anything like that?"

Barry ordered tea and an assortment of sweet biscuits. "Now tell me about Italy, Barbara. And your singing."

"Oh. That. Well, Italy turned out to be nothing like I'd expected. It's a beautiful country, but I didn't get to do any of the things I wanted. And I'm not going to be an opera singer after all."

"Oh, Barbara, I am sorry."

"I did my best," she said petulantly. "But every time I made a little progress I was sent to a new and supposedly better voice coach. Practice practice practice. I was always singing—except when I was working on my breathing, or my diction, or studying foreign languages. There was no time for anything else." She gestured constantly as she spoke. Finger butterflies fluttering in the air.

"I thought Milan would be wonderful. I was going to go to lots of fashion shows and learn to ski in the Alps and meet lots of gorgeous Italian men. Instead I might as well have been a nun." Barbara broke off when the biscuits arrived and began cramming them into her mouth.

Barry waited.

With her mouth full Barbara mumbled, "No more sugar, that's what my last voice coach told me." She paused to swallow. "He was an absolute dictator, Barry. Have you ever heard of Mussolini?"

"The Italian dictator? I have of course."

"Well, Maestro Antonelli was Mussolini Junior. He ruined my life."

Barry felt as if a petrol bomb had exploded inside him. "Do you mean . . ."

"He made me work hour after hour until I was hoarse, then he said I was too weak and must build up my vocal cords with still more exercises. Eventually I had the most awful attack of laryngitis, I couldn't talk for ages. As soon as it cleared up he started on me all over again. You can't imagine how terrible it was. Finally my voice simply wouldn't come back, it was absolutely shredded.

The doctor said the vocal cords were permanently damaged. Mother's going to sue. Can we get some more of these cookies?"

So that's all, just her voice. Thank God. I thought she'd been raped. "What a dreadful thing to happen," he commiserated. "Your beautiful voice."

"There's a lot more to me than a voice," she said indignantly.

"Of course there is, I only meant . . ."

"Mother's exactly the same. I've had to endure two absolutely awful years and all she cares about is what happened to my God-damned voice."

So she swears, on top of everything else. "Where is Isabella? Is she with you?"

"Mother hated Europe. I knew she would, she doesn't like anything. After a couple of months she went home and left me at the mercy of dictators."

Barry signalled the waiter to bring another plate of biscuits.

"What are your plans when you get back to Dallas?"

"I don't intend to go back to Dallas. Would you like to sit around the house all day with your mother?"

Barry gave a wry smile. "Surely you have other options."

That was when Barbara asked if he wanted to make love to her.

I *am not going to take advantage of this girl's naïveté,* Barry told himself sternly. *Besides, she's Henry Mooney's granddaughter, which makes her practically family. If I laid a finger on her, Ursula would have my guts for garters.* "I'm flattered, Barbara, but . . ."

"Don't you want to have sex with every beautiful woman you see?"

He was disconcerted by her bald use of the word *sex.* "Of course not!"

"You're lying. I don't mind, I'd expect you to. You have such good manners."

She made good manners sound like a character flaw. "I am not lying, Barbara. You should know better than to accuse anyone of—"

"Signore Favarelli accused me of lying when I said he was hurting my throat."

"Must you always interrupt?"

"I don't interrupt. I anticipate."

"Then tell me what I'm about to say next."

"You're about to call me a bloody pain in the ass."

"You're not as good as you think you are," Barry said stiffly. "I don't use language like that around women."

"So you admit I'm a woman."

"You are of course, but . . ."

"Then don't treat me like a little girl. Give me a straight answer. Do you want to have sex with me or not?"

"Feck it!" Barry exploded. Jumping to his feet, he signalled the waiter to bring the bill and strode toward the front desk.

Barbara followed him. "And just where do you think you're going?"

"Home." He flung the word over his shoulder without looking back.

"But you can't!"

Barry whirled around. "I can do anything I want!" His eyes were savage. It was the first time he had let any woman glimpse the other Barry. The one he kept tightly leashed.

Barbara froze like a rabbit in the lights. "Yes," she said in an uncharacteristically faint voice. "Yes, of course you can." The two stood facing each other. The air between them vibrated with tension.

The other occupants of the hotel lobby politely averted their eyes.

Like a musical instrument changing keys, Barbara's tone changed. "Don't look at me like that, Barry. I was only teasing about Italian men. I didn't make love with any of them."

"Really?" His voice was cold.

"Yes, really. Can we sit down again? Please?"

"If you wish." Still cold. He was being defensive, though she could not know that.

They resumed their seats at the small table. Barry picked up his cup. The tea was cold too. *Her fault.*

"I suppose I shouldn't have come out with it like that," Barbara said, "but I've been thinking a lot about you."

He waited. Silently.

"I'm going to make love with somebody sometime."

"Probably," he conceded.

"So I thought . . . well, it might as well be you. At least you can speak English. And you are absolutely the most handsome man I know."

Barry had to bite the inside of his cheek to keep from smiling. *It would be a dreadful mistake to let this girl think she can get around me.* "You sound very determined, Barbara. Don't I have a say in this?"

"Well yes. Of course." She reached for another sweet biscuit, crumbled it between her fingers, and let the fragments fall into her teacup. "I just thought you'd want to." Now there was a defensive chill in her voice.

The sooner she goes back to Texas the better, Barry told himself.

"Let's look at this realistically, Barbara. I'm eight years older than you, we hardly know one another, and you've just been through a difficult time so you may not be thinking clearly. You may not want to go home but you really have no option, so . . ."

"Of course I have an option. My grandfather left me a trust fund, so I can stay here if I want to. And I do."

"But your mother . . ."

"My mother," said Barbara, "is a snakes' nest of resentments that make her impossible to live with. Oh, she doesn't complain openly, she's too much of a lady for that. But she makes certain everyone in a five-mile radius knows exactly how she feels."

"What could Isabella possibly have to resent?"

"Everything. When she was growing up she resented her own mother for being more beautiful than she ever could be. I figured that out from things she's said over the years. She still resents Aunt Hank for being the one who was named for Grandpapa Henry, although I don't see how the poor woman could help it. Mother resents that Hank will always be richer than she is, because Hank's husband makes a lot of money. She resents me for being young and having my whole life ahead of me. She even resents the law of gravity. But most of all my mother resents yours."

"Mine?" Barry was astonished. "You mean Ursula?"

"Yes of course. Mother positively hates her. Didn't you know?"

Barry shook his head. "I'm beginning to think the female mind is beyond my comprehension."

Barbara gave a low, throaty laugh. "Your speech is so elegant compared to the way they talk in Texas. I just know I'm going to be happy here."

That night Barry telephoned Ursula. On the notepad beside the telephone in the hall, he wrote down the length of the call so he could pay Mr. Philpott. Otherwise he would lose phone privileges.

When Barry gave his mother a severely edited version of his encounter with Barbara, she laughed. "It sounds as if the girl has a crush on you, Barry. Surely you can handle it."

"But she plans to stay here, Ursula. What am I going to do?"

"Nothing. She's not your responsibility. I can't imagine Barbara could ever adapt herself to our ways—or our standard of living. Simply keep an eye on her so that no harm comes to her. She'll be on her way home soon enough."

Simply keep an eye on her. Ursula doesn't understand the situation.

He was not about to explain it to her.

Impelled by the good manners that Barbara derided, he promised to introduce her to his bank manager and help her find a flat—which she persisted in calling an apartment. When he put out feelers amongst his friends, Barry added, "The place must be as far from Harold's Cross as possible."

After several days Dennis Cassidy reported, "We've found the perfect flat. Alice's parents live in Dun Laoghaire, and the people next door to them want to let the top storey of their house."

"You'll like Dun Laoghaire," Barry assured Barbara. "There are some very pretty houses along the seafront, plus the harbour and the strand and . . ."

"Strand of what?"

"A strand is a beach."

"Why don't you just say beach, then?"

"Barbara, if you're going to stay here you're going to have to learn Irish English. It isn't the same as American English."

"It's all English, isn't it?"

"No," said Barry firmly. "It is not 'all English.'"

FOR no reason that Barry could imagine, Alice Green took a strong liking to Barbara. It was Alice who taught the American girl to give the town its correct spelling instead of "Dunleary," and pointed out the best shops. "How long are you going to stay in Ireland?" she asked not once but several times.

"I haven't decided," Barbara told her.

"With America to go back to? I know what I would do if I . . ."

"There are things Ireland has that America doesn't."

"Like a certain man, for example?" Alice giggled.

"I wouldn't stay here for a mere man," said Barbara. "I can have any man I want."

Alice looked her new friend up and down. "I'm sure."

ON the tenth of November, Seán Lemass, plagued by political difficulties and ill health that he refused to acknowledge, stood up in the Dáil chamber to announce his resignation as taoiseach. He followed his announcement with a single sentence in Irish, which he then repeated in English. "I recommend to Dáil Éireann Deputy John Lynch for appointment as taoiseach."[1]

Seán Lemass was a patriot, an old warrior who had fought in the GPO in 1916, in the War of Independence, and in the Civil War. John Mary Lynch, who went by the name of Jack, was eighteen years younger and had fought his battles on the sporting field, winning all-Ireland titles with Cork in both hurling and Gaelic football. The popular former athlete was nicknamed "the Nice Fellow."

Barry joined the throng of reporters and photographers who besieged Lemass on the steps of Leinster House after his announcement. Lemass, who looked tired, continued to smoke his pipe while answering their questions with characteristic brevity.

"Political infighting was bound to bring him down sooner or later," Barry heard one reporter remark to another. "Fianna Fáil's always been rough-and-tumble."

"Give us a few words on the man you've nominated to succeed you," someone called out.

With an enigmatic smile Lemass replied, "If anything, Jack Lynch is a tougher individual than I am."[2]

Chapter Thirty

CHRISTMAS presented Barry with a dilemma. The proper thing to do, since Barbara had no family in Ireland, would be to invite her to the farm for the holiday. But when a man took a woman home with him at Christmas it was considered tantamount to announcing their engagement.

Yet how could he leave her alone in Dublin amongst relative strangers?

And what assumptions would she make if he stayed in Dublin to be with her?

In the end he settled for a compromise. He bought train tickets for himself and Barbara and took her to the farm. There he left her in the company of his mother—who was not too pleased about the arrangement—while he recovered his old bicycle from the barn and prepared to set off for Tipperary. "I have some business that will keep me away over the holidays," he told the two women.

His mother was scowling at him.

BARRY was relieved to find Séamus McCoy still in Ballina. "I was afraid you would go north for the Christmas."

"I thought about it," Séamus said, "but in the finish-up I'm not much of a man for celebrating holidays. So here I am on my own."

"Would you like some company?"

"Are you not going to the farm?"

"I've already been," Barry replied succinctly.

The two men went to Mass together in the Catholic church on top of the hill in Killaloe. At the foot of the street was the Cathedral of Saint Flannan, built in the thirteenth century on the ruins of a still earlier church. Now an Anglican cathedral, it served a dwindling Protestant congregation. An ancient tombstone recessed in the Romanesque doorway marked the burial site of Muircheartach Mor, Brian Bóru's great-grandson.[1]

On Christmas morning the bells of both churches, Protestant and Catholic, pealed as one.

Barry and Séamus took Christmas dinner with the Reddan family. Barry enjoyed being with his old friends and ate two helpings of Peg Reddan's roasted turkey. But like spectres at the feast, thoughts of Ursula and Barbara haunted him.

I've done the best I could, damn it.

McCoy asked no questions. He simply accepted that Barry needed a place to stay for a few days and made him comfortable in the room above the pub. When the weather was fine they went for long walks beside Lough Derg, talking about the Army, or politics, or, occasionally, themselves. Sometimes they did not talk at all, but strolled along in a companionable silence. Barry was deeply grateful to have found such a friend; a man to whom he could say almost anything.

I wonder if my father was anything like Séamus McCoy.

When the rain poured down, the two men stayed indoors and read. Barry was glad to have a chance to browse through McCoy's extensive collection of republican reading material. Evenings were spent in the pub with the hammer on the wall, talking about sports or politics or the weather. But never the Army.

When he could put it off no longer, Barry went back to the farm to collect Barbara. "I have an assignment back in Dublin," he explained to his mother. That was all he explained. He ignored the exasperated look Ursula gave him.

Barbara did not chastise him for going off and leaving her, as he had expected. Her eyes were bright and her skin was glowing and she gave the appearance of being very much at home. Before they left the farmhouse she threw her arms around Ursula in a big hug. The older woman stiffened slightly. Then, seeing Barry watching, she forced herself to smile. "It's been grand, Barbara. Do come again sometime."

She's lying through her teeth, thought Barry. *Obviously they didn't get along very well. But then, I didn't expect they would.*

IT was a most enjoyable bit of mischief. Life had not offered Barry many opportunities for mischief lately, but the little boy buried inside him was still there.

On the train Barry asked Barbara if she had enjoyed her holiday. "It certainly wasn't the Christmas I expected, but it was interesting. Your customs are so different from ours. For one thing, I didn't see Christmas lights on any of the houses. In Dallas we have thousands of coloured lights on everything, even draped around the trees and shrubbery. People put life-sized figures of Santa

Claus with his sleigh on their roofs, or the manger with angels and shepherds on their lawns. Or both at once. Sometimes they play Christmas music over loudspeakers. It's a tradition to drive around the city at night to see the displays. Some of them are absolutely spectacular."

"I'm sure they are," Barry said faintly.

"There's nothing like that in Ireland," Barbara went on. "It's so quiet here. On Christmas Eve I went to church with your mother . . ."

Dear God, I never even thought to ask if she's a Catholic!

". . . And since neither of us is a very good cook, the next day we had our dinner at the Olde Ground Hotel in Ennis. What a wonderful place, shabby and grand at the same time. So very Irish."

"Shabby and grand at the same time is Anglo-Irish," Barry said.

"What's the difference?"

I will not take on the Irish education of Barbara Kavanagh, he told himself. But he knew he would.

At the train station in Dublin he hired a taxicab and delivered Barbara to Dun Laoghaire. He had the taxi wait while he walked her to the door like a solicitous older brother. After a moment's hesitation he gave her a light kiss on the cheek, then walked away before she could invite him to come in.

His nostrils were filled with the perfume of her hair.

JANUARY was a bitter month, with frigid winds and lowering skies. Barry Halloran was indifferent to the cold. Weeks spent shivering in muddy dugouts half filled with icy water had inured him to normal winter weather. But he awoke one morning to find himself worrying about Barbara. *She's from Texas. And Italy's a warm climate, isn't it? Is she able for the kind of weather we have here? Is there enough heating in her flat? I should have made certain she has a working fireplace, or at least a three-bar heater.*

Barbara continued to be on his mind while he read the morning papers.

Taoiseach Jack Lynch had just met with Prime Minister Harold Wilson in London to discuss their countries' respective applications to join the European Economic Community, originally known as the Common Market.

I wonder if it's as cold in London as it is here, thought Barry. Putting the papers aside, he stared out the window for a while. But he was not thinking about London.

IN Switzers' Department Store, where Alice was now a full-time employee, selling women's hats, Barry Halloran felt very out-of-place. He was far too big to be comfortable amongst the little dressing tables and small stools where women sat while trying on their purchases.

Alice was surprised to see him. "Can I help you?" she asked with a nervous giggle.

"Actually you can. I was wondering if you know what sort of heat Barbara—Miss Kavanagh—has in her flat."

Alice's expression of surprise intensified. "What a thoughtful man you are! As it happens I called in to see Barbara over the weekend and she had a lovely coal fire blazing, so I'm sure she's as snug as can be. I'll tell her you were worrying about her, though."

"Don't do that! I mean, there's no need to mention this conversation. I was only making an enquiry on behalf of her mother."

Alice gave Barry a conspiratorial smile. "Don't worry. Your secret is safe with me."

AT the end of January three American astronauts, "Gus" Grissom, Ed White, and Roger Chafee, died in a flash fire that destroyed their space capsule on the launch pad.

Barry Halloran was amongst the many Irish men and women who called at the American Embassy to sign a book of condolence.

The families of the dead astronauts declared that their dream would not die with them.

WITHIN days the Northern Ireland Civil Rights Association was formed. The first meeting took place in the International Hotel in Belfast. Amongst those present were constitutional nationalists, liberal unionists, radical lawyers, socialists, members of the Irish Communist Party, and republicans inspired by Cathal Goulding.[2]

ON the first of February, Senator Margaret Mary Pearse gave the house and grounds of St. Enda's College to the Irish nation. Barry Halloran was amongst those who attended the ceremony.

A member of Seanad Éireann since 1938, Senator Pearse was the last surviving member of her family. She did not encourage publicity and was rarely photographed. Rumour had it that she was not in good health, which was why she was making the donation at this time. It was intended to be not only a memorial to her brothers, Pádraic and Willie Pearse, but also to the dream of an Irish republic.

While the speeches were being made Barry stood off to one side, studying her face. He was hoping for a photograph like the one he had taken of de

Valera; one of those rare and magical glimpses of truth that could only happen by accident.

Margaret Pearse had a sweet, round face beneath a cloud of white hair dressed in the style of an earlier era. The distance between nose and chin was very short. The darkness in the eyes was very deep.

What does she see when she closes her eyes at night? Two young men going off on their bicycles that Easter Monday morning, stopping at the foot of the drive, perhaps, to wave back to her one last time?

At that moment Senator Pearse turned her head and looked straight at Barry. Between them passed a soundless communication like moths courting; less than a breath, more than a thought.

He lifted his camera and took the picture.

I have a job!" Barbara's voice carolled down the phone line. Barry had given her the number with firm instructions never to use it unless she was in trouble. He was not surprised that she ignored his injunction.

"I didn't know you wanted a job," Barry said.

"It was the most amazing thing. I was beginning to feel a little bored—you know—so I went to a fashion show at Brown Thomas. I got to talking to one of the models afterward and guess what?"

"You're going to be a model?"

"Of course not. I'm tall enough but my bones are too big, I could never look willowy. No, this girl told me about a friend of hers who's an impresario in the entertainment business in England. She said he was looking for a singer."

"But I thought your voice was . . ."

"Ruined for opera but not for jazz. Don't you love jazz? I do. Anyway, Moya's friend put together a new trio and they want a singer, so she telephoned him and he came over to Dublin and I sang for him and he was very impressed and . . . well, the upshot is, I've got the job. I'm flying to London tomorrow."

"You're going to London? And you don't know anything about this man. Who is he and what—"

"He's developed a lot of acts and he says my voice is absolutely perfect for the sort of songs Ella Fitzgerald does."

"Barbara, you can't simply—"

"It's all settled, I told you. I'm leaving tomorrow."

"But your flat . . ."

"Oh, I'll let that go. We're going to be on the road for a while, getting established, so there's no point in holding on to a place here."

"That's absurd," said Barry, trying to hide his dismay. "You have no background in jazz and no one's listening to it now anyway. Music today is—"

"Don't be such a stick-in-the-mud, Barry," she said. "Jazz is due for a revival. Jeremy says we have to be ahead of the trend, not following it."

"Jeremy, is that his name? What's the rest of it? And what does he want with a girl who—"

"His name is Jeremy Seyboldt and it isn't sex he's after, if that's what you're worried about. Jeremy's gay."

"Gay?"

"What on earth's the matter with you? Gay! You know, queer. Homosexual. But don't hold that against him, he's an absolutely lovely man."

Jaysus, Barry thought after he put down the telephone receiver. *What am I going to tell Ursula?*

In the end he told her nothing at all. *We Irish are masters of the fudge.*

Two weeks later he received a postcard from Barbara with an address in Manchester. "We'll be here for six weeks, then we're going to Edinburgh," she wrote. "I'm having a great time and the British love me. I may stay forever."

IN May, Ireland and Britain applied together to join the EEC. For the second time, de Gaulle of France said no to Britain. The decision on Ireland was merely deferred.

URSULA'S voice came singing down the telephone wire. "For once we beat them," she rejoiced to her son. "We'll be in the EEC long before Britain—if they ever are."

"Of course they will be, Ursula. It's inevitable."

"I don't see anything inevitable about it. Besides, if we're in and they're out, it's just one more severing of any tie between us."

Barry said, "The ties will never be totally severed, no matter how much we might wish otherwise. We share a language and a concept of government, and English blood flows in so many Irish veins. Besides, did you ever study a map? This island broke off that one millions of years ago and we're still practically right on their doorstep."

"You needn't sound so happy about it."

"I'm not particularly happy about it. But sometimes one must face reality."

Chapter Thirty-one

NINETEEN sixty-seven was a year of growth and consolidation for Barry. Film was expensive so he tried to make every shot count. As his proficiency increased so did his reputation. He travelled throughout the Republic photographing a nation pulling itself up by its bootstraps. In addition to images of a political nature there was always money to be made from photographing a wedding, or fashion models wearing Mary O'Donnell's latest creations. For a time Barry had a huge crush on the stunning Mary, but she had so many admirers that he felt lost in the crowd.

Ireland in the late sixties was high-spirited and forward-looking. The rural lifestyle was being elbowed aside by the hard edge of urban aspirations. The middle class had more money to spend. Television was creating an unprecedented desire for consumer goods. Traditional disciplines—aside from those imposed by the Church, which still held—were beginning to break down. Youngsters found it fashionable to "cock a snook" at the older generation. People who had endured incredible hardships, people who had fought and even died for their country, were fading from the modern frame of reference.

Ireland was attempting to outgrow her past.

The latest census showed the first increase in population since the Famine. Since 1960 more than two hundred companies from abroad had established themselves in the Republic, and 80 percent of private investment was coming from foreign capital. Comprehensive post-primary education, free of cost, was preparing the next generation for a radically different Ireland.

But different did not necessarily mean better.

In spite of the Tourist Board's claim that Dublin epitomised Georgian elegance, Barry's camera discovered an appalling number of beautiful old street-scapes being wantonly destroyed to make room for blank-faced office blocks and so-called social housing designed without any degree of aesthetic sensibility. The new Dublin being erected on the lovely bones of the old had neither character nor grace. The Fianna Fáil government gave tacit acceptance to wholesale architectural vandalism so long as the developers kept slipping brown envelopes under the table.

AT irregular intervals Barry received postcards from Barbara Kavanagh. Almost every postmark was different, but the messages had a certain sameness. She was fine, she was doing well, she was happy.

Nothing that she wouldn't write to a maiden aunt, Barry thought sourly. *I should be thankful she's off my hands. She's far too unsettling.*

Yet whenever he found a postcard with her distinctive American scrawl amongst his letters, his heart leapt.

IN June, Cathal Goulding was the principal speaker at the annual Wolfe Tone Commemoration at Bodenstown, in County Kildare. Since 1962 the IRA as an active organisation had all but ceased to exist, yet attending the commemoration remained a ritual for Volunteers past and present. Séamus McCoy stood in the crowd beside Barry Halloran. McCoy's cough was worse than ever.

In his speech Goulding refuted the doctrine of physical-force republicanism and urged public service work instead.[1] When the speech was over, Barry turned to McCoy. "What do you think about that?"

"Not much, to be honest. I'm a soldier, that's what I volunteered for, not marching up and down carrying a placard, for God's sake. You opted out of active service, Seventeen, and I respect your decision, but I can't. Things may seem quiet enough in the north but . . . remember the Malvern Street murders last year? The loyalists think we're out of the picture so they can do what they like, but sooner or later they'll go too far."

"How far is too far, Séamus?"

"We'll know when it happens," McCoy said. His eyes were bleak, but a tight little smile twitched the corners of his mouth.

The bright sky had clouded over. A sodden drizzle began to fall. Barry said, "You in a hurry to go back to County Tip?"

"Not at all, I'm headed the other way. Connolly Station and the Belfast train."

"Stop at my place first for a chin-wag. I've half a bottle of Jameson's under the bed."

"I'm your man," said McCoy.

They hitched a ride with a fellow Volunteer who was taking several other men into the city, to the Bleeding Horse Pub. "Join us," they urged. "A lot of the lads'll be there."

"Some other time," Barry said. "Séamus has a train to catch." He did not see McCoy very often and did not want to try to carry on a conversation over the rowdy noise of a pub. A short walk from the Bleeding Horse took the two men to Harold's Cross. Barry put a tumbler of whiskey in McCoy's hand and seated him in the one good armchair. "Now, Séamus. What's this about you going north?"

"The commemoration of the Rising stirred up a lot of interest in Belfast. Some of the younger generation want to recover the spirit of 1916, and they're interested in the IRA. Unfortunately nothing's left of the Belfast Brigade but a few old veterans from the forties. However, Sinn Féin has suggested I might give the lads a series of lectures on republicanism."

Barry raised an eyebrow. "Recruiting lectures?"

"Educational lectures. The Army's not actively recruiting, but these are working-class Catholic lads who can't get jobs and they desperately need something. If nothing else comes along they might be drawn into the worst of the militant splinter groups; you know which ones I mean."

Barry nodded. "The IRA dissidents who've become involved in criminal activity that has nothing to do with furthering the cause."

"Aye. And that's no place for decent boys, in my opinion. So we're going to offer the lads a lecture a week and teach them the true meaning of the republican movement."

"I recall the first lecture you gave me, Séamus. You said the Army demanded absolute commitment, dedication, and honour. Or else. You had me scared to death."

McCoy grinned. "You weren't scared, you loved it. Young men always think they can be valiant—until they're pushed to the pin of their collar, that is. But you proved you were able for it, didn't you?"

Barry tried to look modest, though he was intensely pleased.

"My next step," McCoy went on, "will be to explain when and why the republican movement began. I didn't have to do that with you, but I surely will with these lads. Northerners aren't told about the centuries of brutal oppression, or how our land was looted. They're taught only English history, which claims England is the source of all good things. For all they know in the Six Counties, Ireland was inhabited by ring-tailed baboons until Queen Liz and her toadies came along to civilise us.

"Once they're enlightened on that score we'll go into republican ideology and aspirations. For the grand finale I'll explain that being a Volunteer means having little money and few friends, and the distinct possibility of imprisonment or death."

"If you have even two or three still with you after that depressing news," said Barry, "what will you do with them?"

"Teach 'em a wee bit of military drill. Call 'em reservists. Don't look at me like that, Seventeen. You know the struggle's not over."

"I know."

"Don't suppose you'd like to come with me? Help teach history, maybe?"

Barry felt a sudden, almost overpowering longing. For comrades who felt as he did, men who spoke the same language. *Maybe someday we'll drive the bastards out of Ireland once and for all!* It was frightening to realise how quickly the surge of excitement came back, in spite of the man he thought he was. "My place is here now," he said firmly. As much for himself as for McCoy.

"Aye." McCoy slumped in his chair, hugging his midriff. "And you're right too. I can see you're well dug in and making a few bob; that's a new coat hanging on the peg."

"It is a new coat."

"Well dug in," McCoy repeated. "Nice place."

"Next you'll be telling me that all it lacks is a woman's touch."

"That's your business. There was a time I thought of marrying, though. A couple of times, in fact, but it never worked out. The Army. You know."

"I know."

"What about yourself, Seventeen?"

Barry kept his voice light. "What woman would be willing to live the way I do?"

"There's that," McCoy agreed. "I've never heard a single one say she wanted a stone nose under a bell jar in her parlour." He lit a cigarette and began blowing smoke rings. Both men watched the amorphous circles drift upward, lose shape, disappear.

Barry asked, "Would you like to listen to the gramophone?"

"How about the Clancy Brothers and Tommy Makem? You have them?"

"'Fraid not," Barry admitted. "Lately I've been playing a lot of Ella Fitzgerald."

"Let's hear her, then."

McCoy closed his eyes and leaned his head against the back of the chair. Except for the singer's voice the room was quiet. Peaceful.

"Nice," McCoy pronounced with the record ended. "Not as good as Hank Williams, but nice. I'd best get on the road, though. That train won't wait for me."

At the front door he paused. "One of these days," he told Barry, "we may need an experienced engineer to teach newcomers about explosives."

"Nelson's Pillar was my last bomb, Séamus."

"For certain?"

"You have my word on it."

Barry watched the older man walk away down the street. The rain was falling harder. McCoy coughed and turned up the collar of his coat.

That night Barry dreamed he was trying to cut lengths from a roll of commercial fuse with a dull pocket knife. Suddenly the cord pulled away from him and reared up above his head, swaying back and forth and hissing.

He heard Barbara Kavanagh's voice say, "That's a Texas rattlesnake. If it bites you you're dead."

JEREMY Seyboldt was no impresario. Barbara had soon discovered that he was a self-aggrandising hustler with no scruples. His knowledge of music was superficial at best, but this was Swinging Sixties London. The Beatles and Carnaby Street. Anyone who could Keep Up with the Beat stood a chance of Making It Big.

Jeremy spoke in superlatives, unlike most Englishmen but like many Americans. Barbara warmed to him for that reason alone. That, and because he was absolutely determined to succeed at something. Anything. No matter what it took.

She felt the same way herself.

Glowing letters to her mother gave the impression that she was rising steadily in the musical firmament. She made offhanded references to famous people she claimed to have met in Britain. "It's only a matter of time before I'm as big as any of them," she wrote.

Isabella's reply was a short note to the effect that she was planning to have the house painted.

In the latest dreary closet that served as her latest dreary dressing room, Barbara wadded the note into a ball and threw it at the wastebasket. The basket was already overflowing with tissues stained with cold cream and makeup. The letter bounced off and rolled a short distance across the floor.

Barbara folded her arms on the cluttered dressing table and put her head down on them. "I'm going to be a star," she whispered into the darkness between her elbows. "I am."

She was determined not to cry.

BARRY'S photographs covered a wide range of subjects. He was proud of some of them. Others were simply pictures he took because he knew he could sell them. Freelancing was never easy, but he relished the uncertainty. As long as he kept his expenses down he could be his own man.

When Barbara Kavanagh commandeered his fantasies he reminded himself that he could not afford her.

Barry had not crossed the border since his injury, but knowing that Séamus McCoy was in Belfast refocussed his attention. The electronic media and southern newspapers gave little coverage to Belfast and almost none to the rest of the province. As far as southern Ireland was concerned, the north was a planet apart.

As far as the world's concerned, Northern Ireland is a planet apart, Barry thought sourly. *But the problems are still there in spite of O'Neill's efforts. Unfortunately he's too liberal for the unionists and not liberal enough for the nationalists. Séamus is right. Sooner rather than later, there's going to be trouble. Then we'll need someone who can show the rest of the world what's going on.*

I could do it.

The gun's on the shelf, but the camera isn't.

Barry had been confident of his courage, which was rooted in a cold rage he could summon almost at will and aim in any direction he chose. Rage had made him invincible.

But that was before Derry.

Now his body knew on a cellular level the awful dimensions of pain. When he thought of returning to Northern Ireland his bones remembered. *I don't have to go back there. No one expects it of me.*

ON December eleventh, Taoiseach Jack Lynch had his first meeting with Northern Ireland's prime minister, Terence O'Neill, at Stormont. As Lynch's car arrived, the Reverend Ian Paisley bombarded it with snowballs.

Barry Halloran was disappointed that he had not been on hand to photograph the shameful incident.

The following day an opinion poll in the north revealed that if the people were given a choice between O'Neill and Paisley, 90 percent would choose O'Neill.

Chapter Thirty-two

THERE was something in the air in 1968, and the name of it was revolt. Around the world young people were taking to the streets, vehemently protesting injustice. In Paris and Prague and Philadelphia, students, dissidents, and anti-war activists were prepared to shake the foundations of the establishment.

Meanwhile, in the Six Counties the first generation of Catholics to attend university was coming of age.

The British administration was about to see the results of its neglect of Northern Ireland since 1921.

IN February, Father Aloysius wrote to Barry, "The Northern Ireland Civil Rights Association has proposed a programme for one man, one vote, to put an end to gerrymandering. NICRA is also calling for a fair-housing policy for the underprivileged, plus repeal of the Special Powers Act that keeps this province effectively under martial law. Last but by no means least, NICRA wants the disbanding of the B-Specials. There is a rumour that some Sinn Féin activists are working with NICRA now,[1] helping to organise nonviolent demonstrations to call attention to the civil rights issue. You might like to come up and photograph the protests."

Holding the letter in his hand, Barry looked around his comfortable room. On the table was a new edition of Yeats's poems. On the gramophone Julie London was singing "Cry Me a River." That evening he was going to the cinema with one of the young women he took out from time to time. With a bit of luck the evening might end with the two of them in bed. He had reason to believe that the young woman was expecting it.

Barry looked back at the priest's letter. *What about what I expect of my-self?*

Dear Father Aloysius,
When NICRA's plans for a civil rights demonstration are confirmed, please send me the details.

As ever,
Barry

On the fourth of April, 1968, the Reverend Martin Luther King, Jr., was assassinated in Memphis, Tennessee.

THE civil rights movement in Northern Ireland was gaining momentum. Because there was a small but visible improvement in the lot of Catholics in the eastern part of the province, Catholics west of the River Bann felt more disenfranchised than ever.

In County Tyrone hundreds of Catholic families, many of them with a large number of children, had been on waiting lists for as much as ten years in hopes of being allocated public housing. Then a Protestant woman became engaged to an Orange politician and was immediately given a house. Two outraged Catholic families staged a sit-in in protest.[2]

When Austin Currie, a newly elected Nationalist MP, joined in the protest, the result was a flurry of publicity that infuriated the Unionists.

"A sit-in does not offer much in the way of photographic possibilities," Father Aloysius wrote to Barry, "but there may be more dramatic events soon. I'll let you know."

In August the priest informed Barry, "NICRA is joining with the Campaign for Social Justice to hold a full-scale, nonviolent civil rights march in County Tyrone on the twenty-fourth."

County Tyrone.

Derry was close to the northern tip of County Tyrone.

Derry, which lay at the root of his fear.

If I fell off a horse Mam made me get back on as soon as possible. Even if— particularly if—I was hurt. She said it was the only way not to lose my nerve.

I refuse to be afraid for the rest of my life. That would be worse than pain.

In the grey light of dawn Barry packed up his camera equipment. After breakfast he paid his rent for a month in advance.

"You are coming back?" Mr. Philpott asked anxiously. "If not I'll be wanting to let the room."

"I only intend to be gone for a few days, then I'm coming back, I promise." That promise made Barry feel better.

As soon as he boarded the train for the north he took out his book of Yeats's poetry and read with ferocious concentration. Strangely, once he crossed the border his apprehension faded. *I'm committed now. The campaign's begun.*

MAY Coogan answered his knock on the door. "Yes?" she ventured warily.

"Don't you know me, May?" Barry whipped off the knitted cap he had pulled over his hair and stood tall, abandoning the slouch he had affected since leaving the train station. "You took care of me when I was broken in bits."

Her jaw dropped "Merciful hour, it's you!"

Barry laughed. "The proverbial bad penny."

"Just wait 'til I tell Father. He'll be so pleased."

"Is he here?"

"He's taking Mass to his shut-ins, but he should be back in an hour or so. Come through and I'll put the kettle on; I want to hear everything that's happened since we saw you last."

They were still sitting at the kitchen table when the priest returned. May called out, "Father! You'll never believe who's come back to us."

Father Aloysius wrung both of Barry's hands, exclaiming several times, "I can't believe you're really here." Time was not being kind to the priest. He had gone totally bald, while the furrows in his face had deepened dramatically. His head resembled a knobbly hill above a ploughed field.

Barry explained, "I've come to photograph the civil rights demonstration you wrote about. Since Derry's close to Tyrone I was hoping you could put me up for a night or two."

"Gladly. And I can drive you down, too. I have an old car now, a banger, but it will get us there and probably get us back."

"Why, is it far?"

"They'll be marching from Coalisland to Dungannon at the other end of the county. You'd be a lot closer if you stayed in Belfast."

Barry shook his head. "I'd prefer to be in Derry."

"I'm glad to hear it, I'd prefer to have you here. We have a lot of catching up to do."

That evening Father Aloysius invited Terence Roche to join them for supper. Before Roche would even sit down at the table, he insisted on examining Barry's leg with professional thoroughness.

"It's mended much better than I expected, I have to say. Does it give you any trouble?"

"Nothing to moan about."

"You had a narrow escape, young man. You should have been dead. After you left here, I told John you'd be crippled for the rest of your life."

"I'm glad you didn't tell me that. I expected to get well, so I did."

Father Aloysius said, "There's proof of the power of faith, Terry."

"Proof that I'm a better doctor than you'll admit," his friend replied.

If the priest was aging badly, Terence Roche, whose appearance had repelled Barry when they first met, was surprisingly improved. His voice was still a dull monotone, but he was sporting a set of gleaming white false teeth and there was a definite sparkle in his eyes.

"I've taken a wife since I saw you last," he told Barry over dinner.

"Congratulations, Terry. Will I meet her?"

May Coogan gave a sniff as she set a platter of chops on the table. "Chance'd be a fine thing. The new Mrs. Roche isn't one for mingling with the lower classes."

Terry Roche frowned. "She's not like that and you know it. She's just shy."

"And a Prod. I don't know why you couldn't marry one of your own people."

"I love my wife, May," Roche said softly.

The housekeeper swallowed hard. Colour flooded her face and she retired in confusion. When the time came for serving the pudding the priest went into the kitchen and brought it back himself.

Shortly after the meal the doctor excused himself and went home. Barry and Father Aloysius settled down in the parlour for a long talk. Barry asked, "Why is May so upset about Terry's new wife?"

"She's always fancied him herself," said the priest. "I'm sure you noticed when you were here before."

Not a bit of it. Maybe I'm no good at recognising the signals people give out. Are they like a code?

THE following morning the priest's old Morris Minor grumbled like a living thing, threatening to die on every incline as they drove through the Sperrin Mountains. "Must be IRA transport," Barry muttered.

"Sorry? I couldn't hear you over the sound of the engine."

"You didn't miss anything, Father. I was talking to myself. Do you never do that?"

Father Aloysius, who was gripping the steering wheel firmly with both hands, nodded toward a little plastic statuette of the Blessed Virgin affixed to the dashboard. "I have her to talk to," he said.

Barry turned to look at him. "As a matter of interest—does she ever answer you?"

"Of course she does."

"How?"

"Deep in my soul."

"The spirit within," Barry murmured.

"Sorry?"

"Something I've heard my mother say. I wish she could meet you."

By the time they reached the designated meeting place in a field outside Coalisland, a large crowd had gathered. More were arriving every minute. The day was warm and partially overcast. A fitful sun flitted in and out of the clouds like someone peeping through the curtains of a stage set.

Father Aloysius parked the car on a rise at the edge of the field. As he and Barry got out, the priest said, "Help me find some rocks to put behind the wheels. I don't trust the handbrake at all."

When they were sure the Morris would not roll backwards, Barry took out his equipment. He loaded his two cameras and put extra rolls of film in his pockets. "I think the best way for me to do this is to walk with the demonstrators, Father," he said as he slung the cameras around his neck. "Can you meet us in Dungannon when we get there? Or do you want to join the march too?"

"My heart does, but my feet don't." Father Aloysius gestured ruefully toward his feet. His black leather shoes were deeply slashed over the instep. "I'm not up to much walking anymore, that's why I needed the car. Until he saw the condition of my feet the bishop wouldn't hear of it, but one look at them convinced him; the poor man suffers dreadfully from bunions and hammertoes himself. I'll see you off with my blessing, then I'll be waiting for you in the Square in Dungannon. I think it's only two or three miles. Can you make it that far?"

"I can of course, it's a doddle. I'm sorry for taking you away from your parish for a whole day, though."

"Nonsense. I belong here too."

As the crowd continued to grow, Barry scanned faces intently. There was no sign of Séamus McCoy or any of the IRA men he knew. This truly was a march of the people. By the time they were ready to move off, the demonstrators numbered several thousand men, women, and children. Barry photographed young mothers holding small sons and daughters by the hand. "It's for them we're doing this," one woman stressed. "Everything is for them."

AUSTIN Currie, who had organised the event, circulated amongst the marchers, giving encouragement, though they hardly seemed to need it. Excitement was running high. People were laughing and joking as they passed flasks of hot tea around. "Is there nothing stronger, Liam?"

"Not until Dungannon. We'll celebrate in Dungannon."

Someone else remarked, "The Prods aren't going to like this much. They think they have an exclusive right to march in this province."

When the signal was given they formed a column eight to ten deep and moved away up the road. Still laughing, still high-spirited. Barry walked at the edge of the crowd so that he could photograph individual faces.

This is the way we're going to do it, he said to himself. *One step at a time. No guns, no bombs, no violence, just the will of the people.*

A ray of sun danced briefly on the curls of a little blond girl a few steps ahead.

They had gone no more than half the distance when Barry saw the priest's car approaching, far too fast for the country road. Father Aloysius turned into a farm lane and waited until Barry came up to him. "I thought I'd better warn you," he said in an urgent voice. "The RUC intends to re-route the march because the Protestants are staging a counter demonstration. You won't be allowed into Dungannon Square. It's their territory, you see."[3]

The priest saw his friend's eyes go from hot to cold in a blink, as if he had undergone a radical change in internal temperature.

Barry turned toward the crowd. "Do you hear that?" he shouted. "Dungannon Square's Protestant territory. We're not welcome in our own land!" His voice was rolling thunder.

The expressions on faces in the crowd changed. Hardened. Even the children seemed to stiffen their spines. Barry turned back to Father Aloysius. There was a dangerous glitter in his eyes. "Looks like we're going anyway," he said jauntily.

Beads of nervous perspiration began to form on the priest's forehead. "I'll stay with you as best I can, but be careful, this is the north."

Barry gave a snort. "You think I don't know that?"

When the marchers entered Dungannon they saw people watching them from the windows, but the streets were almost deserted. They walked through the town in a silence broken only by the sound of their feet. As they approached Dungannon Square, a fully armed phalanx of RUC men in uniform blocked their way.

Firm faces. Determined faces. The faces of men prepared to do their duty.

I wonder if any of those men were at Brookeborough?

Out of instinct, Barry reached into his pocket for the Mauser. Then he remembered that the pistol was still in Clare. Under the mattress with Ned's rifle.

At that moment a man in the middle of the crowd began to sing the anthem of the American civil rights movement. The other demonstrators linked arms and joined in. A rousing chorus of "We Shall Overcome" rang through the disapproving streets of Dungannon.

A grandmother with thinning white hair and most of her front teeth missing tugged at Barry's elbow. Her face was a road map of hard times. "Will you link with an old woman?"

He turned and smiled down at her. A warm, slow, lover's smile, as if the two of them were all alone and she was the most beautiful girl in the world. "There aren't any old women here," he said gently. "But I'll be proud to link with you."

As he tucked her arm through his, the years fell away from her face.

.   .   .

WORKING one-handed, Barry took picture after picture, aiming the camera back and forth between the resolute marchers and the angry human wall that opposed them. An RUC officer noticed what he was doing and shouted at him to stop. "I'm with the press!" Barry roared back. "You want the world to know you're afraid of the press?"

The officer gave him a hard stare but did not repeat the order.

Although Barry's leg had begun to ache, he ignored it. He kept on taking pictures until the demonstrators, content that they had made their point, turned and marched back the way they had come. Still singing.

Father Aloysius had parked a hundred yards from the Square. When he saw Barry he opened the car door and beckoned him to get in. Barry shook his head. "I'm going back with them," he called to the priest. "All the way."

WHEN he returned to Dublin to develop his pictures Barry still felt something of the euphoria he had enjoyed—they all had enjoyed—on the walk back to Coalisland. The sense that anything was possible.

He put together a portfolio of photographs from the demonstration, including dramatic long shots to illustrate the size of the nationalist crowd and close-ups revealing expressions of naked enmity on the faces of the Royal Ulster Constabulary.

To accompany the photographs Barry wrote an explanatory text which concluded: "The civil rights struggle in Northern Ireland is growing out of the anger and frustration of the ordinary people. Its inspiration comes, not from the writings of Pádraic Pearse and James Connolly, but from Terence Mac-Swiney, the Irish republican lord mayor of Cork who had died on hunger strike in England. In his inaugural speech MacSwiney had said, "This contest of ours is not on our side a rivalry of vengeance, but one of endurance. It is not they who can inflict the most, but they who can suffer the most, who will conquer."[4]

Chapter Thirty-three

$\cdot\!\!\cdot\!\!\prec\!\!\infty\!\!\succ\!\!\cdot\!\!\cdot$

B ARRY sent the Coalisland-Dungannon portfolio to an agency in America that had purchased some of his photos in the past. He was elated when the article was sold in its entirety to a Sunday supplement. Its publication, he felt, vindicated the choices he had made. With his camera he could do more to support the struggle than he had ever done with a gun.

The correlation with the martyred Martin Luther King, Jr., was too obvious to ignore. Barry's photo spread helped attract international attention to Northern Ireland. News editors in the Republic also began to take an interest.

In October a group of Derry Catholics joined with local trade unionists to plan a march through the city, protesting sectarian discrimination in housing and employment. Because they had the support of several liberal politicians, RTE sent a television team to cover the event. Two days before the announced date, the minister for home affairs banned the march. Four hundred demonstrators turned up anyway. This time the RUC did not attempt a passive blocking action. Instead they trapped the marchers between two police cordons and attacked them with batons and water cannon.[1] More than a hundred demonstrators were injured. Pictures of Gerry Fitt, a West Belfast MP, with blood streaming down his face from a head wound were relayed around the world via television.

That night there was rioting for the first time in the Catholic Bogside area.

"I fear things may get worse," Father Aloysius wrote to Barry. "I pray there is no more violence, but the mood in the streets is not good. Civil rights groups are being organised throughout the province. Perhaps most alarming is the fact that foreign journalists have begun to arrive. They would not be here if they did not expect trouble. As I do," the priest added sadly. "God help us all."

Barry packed up his cameras and headed back to the north.

A modest package of reforms intended to defuse the situation was announced by Terence O'Neill on the twenty-second of November. The *Belfast Telegraph* commented, "In just 48 days since the Derry march, the Catholic community has obtained more political gains than it had in 47 years." But the announced reforms were not sufficient to undo generations of injustice.

Eight days later Ian Paisley prevented a civil rights march planned for the city of Armagh. Before the demonstration could get under way, Paisley arrived in Armagh together with carloads of his followers armed with stones and cudgels. To avoid violence, the organisers of the march backed down.

Members of the IRA from both sides of the border were now joining civil rights groups in large numbers.

ON the ninth of December, O'Neill made a speech on television in which he described Ulster as being at the crossroads. The northern premier urged restraint and civility, describing a unionism armed with justice as preferable to one armed merely with strength.

But he said nothing about one man, one vote.

WHEREVER Barry went into the Six Counties he was aware of building tension. The genie was out of the bottle. Nationalists were beginning to sense their power. Unionism was beginning to feel threatened.

Confrontations became more frequent.

As a cameraman covering potentially volatile situations, Barry developed a gut feeling for the mood of a crowd. The higher the adrenaline level, the more distance he put between himself and his subjects. A crowd was like a wild animal: familiarity made it more tolerant. When they were used to seeing him he could move closer without causing a reaction. Yet he never let himself forget what he was dealing with. The RUC in particular hated photojournalists and did what they could to make his work harder.

However, he no longer bothered to disguise himself. He was now well-enough known to feel relatively safe from attack, though he almost hoped someone would try. *If they do they'll be sorry, because I'll fight back.*

Oh yes. I'll fight back.

It was still there, the deeply embedded warrior persona which had been part of him for so long.

A new organisation had appeared, calling itself the People's Democracy and largely composed of Catholic students from Queen's University, Belfast. They decided to stage their own version of the famous civil rights march from Selma to Montgomery in the United States. The students hoped to force London to become involved in the Northern Ireland situation as the Selma march had drawn Washington into the civil rights struggle.

Their plan was to march from Belfast to Derry, a distance of some seventy-five miles. Austin Currie and a teacher of French called John Hume, who was vice chairman of the newly formed Derry Citizens' Action Committee, tried to discourage the idea. They feared the march would pass through loyalist areas and thus be highly provocative.

When he heard this Barry lost his temper. "What about the hundreds of Orange marches that parade through Catholic areas every year, banging their drums and shouting their triumphalism? I suppose that's not provocative?"

He was glad when the organisers of the march announced that it would go ahead.

Knowing he would never be able to walk seventy-five miles in four days, Barry obtained a map of the route and sought out Séamus McCoy. It was easy enough to find him—all one had to do was make enquiries at the Felons' Club on the Falls Road.

"I need the use of a car for four or five days," Barry explained to McCoy, "so I can follow the march."

The older man squinted in thought for a moment. "A pal of mine has a Volkswagen we can borrow, but there's a catch."

"What's that?"

"My friend doesn't know you, so I suspect I'll have to do the driving."

"Admit it, Séamus. You're just eager to drive a car."

"Aye. If I wasn't in the Army I'd have a wee car of my own by now."

"And a wife too?" Barry asked innocently.

"You can laugh now, Seventeen. But your day will come. I promise you, your day most definitely will come."

ON New Year's Day, 1969, between twenty and thirty young people prepared to set off from the City Hall in Belfast.[2] A small police escort had been assigned to them. The event drew little attention from the citizenry, though some well-wishers came forward with sandwiches and packets of soup which they could boil up on the way.

A crowd of Paisleyites was also present, waving the Union Jack and shouting insults.

The "Long March," as the event was being called, was not considered a major news item. Barry Halloran was one of the few photographers who were there for the beginning. He had no difficulty mingling with the students, who, edgy with excitement, were talking to anyone who would listen. Their conversation was revealing. They were not marching on behalf of a united Ireland. All they were seeking was equality with every other citizen of Northern Ireland.

Britain insists that this is part of the United Kingdom and the Catholics in it are British subjects, thought Barry, *so they have a perfect right to expect equal treatment under the law. Something they have never received, any more than the Negroes in America have.*

His attention was drawn to one girl in particular, a petite redhead who could not have been more than twenty-one. The look in her eyes made him think of Joan of Arc. *As Joan must have looked before she was betrayed. Before she was burned.*

A few minutes later McCoy drove up in a borrowed Volkswagen Beetle. He was grinning with proprietary delight. Barry folded his long legs uncomfortably into the small space and prepared to assume the role of navigator. "The route of march is much longer than it need be, Séamus. According to the map, they're taking a lot of detours to avoid loyalist strongholds."

"The Paisleyites will seek them out anyway," McCoy predicted. "The poor sods aren't carrying any weapons to defend themselves with. It's damned brave of them, if you ask me." He slammed through the gears and tromped down on the accelerator.

"If this is how you're going to drive, I think I'm the brave one," Barry gasped.

"Nonsense. The automobile a man drives reflects his personality, and I'm aggressive."

"You may be, but this little car isn't. Show it some mercy, will you?"

McCoy ignored the remark. "Every man feels more powerful when he's behind the wheel of a car. Have you no interest in motors at all?"

"I never really thought about it."

"Sometimes I despair of you, Seventeen."

The first day passed without serious trouble, though there were frequent bands of hecklers along the way. That night Barry and McCoy stayed in a small country inn and enjoyed a good meal, during which McCoy expounded on the merits of various automobiles between fits of coughing.

"You should give up those cigarettes," Barry advised him.

"Not me, I love my bad habits. They're the best thing about me."

The next morning they caught up with the marchers only to find a large crowd surrounding them, shouting obscenities. Some of those in the crowd were no older than the marchers themselves. A score were even younger; a mob of children being trained to hate.

Barry's eyes sought out the red-haired girl. She continued to walk forward with her head up and her eyes straight ahead, refusing to react to the verbal assault. Then someone in the crowd threw a bottle filled with urine.

As if that were the signal, a barrage of bricks and stones was hurled at the students. Barry hardly had time to get his camera focussed before the barrage turned into an even more physical assault. Marchers were kicked and pummelled. Girls' hair was pulled. A couple of male students were seized around the neck and half throttled.

Their police escort watched but made no move to interfere.

Uttering a string of expletives, McCoy started to get out of the car. Barry caught him by the wrist with a grasp of iron. "We can't, Séamus. I'm here as an observer."

"Meaning you can't fight back?"

"Meaning I—and you as my driver—can't get involved. We tell the story in pictures, we can't be part of it."

Muttering to himself, McCoy settled back into the car. "Goes against nature," Barry heard him say.

MEANWHILE, Ian Paisley was addressing a large gathering of his supporters in Derry's Guildhall. A simultaneous protest against Paisley was going on outside. In the City Council Chambers, a number of homeless Catholics had barricaded the door and turned off the lights.[3]

Tempers were raw in Derry City.

Throughout the day the marchers were subjected to increasingly violent assaults. The hostilities were well organised; carloads of men armed with cudgels, billhooks, crowbars, and scythe blades were brought to meet the march at predetermined points.

The escalating violence drew the press, whose numbers swelled hourly. They began to send out bulletins on the progress of the march. As photographs of the marchers, bloodied but unbowed, appeared on television, the courage of the students began to swing public opinion in their favour. Others joined them until there were almost a hundred civil rights demonstrators walking toward Derry. Carrying no placards, inciting no violence. Just walking.

The ranks of police grew too, totalling more than eighty by the end of the third day. Never did the police give the marchers any assistance or make any effort to protect them from their tormentors.[4]

Barry was painfully reminded of the reaction of southern white politicians in America when the federal administration tried to enlist protection for civil rights marchers.

The climax came on the fourth day. With the collusion of the RUC and B-Specials,[5] a mob of more than three hundred, including a number of off-duty constables,[6] ambushed the marchers at the narrow Burntollet Bridge. They ran out from lanes on either side of the road, screaming invective. Wielding iron bars and bicycle chains, they swarmed into the ranks of marchers. Men and women alike were battered to the ground. A few of the marchers managed to break through and run for their lives, but many were driven into the ditches on either side of the road and beaten unmercifully. Others were forced into the River Fahan and attacked on the bank when they tried to crawl out.

The journalists covering the march were appalled. At last several, including Barry Halloran, abandoned their professional objectivity and ran to try to help. Most met with the same violence as the marchers. But the thugs who meant to attack Barry turned and ran when the tall man let out a roar and charged at them instead. His hair was fire, his eyes were ice. The fury on his face was too much for any bully.

One of Barry's terrified assailants stumbled over an earlier victim and fell flat on his face in the dirt. Before he could stop himself, Barry gave him a vicious kick in the ribs.

God, that felt good!

Describing the scene at Burntollet Bridge, a reporter wrote in the *Belfast Sunday News,* "I saw a young woman lying face down in the stream." He went on to relate that before he could pull her out, several men had attacked her with spiked cudgels. "I could see the blood spurt out of the holes in her legs,"[7] he stated.

Although most of the marchers were injured to some degree, they re-grouped and staggered on toward Derry. As they passed through outlying Catholic communities their numbers increased dramatically. When they entered Irish Street, which was strongly Protestant, they were ambushed again by extremists, whose cudgels studded with six-inch nails were augmented by large piles of stones conveniently provided by a local builder.

Yet more men and women—not all of them Catholic by any means—continued to join the march. They were attacked yet again as they passed through the Waterside. But by the time they reached Guildhall Square their ranks had swelled to almost two thousand, a number sufficient to deter any further attack.

As public opinion swung to their side during the course of the march, John Hume and Ivan Cooper, a prominent Protestant and strong proponent of civil rights himself, had hastily organised a public reception in the Square. The dazed marchers stumbled into a hero's welcome.

Eighty-seven of their number were admitted to Altnagelvin Hospital with severe injuries. Miraculously, no one had been killed that day. But something was born that would survive for a very long time.

That night the red-haired girl whom Barry had first noticed in Belfast was invited down to Dublin, together with a couple of other marchers, to tell her story on RTE. She proved to be both passionate and articulate. Her name was Bernadette Devlin.

In the early hours of the next morning some members of the RUC who had been drinking in the pubs all evening went rampaging through Derry's Bogside district. Armed with riot sticks and pick handles, they broke windows, smashed down doors, and battered any Catholic they could catch.

A member of the B-Specials chased a seventeen-year-old girl into a laneway. Calling her a Fenian whore, he hit her on the side of the head with his baton and then tried to rape her with it. As she staggered bleeding from the laneway, she ran into a newspaper reporter who recounted her ordeal in the evening papers. A photograph by Barry Halloran accompanied the story.

When Barry and McCoy returned to Belfast they found three young men waiting for them outside the Felons' Club. "Allow me to present my reservists," McCoy said with mock formality.

A gangly youth with tousled hair told McCoy, "After what happened in Derry, there's gonna be more of us wantin' to join you."

"The Army's not on active service now."

"You will be," the youngster said.

STATEMENT BY TERENCE O'NEILL, PRIME MINISTER OF NORTHERN IRELAND,
5 January 1969

I want the people of Ulster to understand in plain terms events which have taken place since January 1st. The march to Londonderry planned by the People's Democracy was, from the outset, a foolhardy and irresponsible undertaking. At best, those who planned it were careless of the effects it would have, at worst, they embraced with enthusiasm the prospect of adverse publicity causing further damage to the interests of Northern Ireland as a whole. . . .

Clearly Ulster has now had enough. We are all sick of marchers and counter-marchers. Unless these warring minorities rapidly return to their senses we will have to consider a further reinforcement of the regular police by greater use of the Special constabulary for normal police duties. . . .

I think we must also have an urgent look at the Public Order Act itself to see whether we ought to ask Parliament for further powers to control those elements which are seeking to hold the entire community to ransom.

Enough is enough. We have heard sufficient for now about Civil rights, let us hear a little about civic responsibility. For it is a short step from the throwing of paving stones to the laying of tombstones and I for one can think of no cause in Ulster today which will be advanced by the death of a single Ulsterman.

Belfast Telegraph, 6 January 1969

Chapter Thirty-four

BARRY returned to Dublin determined to buy an automobile of his own. To cover the situation in the north he needed to be independently mobile, not relying on public transport or borrowed cars. After the Long March it felt good to be back in Dublin. The home was still the hub of society. Everything was built around the family. Children said please and thank you and were respectful to their elders. Young people did not gather in large, threatening crowds. There was no graffiti on the walls urging "Kill a Taig today."

IN the next road down from Philpott's house was a garage which did motor repairs. Occasionally an automobile was parked on the forecourt with a For Sale sign on the windscreen. After carefully examining his bank balance, one Thursday afternoon Barry walked to the garage with the gait of a man out to take a casual stroll. A man who had no intention of buying anything.

A bright red, rather battered-looking sports car of an inexpensive make was parked invitingly close to the footpath. A sign displayed on the windscreen announced, FOR SALE AT A REASONABLE PRICE.

Barry stopped. Gave the automobile a long, hard look. Ambled into the garage, where he found a swarthy man in greasy coveralls. "How much do you want for the red car out there?"

The mechanic glanced past him as if he had forgotten that there was anything parked on the forecourt. "Oh. You mean the Austin Healey?"

"I do. What do you call a reasonable price?"

"It's not a new car, you can see that for yourself. Clean—washed and polished, I mean—but not new at all. In fact it was modified for rally driving. Road racing, that class of thing."

The jaunty grin of Barry's youth had been replaced by a slight smile and one lifted eyebrow, giving him a gently mocking expression. "Did I say I was looking for a new car?"

The mechanic's eyes narrowed to calculating slits. "But you are looking for a car?"

"I didn't say that either. I just happened to be passing and noticed the Austin. What's the story?"

The mechanic wiped his hands on a rag that hung out of his pocket. "Man brought it in here for repairs months ago. To tell the truth, that car was in pretty bad shape. The gears were shot, the tyres were bald, and it needed a new top. When the owner came back and saw the invoice he tried to wriggle out of it, but like I says to him, parts and labour cost money. I was ready to be reasonable but not robbed."

"Of course not," Barry agreed.

"I cut the cost as low as I could and he said he'd be back with the money the next day. I waited. Not a sign of the sinner. My wife wasn't best pleased, I can tell you. She said I should have been paid up front."

Barry looked sympathetic. "You could hardly take money from a customer at gunpoint."

"Feckin' right! So like I say, I waited. Three months now. No sign of the owner, and the wife giving me cold tea. She tells me, 'Sell the car for what's owing.' And she's right too."

"May I see the repair bill?"

"There's storage charges on top of that, y'unnerstand."

"Of course."

"And like I say, the car ain't been cared for properly. She's small but she's powerful, a real racing machine. Somebody installed a big push rod six-cylinder engine that makes that light chassis fly. Man has a car like that, he should take it to a garage on a regular basis, have an expert give 'er a going over."

"I couldn't agree more," said Barry. "I only live a couple of hundred yards from here. With a car like this I'd be a regular customer, Mister . . . ?" He paused.

"Coates. Paudie Coates."

Barry extended his hand. "Barry Halloran."

A closer examination revealed that the car had been crashed at some stage, but Paudie assured him the damage had not been sufficient to make further driving dangerous. "The axles are solid and the body's not out of alignment."

Barry chuckled. "I wish I could say the same about myself. Is there an owner's manual that comes with this?"

"Lost years ago, I suspect," said Paudie. "There's no jack, either, but I'll throw one in for free if you buy the car."

An hour later Barry was sitting behind the wheel of the Austin Healey, negotiating it through the streets of Dublin. Deliciously aware of the purr of the big engine, and of the admiring glances coming his way. *The automobile a man drives reflects his personality.*

He was whizzing down the quays when he realised, *A man driving around the north in this car could hardly be more conspicuous.*

A muscle tensed in Barry's jaw. If Ursula had been sitting beside him she would have recognised her son's "dangerous look."

Unfortunately, almost every week something went wrong with the Austin. On its fifth trip to the garage in as many weeks, Barry asked Paudie Coates, "Can you teach me to do some repairs for myself?"

"Are you good with your hands at all?"

Barry laughed.

IN the aftermath of the Burntollet Bridge debacle a commission was set up to examine the causes of the violence. Ultimately nothing changed. It remained for prominent Protestants such as Ivan Cooper and Campbell Austin, who owned the largest department store in Derry, to try to encourage a less bigoted and more liberal attitude amongst their co-religionists.

However, the voice of the demagogue was growing louder in Northern Ireland.

On the second of February, Ian Paisley led six thousand supporters through Belfast, demanding an end to Terence O'Neill's premiership.

When a disaffected group of Unionists met in Portadown to demand his resignation, O'Neill called for a general election at the end of the month. Unionism fractured into pro- and anti-O'Neill camps. Most vocal on the anti-side were Ian Paisley, Brian Faulkner, the deputy prime minister, and Lord Brookeborough, who had preceded O'Neill in office.

In the election O'Neill managed to hang on, successfully defending his constituency seat against Ian Paisley, but his majority in parliament was fatally diminished.

New figures were emerging in the political sphere. John Hume—newly elected to Stormont as nationalist MP for Derry—Austin Currie, and Ivan Cooper formed the nexus of a civil rights faction. Ian Paisley roundly condemned them all, claiming that the civil rights issue was merely a front for Irish nationalism. "NICRA equals IRA" was his oft-repeated slogan.

In April, Terence O'Neill announced a new policy of one man, one vote.

That same month, in a Westminster by-election Bernadette Devlin, running as a unity candidate, became the youngest woman ever elected to the British House of Commons. In her widely reported maiden speech in Commons, Devlin said, "I am not speaking of one night of broken glass, but of fifty years of human misery."[1]

When a series of explosions disrupted the water supply flowing from the Silent Valley Reservoir to Belfast, at first the IRA was suspected. Then it was found to be the work of the UVF, which was trying to destabilise O'Neill and put an end to his reforms.[2] People in the city feared that it was part of a larger loyalist plot to deny water to the firemen while the Catholic areas of Belfast went up in flames.

On the twenty-eighth the beleaguered Terence O'Neill resigned.

In June, Ian Paisley was banned from Switzerland during the forthcoming papal visit. Following talks at the Swiss embassy, Paisley said that the Swiss were "dimwits" whose only contribution to the twentieth century was the cuckoo clock.[3]

IN 1969 the ha'penny was phased out to prepare for the introduction of decimalisation. The song topping the Irish charts was Elvis Presley's rendition of "In the Ghetto." Very few in the Republic knew what a Chicago ghetto was like, but some knew what parts of Northern Ireland were like. The parts where the Catholics lived.

A small contingent of IRA veterans from Belfast, led by Joe Cahill, travelled to Dublin to talk to Cathal Goulding. They asked him to release whatever arms the organisation had in its Dublin arms dump for use in the defence of Catholics in Belfast and Derry. Goulding refused. He assured the group that continued civil disobedience would not attract the sort of violence they were worried about. Deeply disappointed, Cahill returned to Belfast to await, with mounting concern, the onset of summer and the Marching Season.

IN 1690 two claimants to the English throne had used Ireland as their battleground. William of Orange, a Dutch Calvinist—who paradoxically had the support of the Vatican[4]—was opposed by the Catholic James II, last of the romantic and doomed Stuart dynasty, who had the support of France. The decisive battle took place on the banks of the Boyne River on the first of July. William had twenty-five thousand men; James fewer than nine thousand. The Battle of the Boyne turned into a rout when James abandoned the field and fled to Dublin. The Williamite victory had assured that a Protestant monarch would rule England's colony in Ireland.

To commemorate that event, the Orange Order annually turned the month of July into Marching Season. Hundreds of Orange parades throughout the Six Counties claimed to be celebrating civil and religious liberty. The fact that only Protestants were entitled to either was unspoken but fully understood.

The spectacle climaxed on the twelfth, the date when Williamite forces had concluded mopping-up operations against the Jacobites at the Battle of Aughrim. Marching Season was a festival for northern Protestants. Over many years, northern Catholics had learned to stay at home behind locked doors.

BARRY drove to Belfast to cover the 1969 Marching Season. This time he checked into a small hotel. Although staying in a hotel for any length of time was expensive, it gave him an aura of objectivity. Besides, the sporty Austin was safe in the hotel car park. In a Catholic neighbourhood it would have fallen prey to loyalist vandals.

On the Twelfth a number of feeder parades marched through Belfast to join into one mass body at the end of the day. The routes were designed to include as many Catholic areas as possible. Barry photographed vast ranks of Orangemen in serge suits and bowler hats, Orange Order sashes displayed across their chests, tightly furled umbrellas carried in white-gloved hands. Erect, sober, and unsmiling, God-fearing men all, they stepped to the rhythm of massive Lambeg drums. Martial drums for commemorating ultimate, and permanent, victory.

Officials of the Orange Order, sword bearers, and pole carriers had pride of place in the parades. Vivid banners depicting Queen Victoria holding her Bible and "King Billy" riding his white horse at the Boyne drew cheers from the thousands of spectators. Small children perched on their father's shoulders, eyes shining with the excitement of it all.

Belfast was en fête on the Twelfth. A day for families and parades and picnics.

Contrast this, Barry thought to himself, already planning the photo spread, *with scenes from Burntollet Bridge. Civil rights marchers being beaten to the ground by the police.*

But Catholics were no longer passively accepting abuse. On this Twelfth of July rioting broke out in several parts of the Six Counties. In Belfast marchers passing through the Unity Flats area were bombarded with bottles while jeering nationalists waved the Irish tricolour. A meeting hall belonging to the Orange Order was burned out in Dungiven and there were violent scenes in the town of Lurgan. In Derry an Orange parade was attacked by youths from the Bogside. One Orangeman had his furled umbrella torn from his hand and was beaten about the head with it.

As they did every year, for weeks gleeful small boys had been building immense pyramids of timber and old tyres and discarded furniture on patches of waste ground. As sun set on the night of the Twelfth the traditional bonfires were lit. While the flames roared into the sky, filling it with a lurid orange glow, loyalists invaded Catholic neighbourhoods to smash windows and beat up men on their doorsteps. In an orgy of killing, pet animals were seized and thrown into the flames. More than one human had been known to disappear on Bonfire Night, later reappearing, if at all, as a few bones at the bottom of a burned out pyre.

As Barry drove out of the city the next day, many fires were still burning. Belfast stank of smoke and burned rubber.

On the sixteenth of July—which coincidentally was also the date of the execution of Nicholas the Second, last czar of Russia, and the date when the first atomic bomb was exploded in New Mexico in 1945—*Apollo 11* was launched from Cape Kennedy.

Chapter Thirty-five

———— ⋘∞⋙ ————

July 21, 1969

"ONE SMALL STEP FOR A MAN,
ONE GIANT LEAP FOR MANKIND"

Neil Armstrong becomes the first man to walk on the moon.

BARRY had nicknamed his automobile "Apollo." *I'm thirty years old, far too old to be so fanciful,* he chided himself. Yet the name stuck.

After buying a set of tools and several hours of Paudie Coates's time, he was confident that he could keep Apollo running—barring a major breakdown. He had to keep it running. With a fast and reliable car of his own, he could go to most places in the north and be back in Dublin the same night.

He spent much of his time driving back and forth between Dublin and the north. More than once he slept in his car. Parking in a lay-by, pulling his cap down over his eyes, wrapping his coat around his body, continually shifting his legs in an attempt to find a comfortable position. The sports car was little roomier than a Volkswagen Beetle, but at least it was his. He packed it with everything he might need for a protracted stay, returning to Dublin only to develop his photographs.

There were plenty of photo labs in Belfast that could have handled the work, but Barry did not trust any of them. Some of his pictures made an obvious political point. He did not want to be informed that his negatives had gone missing.

During July a Catholic taxi driver in Derry died after being beaten by members of the RUC who mistakenly identified him as harbouring juvenile rioters.[1]

While in the Six Counties, Barry was constantly on guard. Every word, every action had to be weighed in the light of the sectarian response it might evoke. *How can people live like this?* he wondered. *Yet thousands do; for all of their lives.*

In the first week of August, running battles between Catholics and Protestants broke out in Belfast. A riot in the Protestant Shankill Road resulted in the burning of an automobile and a van, and a RUC Land Rover was damaged by a petrol bomb. A gang of loyalists swept through the Catholic area around the Crumlin Road, warning families to get out or be burned out.[2] Barry spent several days photographing warfare in the streets while anger on both sides boiled over. The RUC paused only long enough to determine which combatants were Catholic before they began wielding their batons.

Barry fought against the urge to get involved. The struggle was born of fear—his fear of the thing within him, the old savage warrior who lurked under the skin, glorying in battle, eager to kill. . . .

Only by fiercely concentrating on his work was he able to remain objective. Sometimes he simply had to walk away and put his cameras in the car.

On the fifth of August the Ulster Volunteer Force exploded a bomb at the studios of Radio Telefís Éireann in Dublin. Barry hastily drove back to Dublin to take photographs, but by the time he arrived at RTE the damage had been tidied away. He spent a few days developing film and showing his photographs to editors, then returned to Belfast.

As usual, he met Séamus McCoy at the Felons' Club. They subsequently adjourned to a pub across the way for a couple of pints.

"That bomb in Dublin is small peas compared to what's likely to happen in the north," McCoy told Barry. "You know the parade the Apprentice Boys of Derry stage on the twelfth of August?"

"I do of course. Another celebration of another Protestant victory hundreds of years ago."

"Well, this year they're going to meet with organised resistance. When the parade passes the Bogside an army of civilians will be waiting for them. Only civilians, mind you!" McCoy emphasised, looking sour. "Goulding's sent down word that the IRA can't defend the Bogside because we don't have enough men or guns. So it's up to the Bogsiders to organise their own protection as best they can."

Tight-lipped, Barry said, "I'm on my way to Derry, then." Seeing the look on the other man's face, he added, "Just to take photographs, Séamus."

"I hear you. I could come along if you like. Drive that new car for you?"

Barry chuckled. "I wondered how long it would take you to ask. I'd be glad of your company. But I'll drive."

.   .   .

MEMBERS of the Derry Citizens' Defence Association went to Dublin, hoping for a meeting with the taoiseach. They wanted to convince him that the south had a role to play in the protection of Irish Catholics in the north. They were met with courtesy by the taoiseach's secretary. Jack Lynch himself was not available. When the DCDA delegation explained the concerns the organisation felt about the upcoming Apprentice Boys' March, they were sent to the Department of Foreign Affairs to meet with two civil servants described as experts on the north.

Two hours of conversation ensued. By the end of that time the DCDA men were aware that the Fianna Fáil government's expression of support for the reunification of the island was no more than lip service. They also had been warned against blowing the matter of potential trouble in Derry out of proportion.

They insisted on pressing the point. "What will happen if there is an attack and people are killed?"

"We'll not let you down," was the ambiguous reply.

"What does that mean?"

A civil servant said soothingly, "Of course the government will act to protect our people in Northern Ireland."

"Can we take this message back to the people of Derry?" the DCDA representatives asked.

"Yes."[3]

AFTER lunch on the eleventh of August, Barry Halloran and Séamus McCoy set out for Derry. Barry now had four cameras, an assortment of lenses, filters, and other accessories, two tripods, a reflective shield, and a couple of battery-operated portable lights with folding support poles. "You really need all this stuff?" McCoy had asked as he wedged his rucksack into the boot of the car. He travelled with little more than a spare shirt and his shaving kit.

"Be glad I don't work in television, that really involves a lot of gear," said Barry. "I prefer to travel light, myself."

"Light." McCoy sounded bemused.

Barry showed off behind the wheel. Double-clutching with a flourish, accelerating into the curves. The motor, which he tinkered with in every spare moment, purred like a great cat. McCoy looked so envious that at last Barry promised, "You can drive on the way back to Belfast."

They arrived in Derry while the sun was still high in the sky. Barry parked Apollo in a disused service alley behind Father Aloysius's house, where it was unlikely to attract notice. Fortunately the priest was at home when they arrived. He gave them tea and insisted that they both stay with him while they were in the city. May Coogan was sent to make up the two folding beds he kept for visitors.

"A delegation from the Bogside appealed to the Apprentice Boys to call off their parade in order to avoid confrontation," Father Aloysius told his guests that evening, "but they were refused. The Apprentice Boys said it was their traditional right to march when they want and where they want, and that's all there was to it. John Hume has advised all Catholics to stay indoors tomorrow. But I don't think they will. I've already seen some of our local lads collecting milk bottles to use for making Molotov cocktails.

"We're on a dreadful downward spiral in this province, I'm afraid. Every violent incident sparks off a worse one. I've tried to persuade my parishioners of the folly of giving in to this sort of behaviour, but they don't seem to listen to me anymore."

"We're a patient people," said McCoy, "but our patience has finally run out. And I for one am glad, by God! Uh . . . begging your pardon, Father."

The priest nodded. "I'm sure He understands."

"Ian Paisley thinks God's a unionist."

With a small, sad smile, the priest replied, "One would wonder what God thinks of Ian Paisley."

The following day Barry and McCoy went to the Apprentice Boys' Hall to photograph the march forming up. Barry began the afternoon with two cameras slung around his neck, a light meter and several rolls of film stuffed into his pockets. He gave more film to McCoy to carry. Then the two men set out on foot through the Bogside—a nationalist community readying itself for invasion by unionists. Families with small children who lived nearest the parade route had evacuated their homes. Three barricades were being erected: one at the Little Diamond, one at Marlborough Terrace, and one at Rossville Street, where piles of old furniture and broken timber were stacked shoulder high.

The strongest point of defence would be in William Street, the main entrance to the Bogside.

When Barry and Séamus reached Fahan Street they saw, painted in white letters on the black tarmac of the road, GIVE PEACE A CHANCE.

At the edge of the Bogside stood the great wall enclosing what once had been ancient Derry. The wall's bulk partly muffled the derisive rattle of huge Lambeg drums. Warming up. Sending out their message like an advance guard. When the march began it would proceed along the top of wall, directly overlooking the Bogside. There were already several Apprentice Boys standing on the wall, contemptuously throwing pennies at Catholics in the street below.

The Apprentice Boys' Hall was an imposing granite building in the Scottish baronial style which had been erected on the site of a sixth-century Irish monastery. As he admired the perfect proportions of the turrets and the strength of the battlemented tower, Barry thought, *Architecture is the most lasting symbol of conquest.*

He began taking photographs. The Apprentice Boys—in reality middle-aged men for the most part, with the determinedly set faces which seemed to be traditional on members of the Orange Order—pretended not to see him. They were wrapped in a cocoon of their own, waiting to burst forth in all their glory. All the trappings were in place. The banners. The drums. The certainty.

As the first of the television crews arrived, Barry gestured to McCoy. "Let's go back to the Bogside. I've seen all I want to here."

By this time the RUC was out in full force, both in cars and on foot. They erected barricades of their own and took up positions along the route of the march. From their placement it was apparent that they meant to protect the Apprentice Boys, not the residents of the Bogside.

In Marlborough Terrace the local bookmaker was offering odds of ten to one on peace. There were no takers.

As the afternoon dragged on, the tension grew.

From the wall overlooking the Bogside, Apprentice Boys and their supporters hurled taunts into the Catholic ghetto.

Within that ghetto Barry Halloran roved from block to block, switching back and forth between his cameras. "This one's for close-ups," he explained to McCoy. "The other one has a wide-angle lens for showing the whole scene."

"You really enjoy this picture-taking, don't you?"

"I really do."

"As much as being in the Army?"

Barry did not answer.

In Rossville Street he noticed a petite woman in a dark blue pullover and blue jeans. She was being trailed by a television crew. "Look, Séamus; there's Bernadette Devlin over there."

McCoy squinted at her. "Looks like a child in those jeans, don't she? Yet she's brave enough to enter the lion's den. I'd give a year of my life to see her facing down the unionists in Westminster."

Devlin picked up a megaphone and began addressing the crowd, urging the protesters to stand their ground. When she put down the megaphone the streets were ominously quiet in spite of the number of people filling them.

The boom of drums was heard again. Rhythmic and constant now, setting the tempo for marching feet.

Marshals appointed by the Citizens' Action Committee took up defensive positions. DCDA stewards moved through the ever-increasing crowd, hoping to keep it under control. Policemen carrying steel shields tensed in expectation.

"I see a few lads I know," McCoy told Barry. "There's Billy McKee over there, and a couple of others."

"So the IRA is here?"

"Don't think so. They're the only ones, damn it."

"Join them if you want to," Barry said.

He did not have to say it twice. McCoy had vanished into the crowd before Barry remembered to ask him for the rolls of film he carried.

As the parade came into view the nationalists behind the barricades let out a roar. The unionists shouted abuse back at them. Then one threw a stone.

The Battle of the Bogside had begun.

Almost immediately a phalanx of police arrived in armoured vehicles, adding the roar of their engines to the swelling voice of the crowd. They smashed their way through the nationalists' barricades and into the Bogside itself. The defenders who rushed to try to fill the gaps were met with police batons. A baton bash to the head was sufficient to knock a man unconscious—or worse. Within moments several Bogsiders lay bleeding in the street. Their furious companions began hurling handfuls of nails, and then petrol bombs, at the police. One of the petrol bombs struck a policeman full force, setting his uniform on fire. He screamed and staggered forward, then fell to the ground, still screaming.

Barry saw a man in a clerical collar run forward to help put out the flames, and recognised Father Aloysius.

A cluster of stone-throwing Protestant boys had followed the armoured vehicles when they broke through the barricades. Catholic boys, amongst them a young fellow named Martin McGuinness, returned stone for stone.

Petrol bombs were now flying through the air in every direction. Several landed on rooftops, setting them ablaze. A water cannon which the police brought up to quell the rioters had to be turned on the houses instead. From the upper windows of tenements in Rossville Street the Bogsiders hurled bombs down on the RUC. More men and women clambered onto the roof of the ten-storey Rossville Flats, where they succeeded in erecting a makeshift catapult that temporarily halted the police advance. Infuriated, the police batoned everyone in sight.

In a short time the war was no longer between Catholics and Protestants. It was between the nationalists and the RUC.

Trying to keep emotionally detached, concentrating on composing frame after frame, Barry crisscrossed the Bogside. The scene had all the elements of a war zone. Glass crunched underfoot. Petrol blazed in the gutters. Frightened rats scurried like people.

The level of gratuitous violence on both sides surpassed anything Barry had expected. Brutalised for generations, the Bogsiders were brutalising back. Every milk bottle in the area was pressed into service to make petrol bombs. "Tell the milkman me mam wants two pints of milk and seventy-five bottles," a boy shouted.

An improvised first aid station was set up in the Kandy Korner and staffed with local housewives. Their first patient was a member of the RUC.

Barry kept watching for glimpses of McCoy's grizzled head in the crowd, but did not see him. He was not unduly concerned. *If anyone can take care of himself it's Séamus.*

As expected, the fighting was heaviest in William Street. Buildings near the police station in the Strand Road were set ablaze as a depressing drizzle began to fall. Enough rain to dampen the rioters; not enough to dampen their fervour or wash away the stink of the petrol.

When Barry turned his cameras on the police he saw them as a black wave. Black helmets, black uniforms, black raincoats, black boots. Black truncheons looking for Catholic skulls to break.

Catholics with paving stones and pickaxe handles seeking RUC skulls to break . . .

By early evening the RUC had taken a number of casualties. Their thinning ranks were reinforced by B-Specials equipped with machine guns. At midnight the minister of home affairs for Northern Ireland authorised the use of CS gas; the first time it had been employed as a riot control measure in the United Kingdom.

When Barry Halloran came around a corner, he thought at first that someone had thrown pepper in his eyes. Then it was as if he had taken a drink of boiling water. His throat was scalded. He could not speak, could not even breathe.

Eyes screwed shut, he staggered back the way he had come. His stomach heaved with nausea and he kept trying to spit out the vile taste in his mouth. Every inch of his exposed skin began to itch violently. All around him people were choking and retching. And cursing, when they could.

"Tear gas," a man groaned. "They've gassed us, the feckers!"

Knowledge alleviated Barry's welling panic. He leaned against a wall and concentrated on fighting the effects of the gas. At last he was able to draw breath again, though the lingering smell continued to sicken him. He opened his burning, streaming eyes and looked around.

The battle was still going on.

Nationalists headed for the RUC station in Rosemount, some two miles away, and erected makeshift barricades around the building. When they hurled petrol bombs at the door they were met by a barrage of CS gas. "Stop the gas and we'll stop the bombs!" they shouted. When John Hume arrived, urging restraint, he was struck by a gas cartridge and had to be carried away.

In the Bogside a thick fog of CS gas crawled like a living thing up the side of the Rossville Flats.

Other politicians appeared on the scene to assess the situation. They briefly orated for the television cameras, then scurried back to the safety of their automobiles and vanished in a cloud of exhaust fumes. Neil Blaney, TD for North-East Donegal and minister for agriculture in the Lynch cabinet, was the exception. Blaney personally met with many of the nationalists. He listened to what they had to say and promised to do everything in his power to protect them.

Blaney had been born shortly after the War of Independence, while his father was still a prisoner of the British under sentence of death.

Barry was unaware of weariness. Like everyone else, he was fuelled by adrenaline. When he went back to his car for more film he found Father Aloysius standing outside the house. The priest's face and clothing were smoke-smudged and smeared with ashes. "Child of grace!" he exclaimed when he saw Barry. "I was afraid you might have been hurt again."

"Only gassed, Father; that's bad enough. But I haven't seen Séamus in . . . I don't know how long. Is he here by any chance?"

The priest shook his head. "Do you want me to help you look for him?"

"There's no need, I'm sure he's all right. But you look exhausted. You should have May give you a cup of tea and then take a bit of rest."

Father Aloysius smiled wanly. "In a little while, perhaps." He followed Barry back into the Bogside. Into the smoke and flame, the groans of the injured and the stink of the gas.

As dawn broke, an Irish tricolour floated triumphantly from the roof of the Rossville Flats.

Shortly afterwards a senior police officer told his superiors that the army would have to be called in.

In mid-morning Barry photographed Bernadette Devlin breaking up paving stones to resupply the men and women of the Bogside with missiles.

But he still had not found Séamus McCoy. Occasionally someone would beckon from a doorstep and offer him a sandwich or a mug of hot tea. Each time he asked, "Have you seen a short, grey-haired man who squints a lot, wearing a brown jacket and baggy pants?"

The answer was always the same: a regretful shake of the head. Many people in Derry were seeking their loved ones that day.

The hours passed in a cacophony of shouts and curses. Black, oily petrol smoke filled the narrow streets. Grenades of CS gas were hurled from behind metal shields as clusters of defenders fought their way from one area to another. Squads of police advanced and were driven back.

Streams of melted goo dripped from an abandoned ice cream truck and ran down the street. Dogs and cats feasted together.

Immersed in the violent heart of the Bogside, Barry had no clear sense of how the battle was going. If he stopped moving, his left knee locked up almost at once.

Almost as light relief for the brutal images he was recording, he photographed a row of little boys and girls sitting atop a broken barricade. They were watching with undisguised glee something they interpreted as street theatre.

The second day of violence would be over in a few hours. Yet still the fighting went on.

AT nine that evening Taoiseach Jack Lynch went on television to announce that the Irish army was setting up field hospitals near the border of Donegal. They were to handle the overflow of injured people who could not be accommodated in Derry hospitals. Lynch went on to say, "It is evident that the Stormont Government is no longer in control of the situation. Indeed the present situation is the inevitable outcome of the policies pursued for decades by successive Stormont governments. It is clear also that the Irish government can no longer stand by and see innocent people injured and perhaps worse.[4]

AT one o'clock on the morning of the third day, Bernadette Devlin telephoned London to ask the home secretary, James Callahan, to stop the use of CS gas. Because she did not have enough money to pay for the call, she asked the operator to reverse the charges. She explained that she was a member of parliament.

London refused to accept her phone call.

JACK Lynch's televised speech poured fuel on the flames. Loyalists were convinced that the setting up of field hospitals in Donegal was a thinly disguised attempt to arrange staging points for an invasion of their small corner of the United Kingdom.

Nationalists interpreted the taoiseach's remark about the Irish government "no longer standing by" to mean that the Irish army was on its way to take the Six Counties back. Catholic housing estates were evacuated to provide billets for the army from the south.

The violence in Derry had spread to Belfast. On the night of the thirteenth and again on the fourteenth, Loyalist gangs equipped with rifles and stunguns took to the streets, claiming that their intention was to protect Protestants. Instead they entered Catholic neighbourhoods and assaulted anyone they could catch. In reprisal for the failure of the RUC to defend them, Catholics began attacking police stations with petrol bombs.

The Stormont government urgently requested that London send British troops to Northern Ireland.

Chapter Thirty-six

LIKE clouds of poison gas the anger blew across the north, overtaking one town after another. Strabane, Coalisland, Dungannon—where the constables ignored orders and opened fire on a crowd of unarmed Catholics, injuring three—Lurgan, Enniskillen, Omagh . . .

The situation was rapidly spinning out of control. Yet, the Irish government seemed all but oblivious to the gravity of the situation. Contrary to the expectation in the north, there was no mobilisation of the southern army. Lynch's Fianna Fáil government was fully involved in business as usual.

However, Sir Andrew Gilchrist, Britain's ambassador to Ireland, warned the British prime minister, Harold Macmillan, that there was a danger the Irish army might be sent into the north to protect the Bogside. Such a move would have far-reaching ramifications. In spite of Lynch's speech, Sir Andrew believed that the taoiseach did not want to send troops north because he had privately expressed no interest in a united Ireland.[1]

But the minister for finance, Charles J. Haughey, had republican roots and felt strongly about Irish reunification. Haughey, Gilchrist told Macmillan, wielded considerable influence within the cabinet. He might get Lynch to change his mind.

And still they were fighting in Derry. Five civilians had been shot dead and hundreds more had been injured. Attack and counter-attack had become ritualistic; stylised warfare where both sides knew what was expected. But it could not last much longer. Eventually there were no more than 150 nationalists still on their feet, wearing dazed expressions and staggering with exhaustion.

IN Belfast appalling violence was now taking place in the Falls Road area and Bombay Street, where loyalist mobs ordered residents at gunpoint to leave their homes, then set fire to the houses. Soon thousands were homeless. While they ran for cover their local shops were looted and business premises destroyed. A gang of little boys who had followed the adults from the Shankill broke into a liquor store. Children as young as nine years old were soon staggering along the pavement, so drunk that they did not know what they were doing.[2]

The mobs ran from street to street, burning buildings and torching parked cars. The RUC watched but made no effort to prevent what was happening. A new horror appeared when carloads of B-Specials drove down Philpott Street, firing at random. They raked the Divis Flats with 30-calibre Browning machine guns. Nine-year-old Patrick Rooney was shot in the head as he lay in his bed.[3]

Against a backdrop of flames, the residents of Bombay Street struggled to salvage what few belongings they could. In an effort to defend themselves they highjacked a bus at the corner of Bombay Street and the Falls Road to use as a barricade. They pickaxed the tyres to be certain it could not be driven away, but the bus did not entirely block the street. They were about to seize an articulated lorry to complete the barricade when someone shouted, "Don't do that! That truck belongs to the Irish Glass Bottle Company and Jack Lynch is going to come up here and help us!"

Jack Lynch did not come. And though the nationalists waited with pathetic faith, neither did the massive Irish Republican Army with which the demagogue had so frightened his followers. It simply did not exist. The IRA in Belfast consisted of no more than a handful of middle-aged men who had not used their guns since the 1950s. Against the heavily armed loyalist gangs, they were helpless.

While the black smoke of burning neighbourhoods stained the sky, churches and halls all across Belfast began opening their doors to take in the homeless.

On the sixteenth of August, shocked viewers of the news on television saw for the first time what was happening in Belfast. Large areas resembled Berlin in the aftermath of World War Two. Who was to blame for such wanton destruction? Few people in Britain had any knowledge of Irish history or the current political situation. Many believed the televised rantings of the demagogue when he claimed it was all the fault of the Irish Republican Army.

That evening, when it was far too late, the first British troops came marching up the Falls Road in Belfast with fixed bayonets, machine guns, high-powered rifles, and CS gas. The beleaguered Catholics gave them a rapturous welcome. They believed the soldiers had come to protect them from the loyalists.

Not everyone was convinced, however. Catholic refugees began streaming across the border to the Republic.

IN Derry on August fifteenth, British soldiers ringed the Bogside with barbed wire. They set up barricades at strategic locations in the Bogside, the sprawling Creggan, and several smaller Catholic neighbourhoods. The RUC and the B-Specials returned to their barracks as the British army assumed control of the city.

Grimy, exhausted, sometimes stopping to try to remember how to focus his camera, Barry Halloran took picture after picture.

WHEN it was over—as over as it could be—Barry trudged wearily through rubble-choked streets, looking for Séamus McCoy. There was no sign of him anywhere. *He probably went off somewhere with Billy McKee,* Barry tried to tell himself. But he did not believe it. He was filled with foreboding.

I'm getting to be like Ursula. I know things.

He returned to the priest's house, relieved to find it still standing when so many homes had been destroyed. The Cathedral of St. Eugene had been vandalised by B-Specials.

Father Aloysius was slumped in a chair in his small, shabby parlour. His face was pale and his hands were shaking, but otherwise he was all right. "Your friend isn't back yet," he told Barry.

"I haven't seen him either. I'm no good at finding people."

"Have a glass of brandy with me," said the priest, "then we'll look for him together."

They found Séamus McCoy in Altnagelvin Hospital. He was lying on a trolley in a crowded corridor outside the emergency room because there was no space available in the wards. The patients on trolleys had received necessary first aid and been put into hospital gowns, but they had not yet been fully examined. There were just too many of them.

Under the thin hospital blanket McCoy looked shrunken, almost like a child. His eyes were bandaged and he was coughing.

I should have let him drive the car, damn it! Barry bent over his friend. "What happened to you, Séamus?"

"Seventeen, is that you?" His voice was a breathless wheeze. "Get me out of here. I'm behind enemy lines."

"You're in hospital. What happened? Were you shot?"

"Gassed. Like our poor lads in the first war. The bloody RUC threw a cartridge right in my face. Get me out of here, Seventeen, I don't want to be blind in enemy territory."

Barry turned to Father Aloysius. "Can we take him back to your place?"

"He'd be welcome, of course, but he's better off here."

McCoy was growing agitated. "Who's that?" He gave another racking cough. "Who's there?"

Barry leaned over him again. "It's Father Aloysius, Séamus. You remember him."

"I'm trapped behind enemy lines, Seventeen!" wailed McCoy.

"Not for long," Barry assured him. Scooping his friend into his arms, he lifted him from the bed. McCoy reached around and scrabbled with the opening of his hospital gown, trying to cover his naked backside.

Father Aloysius protested, "You can't do this," but Barry was not listening.

Carrying McCoy, he strode toward the nearest exit. After a moment's hesitation Father Aloysius trotted after them, making small, anxious noises. A nurse called out, "Where are you going with that man?" Barry ignored her. He forced his way through a score of milling friends and relatives who looked at him aghast. A doctor in a bloodstained white coat tried to block his way, but the eyes Barry turned on the doctor were so fierce that the man fell back.

"Help, security!" someone shouted.

Barry sprinted toward the exit. A uniformed security guard with outstretched arms tried to intercept him. Cradling McCoy against his chest, Barry rolled one shoulder forward and hit the guard with enough force to knock the man off his feet. "Find Terry Roche," Barry shouted to the priest, "and bring him to your house!" Then he plunged through the doorway and ran to the car park.

THE Bogsiders were jubilant. Lifting the last weary defenders to their shoulders, they carried them through cheering streets. The district was devastated but its sense of community had never been so strong. By forcing the RUC and the B-Specials to call for the British army, they had won. The hated police had been forced to admit defeat and Stormont had cracked under pressure.

In a television interview Paddy Doherty of the Derry Citizens' Defence Association stated, "The writ of the British queen no longer runs in Free Derry."[4] An area in the Bogside was christened "Free Derry Corner."

Nationalist Derry had symbolically seceded from the Six Counties.

BARRY and May Coogan put Séamus McCoy to bed and made him as comfortable as they could. While they waited for the doctor, Barry listened to the housekeeper's radio in the kitchen. The news from Belfast was so bad that he did not dare tell McCoy.

Shortly before eight that evening Terry Roche arrived. He had been manning one of the first aid stations and, like every other member of the medical community, was haggard with fatigue, but he gave McCoy a thorough examination. Then he took Barry aside. "I'm not an eye specialist but I'm pretty sure his blindness is temporary. He told me he's had eye problems before, which is probably exacerbating the situation. The real problem is his chest."

"His lungs? Tell me it's not tuberculosis," Barry pleaded.

"I almost wish it were, there's a lot we can do for TB these days. I palpated a large mass in his chest. Unless I'm very much mistaken, your friend has a tumour."

"A tumour?"

"Big enough to affect his breathing, and possibly malignant. He'll need X-rays and a biopsy, so he'd best go back to Altnagelvin."

Barry stood very still, as if listening to an inner voice. "No," he said after a moment. "I'm taking him to Dublin."

"*You're* taking him to Dublin?"

"I'm accepting full responsibility for him, Terry. He doesn't have any family, so if he's ill I want him with me. Is it safe for him to travel?"

"That's not a good idea, not yet. He's in a bit of shock right now and he needs peace and quiet. I'd recommend several days' bed rest before he's moved for any distance. I'm sure John won't mind having him here, and I can show May how to bathe his eyes and put drops in. Then, if you're certain . . ."

"I'm certain."

"I can recommend a good man in Dublin. A cancer specialist."

An hour later McCoy was asleep and Barry was on his way to Belfast. He left behind strict instructions: "Don't let Séamus listen to the radio, and if he begins to get his eyesight back, don't give him a newspaper. God knows what he'd do if he found out about Belfast."

A cool, cloudless dawn was breaking over the city as Barry drove up the Falls Road. Astonishingly, he saw no people. The streets were eerily deserted. He parked Apollo and, taking his cameras, began walking along Bombay Street. Or what had been Bombay Street.

The smoking ruins, many of which were still burning, resembled photographs of Berlin on the day it fell. A number of shopfronts had collapsed into the road.

Barry knew bomb damage when he saw it.

When his foot struck something hard he glanced down. It was a badly singed canvas bag, fastened at the neck with braided cord. He reached down to pick it up. It weighed at least twelve pounds, maybe more. Curious, Barry set the bag on a pile of rubble so he could untie the cord. It was so burned that he finally had to take out his pocket knife and cut it.

The bag was filled with coins. Shapeless now. Fused together into a solid lump by the heat of the blast. Receipts from some shop, perhaps; being carried to the bank by the shopkeeper when calamity overtook him.

Barry photographed the bag and its contents, then walked on.

People began to appear in twos and threes. They had the same dazed faces he had seen in the Bogside but there was no triumph here. Women with scarves tied around their hair bent over to search through debris, looking for something familiar; something loved and lost. A man kicked at a broken shop sign and cursed aloud.

Another man noticed that Barry was walking in the direction of the Protestant Shankill Road and called out to him, "I wouldn't go any farther if I were you. Unless you have a gun, that is."

Barry stopped. "I don't have a gun."

"What's that in your hands then?"

"A camera."

The man snorted. "Whole lot of good that'll do you."

Barry continued taking pictures, though he did not go as far as the Shankill Road. *Not without a gun.* When his brain fogged with weariness he went back to Apollo. As he drove away from the area he saw a slogan freshly daubed in white paint on a fire-blackened wall: I.R.A. MEANS I RAN AWAY.

Barry's heart sank. *They think we failed them.*

The Belfast IRA was far too small in numbers to have been any help, but the victims of violence did not see it that way. In Belfast in 1969 everything was black-and-white—like the images on the television screens.

Barry checked in to a hotel near the centre of the city and was asleep before his head hit the pillow. He finally staggered out of bed at teatime. After a cold shower and a stiff drink in the hotel bar, he headed back toward West Belfast. At the Felons' Club the door was padlocked and the windows were fastened with shutters, yet he could hear activity inside. When he knocked at the door everything went very quiet. After a while he walked away.

IN Dublin on August sixteenth, gardai used a baton charge to break up an anti-British demonstration outside the British embassy. Fifty protesters were injured.[5]

In Belfast, 427 people were being treated in hospital for serious injuries. Of that number, 108 had gunshot wounds.[6] The Falls, Crumlin Road, the Ardoyne—every Catholic area had suffered.

. . .

BARRY spent two days in Belfast, compiling a photographic essay of a city in shock. He was not allowed to take any more photographs in Bombay Street. When he tried to enter the area he was stopped by British soldiers who firmly informed him, "No pictures for security reasons."

Whose security? Barry wondered.

THERE had been a time when entering the republican movement in the north depended mainly on family tradition. Young men followed their fathers. After Bombay Street, men from seventeen to seventy thronged to the IRA. "We've got to get back at the Oranges!" became a rallying cry. Television images of nationalists being attacked with batons by the RUC became commonplace, along with rolls of barbed wire and lines of grim-faced troops upholding the rule of law.

In Dublin three government ministers visited the Department of Foreign Affairs to ask for rifles to protect Catholics in the north. Their request was refused.

WHEN Barry returned to Derry, May Coogan told him that McCoy was complaining about the food.

"He must be feeling better, then."

"Strong enough to give out to me because I won't put the radio in his room."

"He knows nothing about the riots in Belfast?"

"We've kept all that from him. He keeps asking Father what's happening outside, but Father's good at evading questions he doesn't want to answer. He talks to your friend about God instead."

Barry laughed. "That'll do him a power of good."

Although McCoy was beginning to regain some vision, his cough was no better. Barry congratulated him on the improvement to his eyes and said nothing about the cough. "When Terry gives me the okay I'm going to take you to Dublin with me."

"I thought we were going back to Belfast. You said I could drive."

"There's no way you're going to drive my car until your eyes are clear, Séamus. I have to go back to Dublin to develop the photographs we took, so you might as well go with me. You're not in fit shape yet for anything else."

"I'm as fit as I ever was!"

"That's as may be, but I'd like to have you with me for a few days, just the same. You gave me a bit of a scare, you know."

To Barry's surprise, McCoy acquiesced with no further protest. *He must re-*

ally feel bad, Barry thought. The night before they left Derry he placed a telephone call to Dublin. He wanted to let his landlord know that he was bringing a guest with him. Philpott did not like surprises.

It was Barry who got the surprise.

Chapter Thirty-seven

As they drove out of Derry the following morning, Barry put his foot down hard on the accelerator and kept it there. McCoy slumped in the passenger seat with his arms folded across his chest. The two men exchanged only a few words. Barry was not in the mood for conversation, and McCoy was afraid of setting off his cough again. After a few minutes he reached over and turned on the radio. He fiddled with the dial until he found a country-western programme. "Now that's my idea of music," McCoy said happily. He settled back in his seat and dozed off. When he began snore, Barry retuned to a BBC station that played light classical music.

Alone with his thoughts, he drove south and east. Watching the road with eyes that saw other scenes. When the music eventually gave way to a newscast, he did not notice.

Philpott had answered his phone call on the second ring. Before Barry could say more than hello, his landlord had launched into a tirade. "I won't have this, Mr. Halloran, I simply won't stand for it! You have to come home immediately and sort out your American woman."

It can't be! "What American woman?"

"Miss Kavanagh. She says she's a friend of yours and has no place to stay. She arrived this afternoon, obviously expecting you would take care of her. I could hardly put her out on the street, but come back now and deal with this, or I'll put the both of you out."

·　　·　　·

APOLLO sped along the straight and hurtled around the curves. *What makes Barbara think she has the right . . . ? I never gave her the slightest indication that I . . . Damn the woman anyway. Thrusting herself into my life when it's complicated enough already.*

I wonder if she's all right. Maybe she's ill. Or maybe that bastard hurt her some way. . . .

Suddenly McCoy sat up. "What the hell happened in Belfast?"

THE long days of Irish summer meant that the light lingered until they reached Dublin. As they drove through the outskirts Barry asked McCoy if he was tired.

"Not a bit of it," the other man asserted. "I'm so damned mad that I could walk all the way to Belfast with a full pack on my back. And a loaded rifle."

The red sports car pulled up in front of Philpott's house with a squeal of brakes. A smell of steam came from under the bonnet. McCoy said, "Your car's overheated."

"So am I," Barry replied through gritted teeth. "Wait here in the car, will you? I need to have a little private conversation before I take you inside."

"Listen, if I'm going to be any trouble . . ."

"Don't talk like that, Séamus. I'll be back in just a minute, all right?"

Barry stormed into the house, taking care to slam the door behind him. He wanted everyone to know that he was furious.

Barbara was sitting in the front parlour with his landlord. She looked bored; Philpott wore the expression of an unwilling martyr. "It's about time, Mr. Halloran," he said petulantly. "You can't expect me to entertain your guests."

"She's not my guest. I didn't invite her and I don't know why she's here."

Barbara snapped, "Don't talk about me as if I'm not even in the room!"

"You shouldn't *be* in the room," Barry retorted, struggling to hold on to the shreds of his temper. "You should be in London or Manchester or wherever the hell else, and I should be in the north taking photographs. Now tell me what this is all about before I throw you out myself."

Her defiant expression faded. She looked so abject that Barry would have pitied her if he had had any room left for pity amongst his tangled emotions. "I've lost my job," she said in a barely audible voice.

"Then why not go home? Why come to me?"

"I didn't have enough money for a ticket to America. I barely had enough to get here."

"Jesus Christ, Barbara! The first time I saw you I knew you were trouble, and nothing's changed."

"Everything's changed. Please, can't we talk in private?"

Philpott stood up and brushed imaginary wrinkles from his trousers. "I'll be in the kitchen, there's still washing up to do. But I'm not preparing any more meals tonight, Mr. Halloran," he warned. "If you want something to eat you'll have to go out for it or fix it yourself."

Deliberately turning his back on Barbara, Barry walked over to the window. He could see Apollo parked at the kerb. Underneath its coating of road dust, the car gleamed dull red. *Blood-coloured. I should paint it blue. Or green. Definitely, green.*

Barbara came to stand beside him. "Is that your car, Barry? It's very smart."

Smart indeed. It's a battered banger held together with spit and wire. She's trying to get on my good side.

"Who's that sitting in it?"

"A friend," Barry said tightly, unwilling to give her anything.

"I came to you because I thought we were friends."

He would not look at her. "Even if we are, that doesn't give you the right to disrupt my life without a word of warning."

"I know, and I'm sorry, but . . . oh, Barry, everything went wrong at once! The bookings dried up and Jeremy ran off with the piano player and then I found out they'd taken all the money with them."

"You sound as if it were the greatest tragedy in the world. It isn't, I assure you."

She gave a little sigh. "I know. It's just the worst thing that ever happened to me."

"Lucky you, then." He tried to stay angry with her, but she was standing so close that he could feel the heat of her body. "Well, now that you're here . . ."

"You'll help me?"

"Stop anticipating. I was going to say, now that you're here we'll have to decide what's to be done with you. But not tonight."

"You can't put me out on the sidewalk!"

"Where did you sleep last night?"

"Mr. Philpott let me use your room since you weren't in it anyway."

"Well you can't stay there now. D'you want to go to a hotel?"

"I told you, I don't have any money."

If I pay for a hotel room, Barry warned himself, *I'll be making a commitment.*

He found Philpott sulking in his own apartment. "I don't want women here, Halloran. I've never wanted women here. They disrupt everything."

I couldn't agree more. "I'm sorry about Miss Kavanagh, but she came without my knowledge or permission."

"So you say."

Barry's eyes turned icy. "So I say. Now, however, she is here, and so is a friend of mine whom I did invite. You and I have some arrangements to make." The final sentence was spoken in low growl that was curiously unnerving.

.   .   .

WITHIN the hour Séamus McCoy was tucked into bed in Barry's room, and a separate folding bed had been brought in for Barry so that he would not disturb the sick man. McCoy protested over being treated like an invalid.

"It's only for a few days," Barry had told Philpott privately. "He'll go into hospital as soon as they can take him."

The landlord looked alarmed.

"He's not contagious," Barry hastened to add. "He has a tumour in his chest." He resurrected one of his old, irresistible smiles. "I'm grateful to you for being so kind to a sick man." It was a cynical ploy but it worked. Philpott simpered with pleasure, then said that McCoy could stay as long as he needed.

Barbara was more problematic. At first Philpott was adamant that he would not admit any women to his boardinghouse. "Think of it as an opportunity for you," Barry suggested. "Could you not use some help here? Miss Kavanagh is a strong, healthy woman. She could take a lot of work off your hands, and in return all you need do is give her room and board. Her room needn't be anything fancy, either. I don't think she's enjoyed much in the way of fancy accommodations lately."

Although Philpott was tempted, he would not surrender without a token struggle. "I don't think it would work out, Mr. Halloran. She doesn't seem like the sort who does house cleaning."

"She will be," Barry said in a determined voice. "After I explain it to her."

He carried Barbara's luggage to a dingy cubicle at the top of the stairs, the only empty room in the house. There was no furniture aside from an iron bedstead with a musty mattress, and an old wardrobe. The bathroom was on the landing below.

Barry forced open the only window, which had been painted shut, to air out the room. Then he turned the mattress over and helped Barbara make up the bed. At his insistence Philpott had given her two blankets and a good quilt.

"I think he's afraid of you," Barbara told Barry, "though I don't know why. You're really so harmless."

Barry was nonplussed. No one had ever called him harmless before.

While she unpacked he sat on the edge of the bed and watched. The contents of her luggage—the expensive matched set he remembered, badly scuffed and battered now—were revealing. Her train case was crammed with toiletries and makeup. The larger suitcase contained a tawdry collection of stage costumes made of cheap, shiny fabric and stained with perspiration. The smaller one held a few very short skirts, several brightly coloured tops, a froth of underwear, a worn cashmere cardigan, and a white plastic jacket with an industrial zipper up the front.

Against his will, Barry was moved to pity. "Don't you have a coat? Autumn can be cold."

"I did have a good coat, but I had to pawn it to buy a ticket for Ireland. I spent the last of the money on a taxi from the airport." From the bottom of her suitcase Barbara removed four pairs of shoes, none of them new. For such a tall girl she had very small feet.

Touchingly small.

Barry tore his eyes away. "If there's nothing else you need right now, you'd best go to bed," he said. "You must be exhausted." When he stood up, the bed springs creaked. "Good night, Barbara."

She yawned. "G'night."

If he had expected her to thank him he was disappointed.

Barry did not get much sleep that night. He was too aware of the tinderbox that was Northern Ireland, ready to explode. And of Séamus McCoy, moaning in his sleep.

And of the young woman in the room at the top of the house.

I don't need this, Barry said to God. Or whoever was listening. *I really don't need this.*

SHE came to him in his dreams with her tiger's eyes and her bronze hair. In his dreams, in his dreams.

He took her in his arms and she fought with all her strength but he was stronger, he did what he wanted with her. What she wanted him to do. In his dreams, in his dreams.

And afterwards she loved him.

AS usual Barry was awake at dawn. He dressed quietly and left McCoy sleeping.

Barbara had to be forcefully roused. "I'm never up before eleven!"

Barry ripped the covers from her bed. "You're up now. We have to talk."

As she got out of bed Barry tried not to notice how sheer her nightdress was, or how beautiful she looked without makeup. Her hair all tumbled. He waited while she put on a dressing gown, then explained the arrangement he had made with Philpott.

"Absolutely not!" Barbara actually stamped her foot. *I never saw anyone do that before.* "Under no circumstances! I'm not anyone's housemaid, Barry Halloran, and I'm insulted you would even suggest it."

"It would only be temporary, Barbara."

"How can you be sure?"

"Because everything's temporary. Mr. Philpott could die. Or so could you, for that matter."

The hazel eyes widened in horror. "I'm not going to die!"

"That," said Barry dryly, "would make you unique in human history. What I meant was, the job is just until you return to America."

"You don't seem to understand. I'm not going to the States because I like it better over here. If you try to send me home I'll just come back again."

"You don't seem to understand. I'm not going to send you home because you're not my responsibility. But if you stay here, what will you do for money? Have you really none at all?"

"Not a bean." She sounded unconcerned.

"What about your trust fund?"

"I can't touch the principal at all, but I draw the interest on it in June and December. That means I'll be stony broke for the next four months." She looked at Barry expectantly.

You're badly spoiled, my girl, he thought. *But I won't compound the crime.* "I suggest you work for Mr. Philpott until you have the next payment, then you can find a place of your own and another job."

"Oh." She was silent for a moment. "Do you know anyone who's looking for a club singer?"

"This is Dublin, not London. I don't think there's much demand for a club singer here."

"So where will I find work?"

"In a department store, like your friend Alice. Or in a restau—"

"I'm no waitress." The dark brows drew together.

"Barbara, there's nothing demeaning about honest wor—"

"Well I won't wait tables and I won't clean houses. You'll have to think of something else."

Cutting your throat might be a good place to start. "Very well." He pulled her suitcases out from under the bed. Going to the wardrobe, he began taking out her clothes and folding them as neatly as he could.

"What do you think you're doing?"

"That should be obvious. I'm packing your things."

"Why?"

"Because you can't stay here for free. I'll put them outside and you can take them when you go."

"Go where?"

"That's up to you." He put a stack of costumes into a suitcase.

Barbara watched in disbelief as Barry methodically packed her possessions, then closed the suitcases and began carrying them to the stairs.

"All right," she said in a sullen voice.

He stopped but did not turn around. "Sorry?"

"I said all *right,* God damn it. You win."

He turned around but did not set the suitcases down. "I don't like hearing a woman swear."

"Well, I swear, so you'd better get used to it."

Barry started down the stairs again.

"You son of a bitch," she screamed after him, "do you always have to win?"

"Actually," he replied in an even tone, "I do."

Back in his room, Barry took out Ned's notebooks. *How long has it been since I looked at these? Years, maybe.*

He riffled through the third in the sequence until he came to the page he was looking for. The first time he saw that page Barry had not understood all that it meant, but he understood now.

In the exact centre of the paper, in Ned Halloran's best copperplate hand-writing, was a single word:

Síle.

WHILE Barbara reluctantly attempted to master the vacuum cleaner, Barry telephoned the cancer specialist Terry Roche had recommended. "Dr. Roche already telephoned me," the doctor told him. "After I examine Mr. McCoy I can make arrangements at St. Luke's for an X-ray and a biopsy, if necessary. Can you bring him to see me on Thursday?"

"I'll do better than that. I'll fetch him right now."

"I'm afraid I'm booked solid today . . ." the doctor began.

"I'll have him there in an hour," said Barry. And hung up.

In Barry's room McCoy was sitting in the armchair with his arms wrapped around his chest. He had not yet shaved, which helped disguise his sunken cheeks. "I think that gas went into my chest, Seventeen. It's given me a ferocious case of heartburn."

"Listen, Séamus, I know a good doctor here in Dublin. As it happens I'll be driving past his surgery today on my way to buy some photographic supplies, so why don't you come with me? We'll pop in and let him take a look at you. Maybe he can do something for your heartburn."

"There's no need," McCoy said. Yet he did not resist when Barry shepherded him to the car.

While McCoy was with the doctor Barry sat in the waiting room leafing through back issues of *Ireland's Own* for what seemed like hours. When he discovered a folded newspaper someone had abandoned he seized upon it.

Chapter Thirty-eight

August 19, 1969

DOWNING STREET DECLARATION

Following meetings between representatives of the government of Northern Ireland and the British government, it has been announced that Northern Ireland will remain part of the United Kingdom for as long as that is the wish of the majority.

W HEN the door of the examining room finally opened, McCoy emerged looking paler than ever. "I may have a wee problem, Seventeen." He sounded embarrassed.

Barry hastily refolded the newspaper so that his friend could not see it.

Checking McCoy into hospital meant entrusting him to strangers in a strange world. Battles were fought in Saint Luke's, but not as Barry understood battles. Doctors and nurses fought for life rather than to inflict death. Cancer was the enemy. The weapons used and the language of strategy were secrets zealously guarded by a priesthood in white coats.

Once again Barry was an outsider.

The tests were conclusive: McCoy had a malignant tumour and would need an immediate operation. He took the news with stoic fortitude. "If my number's up, my number's up, Seventeen. Don't look so glum. I never expected to live this long."

Barry went back to Harold's Cross in hopes of snatching a few hours' sleep before the operation, which was scheduled for the following morning. Barbara and Philpott both spoke to him but their words did not register. He made automatic responses, ate food without tasting it, went to bed without sleeping. In the morning he returned to the hospital in time to see McCoy before they took him to the operating theatre.

"How are you keeping, Séamus?"

"I feel better than you look, Seventeen. Did you sleep in a dugout last night?"

"I spent the night developing photographs and forgot to go to bed," Barry lied.

"That's good. I was afraid you were worried about me."

"Why should I worry about you? You're as strong as a goat's breath."

While he waited for McCoy to be brought down from theatre, Barry looked through the collection of old magazines and outdated newspapers, then laid them aside. He exchanged meaningless comments on the weather with another man who was waiting. After a while the man left. Hours passed. A couple arrived; the woman kept sniffling. The man talked to her in a low undertone, then fell silent and sat gloomily staring at his shoes.

There were no windows in the hospital waiting room. Barry lost all sense of time. He did not look at his watch because he did not want to know how long they had been working on McCoy.

Waiting is hell and hell is waiting. For all eternity. Just waiting.

Barry's mind rambled aimlessly. Most of his thoughts were dark ones. He found himself recalling the conversation with his mother about using only one word on a tombstone. *What would apply to Ursula, I wonder?*

Unique.

And Séamus?

Indispensable.

That discovery was so painful that he forced himself to think of someone else. *What about Barbara? How would one describe her?*

The quest kept him amused until McCoy's surgeon entered the waiting room. When he untied his mask his smile was like a sunrise. "I think we got it all, Mr. Halloran. Your friend is very lucky."

Barry caught his breath. "Can I see him?"

"He's still in recovery. He'll probably sleep through until morning, so come back then. We'll be keeping him here for a while, of course, but he should be able to go home in a few weeks."

For Barry, the devastation wrought upon so many in recent weeks had dwindled in comparison to one threatened loss. The lifting of the threat lifted his heart. Apollo became a winged chariot. As he drove home, the charioteer whistled "Tri-Coloured Ribbon.'"

When he pulled up in front of the house he heard "Boléro" wafting from an open window. His window. Barry's good mood evaporated. It was not yet teatime, so the other boarders were still at work. Philpott was probably busy in the kitchen. There was only one person who would be playing the gramophone.

Angrily, Barry flung open the door to his room—to find that it had been transformed into a stage. The beds had been folded away and the furniture pushed against the walls, leaving the floor clear for Barbara.

Barbara. Dancing with wild abandon.

For the second time that day Barry caught his breath.

She was music to his eyes.

An old familiar music expressed in a new form, but recognisable just the same. *I am lost,* he thought.

Oblivious to everything but the compelling rhythm of the dance, Barbara swept around in an elegant half-circle that brought her face-to-face with Barry. She gave a gasp. "I didn't know you were home!"

"I am now."

She recovered her composure almost instantly. "How's your friend?"

"The doctors think he's going to be all right."

"Oh, Barry, I am glad!" She threw her arms around his neck and kissed him. She smelled of perfume and perspiration.

Her heart was pounding against Barry's chest. Racing as his was racing with too many emotions. Relief, joy, passion . . . Between one beat and the next, thought became impossible for him. His arms tightened around her and he bore her to the floor. If she had struggled he would have let her up immediately, he still had that much self-control. But she did not struggle. She gave a deep, throaty moan, and pulled him more tightly against her.

Women in Barry's experience were relatively passive. He had assumed it was because the machineries of their bodies were different from his. They could not possibly understand the forces that drove him: the intense sexual hunger, the blind need.

Barbara Kavanagh did understand. She met him with her youth and strength and an astonishing lust. When he began to fumble with her clothes he found her fingers already there. Then they were on him, making urgent, needful adjustments.

Against his lips, she murmured his name.

All at once he was inside. *Inside!* Inside silken, throbbing heat; lying above her, propped on his elbows—he was so big that he had always been afraid of crushing a woman—but also enveloped by her, melded to her, unable to distinguish any difference between them. Unaware of anything but sensation.

Barry lay perfectly still. *Nothing may ever feel this good again. Make it last.*

As if following the same conductor, Barbara waited too. Then she began to move under him, gently at first, but soon demandingly, capturing him with her rhythm which miraculously was his own rhythm.

His skin was made for this. His lungs and heart and penis and brain . . . yes, his brain . . . all were made for this. Bodies . . . singing . . . together. That was it, singing. Like a choir. Making something larger than their individual selves, a tactile chorus that rose and rose to an unbearable crescendo . . . falling away to diminuendo . . . building again . . .

THREE hours later Barry was alone in his room. Still smelling her perfume on the air. Still feeling her against him. All around him. She had gone to her own room but in some mysterious way she had never left his.

It made no sense, but there it was.

They had both missed tea. He was not hungry—*Not for food anyway*—but he wanted to be certain she was all right. That is what he told himself, though he knew he really just longed to see her face again. And hear her voice, that dark-amber incredible voice, murmuring his name.

When he knocked gently on her door there was no answer. Suddenly anxious—*Maybe I frightened her; maybe she's run off!*—he pounded his fist on the door panel.

"Come in, it's open."

Wrapped in her dressing gown, Barbara was sitting on the bed applying fresh varnish to her toenails. Tendrils of damp hair clung to her temples. She looked up with a quizzical smile. "Do you want something?"

Do I want something?

"I thought you might . . . be hungry. We could go down to the kitchen and . . ."

"Thanks, but I'm going to bed as soon as my nails are dry. I'm really tired. I suppose it gets easier with practice, though."

"Gets easier with practice?"

"Housecleaning. What did you think I meant?"

A muscle twitched in Barry's jaw. "I don't know, Barbara. Half the time I have no idea what you mean. You have me flummoxed."

"What's 'flummoxed'?"

"Baffled. You're not what I expected."

"What did you expect?"

Oh no. I won't go down that road. "Actually, I hadn't given it much thought," Barry said with studied nonchalance. It was a point of honour to sound as emotionally uninvolved as she did. "If you don't want anything to eat I'll wish you good night." Polite; formal.

"I'll see you tomorrow," she called after him. "Do you want me to do your room first?"

Jesus Christ!

He did not think he was in love with her. *In love. Silly, sentimental phrase. Does anyone say that anymore?* He certainly did not want to be in love with her. Yet she was embedded in his pores.

.   .   .

WHILE he waited for McCoy to be released from hospital, Barry concentrated on his photography. Events in the north were spilling over into the southern press now, so he was aware of James Callaghan's visit to the Bogside and his grant of £250,000 for "alleviation of distress." In the wake of such large-scale violence in the Six Counties several government enquiries were under way. The inspector general of the RUC announced disciplinary action against sixteen constables as a result of events at Burntollet Bridge in January.[1] The Cameron Commission placed much of the blame for the more recent violence in Derry and Belfast on the actions of the RUC and the policies of Stormont.

None of this offered opportunities for Barry's camera, which was just as well because he could not go north anyway. He visited McCoy in hospital every afternoon and spent the rest of his time taking local and regional photographs. Sporting events, politicians making speeches, brides on their way to church. The peaceful documentation of a peaceful country.

When he was at home Barry could not help noticing the way the male boarders looked at Barbara. She paid no attention. Barry, however, made a point of intercepting those glances and responding with such an icy glare that the man in question understood perfectly.

ON the tenth of October the report of the Hunt Committee on Policing in Northern Ireland recommended that the RUC become an unarmed civilian police force. It also recommended disbanding the B-Specials and replacing them with a locally recruited part-time military force under the control of the British army, to be known as the Ulster Defence regiment.[2]

The following day three thousand unionists marched from the Shankill Road to attack the Unity Flats with petrol bombs. The British army moved in with guns.

Ian Paisley claimed to have been told by British soldiers that they had been sent to Northern Ireland to keep the Catholics happy.

LIVING beneath the same roof as Barbara was a peculiar torture for Barry. Every day, he saw her face. Heard her voice. Sometimes even heard her singing as she went about her work. Yet she never by the slightest glance indicated that anything sexual had happened between them, or that she would like it to happen again.

To Barry's surprise, she displayed, after some initial difficulties, a talent for housekeeping. The folds of the curtains hung perfectly and the highly polished tabletops sported striking arrangements of flowers and greenery. Even Philpott grudgingly admitted that Barbara was an asset to the house. "I suppose she would make someone a good wife," he told Barry.

"Don't look at me, I have no plans to marry. Even if I did, it wouldn't be to someone as contrary as Barbara Kavanagh."

"So there's nothing going on between the two of you?"

Barry was able to say honestly, "There is nothing going on between us."

"That's good. I won't have anything of that nature in this house. Nothing nasty between men and women. You do understand, don't you?"

Looking down at the fussy little man with his aging, frightened face, suddenly Barry did understand.

He felt a deep pity for Mr. Philpott.

ON the seventh of November more than three thousand Viking artefacts, indicating the ruins of the largest Viking town ever discovered outside of Scandinavia, were discovered on the site of proposed Dublin civic offices at Wood Quay. Barry hurried to take photographs. It soon became obvious that a fight was looming; archaeologists were already planning a strong resistance to any further exploitation of the site. Dublin Corporation was equally determined to build its new facility there, even at the cost of destroying a unique piece of world heritage.

"I've found a new battle to fight," Barry reported when he visited McCoy in hospital the next day.

McCoy was not encouraging. "You'll never beat the government, Seventeen. Any government."

"I don't know about that. Look what's happening in the north, the new concessions Stormont's making."

"Don't you believe it. We're really dealing with the Brits there, remember? The Conservative Party in Britain will back the Unionists in Stormont every time, because they need their support at Westminster. Those concessions are just a bit of window dressing to keep the Catholics quiet for a wee while. They'll be forgotten soon enough. The British never keep their word to the Irish, not when it comes to political power plays."

"It's not like you to be a pessimist, Séamus. Did you ever hear of the great Irish explorer, Ernest Shackleton? He was born in County Kildare and I have a book about him. Shackleton said, 'Optimism is the true moral courage.'"

"What do I have to be optimistic about?" McCoy grumbled. "They've taken my fags away and told me not to smoke for the rest of my life. Every six months I'll have to visit some bloody doctor who'll tell me just how long the rest of my life is likely to be. In the meantime I'm too beat-up to attract a woman and too poor if I did find one who'd have me. What's left to look forward to?"

"For one thing, I've been told I can bring you home next weekend."

"Home?"

"To my house. You'll be convalescent for a while and I want you where I can keep an eye on you."

McCoy shook his head. "That's not on. My friends in the north will look after me, or I can go back to Ballina, there's always a place for me there. If need be I could stay with the Reddans for a while."

"This isn't arguable, Séamus. You're coming with me."

"There's really not enough room for the two of us."

"You're a stubborn man, aren't you? We'll rent another bedsit for you, don't worry. I happen to know one's coming available at the end of the month."

McCoy squinted up at Barry. "And what am I supposed to use for money? I can't afford a place like yours."

"My landlord was willing to give my friend Barbara room and board in exchange for a little housework. I'm sure I can convince him to make some sort of arrangement for you."

McCoy started to laugh, but it hurt. "For a man who claims to travel light you go about it in a funny way, Seventeen. Sounds like you've acquired yourself a whole family."

Barry gave a wry smile. "Maybe I have." But the idea was not unpleasant. He felt as if something inside himself were expanding.

When he arrived home that afternoon he happened to meet Barbara in the front hall. No one else was around; no one to see them. She took one step closer to Barry than he expected. "How was Mr. McCoy today?" she asked in a voice that had nothing whatever to do with Séamus McCoy.

"He's in good form. I plan to bring him home on Sunday."

"And he'll share your room again?"

"Only until I can move him into a room of his own. I'm going to ask Philpott to—"

"So you'll be alone?" The eyes she raised to Barry's were golden with promise. Before he could respond, she headed for the stairs. "Have to run. I've still tons of work to do."

Barry's temper flared. "Don't turn your back on me and walk away."

She paused. Looked at him over her shoulder. "Or what? What will you do?"

He did not stop to think, just strode forward and took her in his arms.

"I told you I would have none of this!" an outraged voice cried.

Barry released Barbara and spun around. Philpott had just entered the hall. "I *told* you," he repeated, his voice quavering. "I don't have to tolerate this sort of carry-on. I don't have to take in boarders at all, I have my army pension."

Barry tried to picture the wispy little fellow in the army. For once, his imagination failed him. "May I speak with you in private, Mr. Philpott?"

"To ask permission to enjoy this doxy you've brought into my home under false pretences? You won't get it!"

The cold anger was summoned; focussed; aimed. "Never speak of Miss Kavanagh that way again. Do you understand me?"

Philpott swallowed so hard that his Adam's apple leapt above his collar like a frightened little animal trapped in a tunnel.

Barbara's fingers groped for Barry's hand and gave it a squeeze. "Thank you," she whispered.

He continued to hold the landlord locked with his eyes. "Now, about that private conversation?"

YOU'RE going to have a room of your own, Séamus," Barry reported the next day. "A better one than mine."

"What's it going to cost me?" McCoy asked suspiciously.

"Now that's where we've been lucky. It seems that Philpott's decided to sell the house. He's tired of the responsibility and he's had a decent offer for the place, so he's going to take it. The new owner will want him to stay on to do the cooking, which is the one thing Philpott really enjoys. But the owner doesn't want to live on the premises, so he'll need someone to take over as manager. Collect the rents, pay the bills, that sort of thing. It's not physically taxing, but it will require a person who can be there all the time. That's where you come in."

McCoy looked appalled. "You've committed me to a job running a feckin' boardinghouse?"

Barry was prepared for this moment. "If you don't take it, I shall myself. Free room and board is too good to pass up. Of course it means I won't have much time for photography, but . . ."

"You don't want to give up your photography, Seventeen."

"I don't," Barry agreed. "But I'm being practical."

McCoy let out a little sigh. "Maybe it's time I started being practical. All right, I guess you can pass the word along: I'll do it. But do you think I'll get along with the new owner?"

"I have no idea," Barry said blandly.

Chapter Thirty-nine

Y OU will be surprised to learn," Barry wrote to Ursula—thinking it wiser to communicate the news by letter rather than a telephone call—"that I am buying the boardinghouse where I live. I am rather surprised myself, but it is a good investment. Although I will have a mortgage the income from the property will meet the payments," Barry claimed.

In truth it would not, since Barry, Barbara, McCoy, and Philpott would be living rent free. *We sound like a firm of solicitors,* Barry thought when he strung their names together.

However, property was cheap in Dublin as it was throughout Ireland, and currently there were six paying tenants in the house. As long as Barry's photographs continued to sell he could stay afloat financially.

"I shall not be able to come down to Clare for Christmas this year," his letter to his mother went on, "but if things go well you will have an invitation to my own house for next Christmas."

December was devoted to talking to bank managers and solicitors, signing papers, getting McCoy settled in, and above all trying to maintain his anonymity as "the new owner." Philpott was sworn to secrecy. "If you tell anyone, the deal's off," Barry warned the little man. "I don't want my friends to think they're getting charity."

"It's not charity if they're working for you."

"Séamus won't be up to much work for a while. Show me what needs to be done right now and I'll do it myself. As for Miss Kavanagh, she can continue to take her instructions from you as the representative of the new owner."

"How long do you think you can keep your secret?" Philpott asked. His eyes twinkled mischievously. Freed of the burden of responsibility, he was beginning to enjoy the situation.

"I honestly don't know, I'm taking one day at a time." *I've always taken one day at a time. That's something one learns in the Army.*

IN December the Army Convention met in Dublin. Although McCoy was anxious to go, the weather was bad and he was too recently out of hospital to risk it. Barry consoled him by promising, "I'll tell you everything that happens."

"That's not the same as being there."

"You may not be missing much. I spoke briefly with Éamonn MacThomáis and he says it's likely to be just another long argument about political philosophy."

"That's what's wrong, Seventeen; all that talking and no doing."

"What would you suggest the Army do?"

"March on the north," McCoy replied without hesitation.

"Maybe that would have worked once," Barry told him, "but not anymore."

"You're not admitting the Six are lost forever?!"

"I'm not admitting that and I don't believe it. But I do believe reuniting Ireland is going to require a lot of work on a lot of different levels. The policy of neutrality that kept us out of the Second World War has ensured that modern Ireland's wars are all fought on this one island. Conflict limited to such a small space is very bitter indeed."

The Army Convention of 1969 was well attended. Barry feared he would not find a seat until he saw Éamonn MacThomáis standing up and looking around. Barry waved to him; MacThomáis waved back and gestured to a seat he had saved next to his own. "I thought for a while that you weren't coming," he told Barry.

"It's not like me to be late," Barry admitted. "Punctuality was drilled into me by my training officer when I joined the Army. But just as I was about to leave the house there was a problem about the plumbing and I . . ."

"What in the name of the holy saints do you have to do with plumbing?"

"It's a long story, Éamonn," Barry said with a wry smile. "I'll tell you some other time. The Army Council are taking their seats up front, so I guess the meeting's about to start."

True to prediction, the main business of the convention was a discussion of republican philosophy and tactics that turned into a heated argument. For Cathal Goulding and the majority of the Army Council, political abstentionism had died in the flames of Belfast. Determined to pursue republican goals through political means, they tabled two motions. The first was to join a national liberation front in alliance with the more radical leftists. The second, and more divisive, motion was to recognise as valid both the government of the Twenty-Six Counties and that of the Six, which would clear the way for republicans to take an active part in both parliaments.

One member of the council held a sharply differing view. Seán MacStiofáin promptly tabled a second motion that upheld traditional militancy. There was a moment of silence in the hall while all eyes turned toward MacStiofáin. Five foot ten in height, a stocky man with greying brown hair and a dimpled chin, he had a rather cherubic countenance. Yet, as MacThomáis whispered to Barry, "There stands a genuine hard man; perhaps the only real terrorist the Army's ever produced."[1]

"Who's going to defend the Catholics in the Six if there's no fighting IRA?" MacStiofáin demanded to know. "You think the Brits will do it? I tell you they won't. Their allegiance is to the crown, not the harp. If they've brought any degree of control to the situation in the north it's only in order to keep the status quo."

Some of the men in the hall, including Ruairí Ó Brádaigh, agreed with MacStiofáin. Debate swiftly became rancorous argument. "We're the Army, damn it!" a Volunteer cried. "We've pledged our lives to fight for Ireland and we don't have all of Ireland back yet. Are you asking us to surrender?"

"Maybe Paisley and his crowd have it right," another man shouted. "What is it they say? 'No Surrender.'"

The slogan became a chant: "No Surrender, No Surrender!"

Pandemonium broke out. With a great effort, Cathal Goulding finally brought the convention under control long enough to demand a vote from the senior officers.

When Goulding's motions passed by thirty-nine to twelve, the hall erupted again.

Two groups of Volunteers began gathering on opposite sides of the room. Barry turned toward MacThomáis. "What are you going to do?"

"I don't know, Barry. There's an argument to be made for both sides—especially when you consider what's after happening in Belfast—but I don't honestly know. I'd like to talk to Cathal. . . ." MacThomáis stepped out into the aisle just as a crowd of men rushed past. Somehow he was caught in their midst and carried along toward the side where MacStiofáin's adherents were gathering.

Barry stayed in his seat. *This is wrong. Dear God, this is all wrong.*

He returned to Harold's Cross late that night. McCoy was waiting for him. "Well? What happened?"

"The worst possible outcome, Séamus."

The older man studied Barry's face intently. "A split? In the Army?"

"You've got it in one." He explained what had happened as best he could.

"What about you?" McCoy wanted to know. "Which way did you go?"

"They're both right and they're both wrong. I came away without committing to either side."

"It's not like you to be indecisive, Seventeen."

"Oh, I made a decision right enough. I decided not to watch the Army I love split itself apart. I have a bottle in my room. Care to join me?"

"You couldn't keep me away," said Séamus McCoy.

That night Barry Halloran, who never got drunk, got very very drunk.

ANTICIPATING the way the convention might go, MacStiofáin had pre-arranged a meeting place where he and the other dissidents could discuss their next move. He then set out for Belfast, where he addressed a meeting of the rapidly expanding IRA there.

On the eighteenth of December dissident delegates from the convention and their followers held a meeting during which they elected a twelve-man executive body. The executive chose a seven-member provisional army council. Seán MacStiofáin was appointed chief of staff.

In Dublin ten days later the Provisional IRA issued its first statement: "We declare our allegiance to the thirty-two county Irish Republic, proclaimed at Easter 1916, established by the first Dáil Éireann in 1919, overthrown by force of arms in 1922 and suppressed to this day by the existing British-imposed six-county and twenty-six county partition states."[2]

CHRISTMAS would be a muted celebration, though Barbara was keen on putting up a Christmas tree. "It won't be Christmas if we don't," she insisted.

Barry told her, "Christmas has nothing to do with trees, that's a German custom Prince Albert and Queen Victoria introduced."

"Well I think it's lovely to have a big tree all covered with lights and ornaments."

"I don't have any lights and ornaments, Barbara, and I'm a bit short of cash right now."

"I'll buy them, then."

"With what?" Barry asked reasonably. "Has your money come from America?"

"Not yet."

"I thought you told me you'd receive it in December."

"Well, usually I would, but," she looked contrite, "I forgot to send my new address to the lawyers who administer my trust fund. I'll mail it off tomorrow, I promise. The money should be here in January."

"You simply can't ricochet through life being that irresponsible," Barry scolded.

She pressed her lips together and turned away.

Two days later he came home to find a beautifully decorated spruce tree in the parlour. "How do you suppose she paid for it?" he asked McCoy.

Grinning, McCoy replied, "She went around the neighbourhood offering to clean people's houses for them after the holidays—if they paid a deposit up front. Y'know, I wasn't too impressed by that lassie at first. But she's got good stuff in her."

"If you say so." Barry sounded unconvinced.

However, McCoy had observed the covert looks he slanted in Barbara's direction. McCoy also had noticed, as Barry had not, the looks she sneaked at him.

"Are you going to ask her to marry you, Seventeen?"

"You must be joking."

"Listen here to me, lad. If you have a chance at an ordinary life, grab it. Grab it with both hands. The Army's falling apart, but you've got your career and you've got your house. You don't know how lucky you are."

Barry raised one eyebrow. "My house? What do you mean by that?"

"I'm an old dog, Seventeen; I can scent markings on a lamppost. Man doesn't replace a frayed sash cord in someone else's dining room window."

"It wanted doing and you aren't up to lifting out one of those heavy windows yet."

"This is me you're talking to, remember? If you don't want to tell anyone else your business, lad, I'll respect that. But I know what I know."

Marry Barbara, and her with that temperament. What a ridiculous idea. Besides, as soon as her money arrives she'll be away.

Won't she?

If she hated it here would she not have sent that change of address immediately?

ON Christmas Day, Barry, McCoy, and five of the boarders went to Mass together. When Barry asked Barbara to join them she hesitated. "I'm an employee here; would it be right for me to—"

This time it was Barry who interrupted. "You're in Ireland now, Barbara. We all go together. The Church of Ireland has reserved pews for the gentry but we don't do that. You are a Catholic, aren't you?" He had never been quite certain. Unlike Northern Ireland, people in the south did not ask one another their religion.

"I'm Catholic," she assured him, "like my father. Mother's rather backslid."

Barbara sat between Séamus McCoy and one of the boarders during Mass. She was intensely aware of Barry on McCoy's other side. When the congregation rose to sing "Adeste Fidelis" she skillfully blended her contralto with Barry's deep baritone.

McCoy heard them singing with one voice and smiled to himself.

IN Dublin on the twenty-eighth of December, Bernadette Devlin was named Man of the Year by the *Sunday Independent*.

On that same day, the *Sunday Press* reported the split in the IRA.

.   .   .

AFTER the split, the Officials controlled the existing weaponry. The Provisionals would have to start over from scratch.

Barry received an unsigned note through his letter box: "Resuming operations in your line of expertise. Are you interested?"

He did not respond. Yet he had to admit to himself that for one brief moment he was tempted.

The following day he wrote to Ursula, "We have three crowds calling themselves republican now. There's Fianna Fáil, who used to be republicans. There's the so-called Official IRA with a Marxist-socialist philosophy. And there's the Provisional IRA, who inherited the dream and not much else."

But, though he never mentioned it to anyone, Barry still had Ned's notebooks with the coded lists of names.

NINETEEN seventy did not have an auspicious beginning in Northern Ireland. Attacks on Catholic communities by Protestant extremists continued. In fear and fury, the Catholics turned on their tormentors and fought back.

The Provisional IRA in Belfast organised itself into battalions and undertook a serious search for weapons and funding.[3]

Meanwhile, the various republican splinter groups continued to fund themselves through criminal activities. The success of these operations was not lost on the Provos.

WHEN Barbara's money arrived from the States she opened a Dublin bank account and asked Mr. Philpott if she could move to a nicer room when one became available. "I'll pay the extra cost," she assured him.

Philpott smirked. "I'll have to contact the new owner and ask him, but I'm sure it will be acceptable."

Following the Sinn Féin Ard Fheis on the eleventh of January, Éamonn MacThomáis telephoned Barry with news of a split in the party mirroring that in the Army. One-third of the delegates had walked out, going to a hall in Parnell Square to hold their own meeting. They would be giving their support to the Provisional IRA.

"Ruairí Ó Brádaigh's now the president of Provisional Sinn Féin," MacThomáis reported, "and he'll be moving their offices to Kevin Street. I'm going with them. The Officials will stay in Gardiner Street."

"Is the whole world splitting down the middle?" wondered Barry.

"I blame everything on partition," MacThomáis said sourly. "Divisiveness is a disease."

The two halves of republicanism swiftly moved further apart. The Provisionals announced the launch of a revived *An Phoblacht,* to keep the physical-force men around the country informed of what was happening. From Donegal, Dáithí O Canaill was one of the first to subscribe.

WHEN one of the Officials passed a Provisional in the street they did not speak, but fistfights broke out in pubs.

Meanwhile, Charles Haughey, acting on his own, was trying to interest various British ministers in coming to Dublin to discuss the problem in the north. His effort was unsuccessful.

LIFE in Harold's Cross continued as before. McCoy was slowly regaining his strength and taking over more duties in the household. Although her work was physically hard Barbara enjoyed it. She felt she was making a needed contribution—something she had never done before. She even persuaded Philpott to let her help with the cooking and discovered a talent for making pastry.

Whatever she did, she did to perfection. Waiting for Barry to notice.

Barry, however, was preoccupied on other levels. Although he took no part in Army activities—on either side—he followed developments avidly, as did Séamus McCoy. Both men were deeply worried over the split, and equally worried about the unresolved problems in Northern Ireland.

At the end of March disbanding of the B-Specials began, but this was counterbalanced by Ian Paisley's victory in a by-election for the Northern Ireland parliament at Stormont.

"One step forward and two steps back," Barry lamented. "For a little while there I really had hopes that there would be changes in the north, but I don't think that's going to be allowed to happen."

"Now who's being pessimistic, Seventeen?"

"Tell me honestly. Do you think there'll be any long-term improvement?"

"Honestly?" McCoy squinted into a dimly perceived future. "No."

At the beginning of April there were three nights of rioting in Belfast which came to an end only when the British army used CS gas against the nationalists. Amongst those nationalists were members of the city's rapidly expanding IRA brigade.

The arrival of an additional five hundred soldiers brought the total of British troops in the north to sixty-five hundred. As if in response, the IRA began a new bombing campaign.

It had been fourteen years since Operation Harvest.

Barry and Apollo headed north again. While he was away, Barbara installed window boxes and filled them with a riot of spring flowers.

"You're a wonder, you are," McCoy told her.

It was not McCoy's admiration she sought. All those years ago she had started off on the wrong foot with Barry and she did not know how to make it right. Having sex with him had only exacerbated the problem, because now Barbara knew she was deeply in love with him.

She told herself she would rather die than admit her true feelings to him. She was certain he did not share them.

When Barry came home from Belfast his eyes saw the flowers but they did not register in his brain. His brain was filled with too many ugly pictures.

ON the first of May, Captain James Kelly, an intelligence officer with the Irish army, was arrested in Dublin under the Offences Against the State Act. He was released within twenty-four hours, but suddenly the word *gunrunning* was on everyone's lips. The suggestion was: "Sure the Army could lose a few hundred rifles and slip them across the border quietly."

Five days later Jack Lynch dismissed two cabinet ministers: Charles J. Haughey, the minister for finance, and Neil Blaney, the agriculture minister. Together with a gaggle of press photographers, Barry arrived in time to capture Haughey and Blaney as they left Leinster House. Neil Blaney looked extremely tired. Charles Haughey was a short man with a closed face and deeply hooded eyes, but there was a quality about him that caught and held Barry's attention. *That man's a ticking bomb,* he thought. *We haven't heard the last of him.*

Subsequently the Dáil debated for almost thirty-eight hours about allegations of arms smuggling. On May twenty-eighth the two ex-ministers were arrested together with three other men for conspiring to import arms and ammunition for use in Northern Ireland.

Chapter Forty

THE Arms Trial rocked Ireland. Never since the foundation of the Irish Free State had a serving cabinet minister been arrested. Now there were two of them in the dock.

"I want to believe they're guilty," Barry told McCoy, "because that would mean at least a couple of our politicians tried to do *something*."

"I'm about ready to do something, Seventeen. The old eyes are as good as they'll ever be, so I'm not much use with a rifle anymore. But the IRA is attracting new men and they'll need training officers. I'm thinking of going back on active service."

"With the Provisionals, I assume?"

"The Officials don't speak for me anymore."

McCoy was standing straighter, coughing less, eating more. But, though he was touched by the older man's bravado, Barry knew he was not fit to return to the Army. He decided to seek an ally in his fight to keep McCoy at home.

He waited until the house was quiet in the evening, then went to Barbara's room and knocked gently on the door. "Barbara? It's Barry. May I come in?"

"Just a minute!"

It was considerably more than a minute before she opened the door. She was wearing a new dressing gown and her hair had been brushed until it shone. "This is an unexpected pleasure," she said.

He could not read her mood. Perhaps she was being formally polite, perhaps she was being sarcastic. With Barbara one could not always tell. "I need to talk to you privately," said Barry.

She stood aside for him to enter.

He took a deep breath. This was going to be surprisingly hard. "Barbara, I've never discussed certain aspects of my life with you, because I don't discuss them with anybody. But now I think you need to know that both Séamus and I have been members of the Irish Republican Army."

The colour left her cheeks. "The IRA?"

"Indeed."

Barbara sat down abruptly on the edge of her bed. "Do you kill people?"

He was taken aback by the baldness of the question. "No, no I don't. I haven't been on active service in years. Séamus was, though, until he fell ill, and now he's talking about going back. The reason I'm telling you is, he thinks the world of you and I need you to help me persuade him to stay here with us."

"With us?"

"You and me."

Her features rearranged themselves in some subtle fashion. "If he does go back, will you go with him?"

It was a question Barry had been asking himself. "I don't know," he said honestly. "I might have to. He's, well, he's the closest thing I've ever had to a father and I feel an obligation to look out for him."

Barbara's features rearranged themselves again. "And if I ask you not to go, would that make a difference?"

"Why would you do that?"

It was her turn to draw a deep breath. "Let me tell you about my father. He was born in America but he was an Irish republican because his father was an Irish republican. Dad raised money for the IRA. I know from my mother that he felt guilty because he wasn't playing a more active part in what he called 'the armed struggle.' When I was still a little girl he couldn't stand it any longer. He made his first trip to Ireland with a couple of his republican friends and never came home again."

"What happened?" Barry asked, expecting the familiar story of a man who had abandoned his family.

Her lower lip began to quiver, though she made a brave effort to control it. "We never knew, not exactly. Dad died of a gunshot in a place called Ballymena."

Northern Ireland. "Oh, Barbara!" Barry reached out and gathered her into his arms.

She was trembling uncontrollably. "Because they got him killed my mother hates the republicans and everything they stand for."

"Yes, of course," Barry murmured into her hair. Meaningless syllables of comfort. "Yes. Of course she does. I understand."

At last the trembling stopped.

"Are you going to be all right?"

"I'll be all right," she whispered with her face burrowed against his chest. "As long as you don't . . ."

"I won't," Barry promised.

"I don't believe you. You'll go away like he did and never come back."

Curiously, her vulnerability touched him more than her sensuality. He realised how adrift she really was. Partly as a result of circumstance but mostly by choice, Barbara was cut off from those pillars of stability which most women of her age and class enjoyed. It was one thing for a man to be independent, as Barry had always thought himself. It was a quite different matter for a woman. *The only woman I know who seems able to manage it is Ursula. Or perhaps she simply conceals her vulnerability better.*

Barbara lay soft and pliable in his arms. Her hair smelled like cinnamon. She was a big girl but he was bigger. Stronger. Man enough to take care of her.

In that moment he felt he was man enough to take care of anything.

"Barbara, listen to me. I'll never abandon you, no matter where I go or what I do."

"How can I be so sure?"

"Because I always mean what I say."

With a snort of derision, she was suddenly herself again. "No man always means what he says."

BOTH Haughey and Blaney were released on bail, pending trial for conspiring to finance the illegal importation of arms. Also charged with attempting to smuggle guns to the north were Captain James Kelly, John Kelly—who was not related to the captain but was a leader of the Belfast Citizens' Defence Committee—and Albert Luykx, a Belgian-born businessman.

Defence counsel argued that the weapons in question were intended for use in Northern Ireland on the specific instructions of the government, according to Captain Kelly, a man with a previously unblemished reputation for probity and integrity. The prosecution insisted that no such instructions had been given. Any official sanction for the involvement of the Irish army in northern affairs was strenuously denied. Documents that could have supported Kelly's contention went missing.

Political insiders hinted that in its conduct of the first Arms Trial the Irish government was not, as it claimed, keeping the state from becoming involved in an island-wide sectarian war. Rather, it was addressing a power struggle within Fianna Fáil. If it could be proved that two senior ministers had financed the importation of illegal guns with the secret knowledge and permission of the taoiseach, the Arms Crisis could bring down Jack Lynch.

A cloud of obfuscation and confusion surrounded the case. The subsequent trials and parliamentary debates did nothing to clarify the matter. Half-truths, outright lies, and political chicanery were in full bloom in Irish politics.

.   .   .

WORKING in concert, Barry and Barbara managed to dissuade McCoy from returning to the north. It was difficult, however. Every scrap of news from across the border brought indications of trouble to come.

In the June elections to Westminster, which brought in a Conservative government led by Edward Heath, Ian Paisley was elected MP for North Antrim—and Bernadette Devlin for Mid-Ulster. However, Devlin's appeal against a six-month sentence for her role in the Battle of the Bogside was dismissed and she was imprisoned.

There was violent rioting in Belfast. In the first sustained military action by the Belfast IRA, snipers were stationed in the Newtownards Road. On the twenty-seventh of June five Protestants and a Catholic were shot dead and twenty-six people were seriously injured. On the following day five hundred Catholic workers who had gained employment through Terence O'Neill's liberal policies were driven out of the Harland and Wolff shipyards by angry Protestants.

A curfew in Belfast was monitored by military helicopters, an ominous sight overhead. The Catholics no longer saw the British army as their saviours, but as an occupying force which made little effort to defend them. Both wings of the IRA became involved in skirmishes with British soldiers.

On the second of July the charges against Neil Blaney were dismissed.

DO you believe in déjà vu?" Barry asked Barbara.

"Why?"

"When I saw you dancing that day, it was as if it had all happened before. Did you feel it too?"

"Of course not," she replied. He thought she answered too quickly, perhaps to deny the truth.

"Well, I do. I've experienced it too many times not to believe that some part of the past . . . continues to exist. In us, through us, I don't know how to explain it. But it's there. And in that past I think I knew you."

He was half afraid that she would laugh, but she did not.

"Yes," she said in a whisper.

BARBARA was still contrary and contradictory, still difficult to fathom, yet from that moment they grew closer, as if a door had opened.

Barry admitted to her that he had bought the house.

"Do you mean I'm working for you?"

"Well, sort of. We're working together, really, we're—"

"I'm not about to be your hired help!" Barbara flared. "Not for one more minute!"

"Then be my . . ."

"Your what?"

He could not bring himself to propose marriage. Not yet. She was so complicated during a time when life itself was complicated. It was better that things remain as they were for a while, Barry thought, with each of them living a separate life.

"Be my partner," he suggested. "Help me with this house and I'll split the profit with you."

Her eyes narrowed shrewdly. "Is there any?"

"A little. But if I can count on you to stay we can increase our profits. I'll talk to the bank about adding an extension to the house; there's room at the back."

"I'll think about it," Barbara promised.

How did my life go in this direction? Barry wondered in the quiet of his own room. Yet he was not displeased. He felt like he was growing.

He moved his gramophone into the front parlour and began to invite other friends to visit. He discovered that he enjoyed the role of host, while Barbara was astonished at the wide range of Barry's acquaintance. She already knew Alice and Dennis Cassidy, but Gilbert Fitzmaurice was very different. The first time he came to visit, Barbara took Barry aside and said, "You once told me that man and I were made for each other. Now that I've met him, I'm insulted."

He could not tell whether she was really angry. Barbara's true feelings, he was learning, were not always reflected by her outward demeanour. "I'm surprised you remembered about that," he told her. It seemed a safe remark.

"I remember everything you say."

I'll have to be more damned careful about what I say!

Paudie Coates treated Barbara to a knowledgeable discourse about rally driving, and had her laughing at stories of near disasters on muddy Irish roads. An evening with Éamonn and Rosaleen MacThomáis provided the most wide-ranging conversation of all, for Éamonn was a splendid raconteur.

Barry had asked Éamonn in advance not to discuss the north in McCoy's presence.

SUMMER gave way to autumn without any improvement in the northern situation. If anything, it had grown worse. In September a riot in the loyalist Shankill Road resulted in two hundred civilians and more than one hundred soldiers and policemen being injured. The following month brought riots in the nationalist Ardoyne that lasted for three nights, during which nail bombs were thrown at the soldiers.

THE four remaining defendants in the Arms Trial ultimately were acquitted. Barry was in the crowd outside the High Court on the October day when

Charles Haughey emerged a free man. As Haughey's jubilant supporters cheered, Barry took his picture. *That is indeed a remarkable face,* he thought. *A Caesar. Or a Borgia.*

Half-concealed by the heavy lids were keen and cunning eyes. Without seeming to do so they scanned all the faces in the crowd. Noting who was there; committing them to memory. When Haughey looked at him, Barry gave the politician a tiny wink in salute.

Charles Haughey's enigmatic features revealed nothing. But he responded with an almost imperceptible nod.

WHAT was it like to grow up in America?" Barry asked Barbara. They were in his room, late at night when the house was quiet. Sometimes they went to hers to make love. There was an unspoken understanding: each had their own territory, not to be invaded without invitation.

"Since I didn't grow up someplace else, I have nothing to compare a childhood in America to," Barbara said.

"Do you judge everything comparatively?"

"Of course, don't you?"

"Certainly not." Against his better judgement, Barry could not resist asking, "How do I compare with other men you've known?"

She tossed her head and laughed. "Better than some, not as good as others."

"You're teasing now."

"Am I?" She laughed again. "Oh, don't look like that, you silly old thing." Reaching out and touching his cheek with her fingers, gently trailing them down to the hard jawbone, down again along the strongly muscled neck to his chest. A touch as light as a butterfly's kiss.

He had no defence against gentleness.

One by one, with artless questions asked during his moments of greatest vulnerability, she was extracting Barry's deepest secrets. He even told her about Feargal's death.

She said, "You must hate the RUC."

"I don't want to hate anyone," Barry replied. Knowing that he could and did. "The constables were doing what they had to do, just as we were," he elaborated. *Which is perfectly true. Seen from their side.*

Barbara Kavanagh had not acquired the intellectual maturity to hold two opposing viewpoints at the same time. "I don't know how you can be so understanding! I would never ever forgive anyone who killed somebody I cared about. Even if it took my whole life I'd find a way to get back at them."

Barry realised with dismay that he had told Barbara far too much. Even about Ned's notebooks.

And he did not know if he could trust her at all.

. . .

TRUE to his word, Barry invited his mother to come up to Dublin for Christmas. He was eager for her to see him as a property owner, a man of substance.

Ursula saw more than that. Although they frequently bickered, she realised almost at once the true nature of Barry's relationship with Barbara Kavanagh. The superficial sparring was an attempt to disguise more tender feelings. There was something deeply satisfying, like the closing of a ring, in seeing the two of them together. Her son and Henry's granddaughter.

With a mental shrug of her shoulders, Ursula set about making friends with Barbara; discussing music, telling family anecdotes, soliciting the younger woman's opinions about fashion.

When Barry heard the two women laughing together over a private joke he felt a sense of relief.

Ursula liked Séamus McCoy, too. In his damaged eyes was the same expression she had seen in Ned Halloran's eyes: the dream that would not be extinguished.

"You've created quite a little family for yourself," Ursula remarked to Barry.

"I have. Do you approve?" The slight, ironic half-smile; the lifted eyebrow.

"I would approve more if you married the girl. Why aren't you at least engaged? This is Ireland, you know; people will talk."

"Ursula, never in my entire life have I heard you worry about what other people think."

"I don't care for myself, but I do for you."

"Never worry about me. I'm quite capable of looking after myself—and all this too." With an expansive gesture he indicated the house and everything in it. "My kingdom," he added, smiling broadly now.

THE coming New Year would bring the introduction of the decimal system in Ireland. Farewell to the crown, the farthing, the shilling. "We're going to have to learn sillymetrics next," Ursula dolefully predicted before she returned to Clare.

Looking back on 1971 afterwards, Barry thought of it as "the Building Year." For him, most of it passed in a haze of construction as the new extension to his house was built in the back garden. He was involved in every phase of the work, from drawing up the plans to helping with the carpentry and tiling the roof. Barbara was in charge of decorating the interior. McCoy kept a close eye on the tradesmen and suppliers and prevented Barbara from being too extravagant. He seemed able to handle her even when Barry could not.

"You're my reserve force, Séamus," Barry told him. "When I'm pushed to the pin of my collar I can always count on you."

Barry was thoroughly enjoying himself. He divided his time between his photography, his building, and Barbara, and still squeezed in a few hours to be with friends. And to follow the news from the north. Always, like a black cloud on the horizon, the north.

THE split between the Official IRA and the Provisionals had surfaced in Belfast. There the Provisionals had gained control in all Catholic areas except the Lower Falls Road. They were made very welcome. They were there to defend.

On the tenth of January the IRA tarred and feathered four men for burglary and peddling drugs.[1]

In February British soldiers who were searching Catholic neighbourhoods for weapons were attacked by women on the Crumlin Road. A few days later IRA machine-gun fire killed a British soldier on the New Lodge Road. When a five-year-old Catholic girl was run over by a British Army vehicle, fresh riots broke out.

In March the escalating feud between the Official IRA and the Provisional IRA resulted in a gun battle in Belfast's Leeson Street. The RTE newscast left McCoy distraught. "Why is this happening, Seventeen? It's the Civil War all over again."

Barry tried to comfort his friend. "It's only teething pains as the two sides stake out their territories. You understand about territories, Séamus."

"Sometimes I think I don't understand anything."

Sometimes I don't either, Barry thought. He wished he could put his finger on the precise moment when events had gone out of control, so that he could photograph it and say to the world, "Here, this is where it all went wrong. Don't let this happen again."

There were times when Barry was certain Barbara loved him, though she never said so. There were times when he was afraid she secretly hated him because he was, had been, surely always would be, IRA. She never said that either.

Chapter Forty-one

March 29, 1971

CALLEY GUILTY OF ATROCITY IN VIETNAM

Lieutenant William Calley has been found guilty of murdering civilians during the massacre of 567 men, women, and children in the village of My Lai in Vietnam. Calley's company of U.S. troops was responsible for the massacre, which took place in 1968. The defence claimed that Calley and his men were following orders.

IN Belfast two marches to commemorate the anniversary of the Easter Rising in 1916 were organised by the two branches of the IRA. Both factions wore the traditional republican emblem of the Easter lily. The Provisionals fastened their badges to their coats with pins. The Officials used self-adhesive paper badges. A crowd of more than seven thousand attended the Provisionals' march. The Officials' attracted only half that number.

Some wit dubbed the two halves of the IRA "Provos" and "Stickies.'"

SHORTLY after Easter, Barry helped to raise the rooftree on the new extension of his house. Afterwards he, Barbara, and McCoy celebrated. Champagne for Barbara, Jameson's for the men. Barry warned McCoy not to take more than a small drink because of his medication.

McCoy defiantly drained a large tumbler full of whiskey. "Now that's what I call 'medication,' Seventeen. Pass me another." He drank that too and showed no ill effects.

"Séamus may not be big but he's a giant," Barry confided to Barbara.

She slept in his room that night.

He awoke before she did and rolled up onto his elbow to look down at her. With a rosy dawn light filtering through the net curtains she was breathtaking. Her hair, glossy with rude animal health, fanned across the pillow; her complexion, innocent of makeup, was luminous.

But the knowing eye could discern flaws. The slight vertical furrows above Barbara's nose would intensify with time. Her deep jaw, which was such a valuable part of her singing apparatus, was heavy in repose. Barbara's features required animation to make them beautiful. When she was lost in sleep she looked almost . . .

Someday she'll be dead and in her grave and we will have missed each other this time!

Barry's hand closed tightly on her shoulder. "Barbara? Barbara! Wake up!"

She opened her eyes and peered groggily up at him. "What do you want?"

Seeing life return to her face filled Barry with an inordinate joy. "To ask you something."

The frown lines deepened. "Fine. Ask me in the morning." She rolled over and turned her back to him.

"This is morning, and besides, it won't wait."

"There's nothing that can't wait until I've gotten up and had a cup of coffee," she said over her shoulder. "But for now I'm going back to sleep."

Barry was fully aware of the huge, recklessly impulsive step he was about to take. Aware and frightened and exhilarated.

"Will you marry me?"

Suddenly Barbara was wide awake.

WILL you be my best man, Séamus?" Barry was holding Barbara's hand as they crowded close together in the doorway of McCoy's room.

"Your wha'?" He was still in bed with a thundering hangover, and as startled at having them invade his bedroom as he was by the question.

"You heard me, old friend. This foolish woman has agreed to marry me, and I hope you'll be the best man."

McCoy's befuddled brain was running to catch up. "Marry? You two? When?"

"We want to have the extension finished first, and we'll have to allow plenty of time for Barbara's mother—and mine—to do all those things they're going to want to do."

"Barry and I are both so unconventional," Barbara interjected, "that we decided we should do this the conventional way and have a year's engagement. We're thinking of the first of May next year."

McCoy's wolfish grin surfaced. "If I'm the best man, why are you going to marry this fellow, Barbara?

She rewarded him with her full-throated laugh. "Because you're too good for me!"

In that moment Barry loved her intensely.

THROUGHOUT the summer and into the autumn riots continued to break out; in Belfast, in Derry, in towns and villages that had no previous history of trouble. Much of the rioting was sectarian, but it also involved both loyalist and nationalist paramilitaries. Sometimes they fought each other; sometimes they fought the British soldiers.

The war was taking on a new dimension.

Amidst the continuing violence, political hardliner Brian Faulkner became prime minister of Northern Ireland.

CIGARETTE advertising on television was banned in the Republic. *Nothing Rhymed* was a top hit on the wireless. There was a brisk trade in contraceptives as women from the Republic crossed the border to do a little shopping in Northern Ireland. A pharmacist in Armagh was asked if most of his new customers were Catholic or Protestant. He quipped, "They're the best Roman Catholic Protestants you could hope to meet."

PREDICTABLY, in Northern Ireland civil disorder increased as the Marching Season approached. Tensions grew unbearably high. All of the IRA units in Belfast were put on standby,[1] as were local community defence groups. In the early hours of July Twelfth, bombs were exploded along Orange parade routes in the city, injuring nine people. Although rioting was taking place in several parts of Belfast, the main parade itself passed off without disturbance.[2] Afterwards, however, marchers returning from the main and feeder parades encountered angry crowds and more rioting. Shortly before midnight the Catholic Short Strand was attacked by swarms of loyalists. An effort was made to burn down Saint Matthew's Church.

BARRY remarked, "Jonathon Swift said it all, Séamus, when he wrote, 'We have enough religion to make us hate, but not enough to make us love.'"

McCoy squinted at him. "Swift? I don't think I know him, Seventeen. Is he a republican?"

·   ·   ·

THE extension in Harold's Cross was completed, to the last curtain rod and lick of paint. It contained four large new bedrooms and a bathroom with both tub and shower. Barry thought this an unnecessary luxury. Barbara insisted it was standard in America.

As soon as the plumbers had left, she and Barry tried out the shower. They soaped each other and clung together, laughing, under the spray. Flesh squirming against flesh and every nerve alive.

"Open your skin and let me in," Barbara chanted.

"You're already in my heart. Won't that do?"

May seemed a very long time away.

ON the ninth of August the Conservative prime minister of Great Britain, Edward Heath, introduced internment in Northern Ireland. Arrest without evidence and imprisonment without trail, for an open-ended period of time. Heath was warned against this move by the security forces, who feared it would make matters worse. The prime minister went ahead as a result of pressure from Unionist politicians at Stormont. His actions served to further infuriate and alienate Catholics, many of whom flocked to join the IRA.

In a series of dawn raids the British army captured 342 men to consider for internment. The majority of them were members of the Official IRA, sucked into the maelstrom whether they wished it or not. The Provisionals had received a tip-off from a highly placed individual at Stormont and sent their leaders into hiding.[3] No effort was made to arrest any loyalist paramilitaries.

There was an immediate upsurge in violence. By the twelfth of August twenty-two people had been killed outright and more than seven thousand, most of them Catholics, were homeless.

Many more people were to die after the introduction of internment than had died before it.

During September, in response to Ian Paisley's call for "a third force to defend Ulster,'" the Ulster Defence Association was formed. The UDA brought together a number of Protestant paramilitary and vigilante groups. Working-class men as most members of the IRA were working class, many of them came from deprived backgrounds. They too felt that something—anything—had to be done to better their situation.

In October still more British soldiers were sent to Northern Ireland, and Ian Paisley announced the formation of the Democratic Unionist Party "to be on the right of constitutional issues."

. . .

AT the end of October an IRA bomb exploded at the Post Office Tower in London.

"That was a damned clever piece of engineering," Séamus McCoy commented. "What do you think, Seventeen?"

"I think using bombs is a mistake. They're indiscriminate; they kill innocent civilians as easily as they destroy buildings and bridges. Let me remind you that the IRA's not at war against British civilians, only against their government."

McCoy squinted at him in surprise. "And you one of the best explosives men of them all!"

"Not anymore," Barry said firmly.

IN November the leader of the British Labour Party and former prime minister, Harold Wilson, announced his fifteen-point plan for Northern Ireland. He stated that the situation would not be resolved without finding a means to give hope for the ultimate uniting of Ireland. "If men of moderation have nothing to hope for," Wilson said, "men of violence will have something to shoot for."

Unfortunately, the Labour Party was no longer in power.

IN December the Ulster Defence Force bombed McGurk's Bar in Belfast. Fifteen people were killed and thirteen badly injured. One of them subsequently died.

The British army began sabotaging roads along the border in an ill-considered attempt to make access from the south more difficult for the IRA.

URSULA came up to Dublin for Christmas. Barbara gave her a warm welcome, and Barry was pleased by the prospect of a tradition in the making. He found a quiet moment to take his mother aside and tell her about Barbara's aversion to republicanism. "And that's all right with you?" she wanted to know.

"It has to be. I don't think it will be an issue anyway, since I've given up active service."

"Have you?" Ursula's impassive face revealed nothing of her emotions. "You come from a strong republican tradition, Barry. Are you turning your back on all that now?"

"Not at all; I believe in the Republic as much as ever. I just think we have to find other ways to bring it about. In time I hope to bring Barbara around to my way of thinking."

His mother gave a wry smile. "You're going to change the mind of a woman like that, are you?"

"Give me some credit, Ursula. I'm more of a diplomat than you think."

There was one bad moment during the holidays when the spectre of the north threatened to rear its ugly head. In response to a casual remark of Séamus McCoy's, Barbara said peevishly, "Why can't men learn to get along with each other?"

Ursula gave an unladylike snort. "You're asking too much of creatures who cannot be trained to put a toilet seat down."

Séamus McCoy laughed.

"Barry puts the seat down," said Barbara.

Her future mother-in-law was astonished. "What have you done to him?"

Before Barbara could answer, Barry said, "I've grown up, that's all. Did you think I never would?"

"There were times I was afraid you might not live to grow up. But that's over now, is it not?"

Barbara put her hand firmly on her fiancé's arm. "It most certainly is!"

URSULA stayed at Harold's Cross through the holidays, sleeping in one of the new—as yet unoccupied, to Barry's chagrin—bedrooms. The extension had cost much more to build than he had anticipated. His finances were stretched to the breaking point, and though his pictures continued to sell, they did not bring in the big money from abroad. That came only from dramatic photographs.

All the drama was taking place in Northern Ireland.

On New Year's Eve, Ursula found her son sitting at the dining table, poring over his accounts. The scene was so familiar that she had to smile. As Barbara came in from the kitchen Ursula exclaimed, "Let's all go out someplace!"

Barry gave her a distracted look. "I can't, I have to bring these up-to-date. I have responsibilities now."

"That's as may be, but I'm bored to buttons with responsibility. I need to frivol."

"Frivol?" queried Barbara.

Barry, who was accustomed to his mother's creative use of language, interpreted. "I think Ursula means she wants to be frivolous for a change."

"So do I," Barbara said as she took off her apron.

With a sigh, Barry closed the ledger. "A man doesn't stand a chance around here." But he was smiling.

A few days after Ursula went back to the farm, Barry received a letter from Father Aloysius. "We are going to do it again but this time we are going to do it right," the priest wrote.

The plural pronoun leapt out at Barry. *What does he mean by "we"?*

"A big civil rights march is being planned in Derry for the end of the month," the priest's letter went on. "The purpose of the march is to protest internment and it will be absolutely nonconfrontational. We must demonstrate social responsibility to counter the violence that is taking place. If our people show the way, with God's help others can take heart and follow our example."

We. Our. He's going to take part in the march.

"I'm going north," Barry told Séamus McCoy.

"It's about time, *avic*! When do we leave?"

"Not we. Me. I'll be travelling around a lot, you know how it is, eating irregularly, sleeping irregularly. . . ."

"You're going to join the Provos!" McCoy crowed.

"I am *not* going to join the Provos, Séamus, I'm heading off to photograph a civil rights march in Derry. A peaceful one this time; that should be newsworthy. Photography is my business, and it's been thin on the ground of late, so I need this opportunity. I'm relying on you to stay here. Look after Barbara and keep everything ticking over until I get back. Can you do that for me?"

"I'd be more use to you in the north, Seventeen. I know everybody, I can help you get pictures you might not get otherwise."

"I appreciate that, but this is where I need you most. Please, Séamus." When the other man still seemed reluctant, Barry said, "When I get back I'll let you drive my car, I promise. We'll go out in the country where you don't have to deal with traffic and you can open 'er up."

I sound like a parent bribing a child with sweets. When did our positions become reversed?

Barbara was more difficult, as Barry had known she would be. He had to stress over and over again that it was necessary for him to go where the photographic opportunities were. "But you're not going to get involved?" she kept asking. "You're not going to have anything to do with Those People?"

Barry knew exactly whom she meant by Those People.

"I'm not, I swear. I'm just going to take pictures."

She would not go to the front door with him to say good-bye—one of her many ways of expressing disapproval. When he was ready to leave he found her in the kitchen washing the breakfast dishes as if they were a matter of the utmost urgency. "I'm leaving now," Barry said to her back.

"Fine." She raised one soapy hand in a nonchalant wave but did not look around.

"Is there anything you need before I go?"

"Not a thing. You'd best be on your way." She still would not look at him.

"Well . . . good-bye then."

"Mmm." Much splashing in the kitchen sink.

Barry carried his camera equipment and a small suitcase out to Apollo. As he raised the lid of the boot to stow his things away he looked back at the house.

The front door remained resolutely shut.

The house itself, his very own house, with smoke curling from the chimney, looked wonderfully warm and inviting in the cold light of the bitter January morning.

With a sigh, Barry closed the lid of the boot and started to go around to the driver's side of the car.

At that moment the front door was flung open and Barbara came running out. She hurled her full weight against him, knocking him off balance. Without saying a word, she wrapped her arms around his neck and drew his face to hers for a passionate kiss that seemed to last forever.

Then she ran back into the house. Leaving the feel of her imprinted on the length of his body; the taste of her burned into his lips.

Shaken to the core, Barry got into the car.

It's like nothing I ever imagined. This woman, this house, the life we're going to have.

Thank you, God! I must have done something right after all.

He put Apollo in gear and drove away. Whistling.

Chapter Forty-two

DERRY looked much the same as Barry remembered, though considerable rebuilding had taken place in the Bogside. It was still poor, however. Still second class. A place to live for people who did not matter.

Barry parked Apollo in the alley behind the priest's house. Once again he had a sense of déjà vu. *But this time it will be different,* he assured himself. *This time we will set an example for the rest to follow. It has to work; the alternative is too awful to contemplate.*

Barry's assumption had been correct. Father Aloysius was planning to take part in the march scheduled for the thirtieth of January. "It's so important that we do this," he told Barry. "Did you hear about the bomb the IRA exploded in Callender Street in Belfast on the third? Some sixty people were injured, including women and children.[1] This can't go on, Barry. Those of us who still have a conscience must demonstrate, once and for all, that we Catholics are decent human beings who can behave in a civilised fashion and deserve to be treated with dignity."

"You're right," said Barry. "You're entirely right, Father." *So why do I suddenly have this terrible feeling in the pit of my stomach?* "What are the arrangements for the march?"

"You'll be walking with us?"

"Beside you," Barry replied. "Photographing everything. Have you any idea how the authorities are going to respond to the march?"

"We've given them every assurance of our peaceful intent," said the priest. "People like Brian Faulkner will take a lot of convincing, though. He's a Unionist through and through."

"Is there any IRA involvement in the march?"

Father Aloysius looked thoughtful. "I was concerned about that so I've made some enquiries. A little while ago I was speaking with a young fellow called Martin McGuinness, who's second in command of the Derry brigade. He confirmed that orders have come down from the top that no member of the IRA is to take part in the demonstration. No guns of any sort, no bombs, no nail bombs, nothing, in fact, that might even be construed as a weapon, is to be in the vicinity of the march.[2]

"McGuinness told me he and another Volunteer have collected all the local weapons and taken them to a safe house. Only the two of them know the location of the arms dump, just to be sure there's no maverick action by Volunteers."

"That's a relief," said Barry. "At least if anything goes wrong we won't be blamed."

"We?" This time it was the priest who noticed the pronoun.

SUNDAY morning dawned full of hope. In Derry the air coming down from the mountains was so sweet and pure one could drink it.

As he left for Mass in Dublin, Jack Lynch paused to sign autographs for some young admirers.

When Barry and Father Aloysius emerged from the priest's house they were aware of a strong security-force presence in Derry. A number of barricades had been erected that had not been there the night before.

The Catholic areas seemed calm enough, though hardly quiet. The hum of thousands of voices was clearly audible. As the march began to form up in the Creggan it was obvious that it would be larger than the organisers could have hoped. In addition to the various civil rights groups, identified by signs and banners, tens of thousands of ordinary people had come from all over the north. Many of them were carrying hand-painted signs, too. Demanding the British army leave. Demanding an end to internment.

Men and women, boys and girls. Some of them heavily muffled against the cold, others wearing only light jackets and jumpers. A number had brought their dogs as if they were out for a Sunday stroll.

Even Barry's wide-angle lens was insufficient to give a true indication of the size of the crowd.

Near the head of the march a flatbed coal truck had been transformed into a speakers' platform. Bernadette Devlin was amongst the activists who addressed the crowd through a microphone that occasionally squawked and squealed. Barry crouched down below the truck to photograph her silhouetted against the sky. *I would rather be here right now than anywhere else in the world,* he told himself. *This is one of those moments I shall remember always.*

Stewards equipped with walkie-talkies and megaphones were working hard to form the mass of humanity into a cohesive body. When the signal came to move off, the march started down the hill from the Creggan toward the Bogside. There was almost a holiday atmosphere. People sang "We Shall Over-come." Young lads gave one another an elbow in the ribs as if to say, 'Ain't this fun?'

Coming to a barricade across their route, the leaders signalled for a halt. It took a while for the word to work its way back through the immense crowd. There was a lot of foot shuffling and throat clearing, and not a little complain-ing, while the organisers negotiated with several men in British army uniform. Barry tried to get close enough to hear what was being said, but a soldier with a rifle waved him back.

He caught sight of Father Aloysius shouldering his way through the crowd, reminding everyone that this was to be a peaceful demonstration.

At last the march got under way again. It had now been rerouted from its original line of march to the Guildhall. A score of youths stayed at the barri-cade to heckle the soldiers and throw rocks, while the main body of marchers took the new route toward the Free Derry Corner. By going this way they were held within the confines of the Catholic ghetto. Herded through narrow streets walled in by terraced houses and high-rise flats.

"They better not try to stop us today," one of the demonstrators called to an-other. "The Brits have rubber bullets, y'know."

"Rubber bullets don't scare me none," came the reply.

Barry tried to stay on the fringes of the crowd so that he could pick and choose his images. The faces in the forefront of the march were so very self-confident. The banners they carried were so very bright.

As Barry switched from camera to camera he was too preoccupied to hear the first gunshot.

But he heard the next one. It seemed to come from the direction of William Street,[3] and echoed through the concrete canyons. He stopped in his tracks and looked around. Members of the security forces wearing visored helmets and carrying riot shields had gathered at the next road junction. They were looking around too.

Meanwhile, momentum continued to carry the march forward. Most of the noisy crowd were still unaware of the gunfire. They did not realise anything was amiss until a swarm of British paratroopers in camouflage uniforms and berets charged into Rossville Street, followed by armoured personnel carriers.

The paratroopers were sweating; it gleamed on their faces in spite of the fact that many were streaked with camouflage charcoal, as if on a training mission. Barry recognised the nervous darting of their eyes. He had been in battle, he knew how it felt.

The march slowed, stopped. People turned in one direction and then an-other, trying to decide which way to go. In Rossville Street an old barricade which ran from Glenfada Park to the Rossville Flats had fallen into disrepair, and there was enough of a gap for one person at a time to go through.[4] Reinforcements of barbed wire had been placed in such a way that a frightened crowd could not get past, however. Marchers gathered like sheep huddling before a blizzard, looking for a way out.

There was more gunfire. Louder now. Very close. At first the paratroopers appeared to be firing at random in an attempt to frighten and create confusion. Then Barry saw one take careful aim at an individual and bring him down with a single shot.

Barry froze. *The bastards have been ordered to shoot to kill.*

Swinging around, he sought to photograph the soldier who had fired the deliberate shot. The man had already disappeared in the melee.

As they ran through the streets the paratroopers were shouting to one another, encouraging themselves and their comrades to violence. The gunfire escalated into a terrifying barrage. No one was safe, neither the marchers nor the bystanders: the men, women, and children who had gathered to watch the "parade" go by. People fled into every open doorway and derelict house. A frantic group ran into a concrete courtyard, but it was a cul-de-sac surrounded by buildings. Several paratroopers followed them in.

Like butchers pursuing cattle into an abattoir, Barry thought with horror.

During the next ten minutes the paratroopers fired 108 live rounds, their own officers later admitted. It sounded like much more.

Seven people were shot at the barricade blocking escape from Rossville Street.

THE cameras were no use—*no damned use!*; Barry had nothing with which to fight back, no way to vent his rage and dismay at what was happening. He was at the heart of panic but he was not panicked. The old cold rage poured through him, filling his veins.

He was familiar with the sharp, high-pitched sound of high-velocity rifles. Recognised the altered *spang* of bullets ricocheting off pavement and walls. Had heard screams of fear before. But not bursting from so many throats at the same time.

He saw four paratroopers chasing people toward the Glenfada Park Flats. After they vanished from sight he heard a fusillade of gunfire.

Gunfire seemed to be coming from every direction. Just like the screams and curses. The leading marchers were trapped in what was fast becoming a killing ground. The damp air of Derry carried the coppery smell of blood; the pungent odour of bowels giving way as people spasmed and died on the pavement.

It was impossible to tell who was injured and who was not, because so many were throwing themselves on the ground.

Playing dead was the only defence they had.

From the other side of the barricades men and boys began hurling stones at the soldiers. They ran into the nearest houses looking for bottles to make petrol bombs. But, though Barry prayed to hear it, there was no sound of retaliatory gunfire being aimed at the paratroopers.

The damned guns were put away. To prevent violence.

Barry thankfully noticed a nervous television crew arriving. For the first time he wished he had entered television himself. There was an immediacy to moving images that the still camera could never convey.

This is real, this is real, he kept telling himself. Yet it did not seem real. It was like the most violent cowboy-and-Indian films out of America. The World War Two films. The horror films.

A British Army helicopter was circling overhead. Armed soldiers and rolls of barbed wire were clearly visible atop walls and rooftops.

People who had been farther back in the march continued to pour into the Bogside. As their stewards learned what was happening up ahead they made desperate efforts to turn the crowd back but it was almost impossible. Hysteria had set in.

From the looks on the faces of the paratroopers Barry realised they were hysterical too.

Gunfire, petrol bombs, water cannon, CS gas, the screams of the injured, the moans of the dying. But ten times worse than it had been in 1969; ten times worse than anything Barry could have imagined.

People tried to carry victims to safety only to be shot down themselves. Barry saw a paratrooper casually walk up to a wounded man lying on his belly and shoot him in the back of the head.

Barry saw terrible things. They began to merge into one another, and then into all the other terrible things stored in his memory.

He was no longer attempting to take pictures; he was not a photographer anymore. He was a Volunteer in the front lines without a weapon, trying to protect those who were more defenceless than he. When a sobbing woman bolted into the path of the paratroopers he dove at her and bore her to the ground, covering her with his body until the soldiers ran on. He found an infant in a pram—*God knows where the mother is*—and pushed the pram into an open doorway, out of the line of fire. Then he picked up a hunk of rubble and hurled it at the nearest paratrooper. It wasn't enough, it made no impression. The man snarled at Barry, snapped off a quick shot that missed, and went on.

A steward with a megaphone was beating it uselessly against a wall. A big strong man in a hooded anorak was bleeding from the shoulder and blubbering like a baby. A priest, bent double, came around a corner waving a white flag, closely followed by several men carrying a youth whose body was dripping blood.

The gunfire did not let up for a moment. Since it began only a few minutes had passed in reality, but it seemed an eternity to Barry. It seemed the world had always been full of killing.

Horror upon horror. Dead and dying, needlessly slaughtered. No way to escape. No mercy.

Soldiers laughing wildly as they fired into the crowd.

A flood of images overwhelmed Barry, superimposed one atop the other until he could not tell which he had seen and which he had only read about and imagined. Brookeborough. Feargal O'Hanlon and Seán South. Derry in 1969. Pádraic Pearse falling to British rifles. McCoy lying in hospital with his eyes bandaged.

My father blown apart by a bomb.

Little Patrick Rooney with a bullet in his brain. Liam Lynch and Michael Collins and Robert Casement. The Famine. The arrogance of the conquerer. The stolen land and the stolen lives.

And the cold rage building and building and building in Barry . . .

URSULA Halloran was looking forward to watching the six o'clock news on RTE. The old farmhouse was quiet. Darkness had long since fallen. The horses and cattle had been fed and her own meagre meal prepared and eaten. Nothing remained but to enjoy a second cup of tea and a long, peaceful evening.

She might use some of the time to write a letter to her papa.

Ned Halloran had been dead for many years, yet the habit of writing to him was deeply ingrained. It was Ursula's way of saying things she could say to no one else, and of staying close to someone she could not bear to lose.

She liked to believe that wherever he was, Ned read . . . heard . . . felt her letters.

In this one she was going to tell him about Barry and Barbara. Would he be glad for their sakes? Was the old grudge he had once carried against Henry Mooney truly forgotten? Surely it was. Even the Irish could not carry a grudge beyond the grave.

Ursula put a cup of tea beside her favourite armchair in the parlour and switched on the television. The screen took a few moments to warm up. Then the news presenter appeared, wearing an expression of barely concealed dismay.

"It has been reported that thirteen demonstrators taking part in a civil rights march in Derry were shot dead today by soldiers of the First Parachute Regiment. A fourteenth man is critically wounded in hospital, not expected to live. A spokesman for the British government has described the march as 'a republican march' and therefore illegal, and claims the soldiers were totally justified in using all necessary force to gain control of a very dangerous situation."

"Jesus H. Christ on a crutch!" Ursula cried. She ran to the telephone to ring Barry.

Barbara answered the phone. "He's not here, I'm afraid. He's gone to Derry."

Ursula almost dropped the telephone receiver. "Derry? Are you sure?"

"That's what he told us; why?"

"Have you been watching the television?"

"We don't have one yet, you know that," Barbara said rather peevishly. "I thought we were going to get one but Barry had his car painted instead. British racing green, only he insists on calling it Irish racing green."

"Have you been listening to the radio?"

"No."

"What about Séamus?"

"He's in his room. Asleep, I think. He usually takes a nap right after supper. After tea," she amended. "Do you want me to call him?"

"I think you'd better," Ursula said faintly.

For the remainder of the evening two households, one in Clare and one in Dublin, avidly followed the news from Derry. The rest of Ireland was doing the same. So were shocked television viewers around the world. The events in Derry were almost beyond belief. Already the day was being described as "Bloody Sunday."

Ursula kept the television on until RTE played the national anthem—whose opening lines were "Soldiers are we, whose lives are pledged to Ireland"—and shut down. Then she turned to the radio, searching frantically for any scrap of information.

THAT night Jack Lynch and Edward Heath had a terse and chilly telephone conversation during which Heath claimed, "The massacre was a result of the IRA trying to take over the country."[5]

Following this conversation Lynch recalled the Republic's ambassador, Donal O'Sullivan, from London, and declared the second of February a national day of mourning.

URSULA got no sleep that night. She did not even go to bed. Instead she went out to the broodmare barn to stand in the dusty dark, stroking the velvet nose of her favourite mare and listening to the deep, gentle sound of breathing. When daylight came she wearily began the morning chores. By the time the Ryan brothers arrived to help she was trembling with fatigue.

"Go inside, missus," Gerry urged. "We'll take over now."

"Barry was in Derry."

"I kinda guessed that when I saw you. Come on, I'll take you inside."

Her legs were too rubbery to climb the stairs, so she sat down on the couch in the parlour and let Gerry build up the fire in the fireplace and bring her a cup of tea. "I wouldn't worry about Barry if I was you," the old hired man said as he tucked a blanket around Ursula. "He'd be too hard to kill. If anyone tried he'd fight with the nails on his toes, so he would."

He left Ursula sitting on the couch. Staring at the blank eye of the television, which would not begin to transmit for hours yet. At last she got up and switched on the radio, hoping—fearing—to hear a list of casualties. For once she did not *know*.

While she waited she fell asleep.

THE roar of a motorcar outside did not wake her, but the slamming of the front door did. She gave a gasp of relief as her son burst into the room.

His hair was fire; his eyes were ice.

After a swift glance at Ursula he ran toward the stairs. She heard him taking them three at a time. "What are you going to do?" she shouted. There was no answer.

Barry Halloran flung open the door to his room. Violently thrust both hands under the mattress.

Took out the rifle.

Source Notes

CHAPTER ONE

1. *The Secret Army*, p. 239
2. *Éire-Ireland*, Spring/Summer 2002, p. 83

CHAPTER TWO

1. *Robert Emmet: A Life*, p. 254
2. *Chronicle of the 20th Century*, p. 795
3. *From Union to Union*, p. 152
4. *Irish Rebellion*, p. 81

CHAPTER THREE

1. *The Secret Army*, p. 300
2. *Ireland in the Twentieth Century*, p. 460

CHAPTER FIVE

1. *The Secret Army*, p. 284
2. *Ireland in Quotes*, p. 104
3. *The IRA*, p. 393

CHAPTER EIGHT

1. *The Secret Army*, p. 299
2. *The Secret Army*, p. 308
3. *Ireland in Quotes*, p. 105

CHAPTER NINE

1. *Stanford*, p. 71

CHAPTER TEN

1. *Revolutionary Brotherhood*, p. 168

CHAPTER ELEVEN

1. *Modern Ireland*, p. 269

CHAPTER TWELVE

1. *Ireland: The 20th Century*, p. 173

CHAPTER FOURTEEN

1. *Northern Ireland; Captive of History*, p. 217
2. *The Secret Army*, p. 316
3. *The Orange Terror, excerpt from The Capuchin Annual 1943*, p. 66

CHAPTER FIFTEEN

1. *Seán Lemass*, p. 155
2. *Hope Against History*, p. 27
3. *Irish Stone Bridges*, p. 195

CHAPTER SIXTEEN

1. *A Monument in the City*, p. 16

CHAPTER EIGHTEEN

1. *Ireland in Quotes*, p. 107

CHAPTER NINETEEN

1. *The Secret Army,* p. 247
2. *Belfast 1969,* Radio Telefis Éireann film documentary
3. *The Secret Army,* p. 331

CHAPTER TWENTY

1. *The Catholics of Ulster,* p. 389

CHAPTER TWENTY-ONE

1. *Ireland in Quotes,* p. 107
2. *Provos,* p. 21

CHAPTER TWENTY-TWO

1. *The Secret Army,* p. 337

CHAPTER TWENTY-THREE

1. *Before the Dawn,* p. 49
2. *Persecuting Zeal,* p. 141

CHAPTER TWENTY-FIVE

1. *The Newspaper Book,* p. 295

CHAPTER TWENTY-SIX

1. *Roger Casement,* Radio Telefis Éireann film documentary
2. *A Monument in the City,* p. 11

CHAPTER TWENTY-SEVEN

1. *Ireland This Century,* p. 239

CHAPTER TWENTY-EIGHT

1. *Cuimhneachán 1916–1966*, p. 27
2. *Ireland This Century*, p. 240
3. *The IRA*, p. 345
4. *1916–1966; What Has Happened?* p. 37
5. *Lost Lives*, p. 28
6. *Lost Lives*, p. 26
7. *25 Years of Terror*, p. 99
8. *No Ordinary Women*, p. 38
9. Direct quote from a personal interview with Éamonn MacThomáis.

CHAPTER TWENTY-NINE

1. *Nice Fellow*, p. 133
2. *Seán Lemass*, p. 339

CHAPTER THIRTY

1. *Historic Killaloe*, p. 13
2. *25 Years of Terror*, p. 99

CHAPTER THIRTY-ONE

1. *Before the Dawn*, p. 82

CHAPTER THIRTY-TWO

1. *The IRA*, p. 357
2. *Ireland in the Twentieth Century*, p. 485
3. *Ireland 1912–1985*, p. 420
4. *Enduring the Most*, p. 115

CHAPTER THIRTY-THREE

1. *Armed Struggle*, p. 100
2. *Bernadette*, p. 150
3. *Paddy Bogside*, p. 85
4. *The Battle of the Bogside*, BBC 4 film documentary
5. *Ireland in the Twentieth Century*, p. 490
6. *Bernadette*, p. 153
7. *Belfast Sunday News*, January 5, 1969

CHAPTER THIRTY-FOUR

1. *A Chronology of Irish History Since 1500*, p. 247
2. *Northern Ireland: A Chronology of the Troubles*, p. 14
3. *A Chronology of Irish History Since 1500*, p. 247
4. *Seventeenth-Century Ireland*, p. 223

CHAPTER THIRTY-FIVE

1. *Ireland in the Twentieth Century*, p. 492
2. *Armed Struggle*, p. 101
3. *Paddy Bogside*, p. 123–24
4. *Northern Ireland: A Chronology of the Troubles*, p. 18

CHAPTER THIRTY-SIX

1. *British National Archives: Papers of Andrew Gilchrist*
2. *Belfast 1969*, Radio Telefís Éireann documentary
3. *Northern Ireland: A Chronology of the Troubles*, p. 19
4. *Paddy Bogside*, p. 151
5. *A Chronology of Irish History Since 1500*, p. 248
6. *The IRA*, p. 364

CHAPTER THIRTY-EIGHT

1. *A Chronology of Irish History Since 1500*, p. 249
2. *Northern Ireland: A Chronology of the Troubles*, p. 22

CHAPTER THIRTY-NINE

1. *On Our Knees*, p. 153
2. *Armed Struggle*, p. 106
3. *Ireland in the Twentieth Century*, p. 546

CHAPTER FORTY

1. *Northern Ireland: A Chronology of the Troubles*, p. 32

CHAPTER FORTY-ONE

1. *Joe Cahill: A Life in the IRA*, p. 198
2. *A Secret History of the IRA*, p. 100
3. *25 Years of Terror*, p. 139

CHAPTER FORTY-TWO

1. *The Troubles,* p. 133
2. Martin McGuinness's direct testimony at the Saville Inquiry into Bloody Sunday
3. *Bloody Sunday in Derry,* p. 100
4. *Bloody Sunday, Lord Widgery's Report,* p. 59
5. *British State Papers*

Bibliography

Adams, Gerry. *Before the Dawn*. London: Heinemann, 1966.

Akenson, Donald H. *Education and Enmity: The Control of Schooling in Northern Ireland 1920–50*. Belfast: Queen's University, 1973.

Allen, Gregory. *The Garda Síochána*. Dublin: Gill & Macmillan, 1999.

Anderson, Brendan. *Joe Cahill: A Life in the IRA,* Dublin: O'Brien Press, 2002.

Andrew, Christopher, and Vasili Mitrokhin. *The Mitrokhin Archive*. London: Allen Lane/Penguin Press, 1999.

Ardoyne Commemoration Committee: *Ardoyne: The Untold Truth*. Belfast: BTP Publications Ltd., 2002.

Bell, J. Bowyer. *The Secret Army: The IRA from 1916*. Dublin: Academy Press, 1972.

Bew, Paul, and Gordon Gillespie. *Northern Ireland: A Chronology of the Troubles*. Dublin: Gill & Macmillan, 1999.

Brown, Terence. *Ireland: A Social and Cultural History, 1922–1985*. London: Fontana Press, 1985.

Browne, Noel. *Against the Tide*. Dublin: Gill & Macmillan, 1986.

Clayton, Pamela. *Enemies and Passing Friends: Settler Ideologies in Twentieth Century Ulster*. London: Pluto Press, 1996.

Conroy, John. *Unspeakable Acts, Ordinary People*. New York: Alfred A. Knopf, 2000.

Coogan, Tim Pat. *The IRA*. London: Fontana/Collins, 1987.

———. *Wherever Green Is Worn*. London: Hutchinson, 2000.

Costello, Francis H. *Enduring the Most*. Kerry: Brandon, 1995.

Cuimhneachán, 1916–1966. Dublin: Department of External Affairs, 1966.

Curtis, Liz. *Ireland: The Propaganda War*. Belfast: Sasta, 1998.

Dillon, Martin. *25 Years of Terror*. London: Bantam Books, 1996.

———. *The Shankill Butchers*. London: Arrow Books, 1990.

Doherty, J. E., and D. J. Hickey. *A Chronology of Irish History Since 1500*. Dublin: Gill & Macmillan, 1989.

Doherty, Paddy. *Paddy Bogside*. Dublin: Mercier Press, 2001.

Doyle, Colman, and Liam Flynn. *Ireland: 40 Years of Photo-Journalism*. Dublin: Blackwater Press, 1994.

Dunne, Derek. *Out of the Maze*. Dublin: Gill & Macmillan, 1988.

Elliott, Marianne. *The Catholics of Ireland*. London: Allen Lane, 2000.

English, Richard. *Armed Struggle: A History of the IRA*. London: Macmillan, 2003.

Fallon, Brian. *An Age of Innocence: Irish Culture, 1930–1960*. Dublin: Gill & Macmillan, 1998.

Feeney, Brian. *Sinn Féin: One Hundred Turbulent Years*. Dublin: O'Brien Press, 2002.

Fitzpatrick, Brendan. *Seventeenth-Century Ireland: The War of Religions*. New Gill History of Ireland (series). Dublin: Gill & Macmillan, 1988.

Foster, Robert F. *Modern Ireland, 1600–1972*. London: Allen Lane/Penguin Press, 1988.

Gillespie, Elgy, ed. *Changing the Times*. Dublin: Lilliput, 2003.

Girvin, Brian. *From Union to Union*. Dublin: Gill & Macmillan, 2002.

Geoghegan, Patrick M. *Robert Emmet: A Life*. Dublin: Gill & Macmillan, 2002.

Holland, Jack. *Hope Against History*. London: Hodder & Stoughton, 1999.

Inglis, Brian. *Roger Casement*. London: Hodder & Stoughton, 1973.

Kelly, James. *Orders for the Captain*. Dublin: Kelly, 1971.

————. *The Thimble Riggers: The Dublin Arms Trials of 1970*. Dublin: Kelly, 1999.

Keogh, Dermot. *Twentieth-Century Ireland: Nation and State*. Dublin: Gill & Macmillan, 1994.

Kierse, Seán. *Historic Killaloe*. Killaloe: Bóru Books, 1983.

Litton, Helen. *Irish Rebellions, 1798–1916*. Dublin: Wolfhound Press, 1998.

MacEoin, Gary. *Northern Ireland: Captive of History*. New York: Holt, Rinehart and Winston, 1974.

Mahoney, Rosemary. *Whoredom in Kimmage*. New York: Doubleday, 1993.

McCann, Éamonn. *Bloody Sunday in Derry: What Really Happened*. Kerry: Brandon Publishers, 1992.

McClean, Dr. Raymond. *The Road to Bloody Sunday*. Derry: Guildhall Press, 1997.

McCoole, Sinéad. *No Ordinary Women*. Dublin: O'Brien Press, 2003.

McDonald, Frank. *The Destruction of Dublin*. Dublin: Gill & Macmillan, 1985.

McDonald, Henry. *Trimble*. London: Bloomsbury, 2000.

McKay, Susan. *Northern Protestants: An Unsettled People*. Belfast: Blackstaff Press, 2000.

McKittrick, David, et al. *Lost Lives*. Edinburgh: Mainstream Publishing, 1999.

McNiffe, Liam. *A History of the Garda Síochána*. Dublin: Wolfhound Press, 1997.

Mercer, Derrick, editor-in-chief. *Chronicle of the 20th Century*. London: Longmans, 1988.

Moloney, Ed. *A Secret History of the IRA*. London: Allen Lane/Penguin Press, 2002.

Morrison, Danny. *All the Dead Voices*. Cork: Mercier Press, 2002.

O'Brien, Joanne. *A Matter of Minutes*. Dublin: Wolfhound Press, 2002.

O'Brien, Justin. *The Modern Prince*. Dublin: Merlin Publishing, 2002.

O'Clery, Conor. *Ireland in Quotes*. Dublin: O'Brien Press, 1999.

O'Dochartaigh, Niall. *From Civil Rights to Armalites*. Cork: Cork University Press, 1997.

O'Keefe, Peter, and Tom Simington. *Irish Stone Bridges: History and Heritage*. Dublin: Irish Academic Press, 1991.

O'Regan, John, ed. *A Monument in the City: Nelson's Pillar and Its Aftermath*. Dublin: Gandon, 1998.

Pearson, Peter. *The Heart of Dublin*. Dublin: O'Brien Press, 2000.

Redmond, Adrian, ed. *That Was Then, This Is Now: Change in Ireland, 1949–1999*. Dublin: Central Statistics Office, 2000.

Rose, Richard. *Governing Without Consensus*. London: Faber & Faber, 1971.

Ryder, Chris. *The RUC, 1922–1997*. London: Mandarin, 1997.

Stanford, William Bedell. *Stanford*. Dublin: Hinds, 2001.

Staunton, Enda. *The Nationalists of Northern Ireland, 1918–1973*. Edinburgh: Columba Press, 2000.

Sweetman, Rosita. *On Our Knees: Ireland 1972*. London: Pan Books Ltd., 1972.

Target, G. W. *Bernadette*. London: Hodder & Stoughton, 1975.

Taylor, Peter. *Provos: The IRA and Sinn Fein*. London: Bloomsbury, 1997.

Toolis, Kevin. *Rebel Hearts: Journeys Within the IRA's Soul*. New York: St. Martin's Press, 1996.

Townshend, Charles. *Ireland: The 20th Century*. London: Arnold, 1999.

Wood, Ian S. *God, Guns and Ulster*. London: Caxton Publications, 2003.

PERIODICALS AND PUBLICATIONS:

Bloody Sunday; Lord Widgery's Report, London: The Stationery Office.
1916–1966: What Has Happened? Dublin: Trinity College Dublin Publishing Company.
Testimony given at the Saville Inquiry into Bloody Sunday, 2003.

Belfast Sunday News.
Belfast Telegraph.
Cork Examiner.
Éire-Ireland, New Jersey: The Irish American Cultural Institute.
Irish Independent.
Irish News.
The Irish Times.
The Times (of London).

ARCHIVES AND RELATED MATERIAL:

Irish National Archives, Dublin.
British National Archives released through the British Public Records Office.

FILM AND DOCUMENTARIES:

The Battle of the Bogside, film documentary for BBC 4 (British Broadcasting Co.).
Belfast 1969, film documentary for Radio Telefís Éirean.
Mise Éire, Irish government production.
Roger Casement, film documentary for Radio Telefís Éireann.